The Pas de Deux

❧

Katy Leen

Anie,
Happy Reading!
Katy
Leen

ISBN: 978-0-9936165-3-2

Dedication

As always, for the girls upstairs. And the guys too.

ONE

WHEN CAMILLE CARON told me the next case I'd be working on involved an identity theft, I didn't think she meant mine.

"What kind of a name is Bunny?" I asked her. "That's not a real name."

Camille shrugged. "Laurent chose it," she said, her blasé air as French as her accent.

I picked up the other I.D. on her desk. "Léon? I have to be Bunny and he gets to be Léon?"

She tipped back in her chair and fingered the multi-colored slinky she kept on her desk. "You should have said something sooner if you didn't like the name. It's all done now. Everything's arranged."

"I didn't know about it until just now. Nobody told me."

Camille's brother Laurent strolled into her office and slipped an arm over my shoulder. "Ready?" he said to me. Then he eyed my outfit, jeans with a white pullover. "Is that what you're wearing, Lora?"

I turned to see what he was wearing. Jeans and a blue-striped dress shirt over a tee with a scarf loosely draped at his neck. "We're practically matching," I said. "What's the problem?"

He gestured at himself. "These clothes are fine for "Léon" but look at you. You look like Lora not "Bunny.""

Seemed to me his "Léon" look was pretty much the same as his regular Laurent one. Right down to the dark, unkept hair fringing his shoulders and the slight scruff.

Camille got up and crossed the room to a small armoire on the far wall. In contrast to Laurent, her hair was short and blonde and her eyes a lighter shade of brown. At thirty-one like me, Camille was younger than Laurent by two years and a nudge shorter, but their sibling connection was visible in their sleek, muscular builds and chiseled features. She pulled out some clothes and passed them to me. "*Tiens*," she said. "Try these."

I held up a slinky pink blouse and a black mini skirt. "What? No garter?"

She stepped back over to the armoire and returned with a pair of black stockings with a seam up the back and a black lace garter belt.

"Funny," I said.

"Lora, it's January in Montreal. There's three feet of snow outside. You want frostbite?"

I grabbed the stockings and went off to the washroom to change clothes. Not that I believed a little Lycra was going to save me from frostbite, but it was better than nothing. When I got back, Laurent was in his own office, and Camille sat me down in the window seat across from her desk and started in on my makeup.

"Your eye's twitching," she said. "Stay still or I'll poke it out with the eyeliner."

I reached up to steady the skin near my temple. "I can't help it."

"*Mais voyons*, Lora. This is what you wanted, remember?"

I nodded. True. But trading in my previous career as a social worker to become a PI was a smidge harder than I thought. And going undercover like I was now was even trickier. It always looked fun in the movies—pretending to be someone else, wisecracking, and chasing down perps. In real life, there was more to it.

Camille stood back, cocked an eyebrow at me, and tapped the eyeliner pencil on her knee. "*Écoute-moi*," she said. "If you don't stay still, I'll have to start over."

I willed my eye to relax. "I'm trying." The twitching slowed, and she came at me with the eyeliner again. I grabbed her wrist before the black pencil reached my skin. "But don't make me look like a hooker, okay?"

Camille crooked an eyebrow at me and leaned forward to get back to work. When she was done with my makeup, she freed my hair from its ponytail, fluffing out the auburn waves so they skirted down my back and pulling a few tendrils forward to rest on my face. Then she passed me some silver hoop earrings and held out a ring. What looked like a diamond ring.

I slipped on the earrings and glanced at the ring. "Is that real?" I asked her.

"*Bien sûr.*"

I checked out the ring again. Simple, elegant white gold band, not too flashy stone. Just enough shimmer. I wasn't born with the diamond-loving gene, but I was born with a flood of sentimental genes and every one of them was melting into a big gooey puddle thinking about wearing the ring.

"*Attends,*" Laurent said to Camille as he came back into the room and took the ring from her. "She's my fiancée." He came over to me and reached for my hand. "That's my department," he said as he slipped the ring onto my finger.

"Don't you mean Léon's? Bunny is Léon's fiancée," I said, correcting him and trying to ignore the heat from his hands that flared through me like a shot of brandy. Laurent was hard wired with the French flirt gene, and I knew better than to take it personally. Not that he made it easy. The man should have a "Danger: High Voltage" sign stamped on his forehead.

A glint played in his eyes and he released my hand. "Of course."

"*Bien,*" Camille said, darting a look at her brother and edging her way between us. She zipped me up in black knee-high boots and steered me towards the full-length mirror on the back of her office door. "I present Mademoiselle Bunny Bosworth, future wife of Léon Clément."

I looked at my reflection in the mirror, twisting and turning to get a full sense of the outfit, my eyes stopping at my feet. "These boots fit remarkably well for loaners," I said, knowing Camille and I were usually off by a size.

"*Non, non,*" Camille said. "The boots are not mine. Those I bought for Bunny."

I glanced at Camille's image in the mirror, wondering just how much work had gone into planning for my new alter ego, and my eye twitched again. Then again when I went back to sizing up the new "me" and realized going undercover didn't seem to include actual coverage. Lucky for me, I was wearing a good bra because it was barely shielded by the blouse. Also lucky for me, the height difference between Camille and me meant her mini skirt wasn't so mini and came down nearly to my knees. I had to tug it up some to cover the new blue, fleur-de-lys tattoo I'd gotten recently on my backside, though. The only parts of my body the new look covered well were my eyes where smoky lids and thick, black liner made my blue eyes and pale skin appear lighter.

I pulled some of my hair around from the back and tried to arrange the waves to hide my bra. "Hmm. Bunny Clément," I said, unintentionally aloud, trying on my future pretend married name.

Camille picked a piece of lint off my skirt. "*Non, non,* Lora. In Québec a woman is not given the man's name when she marries. She is still considered independent. *Le mariage* is a partnership of equals."

"Really?" I said, feeling more respect for my adopted home. Back in New York, I'd known women who'd chosen to use their maiden names after they married, but their independence wasn't written into the law. "That's really progressive of you guys. Is that the same all over Canada?"

Camille shook her head. "Only in Québec I think. Didn't Adam ever tell you?"

"It never came up," I said.

"You've lived together for what, almost two years now, and you've never talked about getting married?"

I thought about it. "Not seriously, no."

Her eyebrows rose and fell so quickly someone who wasn't her best friend may have missed it.

"What?" I said. "Since when are you so big on marriage?"

Camille had an on-again off-again man in her life, but during the off times she had no shortage of men offering to keep her company. The last one she met on a case a couple months back, and she'd been seeing him ever since.

"I'm not," she said. "But you and Adam have been together a long time. I just thought that's where you were headed."

My boyfriend Adam and I had been together nearly three years. Somehow that hadn't felt long to me but maybe Camille was right. Maybe that was a long time. I looked down at the engagement ring on my finger. "Well. We might be."

Laurent handed me my coat. "Not tonight. Tonight you're mine."

"You mean Léon's," I corrected him again.

"Right," he said.

OUTSIDE, THE SNOW flurries had stopped and the street lights were on. Sidewalks were busy with local residents coming home and passers-by heading to one of the many restaurants that filled The Plateau neighborhood where Camille and Laurent's PI agency, C&C, was located. The area bordered the mountain Montreal was built around and local development picked up in the 1800s and hadn't stopped since. Over the years, many immigrants started their new lives in The Plateau. Nowadays, it attracted lots of artistic and bohemian types. Buildings were mostly stone or brick, many attached in long rows of triplexes with winding metal staircases out front. Housing prices were on an upward swing, and lucky investors were reaping the benefits. Unfortunately, parking spaces were rarely one of the benefits, and we were all forced to fend for places on the street.

Laurent and I walked nearly half a block before he stopped beside a sporty little black car I didn't recognize. He unlocked it with a remote, pulled the passenger door open, and grabbed the ice scraper from the seat before ushering me in and closing the door.

I watched him clear the snow and frost from the windows, his arms shifting seamlessly from the brush to the scraper, accomplishing the job in a quarter of the time it would have taken me. Then he walked around to the driver's side and got in beside me.

"Something wrong with your car?" I asked him. Technically, Laurent owned two cars, but one was a plain sedan he shared with Camille used mainly when they needed to go unnoticed like on stakeouts or when trailing people. The rest of the time Laurent drove a Beamer.

He took off his tuque and shook out his hair. "Rule number one when you're undercover is not to give yourself away." He made some adjustments to the seat and mirrors, buzzed his window down an inch, and pulled out. "This is a rental."

That explained the smell. A mix of talcum powder, cheap perfume, and chemistry class. I cracked my window to match Laurent's and pulled my coat tighter around me to offset the influx of cold air. It had been nearly two years since I moved from Soho to my boyfriend Adam's hometown of Montreal, but I still wasn't used to the harsh Canadian winters. The cold here seeped into your bones, and the abundance of snow piled everywhere narrowed streets and sidewalks and could cause near blindness when the sun reflected off of it on clear, sunny days. But on evenings like this, the snow could also feel protective and insulating, which I hoped would bode well for my first foray into undercover work.

I'd been working as an assistant for Camille and Laurent for over eight months and only recently told them that I wanted to become a full-fledged PI. In a while, when sessions started up again, I planned to take the mandatory courses to get my license. But it wouldn't be easy or fast. Québec had rules about licensing that didn't favor quickie weekend seminars. So in the meantime, officially, I remained on part-time assistant status with all its ensuing duties, and any major fieldwork I did required supervision by a licensed professional and fell under training. Up until now, Camille had been my mentor. But since she was also my best friend, she cut me a lot of slack. This was my first time working a case with Laurent, and as an ex-cop, he had a penchant for regulations and little patience for rule bending. Which could be a problem because I had a penchant for rule bending and little patience for regulations.

"So, what's on the agenda for tonight?" I asked him.

We stopped for a red light, and Laurent leaned across me to pop open the glove compartment. He pulled out a spiral notebook and dropped it in my lap. "How much do you know about the new case?"

I fingered the pad. "Just that we're working for your cousin Michel, that someone at his wedding planning company *Prêt-à-Marier* is committing identity theft, and that we're posing as clients to try and find out who's responsible."

Laurent smiled. "I see Camille has given you her version."

"Is there another version?"

"Of course. What Camille didn't tell you is that Michel may be wrong. He only *thinks* someone is stealing personal information from his customers and either selling it or using it to commit identity theft. Michel doesn't know for sure. Nobody has traced the thefts to *Prêt-à-Marier* yet."

"So why does Michel suspect it?"

"Some of the victims happened to have been his clients," Laurent said. "But that's not enough to link it to his company. Could be a coincidence. Personal information is stolen every day. First, we need to find out if Michel's suspicions are true. For now, we'll keep things quiet. He's afraid if word gets out, he'll lose business. But if he turns out to be right, he'll have to go to the police."

Sounded reasonable. "What are the thieves doing with the information?"

"Some victims reported debts racking up or new credit cards taken out in their names. Others found dummy versions of themselves being used to apply for driver's licenses and other legal documents. One woman was refused a mortgage because her credit report said she was a bad risk. She knew that was wrong. She paid all her bills on time, but she still lost out on her dream home because someone using her info ruined her reputation."

Wow. That was serious stuff. No wonder Michel was worried. "But when the woman explained it to the bank, they understood, right? Couldn't she get her mortgage then?"

Laurent eyed me. "*Non.* It doesn't work like that. It can take time and lots of proof to clear your name after identity theft."

"That's not fair," I said. "The one who committed the theft should be penalized, not the victim. That's crazy."

He slid his eyes to me again and shook his head. "*Ah*, Lora. There you go believing in fair again. First victims have to prove they're victims. And that includes companies. Michel can be held responsible if a breach is found at *Prêt-à-Marier* and he could have to cover the victims' financial losses. That could put him out of business. He needs to get to the bottom of this to protect his company as much as to protect his clients."

I didn't know much about identity theft, but what I did know made me think of it as personal. I'd never thought about it from a company's angle before. The financial costs could be bad, but seemed to me the real challenge would be recovering public trust. I hoped for Michel's sake he was wrong, and we could prove *Prêt-à-Marier* was in the clear. "So how do we help?"

"Already we've checked accounts for obvious breaches and found nothing. Now we go on the inside. There are three main ways to go: to pose as employees, trades people, or clients. Camille's going into the office as a computer consultant checking for a bug in their system. That gets her access to everyone's files. You and I will be clients. That buys us time with the wedding planner with the added benefit of presenting ourselves as bait. We'll also check out the suppliers the victims had in common. It's possible the problem is on their end. We're hitting one of those tonight. The *Danser* dance studio."

Dance studio? I was going to have to dance in this outfit? I'd had a hard enough time bending to get into the car. Between the boots hugging my knees and the skirt hugging my thighs, my legs had about as much flexibility as Barbie's.

He pointed to the notebook. "Flip through that, and you'll see a guy named Sylvain is the owner. He's also the main dance instructor."

I skimmed the pages. "So he teaches ballroom stuff? Arthur Murray? That kind of thing?"

"He's more of a choreographer. Couples choose three songs each that they want to dance to at their wedding, and he choreographs them."

"Why three?" I asked.

"The first dance as husband and wife, the last dance of the night, and one freebie."

I read through the bio for Sylvain, and despite the cold air circulating in the car, mists of sweat started trickling out of my pores and christening my outfit in various places. Sylvain was no slouch; this was going to be some serious dancing. Fabulous. It had taken me months to convince Laurent to let me go undercover, and I was going to blow it my first night. I'd never taken a dance class in my life. Not that I couldn't follow a beat. I made out pretty well at a club or a party. But that was different. More freestyle. Probably the first and only bona fide dance move I'd learned was the hokey pokey at summer camp when I was ten years old. And I never did get my "shake it all about" timing to match everyone else's.

"You don't look so good," Laurent said, glancing over at me.

I shifted in my seat. "I'm not much of a dancer."

He smiled. "Your Anglophone does not take you dancing?"

By my Anglophone he meant my boyfriend Adam. Laurent liked to tease me now and then about my relationship. I suspected it was partly because he didn't have a committed relationship of his own. Not that many women hadn't tried to hitch themselves to him. But Laurent wasn't interested in getting hitched. At least not yet. Probably because he enjoyed the untethered life so much.

"Adam and I dance at parties and stuff," I told him. "But nothing formal. Nothing that takes specific steps or great rhythm or anything."

Laurent shot a glimpse my way again, still smiling. "Rhythm is very important, Lora. A pity you don't have it with your Anglophone."

I rolled my eyes. Laurent never missed a chance at a crack. "We *have* rhythm," I said. "I just meant that we never took lessons."

"Not a problem." He let his gaze slip briefly from the road to where my hands tugged at the hemline of my skirt trying to pull it as close to the boots as possible. "Tonight's just a meet and greet for all the couples who signed up. Our goal is to see how they run things and establish ourselves as Léon and Bunny."

I stopped fidgeting and let out a deep breath. That didn't sound bad. I could handle that.

"The instructor needs some time to work on the choreography. We don't start dancing until the next lesson."

I guess I could YouTube something before then. Maybe some kind soul put up a *Dancing for Dummies*.

"Okay," he said as he pulled into a side lot bordering a wide, brick building three-storeys high and probably at least a century old. "This is it. Show time."

He took the notebook from me and stuffed it back in the glove compartment before getting out of the car. I hung back and took another deep breath to quell the stage fright brewing in my gut. No worries, I assured myself. Show time was just an expression. Going undercover didn't really take true acting skill. This would not be like the high school drama class I nearly failed. After all, this was work, not school. No one was grading me.

But when Laurent appeared at my door and extended his hand to help me out of the car, I caught the look on his face and knew that last bit was a big fat lie.

TWO

INSIDE, THE BUILDING was all lobby with a staircase straight ahead and a long hallway heading left and right. A small glass-enclosed directory on the immediate wall was the only give-away that the place was tenanted by businesses. The directory listed the dance studio on the second floor, but I stopped short at the base of the long flight of marble stairs in front of me.

"Isn't there an elevator?" I asked Laurent.

"*Non*. A lot of these old buildings don't have elevators," he said as he started up.

The stairs were flanked by the wall on one side and an iron and wood railing on the other. I made my way over to the railing, grabbed onto the banister, and tried a step. I thought the boots would undermine my sense of balance because I wasn't used to walking in stilettos, but it turned out to be the skirt that posed the bigger problem. It had very little give and my legs couldn't quite clear the steps.

Laurent turned back when he noticed I wasn't beside him. "Problem?" he said.

I didn't want to admit a skirt was slowing me down. What kind of PI gets waylaid by her own clothes? "No. I just need a sec."

He joined me back at the bottom of the stairs, reached down, and hiked up my skirt a few inches.

"Hey," I said, darting my eyes around for onlookers and trying to pull the skirt back into place.

"Just try it," he said.

I checked the staircase again to make sure no one had appeared, slipped the skirt back up, and tried the step. Perfect.

He grinned at me, and I fixed my attention on the stairs as I went up. Big whoop. So he thought of the skirt raising bit before I did. I would have thought of it too if I wasn't so busy quelling my stage fright.

At the top of the stairs, I pulled myself together and paused to straighten my clothes. I had just about centered the seam in the back of my stockings when I felt Laurent's hands pulling at my coat.

"First impressions," he said to me as the coat slipped from my body.

I shot him a look. That coat was my protection, my camouflage. Without that coat I felt on display. Naked even. Which was fair since parts of me nearly were. When I'd pictured going undercover, I'd thought wigs and dark glasses, not peek-a-boo blouses and short skirts. What had I gotten myself into?

Laurent added my coat to the clothes rack just inside the door to the dance studio and followed it with his own. I folded my arms across my chest and tried not to sway in my heels while I waited for him. He turned back to me, smiled, and gestured for my hand. I reluctantly gave it to him, sorry for the loss of chest coverage but glad for the added mooring that would save me from ending up spread eagle on the floor giving everyone a peek at the rest of my underwear.

We headed over to a bank of metal chairs that had been set up near the far wall and took our seats. A draft from the old windows that lined the wall spilled onto me, and I inched my chair closer to the radiator. Not that it helped really. The room was enormous and poorly insulated. The exterior wall of windows, punctuated only with rows of whitewashed bricks, were picturesque but provided little protection from the winter chill. And whatever heat was in the room seemed to be wafting up to the high ceiling of white ornate tile painted to match the far walls and wood floor, only the latter was sun faded and scuffed and reminded me of bruised banana.

"Relax," Laurent whispered to me when he noticed me fussing with my chair near the radiator.

"I'm cold," I whispered back.

He reached for my chair and quietly slid both it and me over to him, encircling me with his arm and pulling me into his body. "Better?"

I nodded. It was. Much. The radiator had nothing on Laurent. Plus, I felt safer, more covered again. Still nervous, though. If it was even possible, my stomach seemed to be doing more flip flops. This undercover work was going to take me some time to get used to.

There were two other couples settling themselves in the chairs around us and another man and woman standing over by a table along the side wall. The woman at the table was young, tall yet slight, and dressed in street clothes. The man had on a blousy shirt, form-fitting dark pants, was maybe mid-thirties, and sported a Baryshnikov wave in his hair. When he crossed the room towards us, he walked straight-backed and pigeon-toed.

"*Bonsoir,*" he said to the group and introduced himself. "*Je m'appelle* Sylvain."

The woman came up behind him, carrying a stack of clipboards. "*Voici* Cindy," he said, motioning towards her. Then he paused, noticing another couple just arriving. While he waited for them to join the rest of us, he had Cindy pass out the clipboards to each couple.

I looked down at the clipboard we were given and scanned the sheets attached. They were in French. Which did me no good since learning French was slow in coming for me. Very slow. That's why I wasn't a social worker anymore. Bilingualism was required to work for most social services here, and I was far from bilingual. I squinted at the sheet trying to pick out some meaning from the few words I recognized.

Laurent watched me a minute, shook his head, then flipped the paper over. The other side was in English. In Montreal, people often slipped seamlessly from one language to the next in conversations, but not all paperwork did the same. I was grateful this did. I smiled at him and started to read. The first page was a standard release form exempting the studio from any accidents that may befall us during our lessons, and the second page asked how we'd heard about their services, what motivated us to take the class, and other marketing related questions. We were asked to sign and date the first page and fill in the second.

I signed the first page, deciding Bunny Bosworth had a slanted, messy signature with only the two Bs large and legible, and passed the clipboard over to Laurent and watched him sign for Léon Clément. Then we both spent some time surveying the second sheet for any questions that asked for more personal information. Things that might be used for identity theft. It asked for basic info but nothing out of the ordinary, so Laurent filled in the blanks with random answers and handed our clipboard back to Cindy.

She twirled a strand of her streaked-blonde hair with her finger and flashed him a smile—all plumped lips and no teeth—then slowly moved on to collect the other forms.

When I directed my attention back to Sylvain, he was asking each couple to introduce themselves to the group and share a bit about each person.

The couple to my right went first. Sébastien and Juliette, an attractive twosome probably barely out of university. Sébastien was in banking and Juliette was a teacher, and they were getting married early April. Then we met Emmaline and George, two preppy, thirtysomething computer programmers who were to be married mid March. And beside them, Anna and Peter, the only completely Anglophone couple in the group who appeared to be a nearly May-December pairing. She was a freelance accountant and he ran a store, and their wedding was planned for the first week in March.

When it was our turn, Laurent spoke for both of us telling them that I was an office assistant and he was a carpenter, and apparently we were less than four weeks from our wedding date in February.

Sylvain let out a small squeal and looked down at his own clipboard.

"*C'est bientôt,*" he said. Then, probably prompted by his notes reminding him I only speak English, he switched languages. "You won't have much time left to practice before your big day. Let me make sure I have your song choices right. You have *When you Love Someone* by Bryan Adams, *I'll always be There* by Roch Voisine, *et puis* another Bryan Adams *If you Wanna be Bad, You gotta be Good.*" He looked up, his eyebrows arching. *"C'est plutôt original."*

I turned to Laurent. "What was that he said?"

Juliette beside me smiled. "He said that last song choice was quite different."

I wasn't very good with song titles, so I didn't even know which song they were talking about. I knew some Bryan Adams tunes, but I couldn't place this one. And I had no idea who Roch Voisine was at all. The way Sylvain said the singer's name, it sounded like "Rock," and the only Rock I'd ever heard of was Rock Hudson. I eyed Laurent who was curiously silent.

Wondering what Sylvain could have meant by his remark, I barely took in what he said next as he went over the other couples' song choices. Only that the Anglophone couple picked all Céline Dion hits.

Sylvain ended his talk by explaining that there were some rehearsal rooms down the hall that we would also be using so that although we'd all come three times a week at the same time, we'd each practice individually to our different songs. And at the end of each lesson we'd come together in the big room to showcase what we'd learned and get used to dancing in front of a group. He added in a reminder to dress comfortably and bring the right shoes before he invited us to stay and get to know each other over some coffee and cookies laid out on a table in the corner.

As soon as Sylvain stepped away, a few people headed over to the refreshment table, and I motioned to get up too, but Laurent placed his hand on my leg to stop me. I turned to read his face and followed his eyes across the room to where Sylvain and Cindy were now huddled together in deep conversation. Sylvain was working hard to restrain his gesticulations and Cindy's cheeks were reddening.

I was about to ask Laurent if we should try to get closer to listen in when Sébastien leaned across Juliette and said, *"C'est une belle chanson t'est choisi, n'est-ce pas?"*

Laurent moved his hand further up my thigh with subtle strokes. "What could we do? That's our song. Bunny wanted it in the wedding, and I couldn't disappoint her."

I shot Laurent a look and put my own hand on top of his to still it. And since I didn't have a clue about the mystery song they were talking about, I had nothing to add, so I just plastered a smile on my face to appear friendly. Which apparently encouraged Sébastien to grab a peek at my cleavage and shoot a wink to Laurent.

Ugh. I crossed my arms over my chest again and suppressed the urge to sock Sébastien in the eye.

Juliette stood, either unfazed by Sébastien's behavior or unseeing, and stretched her long limbs before heading over to the refreshment table. I watched a minute then followed, figuring Laurent wouldn't object now. Not when Sébastien had launched into some kind of nattering in French. This way at least one of us could keep watch on Cindy and Sylvain. And I could do that way better from over by the table without the distraction of the winking and man talk.

I poured myself some coffee, popped a cookie in my mouth, and discretely scanned over to Sylvain and Cindy. They were still across the room, but now they sat calmly and seemed to be going over paperwork.

"What do you think they're talking about?" Juliette asked me, her long, sleek dark hair leaning with the tilt of her head.

"Excuse me?" I said.

"Our fiancés," she said. "They look pretty intense. What do you think they're talking about? Me, I think it must be hockey."

I looked over at Laurent and Sébastien, still seated and chatting amiably. "Probably." Seemed to me, Montreal men talked about two things in the winter—hockey and more hockey. Laurent had played in the minor leagues and still played with a local team every week. Hockey was serious sport, serious fun, and serious talk. Knock a guy's family and probably he'll forgive you eventually, knock his favorite team and maybe not.

"My Sébastien is a big fan," she said. "What about you? Your fiancé a fan or a player?"

"Both."

"Ah," she said. "I thought so. He's got good muscles."

Yeah, women were always noticing Laurent's muscles along with everything else. The Carons were French Canadians stretching back generations and somewhere along the line some Native heritage got mixed in. Laurent got his dark eyes, even darker hair, and solid body from those genes. Add in his quiet confidence and edge of mystique, and he was hard to miss. He stood out even more than usual in this crowd, though. Juliette's fiancé seemed pretty fit, but the other two men looked more like eating was their chosen sport. Peter, the other half of the Anglophone couple, more so than George the computer programmer. George had the body of a bulldog, but Peter had a gut. Peter was also easily the oldest. Early fifties maybe. Plus, he was bald and not in the good way. His fiancée Anna looked to be about twenty years younger. She was also eerily thin and moved like a cell phone left on vibrate.

Juliette turned to see what was keeping my attention. "Those two are quite the story," she told me. "Before class, Cindy and Peter were getting caught up. This is Peter's fourth time taking the class."

Wow. Must be some bad dancer. Was it wrong I found that comforting?

"And he met Anna here on round three," she added.

Wait. Maybe I had this wrong. "You mean he's been married three times before?"

"Not all of the relationships made it to the marriage stage. But Anna's not the first fiancée he met here. He met wife number two when he was taking lessons for his wedding to wife number one."

I looked down at the other end of the table where Peter, Anna, and the other couple were talking. Must be something about Peter that made him attractive to women. Something I couldn't see. Not his table manners, clearly. Fresh coffee stains dotted down his shirt and onto the front of his slacks. No doubt leaking from his mouth which was open wide enough to make out that the type of cookie he was munching was chocolate chip.

Our eyes caught, and he closed his mouth, nodded his head at me, and winked.

What was with all this winking? Seriously. Were people really still doing the wink thing?

I turned back to the table to cut off any further face gymnastics with him and reached for another cookie. I nearly dropped it when I heard a loud clap.

"People, people," Sylvain said as he strode into the center of the room and clapped his hands again. *Merci d'être ici ce soir.* Thank you for coming tonight. I must leave now, but I look forward to seeing you all next time."

I finished my cookie, surprised the meet-and-greet was over so soon. Aside from the brief skirmish earlier, nothing about Sylvain or Cindy raised any red flags with me yet. As far as I could tell, the evening netted us nada.

As we gathered our coats and filed out, George, the programmer, tapped me on the shoulder. "Can't wait to see your dance," he said, smoothing his crew cut. "Bet it'll be real steamy."

Beside him, his fiancée Emmaline gave my outfit the once-over as she linked her arm through George's, her long, manicured nails resting on his jacket sleeve. She pressed her thin lips together, her eyes hawk-like under heavy black bangs, and threw me a smile with slightly more judgment than pity.

I didn't care for the look or the comment. What did George mean by steamy? I looked up at Laurent for an explanation.

He slipped his arm around my shoulder and bent down. But all he said was, "Good work tonight, Bunny," as his lips brushed across my cheek.

Figuring I could quiz Laurent better in the car, I made my way over to the stairs and angled past Juliette to get to the banister. I grabbed hold of the railing and tried not to look at my feet as I started down so I wouldn't lose my balance on the spiky heels. I looked in the distance instead, like I was driving my car rather than my body. Only my view wasn't some far off horizon, a cool new hybrid, or an archaic gas guzzler. It was the back of Peter's balding head with its die-hard strands of hair wafting to and fro as he made his way down, huffing and puffing, ahead of me.

When he stopped mid-stair and pitched forward, I instinctively put on my brakes and came to a halt, tightening my grip on the banister. Then his head disappeared from my view, and I watched in stunned horror as his body tumbled the rest of the way down the stairs and crumpled into a motionless heap when it reached the lobby. I blinked, hoping when I opened my eyes Peter would be in front of me again. But he wasn't. I let go of the railing and raced down the stairs, my heels never touching marble until I reached the landing, where a stream of blood circled the toe of my boots.

THREE

BY THE TIME Laurent dropped me at home, I was exhausted. Witnessing a death did that to me. And Peter was dead all right. Heart attack probably, the paramedics had said. Or maybe brain injury during the fall. Given that Peter had no vitals, there wasn't anything they could do for him. They went through the motions of trying to revive him, but it was wasted effort. Said he must have died instantly, which seemed right because he hadn't responded at all when Laurent had tried CPR on him. And Laurent had been fast about it too, being careful not to move Peter's body too much in case something was broken, and working around the blood that was leaking from Peter's nose. I hoped the paramedics were right about the death being instant. It was better than thinking of how Peter must have felt to slowly lose consciousness while he hurtled downward. It's not that I knew him well, but I wouldn't wish that on anybody.

I stepped into the house I shared with my boyfriend Adam, closed the front door, and leaned against it for support. The door was good and solid like the rest of the house. With three bedrooms and only one bath, the two-storey brick home wasn't huge, but it had been built from sturdy material by men with sturdy hands. It was nearly a hundred years old and Adam had inherited it from his mother only a few months after we came to look after her in her last stages of cancer. We'd done some painting and made some repairs, but the house still held the protective aura of a mother's loving arms. Something I found comforting now.

Instinctively, I reached for the locket I'd inherited from my own mother after her death and lost a breath when it wasn't around my neck. Then I remembered I hadn't worn it in preparation for going undercover and felt myself shudder with relief. One emotional trauma for the night was enough.

I heard a noise upstairs and looked past the vestibule door to see Adam at the top of the staircase.

"I thought I heard you come in," he said and made his way downstairs. His cropped brown hair was damp, and he had on gray sweats and a T-shirt from an old U2 concert. He stopped a minute to pull on some socks before coming over to me. "You look tired. Long day?"

I stepped into the hall, not bothering to shed my outdoor gear just yet. "You could say that." I said and explained what happened to Peter, still not quite believing it myself.

"Shit," he said. "Come on. Come sit down."

He brought me over to the couch in the living room and we both sat. He leaned over, switched on a table lamp, and reached for me.

As a social worker, I'd been around my share of trauma and people in distress. I had techniques to handle it. But seeing someone die right in front of me was a new experience. One I didn't like. "I think the surprise of it all just got to me," I told Adam, nestling into him.

"I guess," he said, sounding unconvinced.

"What do you mean?"

"Well, it's not really a surprise, is it? What did you expect when you decided to get into this PI business? It's not like your old social work job didn't have its hazards, but at least you weren't dealing with criminals all the time. Criminals attract trouble."

Actually, as a counselor I'd occasionally worked with clients who had broken laws. Just not when they were in the midst of breaking them. But I didn't deal with criminals all the time now either. At least not serious ones. Mostly, C&C tracked cheating spouses and insurance scammers and worked for employers or lawyers doing background checks or finding witnesses, inheritors, and the like.

I loosened Adam's grip on me, unbuttoned my coat, and sat back. "I never said this guy was a criminal. He was just a regular Joe. Probably had a heart attack. It could happen to anyone. The guy wasn't exactly mister fitness. You should have heard him straining on the stairs. I have no idea how he thought he'd manage a dance class."

Adam leaned away some and got a better look at me. "You were at a dance class? I thought you were working."

I tried to pull my coat closed, but it was too late. He'd already registered the Bunny outfit. "I *was* working."

His eyes went to the ring on my left hand, and he backed away a bit more. "Something else about tonight you want to tell me?"

I pulled off the ring and put it on the coffee table. "This? This is nothing. Just part of the disguise. You remember? I told you I'd be going undercover on this case."

"Undercover you told me about. An engagement you did not."

"It's not a real engagement. It's just pretend."

He looked over at the ring. "That doesn't look very pretend."

"Well, yeah, the ring is real. But I'm only pretending to be Laurent's fiancée."

"I see," he said. "And you have to marry him for pretend too?"

"Of course not. It's just part of our cover." I explained about Michel and his suspicions about the identity thefts.

"Isn't that traceable by computers or identity theft specialists?" Adam said. This was less a question and more a statement. Adam created educational software, so he knew a lot about tech stuff.

"Michel doesn't want to go outside the family on this yet. He's afraid of losing clients. Plus, he's not a hundred percent sure about his suspicions." Or, at least Laurent wasn't sure of Michel's suspicions. "It may have nothing to do with Michel's company."

"So in the meantime, you're going around telling the world that you're engaged to Laurent?"

"Well, not me Lora. I've got an alias."

"Which is?"

I was so hoping he wouldn't ask me that. "Umm, it's Bunny. Bunny Bosworth."

"Bunny? You named yourself Bunny?"

The furnace was cranked pretty high and the heat was starting to get to me. I wanted to take off my coat but thought better of it. A partial view of my outfit through the open coat was already getting me into trouble. "I didn't exactly pick the name. It's just the name I got from C&C."

Adam's voice dropped down. "From exactly who at C&C?"

This was the bit I really didn't want to tell him because I knew he'd get the wrong idea. I trained my eyes on the floor. "Laurent, I think."

"I see," he said for the second time that night. This was not a good sign. When Adam said "I see" it had nothing to do with understanding. It meant he was conjuring up his own take on a situation. He stood and started tidying the room, collecting remotes, straightening books. "And I take it he's the one you're taking these dance lessons with?"

"Well, yeah."

"You learning classics?"

I knew what he was getting at. He was thinking slow dancing in each other's arms.

"No. It's not like that at all." I went on to tell him that Laurent had an alias too and about the three songs and the choreography.

Adam stopped tidying and looked at me. "What three songs?"

I rattled off the names.

He didn't look especially pleased about any of them, but his eyes widened on the last one. "You're kidding me, right?"

I was pretty sure I had remembered the right titles. "Why? What's wrong with them?"

He came over and took my hand, propelling me up, and led me to his home office upstairs. The door was closed and when he opened it, our dachshund, Pong, dashed out and body-checked my legs. A few feet behind her, our cat Ping, curled up on the sofa bed, opened one eye by way of greeting then went back to sleeping. I sat beside her and stroked her back while I waited for Adam to explain the room change.

He sat in his Aeron chair and fired up his computer. A minute later, the speakers blared out one of the Bryan Adams' tunes. I didn't recognize it, so I was guessing it was the second one. The one Sylvain had said was different. I hadn't really placed the first song either, but I did have a vague recollection of it being popularized in a movie with Sandra Bullock, and I knew if I heard it I'd remember it. The tune playing now had a sultry beat. I tried to keep my face from showing my surprise while I listened to Bryan describe a woman with a nasty reputation and a talent for sin and sing out about making a night to remember from January to December.

As it occurred to me that I was supposed to dance to the song at my wedding, it got harder to rein in my emotion. I knew the wedding was fake, but the other couples at the dance class didn't. Now I understood the programmer guy's steamy comment. The music was more striptease than soft shoe.

To busy myself so Adam wouldn't pick up on my reaction, I slipped out of my coat and yanked off my boots, letting them drop to the floor. When I looked back up, Adam had his chair swiveled my way and was watching me, and I remembered I'd been keeping my coat on for a reason.

"What?" I said, my voice a mix of attempted indifference and irritation.

He held my gaze. "You come home looking like a hooker, calling yourself Bunny, and telling me you're off pretending to be engaged to Laurent and dancing to sexy songs, and you can't figure out what's wrong?"

Naturally, I zeroed in on the most important point first. "You think I look like a hooker?"

He ran his hands over his hair and gave me the once-over. "Maybe not a hooker, but you don't look like you."

"That's kind of the point when you're undercover," I said to him as if I was speaking from great expertise on the subject. I got up and headed out of the room. "But if it bothers you so much, I'll change."

I went into the bedroom, grabbed some leggings and a roomy T-shirt, then stomped off to the bathroom to shower and change. I started the water running and the old pipe let out a groan. I groaned back and wiped off my makeup while I waited for the water to heat. The face in the mirror wasn't familiar, but it was definitely *not* hooker. Camille had come through and been careful putting on my Bunny face. True, it was more makeup than I usually wore, but then that didn't take much since sometimes I didn't wear any. And I guess the clothes did their bit to create the image too. Even I felt like my goods were on display in the clothes. But not on offer. There was a big difference.

I peeled off the Bunny clothes and got in the shower. As the warm water streamed over me, it hit me that I might be overreacting to Adam's comments. He had a right to his feelings. If the situation were reversed, I'd be giving him a hard time too. I'd certainly felt pangs of jealousy over far less. He was actually having a pretty tame reaction by comparison. Most likely, my overreaction was simply a diversion tactic to get my mind off of Peter. It would be a long time, if ever, before I got the image of his tumbling body out of my head. Probably I was in some kind of shock. A part of me was even grateful Adam had brought up the Bunny thing. It seemed easier to think about that than about Peter's death.

I thought about Peter's fiancée, Anna, and how she'd stood off to the side watching as first Laurent and then the paramedics tried to save Peter. She seemed oddly small, her face elfin-like. Not once did she rush to Peter's side. And she never cried. She just stood, clutching her purse, until the paramedics led her away after they'd removed Peter's body. Poor Anna. She must have been in shock too.

FOUR

"**I MOVED YOUR** car down the block," Camille said when I got to the office the next morning. "It's on the other side of the street about halfway down."

"Thanks," I said. My Mini had been left behind the day before when I went over to the dance studio with Laurent in the Léon car. But street parking around the C&C office had all sorts of restrictions at the best of times, and in winter, snow clearing added even more. Avoiding parking tickets and towing could have been its own seasonal sport. I'd learned that the hard way enough times to have finally given in and left a spare car key at the office.

I took off my coat and hooked it onto a peg in reception alongside Camille's jacket. An old converted house that had been two semis in its prior life, the C&C office was a lower unit of four suites, one up, one down on either side. The house had lots of stone on the outside and lots of hardwood on the inside, and the renovation did little to tamper with either. The small reception was in an alcove off the hall with access to the basement, the original living room at the front of the house served as Camille's office, the old dining room in the middle as Laurent's office, and the kitchen at the back had been compacted to allow for a bathroom addition alongside it. I worked out of the office for the most part, so no space had been designated for me. But I did recently get my own voice mail line—an event I took as a major sign of career advancement.

I headed to the kitchen to nab some coffee and took it over to the bistro table where I sat and watched Camille rummage through the fridge. When she bent to reach for something on the second shelf, her short blonde hair got a highlight boost from the fridge bulb and looked almost platinum. It went well with her tailored dark pants and stylish red cardigan. I looked down at my jeans and turtleneck sweater that had seen better days and felt a twinge of envy.

She pulled out some cream cheese and put a bagel into the toaster. "I heard about last night," she said, turning to face me. "*Horrible*, no?"

I nodded.

Her bagel popped, and she pushed it down again and stepped closer to me, her face intent on mine. "You okay?"

"Yeah," I told her. And I was. No sudden flashes of dead bodies or bouncing heads all morning. "Any more info on exactly what happened to Peter?"

"Not yet. Laurent's out now seeing what he can find out. Us, we're pushing on with Michel's case." She came closer still and pivoted the laptop she had on the kitchen table so I could see the screen. "This is the *Prêt-à-Marier* website. Have a look."

I flicked through the site she had up in her browser, getting to know a bit more about Michel's company and reading through the short bios on his employees. He had five by the looks of it: a receptionist, and two wedding planners, each with an assistant. I remembered Laurent telling me Camille would be working onsite and that he and I would be working the supplier angle alongside one of the wedding planners, so I asked which wedding planner was ours.

Camille pointed to a picture of an older woman, dark hair pulled back, no smile. "*Celle-là*," she said. She moved her finger along to other photos in turn as she continued. "The other wedding planner isn't a suspect. He's a good friend of Michel's. And the receptionist is family, away on vacation now with the friend's assistant." She withdrew her fingertip from the last picture—a man in his twenties, crooked teeth, mellow eyes. "Those two are clean also."

While Camille went to tend her bagel when it popped for the second time, I leaned in to get a closer look at the photos. If I

27

excluded the second wedding planner along with his assistant and the receptionist, that left only two employees to investigate. The older woman with no smile and a young woman with lots of smile. Which probably meant the bulk of the legwork on the case would fall on Laurent and me as we planned Bunny and Léon's faux wedding and checked out suppliers. Which meant I'd be playing Bunny. A lot.

Camille slathered her bagel with the cheese, brought it over to the table, and sat across from me. "You sure you're okay?" she said. "You look distracted." She reached out, closed the lid on the computer, and kept her eyes on me.

I stalled while I collected my thoughts, blowing on my coffee and taking a few sips. Mostly I'm a tea drinker, but Camille and Laurent almost always had fresh coffee in one form or another sitting in wait, and over time I'd defaulted to drinking it more and more. Nothing like the appeal of no prep time to lure a gal over to the darker side. Only the extra caffeine boost held less appeal, so I was careful to let it ease into my system. Especially the batches Camille made, which could turn a narcolepsy sufferer into an insomniac.

"I'm fine," I finally said, keeping my eyes glued to my coffee. Camille could spot a fib at fifty paces. And I was fibbing big time. Ever since my run-in with Adam about Bunny, I'd been thinking about this whole undercover gig. Adam was right. I was no Bunny. It was one thing to pull off the role for a few hours. But every day? I could barely walk in the clothes and the stilettos. I couldn't dance. I was cold all the time. And the wedding song Adam had played for me gave me nightmares of stripper poles.

None of this I wanted to admit to Camille.

She took a bite of her bagel and drummed her fingers on the table. "Spill," she said.

"There's nothing to spill. Really, I'm good." Doubts or not, no way was I going to cop to them. I didn't want Laurent to find out I had reservations and think I didn't have the chops to work undercover.

Camille's finger drumming grew louder. "This isn't still about the Bunny name, is it?"

"No," I said. True, at first I hadn't been so keen on the name, but now that I'd given it more thought, I knew there was nothing wrong with it. Probably lots of women were called Bunny. Lots of perfectly nice, smart women. I never heard of a CEO named Bunny, but I'm sure there was at least one out there. Somewhere.

"Look, it's nothing okay," I told Camille. Knowing she wouldn't let it go if I didn't give her something, I reached for the first thing that popped into my head. "Adam wasn't thrilled when I got home last night, that's all. He thought the Bunny clothes made me look tarty."

Camille's finger drumming stopped. "Those were *my* clothes," she said.

Okay, maybe I should have reached a little deeper before letting that pop out. I shrugged and tried to put a positive spin on my gaffe. "I guess Adam just thought the clothes were too sexy."

"Your Anglophone is wrong, Lora. Clothes are not sexy," Laurent said from behind me.

I hadn't heard him come in. No surprise. Somewhere along the line Laurent had done some SWAT training, and the man could sneak into a convent without being noticed. I turned to see him leaning against the kitchen doorframe, wearing his coat open over his jeans.

He met my eyes and continued, "It's the people in them."

He was way off base if he was trying to direct that line at me. I was more the all-American-apple-pie-girl-next-door type. Sexy was for cheerleaders and prom queens.

The front door opened behind Laurent, and he pulled his eyes away from mine to take in the man walking in. The guy was tall, with short blonde hair, angular cheekbones, the palest blue eyes I'd ever seen, and he was wearing a tailored trench coat over navy slacks. His name was Luc, and he was a cop. He was also Camille's ex. He and Camille had shared house and home a few years ago. Since then, unofficially, they still indulged in their favorite contact sport when no other partners were in play. Officially, they consulted when C&C cases crossed paths with police matters.

Luc greeted the group of us then tipped his head at Laurent, gesturing towards Laurent's office, and both men went inside and closed the door.

Camille's eyes squinted, the rest of her body rigid in her chair.

"Any idea what that's about?" I asked her.

She shook her head, her chin set, before standing and clearing her dishes. I watched as she loaded the mini-dishwasher and slammed the door shut, the top of it bouncing back open. She let out a stream of air and French expletives, flipped the dishwasher door back up, and made a beeline for Laurent's office.

I smiled and waited at the table. Camille didn't take well to being left out of anything and Luc knew it. And if he didn't remember, he was about to. Camille's rapid-fire French started up, and a minute later Laurent came into the kitchen and sat down beside me. We both looked up at the sound of his office door clicking closed and voices rising, both of us pretending not to notice.

Laurent reached over the table and adjusted the neck of my sweater. "Bunny doesn't wear turtlenecks," he said. Then he slipped his hand into the back pocket of his jeans and pulled out his wallet. He extracted a credit card and held it out to me. "*Vas-y*. Go shop. You've got about an hour before Léon and Bunny have their next appearance. Get something good. *Et plus qu'un* outfit. This case could take a while. Turns out, Peter was one of the identity theft victims and his parents have been to the police. They say he was murdered."

"Murdered?" I said, my voice a mix of confusion and surprise. How could slipping down a flight of stairs be murder?

Laurent arched his eyebrows and waited for me to take hold of the credit card. I reached for the card, and he held onto it a beat before releasing it to my fingers and sitting back, his dark eyes on me. "*Oui, ma petite* Lora. Murdered."

FIVE

MURDERED. I COULDN'T get the word out of my head. Peter's parents had to be wrong. How could he have been murdered? The man just fell down a flight of stairs. I saw it myself. He wasn't tripped or pushed or anything. I know because the only one close enough to do any of that was me. "I still don't get it," I said to Camille as we shopped for my Bunny clothes.

"*Moi non plus.* Luc explained nothing. He said it's not official until the autopsy comes in. Until then he can share no details. Procedure, he said." She slid hangers back and forth on the rack in front of her so fast they squeaked. "Pffft. Procedure nothing. It's because of Bell."

Bell was Camille's name for Paul Bell, aka Puddles, a man we'd reconnected with his daughter on an earlier case, following which he and Camille did a little connecting of their own, and they were still together.

"Maybe," I said, shifting over to look through some folded shirts on a round display. "Or maybe Luc really is following procedure. He's a good cop."

Camille stopped her hanger sliding and glared at me. "*Oui*, he's a good cop. But we're working the same case. *C'est ridicule* to not tell me more. It has to be about Bell."

"You're probably right," I said, not sure if I believed it but seeing no point in speculating further about Luc's motivations.

"*Celle-là?*" Camille said, getting back to her hangers and holding up a pair of dark stretch jeans that looked small for a five year old.

I shook my head.

"*Mais voyons*, Lora. Pick something already. All you have so far is a sweater and two skirts."

I looked over at the pile I'd set down on the chair next to the sale rack I was back to skimming. "There's not a lot left in my size."

Camille did an arm sweep move like a model showing merchandise on a game show. "There's a whole store of your size. *Allez*. Get out of the discount corner and look."

She was right, of course. There were probably lots of choices. The store Camille had brought me to was compact but crammed with diverse offerings. All trendy and all expensive. The few price tags I'd checked on my way to the racks in the back were all in the three figures. But it didn't seem right to spend that much on Laurent's C&C credit card.

Camille pulled out her phone, tapping the toe of her Doc Marten on the tile floor. "Enough already. Laurent will be here for you in twenty-five minutes." She dropped her phone into her bag and set off, flipping through items, occasionally pulling something out and draping it over her arm.

I hurried over to see what she was collecting, and she hugged the pile to her body.

"Not to worry," she said to me. "It's all good." She gestured with her free hand. "You go grab some jewelry over there."

I skimmed her heap, recognizing bits of clothes I'd noticed on the way in, things I would have considered myself if the price had been right. Anything else she included that I didn't want would be easier to return later. So I picked up my finds and headed over to check out the jewelry, finding some earrings, a couple of necklaces, and a silver cuff bangle bracelet that I decided would make a good signature piece for Bunny. Camille was already at the cash when I was done, leaving me just enough time to add my finds to our purchases.

When we stepped out onto Rue Saint-Denis, Camille made a hard left and a few storefronts later, disappeared into another store. I looked up at the awning overhead as I walked over. *Lingerie de Lisette* stretched the length of it in purple script. I didn't recognize the name. Not a surprise since Camille didn't do chain stores, and Montreal was full of boutiques I didn't know. I sighed, hoped this little pit stop was for her benefit not mine, and followed her inside in time to see her park our bags with the cashier and motion to me.

I caught up with her, and she hustled me into a dressing room.

"*D'accord*," she said. "Strip down to your bra."

"What?"

She whipped a measuring tape out of her handbag and twirled it at me. "*Vite, vite.*"

I frowned. "I don't want any new underwear."

"You'll thank me later." She twirled the tape measure at me again. "Now hurry up."

After a sigh of resignation I said, "I already know my size."

"Everybody thinks that. And they're usually wrong."

I started undressing, my eyes on the tape measure. Camille worked a summer for some hotshot lingerie store during a college year she spent in France, and she took proper fitting seriously. Arguing with her would be time consuming and pointless. I barely had my turtleneck hooked onto the peg on the back wall before she went to work sizing me up.

"Okay," she said when she was done. "Get dressed. We don't have enough time for you to try everything on. We'll just grab and go." And she slipped out.

I got my clothes on as fast as I could and joined her in the shop, afraid she was going to pull out a bunch of push-up bras and a set of enhancers. But instead, she gathered up delicate lacy pieces with fine detailing. Not an underwire in the bunch.

"Nice," I said. "But seriously, I don't need any of this."

Camille cocked her head at me. "*Mais voyons*, Lora. You want to do undercover work, you need the tools for the trade."

Not the kind of tools I thought about when I thought about PI work. "I want to be a PI not a lingerie model," I told her.

"*Exactement.* A good PI uses her assets to her full advantage. *All* her assets. Flirting and distraction can be very helpful in disarming people. Everybody underestimates the fun girl, eh. Trust me, these will make the job easier."

That was Canada for you. With all the gun laws, packing heat had a whole other definition. No guns and ammo but plenty of garters and bustiers. Not that any of them would be of help to me. I couldn't see myself packing either set.

Camille nudged me towards checkout. "Anyway, it won't hurt for you to get some nice things."

"I already have nice things," I said.

She cocked an eyebrow at me. "*Vraiment*, Lora, I've seen your closet. You've got functional things. Your bras are for support, your camisoles are for warmth, and your panties are all white briefs."

"Hey, white cotton underpants are healthy," I said. "You're supposed to wear those."

She shook her head to dismiss the idea and moved up the line to pay. "Every woman should have fine lingerie. Good pieces that caress the skin and fit her shape. Not to wear to please a man, but for herself." She pointed to a mannequin nearby wearing a bra that looked like it had been designed by an architect. "*Ça, là,*" she said. "*C'est ridicule*. It's not natural. Natural is sexy."

The cashier frowned in the middle of ringing through our purchases, glanced at the bra Camille dissed, and scanned the area, probably to see if other customers had overheard.

I gave the cashier an apologetic smile as we finished up. Probably like me, she agreed with Camille about the bra. But her job wasn't to like the merchandise, it was to sell it.

When we stepped back outside, Camille directed me to a café and led the way to the washroom in the back. "You can change for your meeting in here." She placed the bags on the counter and stepped out.

I locked up behind her, and I changed into gray stretch jeans and a peasant blouse that showed more cleavage than I was used to but not so much that my "assets" were in full view. I paired the outfit with ankle boots that had less heel than the knee-highs and finished off with large silver hoop earrings, the bracelet, and a new coat Camille insisted I get that had more form than function. Then I touched up my makeup, gathered my things, and stepped out.

"What do you think?" I asked Camille when I found her at the counter that lined the window front of the café.

"*Très beau*," she said, extending a small white box at me, a red ribbon dangling off the side. I peered inside and saw it was filled with chocolate truffles. I looked up at her, and she shrugged at me.

"I had to buy something while I waited for you," she told me.

I smiled, snatched a truffle, and popped it into my mouth.

Camille closed the box and tucked it into one of our bags. "Now let's get out front. Laurent's probably already waiting."

"This must be costing a lot," I said as we made our way out. "And you don't even know for sure yet that your cousin's business is connected to this identity theft stuff or Peter's death. You think all this expense is really necessary?"

"Everything is necessary when it comes to family," she said. And she should know. She came from a large Roman Catholic family that made the Osmonds look fertility challenged.

"**LESS THAN A** month doesn't give me a lot of time to plan a wedding," the sixty-something woman sitting across from me said in a thick Middle Eastern accent, her glass-rimmed eyes skimming down to my belly. "Is there a reason for the rush?"

I automatically sucked in my stomach and pouted out my lips, readying to defend myself. When I had put on the peasant blouse, I was going for fetching, not expecting.

"When you find the love of your life, Madame Shakiba, there is no reason to wait," Laurent said before I got out a word. He reached for my hand and squeezed it. "*N'est-ce pas, mon lapin?*"

I rearranged my lips into a smile. "Sure."

We were at *Prêt-à-Marier* meeting with Michel's wedding planner number two—wedding planner number one, Kai Chin, being the friend of Michel's that he trusted implicitly and was low on the list of suspects.

Madame Shakiba turned to her computer monitor, tapped away on the laptop she'd connected to it, and said, "At least your wedding is not set for Valentine's day." She stopped typing and fixed on me. "Do you have a theme?"

My mind went blank. A theme? Of course I should have a theme, but I hadn't given it any thought. I felt Laurent's grip on my hand tighten. "Hmm," I said. "A theme, right. Well, I want something nice."

She studied me, waiting for more, and I shifted in the hard wood chair. Michel had outfitted all the offices at *Prêt-à-Marier* in antiques which were easy on the eyes but not so easy on the derrière. The antiques fit well with the beamed ceilings, wood plank floors, and the exposed stone wall that ran the length of the main space and was original to the building. Square footage didn't come cheap in the *Prêt-à-Marier* neighborhood of Old Montreal, but charm was aplenty.

Madame Shakiba darted her eyes to the clock on the side wall, and I followed her gaze. Hard not to. Her office was small with only a desk, one large cabinet directly behind it, and enough chairs for Madame Shakiba and a couple of visitors. Sitting in the loft section of the suite, the office also had no exterior windows. And aside from the clock, the walls were bare except for a giant whiteboard and multiple magnetic bulletin boards, each filled with wedding details and various photos. Most looked similar and had the same effect on the eye as wallpaper. But now that I looked closer, one board stood out. It featured pictures of a bride and groom dressed in Victorian garb.

"There's no time to arrange something like that for you," Madame Shakiba told me, obviously noticing where my eyes had strayed.

"Oh, no," I said, a small laugh slipping out. "That's not what I want." And it wasn't. I liked period dress as much as the next gal, but I found bras confining enough. Forget corsets.

Madame Shakiba lifted her glasses and rubbed at her eyes. "All right, then. Why don't we start with something simple and see if we can't find our way to a concept. How about colors? Have you got any in mind?"

"Pink," I told her, remembering the blouse I'd worn to *Danser*.

"Okay. That's one," Madame Shakiba said, typing it into her computer.

I looked at Laurent, hoping he'd ante in. Why was I the only one on the hot seat? He sat back, seemingly happy to let me handle things. I looked at the scarf around his neck and briefly thought about strangling him with it before I noticed the color. "And burgundy," I told her. "Pink and burgundy. I'll have a pink bouquet and burgundy flowers on the tables. And I'd like the invitations to be a pale pink. And, of course, my dress will be white."

Madame Shakiba eyed my midsection again. "Have you already chosen the dress?"

"Not yet."

She sighed and adjusted the lid of her laptop wider to give her fingers more room. The back of the laptop had a long scratch slicing through the centered logo, but it didn't disguise that it was a cheap compatible, and I wondered if it was all Michel could afford to get his staff after his outlay on antiques.

Her fingers started typing again. "What about music and food? Do you want a live band or a dj? Will it be a sit down dinner? And how many guests are you expecting?"

My foot knocked something poking out from under Madame Shakiba's desk as I shifted in my chair again. I looked down at the edge of a mottled shoulder bag and withdrew my foot, the cramped quarters getting to me. Or maybe it was her slew of questions that had me wishing I'd watched more of those reality wedding shows on TV. I would have been better prepared for her grilling. There was a lot to decide and organize. And Madame Shakiba was right, too. A month wouldn't be enough time. If I actually needed to arrange things for real, I'd be in big trouble.

I glanced over at Laurent, and he registered the look of anxiety creeping into my eyes.

"Maybe you have some recommendations?" he said to Madame Shakiba.

She twirled her chair around and sighed again before opening the cabinet behind her desk and heaving out a giant binder. She dropped it in front of me and hefted out another that landed on top, sandwiching the charm dangling from her bracelet between the two albums. She muttered something in a language I didn't understand

and tried to yank her arm away. When that didn't work, she moved to raise the top binder with her free hand, but Laurent got there first and lifted the tome as if it was a piece of paper.

Madame Shakiba thanked him, bent the released arm towards her, and examined her bracelet for damage.

I moved to get a better view around the pile of binders, more curious than concerned. A broken bracelet not being on the same level of urgency as, say, a broken bone. The bracelet looked fine to me. Built to withstand much worse. The golden band had to be at least an inch wide and decent-sized stones adorned it, held in place with sturdy settings. The charm, a miniature gold coin, dangled from the clasp like a chained plug from a bathtub faucet.

Seemingly satisfied the bracelet was in order, Madame Shakiba repositioned herself and pointed to the binders. "Most couples find the venue sets the tone for the reception. That first book will help with that. Don't let the grounds influence you. In winter, only the interior counts with most of them. I'll have to check the computer for availability if you find one you like, but the pictures in there will give you some ideas of how the facilities look and how many guests they can hold." She flipped open the cover and pushed the top album at me. "You do know how many guests you're inviting, do you not?"

I was starting to wonder why Laurent and I hadn't gone over these details beforehand. Worked up a backstory. It was hard thinking up everything on the fly. I glanced at Laurent, now sitting with his arm draped across the back of my chair, and saw he was composed. And calm. Unlike me. Butterflies were touring my stomach again. I had no idea what I was doing. How was any of this supposed to help us find Michel's thief or Peter's possible murderer? All we were doing was sitting here answering questions like any couple in wedding prep mode.

I raised my eyes to meet Madame Shakiba's, determined to give her some kind of an answer, and watched as her nostrils flared and she toyed with her bracelet. That's when it hit me. We weren't just sitting here, we were observing. Learning how things worked. Watching for behavior that was out of the ordinary. Assessing the situation. Just like I did back in my social work days. And I was good at that. Better than good. But I couldn't just stick to answering her flood of questions. I needed to ask a few of my own if I wanted to make a real assessment. "Two hundred," I said in reply to her question about the guest list.

At this, Laurent raised an eyebrow.

"Good," Madame Shakiba said and turned to type it into her computer. "That should narrow things down a bit. And this is an evening reception?"

"Absolutely." I was smiling now and flipping through the binder. "And I'd like a dj not a band." That last bit was actually something I'd thought about for when I got married for real. If I ever did. I'd been to enough weddings where bands did awful covers of songs. I wanted to hear nothing but the real thing at my reception. I stopped on a page in the binder showing a photograph of a room featuring multiple round tables dressed in lace cloths set with china and silver. Very vintage English tea. "And a sit-down dinner like this."

I tapped the page, and Madame Shakiba sat forward to peer at it then peered back up at me, her eyes swinging to my hoop earrings then heading south to my cleavage and belly.

"That's quite elegant," she said, glancing at the photograph again. "Are you certain that's the theme you'd like?"

I restrained myself from narrowing my eyes at her. How she kept her job was beyond me. Weren't wedding planners supposed to be perky and supportive? "It's exactly what I want," I told her.

She shook her head and went back to typing. "And your budget?"

This I thought Laurent should probably answer, but I was on a roll now and still annoyed at being left to handle Madame Shakiba practically alone so I blurted out, "forty thousand."

This got two raised eyebrows from Laurent, but Madame Shakiba's face brightened as she keyed the number into her computer.

"I think I can save us some time," she said, picking up her phone and punching in numbers. "I can think of a few venues that might work that I'd like to show you. It's important we get that decided right away because we need a location before we can do the invitations. I have a cancellation tomorrow morning. I can line up something to see then. How does that sound?"

Sounded fine to me, so I agreed without even looking at Laurent for confirmation. I figured the sooner we met more of the suppliers the better.

She paused and spoke quietly into the phone briefly before hanging up. "Then we'll get going on the dress," she said, turning to face me. "The seamstress will need time to make adjustments." She cast another fleeting glimpse at my stomach, moved the top binder aside, and motioned at the bottom one. "Take this with you. It has dresses in it. Find some you like. It will give me an idea of the best place to shop. There's too little time to have something made."

I nodded. "Actually, I did have a thought about my dress," I told her, working up a little fib. "I was talking to one of the women at our dance lesson last night, and she said you'd helped her find a dress that sounded perfect for me too."

Her eyes darted to her monitor. "You've already started your dance lessons?" she said, more confused than questioning.

"Uh huh. Yesterday. I can't remember the name of the woman I spoke to, but she said you were helping her with her wedding plans too." I crossed my fingers on that lie, hoping it wouldn't affect my karma.

Madame Shakiba pinched the edge of her lip with her teeth and worked her computer some more. "There's no note here about dance lessons," she said. "Somebody should have told me about that." She shot me another look over her glasses, disbelief flitting my way, then skimmed back over to her computer screen. "Which studio are you with?"

"*Danser*," I said. "The one with the choreographer."

After a few more clicks from her computer she said, "I don't see any of my clients signed up for lessons at *Danser*. Are you sure the woman told you *I* was her wedding planner?"

The look in her pinpoint eyes reminded me of a teacher two breaths away from sending a pupil to the principal's office for misbehavior. I felt my cheeks grow warm and nodded, trying to stick to my story but wavering. "Umm. I thought she said it was you."

Laurent's arm around my back tightened some.

"Well, I can't help you without a name, Miss Bosworth." She pushed the dress binder towards me. "For now, we'll just have to work from the book. If you can get me a name, I can check the records again. But there isn't a lot of time. And you'll likely need more than one fitting."

Okay, it was one thing not to fall for my lure, but did she have to keep making digs about my body? I smoothed a hand over my belly thinking maybe Bunny's blouse wasn't the problem, maybe it was the prescription for Madame Shakiba's glasses. Maybe she had distorted vision, like how side-view car mirrors changed perspective. Maybe her glasses should have tiny writing at the bottom of the lens warning her that objects are slimmer, er smaller, than they appear.

Well digs or no digs, I was not going to let this woman get to me. I had a job to do. I wanted to gauge her reaction to Peter's death. I leaned forward as much as Laurent's arm would allow so I could get a better view of Madame Shakiba's face. "I'm sorry I can't remember the wedding dress lady's name," I said, watching her. "But with the accident and all, I felt a bit frazzled after the lesson."

The set of her jaw changed slightly, her gaze fixed on her computer, and she was silent for a beat before speaking. "Yes. I heard about that."

Interesting. "Did you know the man who fell?" I asked her.

"Not really," she said. "He worked with our other wedding planner. Mr. Chin." She busied herself with her keyboard and rushed to add, "I think we've done all we can for today. After I show you some locations, we'll take things from there."

Before I could get in my next question, there was a short knock on the door, the door opened, and in walked a woman. Mid twenties, brown hair pulled into an efficient pony tail, dress off the set of *That Girl* with shoes to match. She crossed over to Madame Shakiba's desk and passed her a few sheets of paper before turning a smile towards Laurent and me, her eyes lingering on Laurent as her smile brightened.

"This is Chantal," Madame Shakiba said. "My assistant. She'll contact you with the details for tomorrow once I have things set up."

Chantal gave a small wave. "The Clément Bosworth couple, right? Nice to meet you." She had no discernable accent when she spoke, but the way her English flowed I was guessing that was her preferred language.

Laurent and I smiled and reciprocated the greeting.

"You guys are getting married real soon, right?" Chantal said. "One of those whirlwind things I bet. That's so romantic."

Laurent pulled me closer and trailed his thumb along my upper arm. "*Oui. Un coup de foudre* that will burn always." He leaned in and kissed my cheek, his warmth lingering on my skin after he pulled away.

"Aww, that's so sweet," Chantal said.

Madame Shakiba shot Chantal a look of impatience and stood. She headed for the door and ushered Chantal out, mumbling something about another account. Then Madame Shakiba turned back and eyed my belly from her new vantage point and finally glanced Laurent's way, her eyes somewhat lowered. "Forgive me for asking, Monsieur, but are you sure dance lessons are a good idea for your future wife?"

Laurent leaned forward, his arm around my shoulders loosening, and reached over to my stomach with his other hand. "A little exercise is good, no?" he said, his thumb moving in small circles around my belly button. "But not to worry. We'll keep our dancing nice and slow."

SIX

CAMILLE LAUGHED WHEN I told her and swiveled back in her office chair.

"It's not funny," I said, plunking into the window seat across from her desk. "It's not enough I'm supposed to be a flirt who dances to stripper songs. Now I have to be pregnant too?"

Laurent took off his coat and draped it over his forearm, a look of confusion on his face. "I said nothing about a flirty stripper."

"No, that's right," I said. "You barely said anything the whole time. You left me out there floundering on my own."

"You did fine."

"Yeah. No thanks to you. You're the one who got me pregnant."

He smiled and winked at Camille who smiled back.

"*Mais voyons*, Laurent," Camille said. "When I told you to take baby steps with her, that's not what I meant."

"Hey," I said to her. "Cut that out. You're my best friend. You're supposed to be on my side. And what did you mean by baby steps? I don't need baby steps. But somebody could have told me I'd have to give the woman a full wedding agenda. I could have been better prepared."

Laurent shook his head and met my eyes. "I wanted to see how you'd handle it."

Instantly, my irritation deflated. My anxiety about playing Bunny was making me lose sight of the bigger picture. I was supposed to be proving I could handle undercover work, not reaming out my boss, the man who was grading me and would decide if I moved up to full time PI or not. I had to get a grip. "You were testing me?"

"I was giving you rope. It's part of your training," Laurent told me, his tone completely unapologetic.

At least now I knew why he'd been so quiet. I'd been treated to the sink or swim method of PI apprenticeship. "So how'd I do?"

He rubbed the back of his neck. "*Pas mal.* A few slip-ups, but nothing I couldn't recover if it came to it."

Slip-ups. Uh oh. "Like what?"

He shifted his weight and let his hand drop to his side. "Your confidence needs work. You almost caved when Madame Shakiba challenged you about your dress lie. And you need to be more careful about asking questions. Be more subtle. Undercover work has its own set of rules. We don't have the same freedom to be direct in our investigating. We need to watch, to be discrete in our questions and poking around. This isn't television. We don't solve crimes in forty minutes between commercials. It takes time and finesse."

I had plenty of finesse. But I could work on the time thing. My aptitude for patience was probably on par with my aptitude for learning new languages. I also didn't fare well with rules unless they suited me. I was hoping these undercover ones would. "What set of rules?"

Laurent came over to the window seat, placing his coat alongside where I'd chucked mine earlier, and sat beside me. "Okay" he said. "Remember rule number one?"

Sure. I was good with that one. "Don't give yourself away," I said.

He nodded. "*Bien.* Now undercover rule number two: Be ready for anything."

That sounded flexible enough. "Got it."

He locked eyes with me. "And rule number three: Take advantage of every opportunity."

I did my best to hold his gaze without breaking away. Greater women than me had gotten lost in his eyes and this was no time to lose my focus. "Right."

"That's what Madame Shakiba gave us today," he said. "An opportunity. If she thinks you're pregnant, we use it. Who knows what it will get us? Her motherly concern for you could break down her defenses and get her talking about co-workers. Or, if she's part of the scam, she could peg you as a vulnerable victim and make you her next score. Either way, we win."

I thought motherly concern was stretching it. The only real interest Madame Shakiba had shown in me the whole time we were there involved the size of my belly. And she hadn't even shown polite sympathies for Peter, or his fiancée Anna either for that matter. She showed more concern for her charm bracelet than any of us. So far, it seemed that if Madame Shakiba was the mother of anything, it was assumptions.

"The woman has the warmth of a popsicle," I said. "That wasn't concern you saw. That was judgment. I thought Michel only had two wedding planners. Why does he even keep her?"

"Contract," Camille said, standing and rounding her desk. She leaned against the desk front and rested her hands around the top on either side of her. "Shakiba was a clause in the conditions of sale when Michel bought the business. He's supposed to keep her on for two years. She works mostly on traditional weddings."

"Traditional weddings?"

"Young couples married off by their parents who still follow traditions of their old country. Brides newly imported for sons to marry. Those types."

Laurent reached over and massaged my knee. "Probably our sexy little Bunny shocked the poor woman."

"Me? I did nothing. You were the one letting her believe I was carrying your prenuptial baby and with the talk about burning *coup de foudre*."

Laurent grinned, and Camille raised an eyebrow at me.

"That's what Laurent told the assistant about us," I told her. "That our love was a *coup de foudre* thing."

Camille looked at Laurent's hand on my knee then stepped forward and grabbed my arm. "*Allez*. Let's take lunch and you can tell me more. I want to know everything you learned about Shakiba and her assistant before I go to *Prêt-à-Marier* to play computer doctor."

I got up and let her lead me to the door where she paused and stepped back over to her desk, opened the top drawer, and took something out.

"*Tiens*," she said, passing it to me.

I looked down at a cell phone now filling my palm. It was covered in a cheery pink and white polka dot skin, and it looked nothing like the plain, black, flip-open style phone I already owned. It was more lightweight and the candy-color cover had me nearly giddy. Which was wrong. I didn't need a new phone. I already had a perfectly good phone. It had taken me a while to get used to, but now I carried it everywhere. We had a bond. We had a history. "Thanks," I said, holding it back out towards her, "but the phone I have works fine."

"It's not for you. It's for Bunny, and it's only short term. We needed a contact number for Léon and Bunny that wouldn't be traced back to us."

My eyes trailed over to Laurent where he was now standing near the door, and he nodded.

Well if it's for a good reason, that's completely different. "Right. Absolutely," I said, holding tight to the phone and trying to keep my smile down to only a notch above a grin. This undercover stuff may have some tricky bits to learn but the perks were fabulous—new ring, new boots, new phone... Temporary or not, I could get used to this way of life.

A phone rang, and a spark went through me at the thought of fielding my first Bunny call. The spark went out when Camille reached across me to pick up the receiver on her desk. She did a lot of listening and little talking before putting down the phone.

"It's time," she said over her shoulder to Laurent as she took a coin out of her top desk drawer. "Call it."

He took a step deeper into the room. "Tails."

"*Ah, zut.*" Camille shook her head and squinted at him. "Cheater."

"How could I cheat?" he said. "You were the one tossing the coin."

"You've always cheated. Since you were nine years old."

Laurent smiled. "*C'est pas vrai.* You've just been a sore loser since you were seven."

I'd seen the sibs go through this coin toss business before. And every time it went Laurent's way, they went through the same schtick. I'd learned it was better not to interfere and started heading for the kitchen to grab some lunch, but Camille waved at me to stop in reception.

"*Allez,*" she said. "We better hurry or we'll be late."

"Late for what?" I asked.

Camille zipped past the receptionist's desk over to the bank of hooks where she'd left her coat and said, "We'll have to grab lunch on the way, we're due at *tante* Claudette's."

My appetite dimmed, my stomach quieting mid growl. I so did not want to go see Camille and Laurent's aunt Claudette. *Tante* Claudette was their mother's sister. She kept an immaculate house, cooked rustic food, and headed up her own pew in the local church. She also may have taken her religious leaning a tad too much to heart because she was known to favor feuds of biblical proportions. And she was in the middle of one of those now with Camille and Laurent's mother. I was guessing this little visit would have something to do with that.

"But don't Bunny and Léon have another meeting after lunch?" I said, looking hopefully at Laurent who had come up behind us and was handing me my coat and hat.

He shook his head. "Tomorrow morning. This afternoon I have background to do and some work on another case."

Another case? How could he work on another case? We could be talking about murder here. I narrowed my eyes at him, wondering if he was fibbing. He winked at me but said nothing. I sighed and held the Bunny phone up again, thinking it was probably more bribe than perk, something to lure me into the rendezvous with *tante* Claudette. I turned the phone over in my hands, taking in the pink and white polka dots and trying not to like the phone so much, but the same giddy excitement came back to me and I knew I was a goner.

I looked up at Camille's smile and wished she didn't know me quite so well.

CAMILLE PULLED HER silver Jetta into her aunt Claudette's driveway and parked. Not far from C&C in distance, the neighborhood was about as far as you could get in style. It bordered on suburban. City suburban, at least. No track houses, but a mix of mid-century bungalows with older two-storeys thrown in here and there. Streets were wider and fewer houses were attached.

I glanced at the tiny brick bungalow Claudette had lived in most of her adult life and saw the living room sheers flutter. Moments later, the front door opened and a little white poodle jumped onto the stoop, yapping out a tune that left little room for breathing.

Claudette, a small woman with high cheekbones, a nose more prominent from age, and silver hair knotted into a bun, rushed out after him. "*Arrête, Mignon*," she said to the dog. "*Ça suffit!*"

The poodle danced around her in circles, still yapping. Apparently, *Mignon's* French comprehension skills were even worse than mine.

Claudette bent down and swooped the dog up as we started up the steps. When we were close enough, Camille reached out and patted the dog's head and *Mignon* switched from barking to lapping his tongue in the air, his tiny coiffed rear end wagging back and forth in time with his tail. We made our way inside, and Claudette released the dog and greeted us properly with cheek kisses and light hugs.

"*Venez*," Claudette said, turning to cross the hall and motioning for us to follow, "it's all ready." She, like the rest of Camille's family, switched to English for my benefit, but unlike the younger members of the Caron Clan, Claudette's English was quite broken and her French accent very heavy.

We slipped off our coats and boots, laid the coats on the entryway banquette, and followed her into the kitchen where she had tea brewing. On the way over to the house, Camille had explained to me that coming for tea was the only way Claudette would agree to see Camille or Laurent. A few months back, Camille's mother and *tante* Claudette had had a falling out and hadn't spoken since. Their respective children had been put on warning that Claudette had no intention of talking to them about the split either. This kind of thing tended to happen from time to time, and usually no one interfered and everyone waited for things to blow over between the sisters. Problem was, Claudette's daughter, Arielle, worked reception at C&C and in loyalty to her mother had quit and taken another job until things cooled down. And Arielle pulled a fit when Camille and Laurent tried to cover her duties with a temp, leaving them sans receptionist for nearly two months. Now C&C needed Arielle back. And the only way to get her back was to mend the rift between the sisters.

So, Camille and Laurent had done what all good nieces and nephews do—agreed for one of them to have their tea leaves read by *tante* Claudette as a ruse to make peace. Evidently, Camille was the lucky one the coin toss chose to go. And she'd dragged me along to sweeten the deal.

I sat down at the Formica table in Claudette's kitchen, and a sharp edge from a slight tear in the vinyl covering on the chair poked into the underside of my thigh. I shifted to avoid it, and my chair started spinning on its round base, not enough to turn a complete circle, but enough to throw me off balance until I planted a foot on the floor and righted myself.

Claudette turned from the counter where she was gathering cups and saucers from the dish drainer. She frowned at Camille and squawked something to her in French. Camille motioned for me to get up, and we switched chairs. From my new vantage point, I had a clear view out the window to the clothesline out back that even in this cold weather had a few items hanging on it. Probably stiff as a board. I also had a good earful of the refrigerator motor which sounded like it had enough juice to power a tank. Appropriate, since it was the color of one. The range matched and the porcelain sink wasn't far off.

I smiled at Claudette as she set out the tableware. She was widowed about seven years back and had taken up reading tea shortly after that, making me wonder if her initial interest was kindled by an attempt to connect with her dear departed husband. "It's very kind of you to include me," I said to her.

She smiled back and nodded. Then she finished placing the cups, took her seat at the table, and lifted the lid on the teapot. Seemingly satisfied that it had steeped long enough, she poured it out equally between us.

"*Ma tante* is very good with the leaves," Camille said to me. "People come from all over the neighborhood for one of her readings."

"Really?" I said, playing along. I knew Camille had little belief in tea reading or much else in the psychic realm. She was just buttering up Claudette.

Camille tapped her aunt's hand. "Tell Lora about the Swedish lady down the street."

"Ah, well," Claudette began speaking each word slowly. "That one was good. The poor woman got told by her doctor that she and her husband never have childrens. He told her not even the treatments for fertility would help. Then she came to me all crying and upset. But we see in her leaves lots of kids. She does not believe it. She makes me do it over and over again. Every time it's the same thing. Even two months later, the same thing. Then she comes back to me again after another couple months and I think enough already, but this time she tells me she is pregnant. And that time it was with twins. Then a year later, she has another one, and now she has five." She shook her head. "That was just crazy, eh."

"Wow," I said. "That's incredible."

"*Ben non*," Claudette said, pulling her wool sweater tighter around her. "That is the leaves." She checked our cups. "Drink, drink. You will see."

I took another sip of my tea and watched Camille do the same. She had explained to me that this was part of the process of the reading. That we were supposed to leisurely drink first. Something about infusing the leaves better. Only I was guessing leisurely was a subjective term because Camille was pretty much done already. I watched as she swirled the remainder around in her cup, turned it upside down briefly, then righted it again before sliding it over to Claudette.

"Claudette looked at the leaves and looked back up at Camille. "A trouble is coming," she told her. "Maybe not too big but important. And soon."

Camille nodded understanding to her aunt and Claudette went back to examining the leaves.

I gave Camille a worried look and she shook her head slightly, dismissing the credibility of the prediction.

"And still, I see no family. Only work. But work is good. Busy." She looked back up, pushed the teacup away, and checked mine. "*Regarde moi ça,*" she said to me. "You finish enough now. You need a little left in the bottom. Now, let the *liquide* pass around three times."

I picked up my cup and gently tilted it from side to side.

Claudette moved on to a circling motion with her hands. "Okay, now upside down on the plate for the water to run out, then flip it back up again."

I followed the instructions and when I was done, I moved the cup to sit in front of her.

She turned it so the handle faced towards her and peered inside. "I see a man," she said. "Not a new man. Someone you already know."

Adam, I thought and smiled.

"He is coming into your life in a big way," she continued. "You will be very close. Like soul mates."

Wait. What does she mean coming?

"And for you too I see lots of work. And danger. Big danger." She looked up and caught my eye before returning her large brown eyes to the teacup. "You need to be very careful. It is bad. I don't know what. The leaves are no good now." She looked up, pushed the cup away, got up from the table, and left the room, her little *Mignon* following after her.

That's it? She tells me I'm in danger and that's it? No more details? A man, work, and danger. That's what I get? "Is it over?" I asked Camille.

She stood and stretched. "*Oui, oui.*" She went over to the counter and lifted the lid off a cookie jar shaped like a dog and tossed in twenty dollars.

I rooted around in my pocket and pulled out a ten dollar bill and some loonies, the Canadian equivalent to dollar bills. "Does she take coins?"

"She takes anything. Whatever a client can pay."

I added my money to the jar and Camille replaced the lid. We cleared our cups away and Camille started to wash them, but Claudette scooted back into the room and brushed her away. Camille shook her head at her aunt. Then they exchanged a little family gossip followed by more cheek kisses and we left.

"YOU DIDN'T EVEN talk about your mother," I said to Camille on the ride back to the office.

"*Pas encore.* Next time."

Next time? No way. I did not want to go back. I could understand the romance bit. Claudette probably just got mixed up about Adam. But the danger stuff spooked me. Camille may not believe in psychic stuff, but I wasn't so sure. "Next time *you* see her, you mean."

"No. When we go back for the next reading."

"What next reading?"

She stopped for a red light and adjusted the heater. "That's how it works. *Ma tante* tells people something dramatic but gives no details so that they have to go back again to find out more." The light turned green, and we were moving again. "And that's when we'll find out about the fight with my mother."

I glanced at her, knowing that was highly unlikely. Ever since Claudette had backed out of a European cruise she was supposed to take with Camille's mom, she had refused to speak about why. They had both lost their deposits, which for two older women on budgets was a big deal. Camille's mother thought the least Claudette could do was explain why, and Claudette thought the least her sister could do was mind her own business. And both women were too stubborn to even consider the other's point of view. "What? You think your aunt will just start talking about it all of a sudden?" I said.

"*Non, non.* You'll get all emotional about being in danger and finding the man of your dreams, and she'll look harder at your tea leaves trying to answer all your questions. And while you keep her busy, I'll snoop."

"Great plan," I said. "Except I already have the man of my dreams and I sure don't need to hear about any danger."

"*Mais voyons*, Lora. It's not real."

"What about the lady with fertility issues who had all those kids? That was spooky."

"Not so spooky. Her husband is Native, and all her kids are fair and blonde."

"So?"

Her eyes slipped from the road to me and back again. "So the neighbor man who lives beside her is fair and blonde. Not such a miracle."

I smiled with relief, a twinge of sadness for the woman's husband cutting in until a thought occurred to me. "Wait. Didn't you say the woman was Swedish. Aren't a lot of Swedes pale and blonde?"

She pulled over and parked a few doors down from C&C. "Maybe."

"Well, is she?"

Camille grabbed her purse and opened the car door. "I guess."

"Then why did you tell me about the man next door?"

She pulled the car door closed a bit to keep out the wind. "I wanted you to feel better."

That so did *not* make me feel better.

SEVEN

AFTER AN HOUR of listening to undercover tips from Camille at C&C, I skipped out a bit early and went home to mull over the day's events. I had a lot of information to process and Claudette's prediction still gnawed at me. But truth be told, it was the whole murder thing that really had me nervous. I'd expected to cut my undercover teeth on a small family case, not a murder. I wasn't sure I was ready.

I tried not to dwell on that and told myself to focus on the identity theft angle of the case instead, hoping the two crimes weren't really related. Or that there'd been a mistake and that there was no murder. Which was easy to believe because I still didn't see how Peter could have been killed. Or why, for that matter. Identity theft seemed like a small crime in comparison. Would it really drive someone to murder?

Clearly, the police thought so or they wouldn't be investigating it. But with Luc not sharing details about the case yet, I was at a loss to piece it together. What I did know was that Laurent was right, I had to get more confident about this undercover thing if I wanted to help. And my first step towards that was to get Bunny organized. Under stress, some people shopped, some people drank, some people exercised. I organized. It made me feel more calm, more in control—feelings I was quickly learning were in short supply since I started this case. But I got it now. Undercover work was a more "go with the flow" thing. I could do that. Only I could do it better if I was organized first. And after all, if I was out to catch an identity thief possibly turned murderer, I didn't have time to hem and haw over clothes. I needed to swallow my reservations, put on my big girl pants, and get on with the case.

To start, I dumped out the bags of clothes from the morning shopping onto my bed and picked through everything. The pieces I'd found were a good start, but Camille's fashion sense had netted me even better, and it didn't take me long to put together a look for Bunny. I decided Bunny had a thing for pink. She also liked shirts with a touch of embroidery or a design, but nothing plain. And she wasn't afraid of a little shimmer. In skirts, she wore short but not mini, and she liked her pants to have some flair. And the chunky, silver cuff bangle I'd gotten as her signature piece went perfectly with all of it.

Now that I had gotten used to the idea, playing Bunny Bosworth didn't seem so bad. Her eyeliner was a touch thick and she did like heels, but I could live with that. As long as she was my creation and her flirty side was more sweet than tart, I could make this work.

I set aside the clothes that didn't fit in with the look I was going for and lugged the rest down to the washer. When I got back to my room, I spotted the lingerie bags sitting on the floor and sighed. I'd forgotten about those. Camille's tools of the trade speech running through my head, I started in on the lingerie, too, reminding myself that I could return anything that felt too risqué.

Ten minutes later, my floor was a sea of tissue paper, my bed rivaled a photo shoot for Victoria's Secret, and my cat Ping was dive bombing the discarded tissue paper on the floor. Not to be left out, my dachshund Pong ambled in from the hall to see what all the crinkling was about. Ping pounced out from under a sheet of tissue and took a clawless swing at Pong's nose, and Pong darted away and went back to watching the show from the hallway. And I turned my attention back to the slew of silk and lace decorating my bed—the whole lot of it looking more suited to under-the-cover activities than to undercover ones.

I held up a one-piece black number, turning it in the air, trying to figure out exactly what it was and how it went on. These things seriously needed to come with instructions. My curiosity getting the best of me, I stripped down and tried to work out how the contraption fit. I had just finished doing up the last hook when Adam walked into the bedroom.

"Wow," he said, stopping in his tracks.

I whipped my head up, my breathing a bit fast and my skin a bit moist from the effort of hooking myself up. A greeting was about all I could manage to get out.

Adam didn't manage much more as he made his way over to me.

The thin strap fell off my shoulder, and he reached over to put it back into place. "Some outfit. Doesn't even cover your tattoo," he said. He let his hand slip down to skim over the right cheek of my derrière that had been recently adorned with a fleur-de-lys in the same blue tone as the Québec flag. "I forget some anniversary or something?"

Now this is where a fib would come in handy. Not something nasty. Just a little white one. We'd patched things up before going to bed the night before and Adam had barely scowled at the ring encircling my all-important finger when he'd dropped me off at C&C after breakfast, but he was not going to like the idea of these being Bunny's unmentionables. Any more than he was going to like the idea that I was still playing Bunny. Never mind that she'd gotten pregnant in the course of the day. Really, I needed more than a fib. I needed a public relations caliber spin.

"No. No anniversary. I just thought I'd try something new," I said.

He stepped back and scanned me. "It's new all right. I never imagined you in something like this."

I cocked my head at him. "You don't like it?"

He came closer and stroked the side of my arms. "I didn't say that. I just didn't expect it. Especially after last night. I thought you'd still be angry at me after all that business about the hooker case you're working on."

Hooker case? There was no hooker case. "What are you talking about? Do you mean the identity theft case I told you about last night?"

"Right. The one where you have to play a hooker."

56

I grimaced. How was I supposed to soothe him about my undercover role if he was going to keep calling me a hooker? "I'm not playing a hooker. I'm playing a woman who just so happens to be called Bunny. And the case is getting complicated, so I'll be doing the whole Bunny thing for a while."

His hands stopped moving. "Which Bunny thing? The name? The slutty clothes? The dirty dancing?"

I wouldn't call it dirty dancing. There hadn't even been *any* dancing yet. Probably not the time to point that out, though. Not now when Adam's eyes were boring into me, his face was reddening, and his muscles were clenching.

"Really, it's not that bad," I told him.

"You still engaged to Laurent?"

"Well, pretend engaged. Yeah."

He went quiet.

I moved over to the bed and tried to brush the remaining lingerie into an unrecognizable ball. "You don't have a problem with that, do you? I mean it's just Laurent. You like Laurent."

"I like him fine when he's not your fiancé."

"It's not like it means anything," I said, figuring this wasn't the best time to mention Laurent was also now the father of my pretend unborn child. "I mean, he's my best friend's brother for goodness sake."

Adam's shoulders relaxed some. "That's true."

"Plus, I'm hardly even with Laurent. I spent most of my day with Camille." This was also true. Of course, Camille and I weren't the ones holding hands in Madame Shakiba's office, but telling Adam about that would only feed his insecurity. And he didn't have any reason to be insecure. We'd been together since we'd met nearly three years ago back in New York when he was getting his Master's degree and I was working as a children's counselor. I'd even moved to a new country for him. Okay, maybe I'd since fallen in love with the place and was happy to have the chance to get a sense of my mom's Canadian roots, but still. The initial moving had to mean something. Sure Laurent was good looking, I'd give Adam that. But he wasn't relationship material. Laurent dated a lot, but I didn't think he'd ever had a serious girlfriend. Probably because of the French flirt thing. Besides, we were both professionals. Strictly employer and employee.

Adam's face softened and his eyes dropped to the line of lace that skirted around my breasts.

"Anyway, I didn't buy this outfit for Laurent," I said. Another accurate statement since I hadn't bought it at all.

"Really," he said, clearly letting his combustible energy flow in a new direction. "Who did you buy it for?"

There was no easy answer for that one, so I kissed him and let him draw his own conclusions. And a half hour later, he'd filled in the appropriate blank to both of our satisfaction. And I'd decided new lingerie wasn't such a bad idea after all.

"I THOUGHT WE were meeting Madame Shakiba this morning," I said to Laurent as he weaved the Léon car through the third deepest level in a downtown underground parking lot, looking for a spot near the elevators. I hoped he found one soon. We'd been through the same routine on two levels already finding no empty spaces, and I hated parking garages with endless cold, dark layers. The only thing with cold, dark layers that I liked had frosting in between.

He navigated the car into a slot and stopped. "Some bride emergency came up. She can't make it. She postponed our other venue tours, but Léon and Bunny are on their own for this one."

We got out and made our way over to the entrance into the building above. Laurent held the glass door open for me with an outstretched arm, and as I passed underneath he smiled down at me. "Nice outfit. I like the scoop of the neck. Very sexy."

I caught a quick glimpse of myself in the mirrored elevator doors. Only the top button on my coat was undone. He couldn't see my blouse, and it didn't have a scoop. He was teasing me.

"*Très drôle*," I said, meaning very funny, one of my few French phrases.

He smiled some more and pressed the "Up" button. The elevator doors opened almost instantly, and we got in.

"So do I get to ask what we do once we get upstairs?" I said to him. "Or is this another no prep deal?"

He pressed the button for our floor and looked down at me, his expression shifting from playful to professional. "We'll see the place, go over some menus, maybe put down a deposit. I arranged for some dummy credit cards with low limits to use at the various suppliers. If someone steals a number, I can trace it back."

"Won't they know the cards are fake."

"They're not fake. Just ones set up in Léon's name."

"I didn't know credit card companies gave out cards to non-existent people."

He reached out and punched the "Close Doors" button, the doors not having the same initiative to shut as they did to open. "Normally they don't," he said. "But I've helped them with fraud cases before and they have a vested interest in putting a stop to identity theft. It costs them billions of dollars in losses too. These cards have just enough on them to cover our deposits, and if any of the charges go through properly Michel will cover the expenses."

Suddenly I felt bad for telling Madame Shakiba we had a forty thousand dollar wedding budget. "Wow. I didn't know Michel would actually have to pay for things. That could cost him a small fortune."

"Nothing compared to the costs of having an identity thief on his payroll. *Prêt-à-Marier* can be held responsible for all costs to a victim whose identity is stolen because of a breach at the company. And having a thief in his supply chain can do a lot of damage to his reputation. The expenses of the investigation are like insurance against greater costs."

"Sounds like you believe there is a thief now."

He shrugged. "I believe something's not right."

"And what if it turns out that the thief really did kill Peter?"

"That's separate. Michel has no responsibility in that. But if we find his identify thief, we find the murderer."

I watched the numbers tick by above the elevator doors that had finally closed. "Isn't that up to the police?"

"Sure. But there's overlap. We often work alongside the police, and in this case it's an advantage that we're already on the inside."

The elevator stopped on the first parking level and three young women stepped in beside us. Two of them checked out Laurent and then quickly looked away. The third woman bumped up against him, offered up a throaty *"Je m'excuse,"* and smiled. He moved closer to me and took my hand, lacing his fingers in between mine. When we stopped again on the main floor and Laurent led me out, the woman looked me up and down and rolled her eyes. I shifted my gaze to the carpet, wondering if she was jealous or trying to diss me. Seemed to me there was a lot of prejudice out there towards "fun" girls like Bunny. I had on the hoop earrings again teamed with a white blouse, black skirt, and the knee-high boots. Not much was visible with my coat on, but probably the boots and makeup gave off enough of a vibe. I walked the length of the hallway with my eyes trained on the floor, still in think mode, until Laurent pulled me up short to keep me from walking into one of the closed doors of the restaurant where we had our appointment.

I looked up to see each door bore the name *Bon Souper.* "Good dinner" I roughly translated in my brain as the right door opened, and I met the eyes of a man in his early twenties wearing black slacks, a white shirt, a blue tie, and hair so slick with gel that I couldn't make out the color. He showed us to a table with two place settings and whisked away the dishes and glassware before dashing off to announce us. Laurent let my hand slip away to help me out of my coat and into my chair, careful to nudge the chair forward slowly over the thin, patterned carpet. He took off his own coat, folded it over mine, and placed both over the back of a chair he grabbed from a nearby table before seating himself across from me.

I got settled, letting my eyes adjust to the bright light streaming in from the windows that framed the street entrance on the back wall, and gave the place the once-over. Tables were draped in fine linen, dishware was pristine white, and the scent of baked apple lingered. Chandeliers hung partway down from the high ceiling, easily leaving at least a nine foot clearance from the floor. A large stone fireplace took up the center of the main wall, and a small, wood-paneled bar stood in the far right corner. Beside it, a set of double swinging doors with porthole windows provided access to the next room, presumably the kitchen. In its life as a restaurant, the place probably hosted some pretty posh folks. Weddings must have been a side business. I wondered which role the site was playing today since we pretty much had it to ourselves save for a few employees flitting about.

A woman wearing a chic wool suit in a vibrant red breezed through one of the porthole doors and headed towards us. Her hair was silver gray and swung free to just above her shoulders in a wavy bob that softened the lines around her neck, along with the help of a silk scarf. Her lipstick and nail polish matched the color of her suit to perfection.

Laurent and I both stood to greet her.

"*Bonjour*," she said and extended her hand to shake first Laurent's hand and then mine.

She introduced herself as Madame Grenier, and Laurent returned the pleasantry by introducing us and adding in a brief explanation about me speaking only English. This got a smile and nod from Madame Grenier who graciously agreed to continue in my language. With a peek at my midsection, she then informed us she'd spoken with Madame Shakiba and understood we had a tight schedule, so she suggested we get straight to a quick tour.

As Madame Grenier showed us around, explaining how the space could be altered to allow for a dance floor and head tables for the wedding party and immediate family, we went over details about our wedding date, our entertainment needs, and the amount of people expected to attend. When we'd circled back to the table where we started the tour, the conversation turned to food, and she placed sample menus in front of us to consider, made a few recommendations, and excused herself for us to talk privately.

"Two hundred and fifty guests?" I said to Laurent when she was gone, referring to the amount of guests he'd just told her we were expecting. "Didn't I tell Madame Shakiba two hundred?"

He shrugged. "Sounded too low. I want it to sound credible. It's supposed to be a typical wedding, no? One of my cousins had three hundred and fifty."

I shook my head. No wedding I had ever been to had that many guests. And mine never would. I'd gone to exactly one family wedding when I was seven and my dad was invited to an aunt's renewal ceremony. The invitation had been a happy surprise since my dad was disowned years before for marrying my mom because his parents hadn't approved of their union. According to my grandparents, my mom was a "liberal hippie" whose Canadian birth qualified her as a near communist—what with her home country's social programs like health care and their harboring of U.S. draft dodgers during the Vietnam war. Turned out, the invitation had been sent out by mistake. We were there all of ten minutes before we were spotted and asked to leave by a groomsman. That was the last I saw of that side of my family. On my mom's side, I could count a dozen or so family members I could round up to invite to a wedding if I included second cousins I'd never met. Good thing I wasn't marrying into the Caron clan for real. My side of the church would have maybe one row of people, and there'd be two-hundred and fifty Carons crammed in on the other.

I picked up the sample menus, happy to let my brain move on to a new topic, and scanned the meals one by one. "Hmm. I don't see any vegetarian options."

"The one with the duck looks good," Laurent said.

"Duck's not vegetarian," I told him.

"So what?"

"So I'm vegetarian, remember?"

He sat back in his chair. "*Ah oui, excuse-moi, mon petit lapin.*"

I shot him a look. Of course he remembered, he just couldn't resist teasing me. I went back to studying the menus, not willing to give Laurent the satisfaction of a response.

"While you're busy," he said, not sounding bothered in the least by my ignoring him, "I'm going to wander a bit. See if I can learn anything. If Madame Grenier comes back, stall her with questions or something."

I told him that was fine, and he walked towards the back of the restaurant pretending to take in the view while I went back to reading the menus. Madame Grenier had given us five to consider.

Each one had several courses and each one featured a fancy main dish. When I was halfway through reading the salmon one, I looked up to check on Laurent. He was leaning against the back wall chatting up a server, his white shirt casually draped over his jeans, his scruff short, his hair grazing his shoulders in disarray. I didn't need to rely on any of my psych courses on body language to see that the poor girl was a goner. Her eyes nearly gleamed. Another few minutes, and she'd not only be spilling the beans on her employer but probably offering up the deed to her parents' house for one date with Laurent, pretend engaged or not.

I looked away, rubbed the sore spot forming in the pit of my stomach, and moved on to read about the grilled chicken. When I couldn't stand reading about sauces and *petits pois* anymore, I looked for the desserts. There weren't any listed. What was up with that? What was a wedding without the cake? And more importantly, what was I supposed to do now with nothing else to read? It was boring sitting here playing lady in waiting.

Checking on Laurent again, I saw he was still in deep conversation with his new groupie. I scanned the room, trying not to appear fixated on them, and spotted the server who'd greeted us when we first arrived now working over at the bar. He seemed to be watching Laurent and his new friend, too.

That's when it dawned on me. I didn't have to just sit here playing backup. This was my chance to take Bunny for a spin and put her flirty side to good use. Maybe make a new friend of my own. I got up, adjusted my clothes, slipped my purse under my arm, and made my way over to the bar.

"Hey there," I said to the guy.

He glanced at me, his arms not losing a beat in restocking bottles under the bar. "Did you want a drink?" he asked me. "We're not really open. I'm not sure I'm supposed to serve anything yet."

Good. He seemed as inexperienced at his job as I was at mine. I gave him a bright smile and mounted the stool, my foot catching briefly in the metal base causing it to tilt to one side and reset itself with a slight thud. I smiled some more, hoping he hadn't noticed, placed my elbows on the bar top, and leaned forward. "Maybe a glass of water then?" I said, trying to imitate the throaty voice of the woman in the elevator earlier. My own voice coming out more choked than throaty.

"You okay?" he said, his eyes showing alarm as he grabbed a glass, squirted some water into it from a spigot, and sent it gliding over to me.

"Fine," I told him, catching the glass and abandoning my throaty voice as a lost cause. "Just a bit dry."

He nodded, relief relaxing his expression, and went back to his restocking as though I wasn't even there.

I resettled myself on the stool. He wasn't making this easy. "You work here long?" I asked.

"*Pardon*?" he said, sounding French for the first time. He had no accent when he spoke English, but that wasn't a surprise. Many Montrealers spoke both languages so fluently it was hard to tell which one was their first language.

"I asked if you'd worked here long?" I repeated, trying for cheerful with a touch of coy this time.

"No."

Chatty fellow he was not. I would never get much out of him this way. What was I thinking? I couldn't flirt. I was more a granola and Ivory soap gal, not a Bond girl. Even with all the right props, I was hopeless. This was humiliating. I should be able to get more than one-word at a time out of this guy. He was young. He had to have hormones kicking around in there somewhere. This should be easy. I felt my confidence ebbing and remembered Laurent's advice to work on that. So I took a deep breath and pretended to drop something. I bent down to retrieve the fake something, undid a couple of buttons on my blouse, and fluffed my hair before popping back up. Then I drained my water glass and asked for a refill. When the server slid it over to me, I moved on to something more my style. Psychological flirting, aka ego stroking.

"You're really good at the glide thing," I said, motioning to how he skimmed my glass along the bar top rather than setting it down in front of me.

"Thanks," he said.

"Think you could teach me?"

He glanced over at Laurent and the groupie then back at me, something shifting in his eyes. "Sure," he said, snatching a clean glass from an overhang above his head. "It's easy." He demonstrated his technique. "Just like the glass is skating on ice. See?"

I nodded.

He reached across the bar and placed his hand over mine, wrapping them both around the empty glass he'd passed to me. "Now you try it."

I knew I could emulate the move without his help and didn't much like the feel of his cold, puffy fingers. But if this was my in with him, I was going to take it. Undercover rule number three I reminded myself, take advantage of every opportunity. I let him guide me and watched as the glass sailed down the bar when it was released.

"Nice," I said. "Fun place to work, I bet. Can I try it again?"

Madame Grenier came streaming back into the room, and my server friend stiffened. "Better not," he said.

I laughed, trying to appear understanding. "I get it. Tough boss, eh?"

"You could say that. She's my mother. She took over the restaurant after my father had his second stroke."

"Oh," I said, my voice dropping, thinking it must have been a serious stroke. "I'm so sorry about your dad."

He shrugged. Probably accustomed to brushing off sympathies. "It was almost a year ago. I'm used to him not being able to do as much anymore."

"Is that him?" I asked, pointing to a photograph of an older man that hung over the sink area on the wall side of the bar. Down the wall, the same man featured in several photos, his arm draped around various people's shoulders. Big shot customers I figured.

My new friend turned to see where I was pointing. "Yeah."

"He looks very nice," I said, meaning it. The man had a softness about his eyes and a kind smile. "And he built up a good business for his family. I guess this will all be yours someday."

He shook his head. "Not if I can help it."

Laurent slipped onto the stool beside me and placed a hand on the small of my back, and my server friend grew quiet. "Ready to go?" Laurent asked me.

I hesitated. I'd finally got the young guy talking and didn't want to end our conversation yet. But he started to back away, his expression cooling, making the decision for me.

"See you around," he said.

"You too." I shot him my best smile. "It was nice meeting you, umm…"

"Benoît," he said, filling in the blank.

I waved as he neared the end of the bar. "Bunny."

Benoît acknowledged our exchange of names with a head bob and a small wave and walked towards the doors to the kitchen.

I jumped off the stool and headed back to the table where Laurent and I had left our coats. How was I supposed to get anywhere with Laurent interrupting me? I didn't bother him when he was shaking down his groupie.

"Did you already leave the deposit?" I asked him, trying to rid my voice of my annoyance and regroup. This was no time to pick a fight with my boss even if I was frustrated. Lucky for me, I'd inherited a gift for tongue holding from my British ancestors. It came in very handy at times like this.

Laurent separated our coats and held mine out for me to slip into. "Not yet. But I told Madame Grenier that I would as soon as I checked with you about our meal choice."

"Doesn't that look odd? Shouldn't it look like we're seeing other places before we make a decision?"

"No need. This was the only one on the venue list Madame Shakiba sent that was common to the identity theft victims. That's why I kept this appointment even when she didn't show. I was going to ditch the others anyway."

He hadn't mentioned that earlier. Now I really wished I'd had more time with Benoît. And that I was privy to Laurent's supplier list before we met Madame Shakiba.

"If you already knew you wanted to check this place out, couldn't you have told that to Madame Shakiba yesterday?"

"*Non*. That would have led her. We needed to see what she would recommend. If she pushed any of the suspect suppliers over others."

I sighed. "Sure would have been nice to know that going in."

He shook his head. "Better that you didn't know. Made the flow of our meeting more natural."

Leaving me in the dark may have been useful for him, but it had me wondering what else he wasn't sharing with me. "Well, if we're going for natural then what about asking Madame Grenier more questions?" I said, thinking maybe I could buy more time and get another crack at Benoît. "You know, to make it look like we're thinking things through."

Laurent began putting on his own coat, his eyes amused. "What kinds of questions?"

I tried to think of something fast. "Like about the cake."

"What about it?" he said.

"There's no cake listed on the menus."

"So?"

"So what's a wedding without the dessert?" I said.

He smiled. "Not to worry. The dessert comes after the wedding."

I shot him a look again. This was so not working. "Look. A real couple would want to know about the cake."

"Fine, I'll ask about cake. Anything else, *mon petit lapin*?"

"I'm still not sure which meal to choose."

"What does it matter?" he said. "We'll just choose the cheapest thing and go."

"The cheapest? Maybe Bunny doesn't want the cheapest thing."

He shook his head. "It's not a real wedding. When Bunny gets married for real, she can have anything she wants. For now, we'll stick with the cheapest. The cheaper the choice, the cheaper the deposit."

He should have thought about that before he decided to add fifty extra mouths to feed to our guest list. "How do we even know what the cheapest is? There are no prices. And don't we get samples? I was expecting samples."

"I didn't ask for samples, and the chicken is the cheapest."

"How do you know?"

"Chicken is always the cheapest."

I looked up to see Madame Grenier hovering a few yards away. She seemed hesitant about approaching us. Probably thought we were having a lovers squabble. I gave up trying to find excuses to extend our stay and smiled at her to signal the all clear.

She returned the smile and joined us. "*Alors*?" she said. "*Des questions*?"

Seems she forgot all about me being English. Or pretended to. She and Laurent finished up the discussion sans *moi,* and she led him away, presumably to process our deposit. I watched as they walked over to the register, Madame Grenier's nails occasionally tapping Laurent's forearm along the way. She had to be at least twenty years older than him, not to mention married, but even she appeared to be falling for his charms.

I paced while I waited, my steps eventually trailing between the tables until I found myself back at the bar. I checked the area for Benoît, but there was no sign of him so I started back, my eyes skimming the wall of pictures and landing on the large one of Monsieur Grenier. So sad to think he'd had a stroke. He probably worked his whole life, hoping for some rest and fun in retirement and instead illness robbed him of that chance. Judging by his varying ages in the photos scattered across the wall, he'd been working in the restaurant biz a long time, too. And he'd built up quite a clientele. I recognized the customer faces in some of the more recent pictures. Movers and shakers I'd seen on TV or in the newspaper, the kind I couldn't remember by name but whose faces were local fixtures. My eyes stopped on one not so famous face, and I did a double take. This one I'd never seen in a paper or on a screen, but it had definitely become a fixture in my brain. I could still picture it laying in a puddle of blood on a marble floor. It belonged to Peter, the dead guy.

"THIS ALL WE'VE got?" I asked Camille.

She finished tying her scarf, checking her reflection in the mirror hanging over the cabinets in C&C reception. "*Et alors*? What were you looking for?"

I swiveled in Arielle's chair to face Camille. "I'm thinking Peter's picture hanging at *Bon Souper* has to mean something. Laurent said *Bon Souper* was one of our suspect suppliers. And Peter was one of the identity theft victims. He must've gone to the place. Probably a lot, to get his picture on the wall." I swiveled back around to scan Arielle's computer monitor, which I had taken to using in her absence. "I don't see anything in your notes that links Peter to *Bon Souper*, though."

For each case, Camille compiled preliminary background notes and entered them into our database where we all added new info as it came in. She was very thorough, too. I had no idea where she learned half the stuff that she amassed on people. Big brother had nothing on Camille. But Peter's file was thinner than most. The same was true for the other people we'd met at *Danser*—no one had criminal records or personal connections to Peter or his fiancée, and none of them were victims of the identity thief.

"There *was* no link until now," Camille told me, moving on to position her hat to limit the hat-hair effect. "And the photograph could be a *coïncidence*. A while back, *Bon Souper* was quite *populaire*."

I smiled. The picture was the first real clue in this case that I'd uncovered all by myself. I knew in my gut it was no coincidence, and it felt good. I eased closer to the computer so I could key in the new info into the file just as Laurent walked out of his office and stood behind me, reading over my shoulder.

"As long as you've got the files up, the *Bon Souper* section needs to be updated."

I closed out the file I was working in and clicked open the *Bon Souper* one. "Ready," I said. "Shoot."

"Six months ago," he began, "*Bon Souper* was nearly ready to fold. Last month they were rehiring staff they'd had to let go over the past year. No new investor. No big upturn in customers."

Camille buttoned her coat and reached for her purse perched on the edge of Arielle's desk. "*Un miracle?*"

"They had to get the cash to stay open somewhere," Laurent said. "Divine intervention would not be my first guess."

I figured his new intel had to come from his groupie, which got me thinking about what I learned from mine. "Maybe Madame Grenier just got better at managing the place," I said. "It probably floundered when Monsieur Grenier first got sick and no one was at the helm."

They both looked at me simultaneously and Camille asked, "How do you know Monsieur Grenier is sick?"

"Benoît told me."

Laurent moved around to face me. "Benoît. Is that the man with his hands on you at the bar?"

Camille's eyebrows rose and fell, and a small smile pulled at her mouth.

"He didn't have his hands on me," I corrected. "He had his hand over mine when he was showing me a bartender move. And yes, that's Benoît. The son of the Greniers. He said his father had a stroke months ago and his mother had to take over the restaurant."

"Why didn't you tell me that in the car?" Laurent asked.

After a small exchange about the picture of Peter with Monsieur Grenier, neither one of us had talked much in the car ride back to the office. I had no idea why Laurent hadn't, but I had been reining in my tongue in fear I might say something that would get me into trouble. I felt like I'd made a blubbering fool of myself going on about the cake and the chicken back at the restaurant. Which was so not like me. Usually I could pick and choose when to express myself and when not. And I liked it that way.

"I didn't think it was important," I told him, squelching my urge to add that he hadn't shared his discovery about the financial situation with me in the car either. Including that observation would have defeated my renewed attempt at tongue holding.

He took a step back and crossed his arms over his chest, pulling the fabric of his shirt tight against his pecs. "Did this Benoît say anything else?"

I thought about it. "Not really."

Camille nudged Laurent aside to pass him and get to the front door. "*Bien.* I'm off to give Michel's employees a good frisking. Maybe that will turn up something more."

With Camille, I knew that frisking was just the beginning. By the time she got through with Michel's employees, each one would not only have their computers searched but anything else Camille could get her hands on—purses, phones, drawers. Nothing was off limits to Camille when she was playing doctor—computer or otherwise.

After she left, Laurent retreated into his own office, leaving open both the door and the eyeline between his round glass desk centered in the room and Arielle's desk in reception where I sat.

"I'm expecting Luc around lunch," he said, revving up his computer. "Then I'll be going out too."

"What about me?" I asked. "You need me later?"

He looked up from his computer, pausing before he spoke. "Our dance lesson tonight has been canceled. Pushed to tomorrow night because of Peter's accident. In the morning, Bunny and Léon are going to the florist with Madame Shakiba. But your time for the rest of today is flexible."

I wasn't surprised to hear about the dance lesson reschedule given the upset of Peter's fall, and truthfully, part of me was relieved. I didn't look forward to facing those marble stairs, and the dancing in front of people thing still daunted me.

Tempting as it was to hang around trying to eavesdrop as Laurent and Luc talked shop when Luc arrived, I decided to use my bonus free time to work some more on my lead. I had to run home to put Pong out, but then I could get to work. And I knew exactly where to start. Maybe Camille hadn't found anything that linked Peter to *Bon Souper*, but that didn't mean I couldn't.

EIGHT

MORNINGS COULD BE brutal. Winter mornings in Montreal when the expected high temperature for the day was minus twenty-five degrees Celsius were beyond brutal. I didn't even know what temperature that was because I still hadn't figured out the whole Celsius/Fahrenheit conversion thing. But I knew it was cold enough to make my lungs contract and threaten to go into hibernation. Which was probably why I was still hunkered down under my quilt twenty minutes after Adam had left for work and only half an hour before Laurent was due to pick me up for our next appearance as Bunny and Léon. Okay, maybe I was also a tad disappointed about the fact that my attempt to flesh out my lead the afternoon before had led nowhere. But mostly I was hiding from the cold.

And if it wasn't for that annoying grating noise seeping in through the crack in my vintage window, I might have stayed good and hunkered until time ran out completely. But curiosity got the best of me, so I eased out of bed, swaddled myself into my robe, and tiptoed along the cool wood floor over to the window. Lifting an edge of the curtain, I peered out, letting my ears guide my eyes to the source of the sound. Which took all of two seconds to locate. It was coming from my very own driveway where Laurent was scraping off the ice from my Mini. Doing a good job too, clearing the entire windshield. Not just the central area like I did, but frame to frame. My shoulders sank and guilt set in. Here I was avoiding work, and there was my boss doing me a favor. Not a completely necessary favor since I figured we'd be taking the Léon car to our meeting, but still, a nice gesture. I looked out again and saw that he was finished and leaning against the car, his arms crossed over his chest and his gloved hands tucked up towards his armpits.

I pulled on some socks, tightened my robe, and made my way downstairs. I yanked open the front door, cupped my hands around my mouth, and called out to Laurent to come in.

The tuque covering his ears must have muffled my voice because he didn't show any sign of acknowledgement. I tried waving my arm to get his attention and yelled louder. This time, his head turned, and he made his way over.

"It's freezing out," I said as he stepped onto my porch. "What are you doing out there?"

"I'm early," he said, his words floating on clouds of warm air wafting out into the cold.

I opened the door wider to allow him in and closed it quickly when he was through. He shook his boots to get off the loose snow and rubbed his hands together. When he bent to kiss my cheeks hello, bits of melting snow lingered on his scruff and trickled, cold and wet, onto my skin.

"I'm not ready yet," I told him. "Come in, and I'll get you some tea to warm up."

He slipped off his boots, placed them on the draining mat behind the door, and added his coat to the iron stand, stashing his hat in his coat pocket. Minus the outdoor gear, his hair bordered on bedhead, his jeans were clean and professional, and his sweater expensive. Classic urban casual except the hair. The hair and scruff added an edge. I wondered if back in his cop days, he had gotten away with that look. He made an after-you gesture, reached down to pet my dog Pong as she greeted him, and followed me down the short hall to the kitchen at the back of the house.

The kitchen was large and still fitted with the original wood cabinets, now painted dusty blue, and a massive white porcelain sink. Adam and I had put in new appliances when we took over the house and updated the counters to granite, but the counter height dated back to earlier days when people weren't quite as tall, which suited me perfectly. Windows ran the back wall with a door leading out to a small three-season sunroom. I'd added some café curtains in a crisp cotton with a pale French Country floral pattern, but they still allowed for plenty of light, which at this time of day was just starting to filter in. I put the kettle on and grabbed two mugs from the cupboard and a tea bag from the tin.

"You hungry?" I asked Laurent. "Want some toast or something?"

"Sure."

I plopped four slices of bread into the toaster, got out plates, and set some butter and jam on the table along with a couple jars of nut butters. When everything else was ready, I joined Laurent at the round pine table.

"This is good," he said, munching on the toast he'd slathered with almond butter and strawberry jam. "I don't eat before the gym."

My eyes wandered over to the clock on the stove. Nearly eight-thirty. He'd probably been here about ten or fifteen minutes, and his gym was in the Plateau and I lived in NDG, which meant at least thirty minutes travel time at this hour. Laurent worked out for an hour, so he had to have been at the gym by latest six-thirty. Compared to him, I was a slacker. Not that I hadn't tried the early exercise thing. A while back, I'd taken some morning yoga classes. It's just that I kept nodding off during the deep breathing and decided the extra sleep served me better.

I blew on my tea and took a sip. "I don't know how you do it," I said to him. "Aren't you tired?"

He rested his back against the wood spindles of the chair. "*Non.* The exercise, it gives me energy."

I reached for the tahini and worked the lid with no success. He took it from me and twisted the cap off in one move. Exercise kept him fit too.

He wiped his mouth with a napkin and set aside his empty plate. "So, your Anglophone off to play his computer games already?"

I slid my eyes to his. "He doesn't play them, he creates them," I said. "And they're educational games." Technically, Adam played them too, along with a bunch of more recreational fare, but those were for research. At least that's what he told me.

Laurent smiled. "Either way. He's left you all alone."

I sighed and avoided his eyes, not wanting to get caught up in his tease. "I'm not alone."

He raised an eyebrow. I pointed to Pong resting under the table and Ping sitting on the chair beside me as if they were exhibit A and B, and I smiled. "A person's never alone when she's got pets."

Then before Laurent could take the topic any deeper, I went on to ask him if there was any more news about Peter or our findings at *Bon Souper*. My own efforts to find more info at my go-to place— Internet social sites—had netted a big nada. Nothing on Facebook, Twitter, LinkedIn, or any of the other biggies. And nothing when I Googled Peter or the restaurant. I was hoping with Laurent's fancier computer programs and better connections, that he would have had better luck.

But Laurent offered up very little, saying only that the *Bon Souper* financials were taking time to track and Camille's frisking at *Prêt-à-Marier* found nothing so far. And he stayed mum on whatever he may have learned from Luc.

So I switched gears and asked him for preliminary info on the florist we were set to see in an hour, but his cell phone rang and I lost him to the caller before he could answer. Leaving me to down the remainder of my tea and get up to clear the table while he conversed with his caller in French.

As I tidied up, my thoughts shifted to the day ahead, and I resisted the urge to go back upstairs and slither into bed. Our second dance lesson loomed in less than twelve hours, and I so did not want to go. I'd used my unexpected night off to watch one of those dancing shows on TV, trying to emulate a few moves. Only the dancers were too fast for me. I tried to follow the steps, but I couldn't tell when one ended and another started. Let alone how to stream them together. Plus, the outfits distracted me. How did women dance in such high heels? And weren't they worried about their butts showing as they twirled about in the flimsy skirts? I'd become so discouraged that I'd given up and shut off the TV before the end of the show, resigned to live out the rest of my days steering clear of any dance floors and hoping this case would be miraculously solved before I ever had to set foot in the *Danser* studio again.

Now, in the snow-bright light of day, I knew that would never happen. I'd have to go to the lesson. And I'd have to try to follow instructions. In front of people. In one of my Bunny outfits. With Laurent, who was fit and probably capable of flinging all nearly five foot two and a hundred and ten pounds of me around the studio like a rag doll. Laurent, who was probably an expert dancer from all the practice he'd had at the gazillion family weddings he'd attended. Laurent, who was now shouting my address into his cell phone.

I turned back to the table and watched as he snapped his phone off and stood.

"That was Michel," he said. "He's coming."

My eyes darted back to the clock. "Coming here? Why? Is he coming with us to the florist?" I gave the last dish a quick rinse, put it in the dishwasher, and swiped some paper towel over the counter, glancing at the table to make sure I'd stowed all the food jars back in the fridge.

Laurent walked into the hallway and headed towards the front of the house. "*Non*. Michel is upset. Some new fuss about Peter."

I went into the hall and paused in the living room doorway. Laurent was peering out the window. "What kind of fuss?" I asked him.

"Not sure. Michel wasn't clear on the phone." He stepped back from the window. "He's here."

That was fast. Must have been nearby. I went to answer the door, but Laurent stepped in front of me before I had it open all the way and pushed me back behind him. I tilted my head, trying to make eye contact with Michel as he stepped in, Laurent still blocking my view.

"*Un instant*," Laurent said to Michel, pushing me out of the vestibule and back into the hall, pulling the anteroom door closed behind him and leaving Michel alone in the tiny space.

I gave Laurent a confused look.

"Your clothes," he said, gesturing at my robe. "You need to get dressed."

I looked down at myself. I'd forgotten I was wearing my robe. But it was a fine robe. Comfy even. A white stretch cotton with little pink flowers. And I was sure it wouldn't be the first time Michel had seen a woman in a robe. "I'll get dressed after," I told Laurent. "I want to know what's got Michel upset." I reached for the doorknob, but he waved my hand away.

A flush of annoyance went through me heightened by impatient curiosity. "Later, okay. Let Michel in. He's never met me before, and he's going to think I don't want him in my house." Or worse. Like I'm a bad housekeeper or something and am furiously dashing about hiding the evidence, grabbing up balls of pet hair as I go, to prepare for his unexpected visit.

"*Non*," Laurent said, now fully blocking the door like a bodyguard protecting his charge.

"Sorry, Michel," I yelled through the door. "This'll just take a second." Then in a lower voice I said to Laurent, "It's a robe for pity's sake."

"It's not appropriate."

This coming from the guy who had me dressed like a hooker two days earlier. "You didn't have a problem with it five minutes ago. Anyway, it covers more of me than that outfit you and Camille put me in for dance class."

He shook his head. "Not the same thing."

"Oh, really. How so?"

"That outfit had underwear."

I felt my face flush. "Fine," I said, starting up the stairs. "I'll change. But don't get into any good stuff while I'm gone."

As I raced into my bedroom, I heard Michel come in below and the two men start talking. I threw on a bra and panties and the first Bunny outfit I saw—a woven black skirt, black stockings with subtle wide striping, and a white v-neck sweater embroidered with pink stitching. Then I made a quick stop by the bathroom to wash up, brush my teeth, put on my Bunny face, and pull my hair into a ponytail. I had to have taken less than ten minutes, but by the time I got back downstairs, both men were in the thick of conversation, their words coming out at a speed an auctioneer would envy.

Laurent noticed me first, his eyes loitering on my outfit long enough to register approval. He let Michel finish whatever comment he was in the midst of making then offered introductions.

Michel hadn't taken off his parka, and it looked mismatched with his navy suit pants and gray socks. He held his hat in his hands and his round head was covered in dark blonde hair styled into a boyish cut that had him looking considerably younger than his forty years.

I smiled at him and told him I was glad to be working on his case.

He frowned, worry furrowing his brows. "*C'est une catastrophe,*" he said.

I looked to Laurent for more details. He explained that Peter's autopsy report had come in with enough evidence to point to suspicious death, launching a murder inquest.

Michel started pacing over my area rug and wringing his hat with his hands.

"Didn't we already know this was likely?" I said.

"We did," Laurent said. "Michel didn't. Nobody wanted to tell him until it was official. Michel doesn't take bad news well."

I sat down on the couch, pulled a pillow onto my lap, and watched Michel pace some more and mutter to himself. Sweat glistened on his forehead, the strands of hair above his eyes becoming damp and starting to curl at the ends. A shade of red resembling frostbite crept into his cheeks. And the hat in his hands started to look as though it had been through a spin cycle. For a minute, I worried he might keel over like Peter and felt my own anxiety meter start to rise. It couldn't be good karma to have two men dead at my feet within days of each other.

I stood and went over to Michel, trying to pat him soothingly on the back as he paced. "It will be okay, Michel. We'll find out who's behind all this."

Michel's pacing picked up, his muttering increased, and his arms started swinging like a toy robot gone out of control. I lost my grip on him and stumbled.

Laurent moved forward to catch me and pulled me back over to the couch. We both sat, our eyes following Michel's movements.

"That's what's got Michel upset," Laurent said. "He doesn't want us to investigate anymore. He wants us off the case."

"Why?" I asked.

"Michel thinks Peter was killed because he knew something about the identity thefts. Maybe something he didn't even know was important. And Michel thinks the same thing will happen to us if we poke around the case."

"So what does he want to do about the identity thefts?"

"Nothing. He's hoping it will all just stop and go away like a bad dream."

I tilted my head to catch Laurent's eye. "And what do you think?"

"I think Michel should take a vacation in Tahiti while we sort this out. A man's been killed. There's more going on here than identity theft. We can't just turn our heads and walk away."

Michel stopped pacing, said something I couldn't make out, made his shaky hand into a gun, and waved it at Laurent and me.

Pretend gun or not, the image was disturbing. Especially coming from a sweaty, red-faced man with panic in his eyes and a Charlie Brown hair curl on his forehead. I inched closer to Laurent, thinking maybe dropping the case wasn't such a bad idea.

OKAY, MAYBE MICHEL was just paranoid. Or maybe he was overindulging a predisposition for the dramatic—which would be no surprise since it was a dominant gene in the Caron clan—but I was glad when Laurent decided to take him home. Between *tante* Claudette's danger predictions and Michel's finger gun, the Caron family had me a tad unnerved, and I was happy to have a bit of time to myself to regroup. Especially since Laurent had no intention of dropping the case. His plan was to ferry Michel home then swing by the police station to get more details on Peter's autopsy report. Like precincts in New York, police stations in Montreal—or Poste de Quartier and PDQ for short as they were known here—were numbered, and Laurent was headed to PDQ9 in the west end. Which was handy because it wasn't too far away, and he figured if we pushed back our meeting with the florist about two hours, he'd make it back to pick me up in plenty of time.

After he and Michel left, I pulled the Bunny phone out of my purse, scrolled through the numbers Camille had programmed into the phone, and called the florist to reschedule. Then, since Madame Shakiba was supposed to join us for the meeting, I called her and left a message about the time change. That done, I skipped over to see if Camille had entered a number for Peter's fiancée Anna. I still had the image in my head of her tiny elfin face staring down at Peter's body, and I worried what hearing that his death was no accident would do to her. Maybe it was the social worker in me, or maybe it was because of a bond from sharing in the trauma of seeing Peter die, but I felt a connection to Anna. The least I could do was check in on her and give her my condolences.

I found Anna's number and called, not surprised when my call went directly to voice mail. Probably she was screening. I listened to enough of her message to peg the voice to be sure I'd reached Anna and clicked off before the beep. Then I toggled over to Bunny's browser, logged into the C&C case files, and checked Anna's address. Her home and work addresses were listed as the same place in Montreal West, not too far from me. Handy since I had two hours free. Just enough time to swing by in person.

I stowed the phone back in the Bunny purse and got ready to go out. As I locked up and scurried through the cold to the protection of my car, I felt immense gratitude to Laurent for clearing all the snow and ice off my Mini. That would save me a lot of time. Which was good. Not only because my time was tight, but Michel's worries were starting to whirr in my head and got me thinking he could be right. If Peter was killed because he knew something about the identity thief, anyone who knew anything could be a target. And if Peter had shared whatever he knew with anyone, that anyone would be Anna.

NINE

FROM THE LOOKS of it, Anna worked out of a detached lower duplex that was bordered by other duplexes on either side. Farther up the street, a few stores were sprinkled in before the strip turned residential again. I drove past her place and went around the block to park, remembering undercover rule number one not to give myself away. Not that I actually thought Anna would even notice my car, let alone somehow know it belonged to me and not Bunny, but if I was going to be a good PI and prove I could follow rules I needed to start somewhere.

When I finally made it back on foot, I noticed the flat above Anna's had a balcony directly on top of the entrances to both units, and a set of Samoyeds stood on the porch poking their noses out between the wood rails and barking at passers-by. The white fur on the dogs' legs blended in with the snow nobody had bothered to shovel, giving their torsos the appearance of floating in mid air. As I neared the porch step below, the barking grew louder.

Anna's head appeared in the glass portion of her front door when I reached her entrance. The canines upstairs posing as doormen saving me the trouble of ringing her bell. She yanked the door open when she saw me, a glimmer of recognition in her eyes. "Yes?"

"Hi Anna," I said, my voice uncomfortably loud in an effort to be heard over the barking. "Remember me? We met at the dance lesson. I'm Lo...errr Bunny."

She scratched at her forehead and a heaviness briefly darkened her face. "Yeah, sure."

I shifted my feet to keep warm. "I didn't mean to bother you, I just wanted to see how you were doing."

"I'm okay," Anna said, the red puffiness and dark circles around her eyes suggesting otherwise. She paused before adding, "Want to come in?"

I nodded and thanked her, stepping inside, relieved to find her safe and sound. She closed the door behind me and retreated into the house while I waited, unsure whether to follow her or stay put.

She hurried down the long hall towards the back of the house, her blouse billowing over her leggings, and disappeared through a doorway just before the kitchen that bookended the house with the vestibule. A minute later, she poked her head out. "Sorry. I thought you were right behind me. Just come on back. I'm in the middle of a calculation."

I pulled off my boots and went in, glancing in the rooms that shot off from each side of the long hallway as I made my way to the back of the house. Some of the doors were closed, bedrooms I figured, since Anna worked out of her home. Although, home may be stretching the term. The place was sparsely furnished and missing the typical amount of personality that comes from pictures on the walls or knick-knacks or even throw rugs. Didn't even see a TV in the living room. The kitchen appeared to be the hub with dirty glasses clustered on the counters, papers strewn over the table, and a coffee pot still brewing.

"Okay," Anna said. "Done." She got up from her desk and brushed past me as she swept through her office doorway en route to the kitchen. "I'll just grab this coffee and be right with you. Want some? It's decaf."

I panned the room, looking for a place to sit and wondering if I should join her in the kitchen instead. She came back carrying a mug in both hands before I had a chance to decide on the coffee or the room change.

I took the mug she offered me. "Thanks," I said. "I didn't mean to disturb your work."

She zipped around to her swivel chair, put her coffee down, and sat, only to spring up and whiz out to the kitchen again. She came back carrying a folding metal chair. "Sorry. The place is a mess. It's coming up on tax season." She opened the chair, placed it between me and a stack of small boxes on the floor, and went back around to her side of the desk.

I set my cup on the edge of Anna's desk, removed my coat, slipped it onto the back of the metal chair, and sat, swinging my purse around to rest in my lap. Watching her, I got the sense Anna was still too numb to fully process Peter's death and probably channeling her grief into work to distract herself. I needed to tread carefully. "I'm so sorry about Peter," I said.

Her eyes froze, but her hands began arranging the papers in front of her into piles. "Thanks," she said. "It's still hard to believe."

"I know what you mean," I said. And I did too. When each of my parents had died, it had taken a while to sink in. And when it did, I'd barely been able to get out of bed for days and didn't see a reason to. It didn't seem possible that the world could still exist without them in it.

She shifted her hands from the papers to the sides of her coffee mug, wrapping her fingers around the cup. "Well, you were there. You saw everything. It was all so quick the way Petey slipped like that."

Slipped? Hmm. It didn't seem like Anna had heard about the autopsy report yet, or about the murder charge Peter's parents had made.

Her eyes flashed and she went on. "Those damn stairs must have just been waxed. Who does that? In the middle of winter? It's insane having marble stairs. They were probably wet too from melted snow off of someone's boot. That's an accident waiting to happen, right? They should carpet them in the winter or something." She paused to chug more coffee before adding, "I bet Petey's family will have something to say about it. They wouldn't let something like this happen to their son without someone paying for it."

I picked up my coffee cup and peered inside, wondering if it was really decaf. "Have you spoken to his parents about it?" I asked.

She shook her head. "Not since I told them about the accident. Petey was their only child. They're just devastated. Their whole family is. Both of his parents have lots of relatives. That's why we were having a big wedding." She stopped and washed down some more coffee, her eyes drifting over to shelves bordering her desk where a photograph sat of Peter and her by a lake. The fragile expression on her face making me wonder if Peter's parents hadn't mentioned the murder to her yet to protect her from more hurt. Problem was, if she might be in danger too, she needed to know.

Exactly when and how to tell her was the big question. The information wasn't public yet, so I had no plausible reason for knowing about the murder charge. I'd blow my cover if I just spilled what I knew. Plus, I didn't have enough facts yet either. Telling her partial information at this point could do more damage to her than good. I needed to try another tack.

"That's tough," I said. "I heard Peter had been having a rough time lately, too. That must have upset them."

Anna set her coffee mug aside. "What did you hear?"

I went quiet a beat while I came up with a fib. "I heard him talking the other night at *Danser* about getting ripped off by someone."

"He did. Some creep bought a bunch of stuff on his credit cards and cleared out his savings account."

"Wow," I said, feigning surprise. "Did he catch the guy?"

She shook her head. "He reported it to the police, but that's it. And the credit card and bank people. After that, he wanted to forget it ever happened. I told him he should try to track the leak. I even started looking through his records myself, but he wanted to just let it go." She let out a long breath. "That's the kind of guy Petey was."

Hmm interesting. Didn't sound like Peter knew much at all. Was it possible everyone was wrong and Peter's death had no connection to the identity theft? "Wasn't he afraid the thief would come after him for reporting it?" I asked, thinking it was as close to alerting her to danger as I could get at the moment.

She shook her head again. "Petey never mentioned it. But why would anyone do that? The scumbag already got what he wanted from Petey. He probably robbed lots of people who told the police. Everyone I know who's had their credit card number or ID info or money ripped off reports it. Why would this guy care about Petey?"

She made a good point.

"Anyway," she went on, "we were both too swamped with work and stressed out with the wedding plans to think much about it." She paused to sip more coffee but set her mug aside when it turned out to be empty. "And now with Petey gone, it all seems so unimportant. Feels like everything's working in reverse with me canceling all the wedding plans we made together."

Seemed to me that's what wedding planners were for. And family and friends. Wedding cancellations were the last thing Anna should have to deal with right now. She shouldn't even be working. And she probably shouldn't have been left alone. "I can help if you'd like. Just tell me what you need."

Her brows furrowed. "What? No. Really, it's fine. My mother is using the guest list to tell the rest of my family about what happened to Petey. Pretty soon everyone we invited will know."

I sat back, relieved to know at least someone was helping Anna. "That's nice of your mother."

For the first time since I'd arrived Anna looked like she might cry. "I think she wanted to catch people before they shelled out money for wedding gifts. Either that or collect on her bets about whether or not Petey and I would make it to the alter."

Now that didn't sound very motherly. I wanted to assure her that couldn't possibly be the case but what did I know? I barely knew Anna, let alone her mom. But I wanted to say something comforting. "This has all been so sudden, I'm sure it's hard on everybody."

"Everybody but my mother. She's relieved. She never wanted me to marry Petey. He didn't have the right genes for her future grandchildren, according to her. She doesn't understand that high blood pressure and high cholesterol aren't genetic."

Maybe. Or maybe she was more concerned about the balding and poor manners being passed on. "If he had high blood pressure and cholesterol, maybe your mom was concerned about his health?"

"No. She didn't have any concern for him. And he didn't have big health problems. He just liked dessert. But he was going to cut back before the wedding."

I flashed on the image of Peter eating cookies at the *Danser* meet and greet. Somehow, it didn't seem to me like he had any plans to give up desserts or anything else. Seemed to me old Petey was the kind of guy who thought of diet as a four-letter word. But I nodded in understanding. Who was I to shatter Anna's image of her dead fiancé?

Anna went on. "He sure did have a sweet tooth, though. You should have seen what Petey chose as our wedding cake. It was beautiful." She rifled through papers on her desk and picked up a photograph of a tiered cake stand filled with dozens of cupcakes. Several different flavors interspersed by the looks of it, and each with a colorful frosting as thick as meringue and decorated with tiny candy flowers. Her eyes misted up again then opened bigger as she passed me the picture. "Here. Why don't you take it? It's already been ordered. I'm sure the bakery can have it ready a little earlier. And they're an awesome company that delivers right to your door. When did you say your wedding was? Around mid February? Mine was set for the beginning of March. That's pretty close."

I looked at the photo of cupcakes, trying to think of a polite way to decline her offer when I caught the hopeful look in her eyes and found myself agreeing instead. What harm could it do? Maybe the bakery would turn out to be one of the suppliers we needed to check out. And if not, the worst thing that could happen is that I'd get stuck with a bunch of cupcakes. That didn't seem so bad. They *did* look good.

"Sure," I said. "That's so sweet of you." And thinking about wedding dessert reminded me of *Bon Souper* and Peter's picture hanging on the restaurant wall. In all my worry over Anna's safety, I'd nearly forgotten my big lead. This was the perfect chance to follow up on it, rule number three and all. "Looks like Peter had really good taste in food," I added to segue over to the topic. "Léon and I are having our reception at *Bon Souper*. I'm a little nervous about the choice. What did Peter think of it?"

Anna started searching through her stack of papers again. "I don't know. We never went there. And he never mentioned it to me, so I don't think he did either." A thoughtful look crossed her face, the moistness back in her eyes, and she smiled a little. "He liked to see himself as a bit of a food critic and always talked about places he tried."

I tried not to let my disappointment show. Maybe the picture had been old, taken before Anna knew Peter. Like Camille said, when the place was more popular. Which probably meant Camille was also right that it was just a coincidence and didn't factor into the case.

"Ah," Anna said, pulling an invoice from her stack. "Here's the cupcake info. I'll give them a call and ask them if the order could be ready early, and if all goes well, I can have them transfer the deposit amount to you." She reached for a stickie pad. "I'll call you when it's all set. What's your phone number?"

Hmm. Hadn't thought about the payment bit. Would have to get Laurent to handle that later with one of his special credit cards. Fingers crossed it wasn't an unnecessary expense. I pulled the Bunny phone out of my bag and called up the number hoping Anna wouldn't think it was odd that I had to look up my own phone number.

She jotted down the number without comment and pulled out another paper from her stack. "Maybe you could use something else. How about the limo rental?"

I didn't know what to say. Anna's face looked so hopeful that I nearly agreed again, but I couldn't take on all her plans. "We've already booked a car," I told her, feeling a tad sheepish about lying. Fibs I could do. Ditto the odd omission now and again. But out and out lies still triggered the same guilt response they had since I was a child and tried to lie to the librarian about losing a rare, out-of-print book.

"What about my hair and makeup appointment?" Anna asked, holding up a business card for La Coupe.

It didn't seem to occur to her that the car and the hair booking were for her wedding date, not Bunny's, and that those kinds of things were not just interchangeable. But then she was grieving. Her thoughts were bound to be a bit muddled. So I just smiled and declined both.

"Probably just as well," she said, reaching up to touch the blonde hair fringing her face. "I could probably still use a visit. My hair is hopeless. It's flat and lifeless. It just hangs there. I had highlights put in last time, but they haven't helped much."

Lifeless would not have been the word I'd use to describe Anna's hair. Straight yes, lifeless and flat, no. Long, dark blonde layers with a touch of gold swept down to her shoulder blades and a fringe of bangs framed her eyes. All neat and tidy. Unlike my hair, which frequently looked like a thick, gnarly bush blazing with fall colors when it wasn't wrestled into a ponytail or clipped up.

Anna lifted a section of hair away from her face. "And see the color at the roots. It's an awful, dingy mess. Not blonde and not brown. Just blech."

Her roots looked fine. But with her bangs out of her eyes, her pupils looked glassy, like shiny black buttons. The thin circular bands surrounding them too narrow to make out the color and adding only the appearance of a glow.

"I think your hair is lovely," I said to Anna as I started to piece things together. Her jittery movements, her fast talking, her rushing around, her glassy eyes all started to make sense to me. Anna wasn't just stressed from Peter's death. Anna was taking something. I scanned the room and zeroed in on a prescription vial nestled among vitamin bottles on a shelf behind her desk. I couldn't make out the label but noticed the cap wasn't completely sealed.

Anna let her hair drop. "My mother calls the color 'sloppy brown.' When I was a kid, she kept it cut short so nobody would notice. She said it made it looked darker. Almost like a real brown." A beep from her computer interrupted her, and she glanced at the screen. "Oh, no. I forgot about this guy. I've got to get back to work. I've got a consultation in five minutes." She sprang up and rounded the desk.

"Oh, sure," I said, standing too and starting to gather my things. "I understand," I said. "I won't keep you. I moved slowly, curious about what pills Anna was taking, and maneuvered my way to the end of her desk to get a look at the bottle label. I bent forward, pretending to search for something in my purse so I could get closer to make out the tiny writing. Fluoxetine, aka Prozac. As a social worker, I'd met many people taking it for depression or anxiety. Anna's prescription dated back more than a month, making me wonder if she was taking it for an ongoing problem or to get through the stress of planning her wedding. And now, to deal with the loss of Peter.

"It was nice of you to stop by, Bunny," Anna said to me as we both made our way out of her office and she led me back to the front door. "It means a lot. And I'll be sorry to miss seeing your dances. Your songs sounded really interesting. You and your fiancé make a great couple. I'll never forget the way your fiancé tried to help Petey. Thank him for me, will you." She paused, her hand on the doorknob. "You're really lucky to have him. And him you. After all, if Petey hadn't been ahead of you on the stairs, you could have been the one to fall off that slippery step."

Barking started up before I stepped out onto Anna's porch, and I nearly bumped into a delivery guy who had stooped over to set a large box in a snow-free spot by his feet. I apologized and headed off to leave Anna to sign for her package. A wedding gift probably. Something else Anna would have to deal with alone. Returning wedding presents. I looked back at the door when I turned onto the sidewalk to trudge to my car, and I felt another pang of sadness for Anna.

TEN

THE LÉON CAR was in my driveway when I got home. At first glance, it was hard to tell if the windows were steamed up or covered in frost, but neither was a good sign. I pulled up in a spot a couple houses down from mine, jumped out of my Mini, and dashed over, locking up with a zap from my remote as I went. The passenger door opened on the Léon car as I approached, and I got in to find Camille at the wheel.

"Hey," I said. "I didn't expect to see you here. Where's Laurent?"

Camille held up a finger and pointed to her ear, and I took in the wire connecting her to her cell phone like an umbilical cord.

"*Non, non,*" she said to whoever was listening at the other end. "*C'est fini.*" She paused. "*Oui.* Okay. *Rappelle-moi.*" She tapped her call off, turned the engine over, and clicked on the defrost before turning to me. "Change of plans. I'm going to the florist with you. I've been waiting almost twenty minutes. Where were you?"

I filled her in on my visit to Anna's, minus my suspicions about Anna's Prozac. That was personal and it didn't seem pertinent. Although I wasn't a practicing social worker anymore, my feelings about respecting confidentiality hadn't changed. I still held to the tenet that private information was only shared on a need-to-know basis.

"We had an agreement, remember?" Camille said, her fingers drumming the steering wheel. "Until you're done training, no client meetings without me or Laurent."

"Anna's not a client."

Camille's finger drumming grew louder. "Semantics. Anna is part of a case. The same rules apply."

Again with the rules. And coming from Camille of all people. "But Anna's in mourning. And nobody's helping her," I said. "And she could be in danger. Someone should look in on her."

"Maybe. But that someone is not you."

I went quiet. We both knew this conversation could go around in circles all day. Neither of us had the time to bother with that, so I cut to the chase. "Look, if Peter was murdered because of the identity theft, Anna could be in danger too and wouldn't even know."

"*Exactement*," Camille said, releasing the parking brake, putting the car into gear, and pulling out. "This is no time for your do-gooder act, Lora. Remember last time you poked your nose into something dangerous without backup? You got into all sorts of trouble."

That was another reference back to the Puddles case. "Everything turned out fine in the end," I reminded her. "You even got a boyfriend out of it."

Camille's foot hit the brake hard as she stopped for a red light, and I lurched forward, remembering too late that I'd gone and used the "B" word.

"*C'est fini!*" she said, her forearms forming an "x" and waving out into a two sticks as her hands cut through the air above the steering wheel like blades on a fan.

I righted myself. "Sorry."

"*Non, non. Pas toi. It's* over. Bell is over."

Bell aka Puddles. And this was news to me. Only last week, Adam and I had met them both for dinner at Schwartz's. Well, they had dinner. Adam and I had French Fries and cole slaw. Schwartz's was a Jewish deli famous for smoked meat with not much fare for vegetarians. But it was close to the office, and Camille and I took turns choosing eating venues to keep things fair. "When did this happen?" I said.

The light turned green and Camille accelerated into traffic. "This morning." She honked to avoid another driver when she glided into his lane and he wasn't going fast enough to leave her space. He sped up, and she acknowledged him with a quick wave. Camille, like many Montrealers, was sparse on blinker use but good with hand gestures.

I studied her face, trying to judge if this breakup was a good thing or not. She kept her eyes on the road, giving nothing away. But it didn't work with me. Camille only avoided eye contact when she was in protection mode. "You okay with it?" I asked her.

"*Oui, oui*. It was fun for a while," she said as she pulled the car to the curb down the street from the florist, *Jardin de Fleurs*. "But then he bought a big screen TV and put it in my *salon*. *C'est complètement fou*, no? I already have a TV."

I stayed quiet and waited. This was not about a TV.

She cut the engine, dug into her purse, and pulled out a bar of chocolate, breaking off a row for herself before extending the package to me to do the same. "I told him to take the TV to his place. He said he didn't buy it for his place, he bought it for our place."

Okay, now I was understanding.

"Our place?" Camille said. "We don't have a place. I have a place and you have a place, but there is no our place." She was replaying their conversation now, her hands flying about almost as fast as her words. "I told him to take his TV and go."

"So he left?"

"*Ben non*. He called me a nutjob and laughed. He said he was staying over most of the week anyway so it made sense to move in. That's when I looked around and saw his stuff everywhere. Shirts in my closet, deodorant in my bathroom, socks on my floor, razors in my medicine cabinet—"

If I was Camille, I would have been grateful for the razors. When we'd first met Puddles, he'd sported a beard à la Hell's Angels that did nothing to showcase his boyish charm which had matured into manly good looks as he made his way into his forties. Most women would be thrilled to have Puddles on their couch, settling in to a committed relationship, big screen TV or not. But Camille didn't do relationships.

She checked her watch and reached for a bag in the backseat. "Hold this a sec," she said, taking off her hat and passing it to me.

"Wait. If he didn't leave, then it's not over."

"It's over for me," she said, pulling something out of the bag, slipping it on her head, and pulling down the visor mirror. "And it will be over for him when I change the locks."

Camille liked to talk tough, but I knew she wouldn't resort to that before talking things through with him. This wasn't her first time bailing when a tryst morphed into a relationship. She spent more time trying to lose a man than most women do trying to find one.

She turned to me, black, straight hair streaming to her elbows, bangs covering her eyebrows, and slipped on round blue-rimmed glasses. "What do you think?" she asked me.

I'd never seen her resort to wigs and glasses to dump a guy before. "I don't think that will fool Puddles," I said.

"*Non, non.* It's for the florist. So Bunny and the *Prêt-à-Marier* computer doc aren't seen together."

Right. Naturally, Camille had more tools in her PI toolbox. When she was undercover, she got to wear wigs and glasses. I had to wear cleavage and spiky heels.

I told her she looked fine and gave her back her hat, and she grabbed her purse and got out of the car.

I got out too, joined her on the sidewalk, and brushed at the sand-stained snow that was already creeping onto my new Bunny boots. "Is Laurent meeting us?"

"He's still at the PDQ. We'll just choose some flowers, and Laurent will swing by later to leave a deposit. He already arranged it over the phone."

Made sense. But I wasn't sure why we couldn't do the whole thing later then. Or maybe place our order by phone or online. Which is what I suggested to Camille as we walked towards *Jardin de Fleurs*.

"We could," she said, adjusting her hat over her wig. "But not all breaches happen like that. Sometimes it's not the business that's at fault. Sometimes employees swipe cards twice or steal PIN numbers. Or target specific clients after they've learned personal details. If we visit the shop, we have a better chance of sizing up employees and seeing how they treat customers."

I stepped up my pace, trying to keep up with Camille's long-legged strides. "Like a sting?"

"*Non, non.* That's entrapment. We don't do entrapment. We're here to watch. But if they happen to steal from us, too bad for them."

We stopped in front of the florist, and Camille went for the door. "You just observe the staff and see if you notice anything odd. I'll do the talking."

I reached for her arm to stop her. "But I'm the bride. Shouldn't I do the talking?"

She sighed. "Fine, you can talk. But leave the details to me."

IF COLORS HAD scents, red would smell like roses, pink like carnations, yellow like tulips, purple like lavender, white like lilies. And all of them blended together would smell like Selena of *Jardin de Fleurs*, who crouched near the refrigerators talking to a little girl.

The girl nodded at whatever Selena had said to her and gripped a basket of flower petals with one hand and tossed some petals to her feet with the other.

"*Très bien,*" Selena said, smiling and rising to stand, flower girl lesson apparently complete.

The girl beamed, then she turned away as an older girl swung open the door to the shop and shot the younger girl an impatient look. Her sister probably, judging by the resemblance. The little one threw a sloppy wave Selena's way, ran for the door, and both girls went out, leaving the store quiet. And minus Madame Shakiba as far as I could tell.

A man emerged from the back of the store and gestured for Selena to join him at the cash. The lines around his eyes suggested he was late thirties, and his red hair and freckles along with his wool turtleneck sweater reminded me of an Irish fisherman just returned from the sea. He wore no nametag, only an apron imprinted with the store's logo and tied at his waist.

Selena headed over to the counter and the Irish fisherman pointed at the computer screen and complained to her about something I couldn't hear, his contorted face and droning tone nevertheless conveying his mood.

Camille circled a display of flowers near the cash and pointed to an arrangement of red roses. "These would make nice centerpieces, no?" she said to me somewhat absently. Probably half her attention focused on trying to catch tidbits of conversation between Selena and the Irish fisherman.

I scrunched my nose, and she moved on to some orange orchids. "These?"

I shook my head, and she picked up a small planter of some blue flowers I didn't recognize. I looked at it and shook my head again, careful to be quiet because I could tell by the cock of Camille's head that she was still listening to the two at the counter.

We continued the same routine with a few more flowers near the cash. None of these would work. Bunny's color was pink. I'd told Madame Shakiba pink for the bouquet and burgundy for the table centerpieces. We needed to branch out and cover more of the store. I shifted to another area that had more promise, not wandering too far so Camille wouldn't look too conspicuous remaining within earshot of the counter.

"*Est-ce que je peux vous aider*, may I help you?" Selena asked, suddenly beside me. I'd noticed her nametag spelling out her first name in large capital letters when we'd come in. Up close, the word *propriétaire* in small print underneath also became visible and signaled she owned the shop. She spoke with an accent I pegged as Spanish. Her coloring was dark, her hair long, coarse, and black, and she moved with a sway to her hips that got me thinking of salsa.

"My friend is getting married," Camille told her as she joined us and went into her spiel. "And we're looking for the right flowers."

"Something pink," I added in.

"Mademoiselle Bosworth?" Selena asked, pausing only long enough to take in my nod before grabbing me into a hug. "*Félicitations*. Madame Shakiba told me all about you and your fiancé when she stopped by earlier. She couldn't come back again, but she picked out some possibilities for you." Selena wrinkled her nose. "But I think we can find something more exciting. Come. You pick out the main flowers, and I'll put together a fabulous collection to set them off." She strode away toward the refrigerators indicating with a wave of her hand that Camille and I should follow.

I knew I was supposed to be observing Madame Shakiba, but part of me was relieved she was a no-show. It would be easier to focus on the task at hand without having her glare staring me down. As I trailed behind Selena, I glanced over at the Irish fisherman and caught him eyeing Camille over the top of his computer monitor, his eyes darting back to the screen when he caught me catching him. Clearly, the wig and glasses did nothing to reduce Camille's cachet with men.

Selena opened a fridge door and withdrew a single pink flower. "Gergeras for the bouquet maybe?" she said and then pointed to another bunch of flowers in one of the tall, thin metal buckets. "Madame Shakiba said you wanted burgundy for the centerpieces. Those calla lilies look amazing on the table. If you want something tall, we do beautiful arrangements in a vase, and if you want something shorter we can use just the heads in a glass bowl. Very elegant." She moved down and opened another door, motioning to another tin of flowers. "Or if it doesn't have to be a solid color, those veronicas would work well."

My eyes veered over to the first cluster of flowers Selena had pointed to then back to the gerbera in her hand, and I pretended to weigh the choices. I had no idea how much time Camille wanted to suss out the store and its employees. But judging by the expression on her face, this phase had gone on long enough. Which didn't surprise me, Camille never spent a minute longer at anything than was absolutely necessary.

Selena looked at me expectantly and I smiled.

"I'd like the gerberas and the calla lilies," I told her.

"I don't think so," a familiar man's voice said as I felt a hand settle on my waist. I looked up to find Laurent's face nearing mine as he kissed my cheek, and I wondered what he was doing sneaking up on me. With his other hand he pointed into the refrigerator. "We'll take Persian buttercups and camellias."

Selena looked at Laurent then back at me. "Your fiancé?"

I nodded, and she passed me the gerbera, collected the new flowers from the fridge, and held them out to me, her eyes quizzical. I had no idea which was which but one sat in a bunch shaped a bit like a ball and was more deep pink than burgundy, and the other had petals in graduations of pink tones. I didn't see how they were any better than the first set. And I didn't like the idea of being overruled. I figured this was the chicken all over again. But how was I supposed to know which flowers were the cheapest? I couldn't see the prices from this angle. Plus, flowers weren't widgets. And they didn't even come in one size. Some flowers may be more expensive but take less to do the job. It would take time to calculate all that. Laurent's choices were probably no cheaper than mine.

I opened my mouth to object to the change when I caught a silent conversation pass between Camille and her brother, and I reconsidered. "You're so right, honey. They're perfect," I said instead, playing along and shooting Laurent a delighted look that was met with a less than delighted one.

"I can take care of the details," Camille said, edging me over to the aisle leading to the door. "If you guys want to head over to your next appointment."

What next appointment? Nobody told me about another appointment, but I continued to play along. "Sure."

"What about flowers for the church? And what about for your flower girl?" Selena asked.

Camille started for the counter, assuring Selena that anything she recommended would be fine, and Selena sashayed away too. Which left me alone to be whisked down the aisle with Laurent's arm at my back while my gloved hand still held firm to the gerbera flower Selena had passed me.

"WHAT?" I ASKED Laurent as the harsh, cold, outdoor air hit my lungs.

He held up his finger in a hold-on-a-minute gesture. "In the car," he said then guided me down the street and around the block in silence.

Normally, I'd have dug in my heels and stayed put following a command like that, but slush and ice didn't make the best surface for heel digging. Plus, the wind had picked up and slashed at my face, my nose started running, and my toes were already going numb. Walking helped some but not much. A lot of Montreal blocks stretched on forever and this was one of them. We reached the corner, turned onto another long street, and kept plodding along. Clearly, Laurent took undercover rule number one seriously, and since he was driving his own car while Camille and I had the Léon one, he had parked out of sight. In Siberia.

When we got to the middle of the second block, I'd had enough. I spotted a café and ducked into the doorway for a moment's respite from the bullying wind. Surprisingly, Laurent moved with me. Too with me. The space was tiny, and he nearly had me pinned to the side glass wall to leave room for customers to access the door. I tried to look up at him in an expression of annoyance, but given our proximity I doubted he could see more than the hat covering the top of my head.

The café door opened and three teenagers stepped out, the last boy holding the door ajar, apparently thinking we were on our way in. I grabbed the door and inched my way over, unsure if we had time to go in or if we really were due soon at another appointment. "Do we have time for a coffee?" I asked Laurent, my voice muffled against the coat covering his chest.

By way of answer, he reached for the door and took hold of it about a foot above my hand, allowing me to pass under his arm when I had the space to move and go in.

Inside, we found our way to one of the few spare tables at the back, the place crowded with other passers-by likely seeking shelter from the freezing weather.

Once we'd taken off our outdoor clothes and settled, I scanned the menu printed on blackboards that ran the width of the wall behind the counter. The soup of the day was lentil. With a croissant on the side, it would make a good lunch. The morning had gone by so fast, I didn't realize how late it was until the panini scent of the place hit me.

"Are we really going to another appointment or do I have time to order lunch?" I asked Laurent.

He didn't answer. But he signaled for a server and waited while I placed my order before ordering a sandwich and coffee for himself. When the server left, Laurent leaned his forearms on the table, took a breath, and finally spoke to me. "Now, tell me about your visit with Anna."

Is that what his mood was about? How did he even find out? Camille hadn't had time to tell him. Their silent conversations weren't that telepathic, were they?

"How did you know?" I said.

His eyes didn't waver from mine. "We'll get to that later. Tell me everything."

"Not much to tell, really," I said, trying to sound casual. Then I replayed my time with Anna, adding in a few more details than I'd told Camille but still steering clear of my observations about the Prozac. The interruption of the waiter placing our food on the table made my retelling feel more drawn out, and by the end of it I felt a renewed sadness for Anna.

"That it?" he asked as I started in on my soup.

I blushed a little, a touch of guilt setting in at leaving out the Prozac bit. Probably it was the probing look in Laurent's dark eyes rousing my guilt. Laurent's eyes were already a magnetic trap for any woman. He was so not playing fair aiming that extra intensity at me.

I pulled my eyes away and fixed them on my bowl as I took another mouthful of soup, hoping the heat of it could be blamed for the rush of pink in my cheeks, and garbled an "ah huh."

"You're sure? She didn't say anything else?"

Now that I could answer truthfully. "Nope. Not that I remember."

Laurent picked up his sandwich and started eating in silence, waves of frustration floating over to my side of the table.

Great. The silent treatment force field. That seemed uncalled for. He may not be happy that I went over to Anna's, but he didn't have to stew about it. People had to matter more than rules and procedures. And caring about someone in grief wasn't a crime. And neither was worrying about someone who may be in danger. I didn't need this.

I stood as I finished the last bite of my croissant. "Well, if we're done here and we don't have an appointment, I'm off."

His sandwich done too, Laurent took a gulp of his coffee. "I'll pay and get the car."

And sit side-by-side trapped in the car while he practiced his mister mute act some more, no thank you. "No need. I can hail a taxi." I lifted the bill off the table, calculated my portion, and rooted around in my purse for enough cash to cover the meal and leave a nice tip.

Laurent watched me then stood too. "Forget it. Business lunch."

I ignored him, slipped the tip on the table, and handed him the rest of the money.

He sighed and took it. "What am I going to do with you? You never listen."

"You don't do much talking," I shot back, immediately sorry for my tone. Laurent was my boss. The boss it took me months to convince to let me go undercover, I reminded myself. Again. What was wrong with me? I softened my voice. "You haven't even told me how you knew I saw Anna."

"Brassard told me," he said. "He saw you leaving when he arrived at Anna's."

Samuel Brassard was a cop friend of Laurent's. They'd trained together at the police academy. He was another stickler for procedure and apparently a tattler, too. I busied myself with getting on my coat. "Oh."

"*Oui.*" Laurent calmly buttoned his jacket, keeping his eyes on me. "Brassard wanted to know what we were doing with his murder suspect."

I whipped my head up and looked at him, whispering, "Suspect?"

100

He reached over and adjusted my scarf, keeping his own voice low. "That's right. Suspect. Anna's the one Peter's parents think killed him."

Anna? That didn't make any sense. "I thought Michel said it was the identity thief. I thought everybody thought that."

Laurent shook his head. "That's only one theory. Peter's parents think Anna did it."

"She was nowhere near Peter when he fell. How could she have killed him?"

"Drugs. Peter's parents say she gave him something that caused a collapse. They say she had an arsenal of stuff. That she had awful panic attacks and was always taking something for something."

Uh oh. That didn't sound good. An image of the Prozac bottle at Anna's amid the forest of other tiny vials flashed in my head. "What do you think?"

He used his hold on my scarf to pull me to him. "The autopsy report backs it up. What I want to know is what you know about it."

ELEVEN

"**I'M TELLING YOU,** Anna didn't do it," I said.

Camille looked at me from across the kitchen table at the C&C office and shook her head. She hadn't learned anything more at the florist after Laurent and I had left and said the only tidbit she'd overheard from Selena and the Irish Fisherman was something about an order mix-up, so Anna wasn't just the hot topic when we regrouped, she was the only topic.

"*Mais voyons*, Lora," Camille said. "You've got to stop taking pity on every sad sap you meet. You just said Anna's taking Prozac."

"I didn't say she was taking it for sure. I said I thought she might be. I never actually saw her take anything. I just saw the bottle." And I hated saying even that. It made Anna look guilty and my instincts were telling me she wasn't. Now that drugs were involved, though, it could be pertinent and I couldn't hold back possible evidence. This definitely qualified as a need-to-know scenario.

"Again with the semantics." Camille waved her hand in the air. Caron sign language meaning the recipient was being ridiculous.

As the recipient in this case, I didn't care for her insinuation. "Even if Anna does take meds, it doesn't mean she gave any to Peter. Let alone enough to kill him. She loved him. I could tell."

Camille stirred the *café au lait* in front of her. "So? Maybe he did something hideous and she snapped. The same passion for love can be turned into hate."

True enough. It wouldn't be the first time. Damn Camille and her good points. Still, I thought about the look on Anna's face the night Peter died. And the tenderness in her voice when she spoke about him at her house, and the sadness in her eyes when she told me about her mother not accepting him. None of that fit with a woman in hate.

"Isn't this all a bit premature?" I said. "Just because Peter's parents are claiming she murdered him doesn't mean she did. What exactly did they find in him anyway?"

"Blood pressure medication, Prozac, and some vitamins," Laurent said.

"And the Prozac, was it an overdose?"

Laurent shook his head. "I didn't see the word overdose. Could have been an interaction that killed him. They're still running more tests. But there's no doubt that he collapsed from something he took."

I mulled that over. "Well then, see, it could have been an accident."

"Not if Prozac caused it. Peter wasn't taking Prozac," Laurent said. "His medical history shows no history of use and no current prescriptions. So how did it get in his system? Suspicious, no?"

Well okay. I had to admit that looked odd but not necessarily unexplainable. "That still doesn't prove Anna had anything to do with his death," I said. "He could have got the Prozac somewhere else. Anyone could have given it to him. Or he could have taken some of Anna's pills by mistake. Maybe he grabbed for his blood pressure medicine and took from the wrong bottle."

Camille and Laurent exchanged a look.

"And does Anna even know his parents accused her?" I went on. "She said nothing about it when I saw her."

"The police have questioned her," Laurent said. "Whether they told her why I don't know. They might not until they have enough to arrest her."

That didn't sound good. "Surely, the police will cover all the angles, right? They won't limit their investigation to Anna. Even if it was murder, they'll check out other possibilities, right? Like the identity thief?"

Camille shrugged. "They will if there's any good evidence. But probably Anna will be their main focus."

I sat back. That sucked big time. But main focus was one thing, sole focus was another. "Okay, then all we have to do is find some good evidence."

"You already found good evidence," Camille said. "Your little tidbit about Anna shows she had access to drugs. And we know she had access to Peter. That's opportunity, no?"

Beside her, Laurent held up his hand as though it were a stop sign. "Not so fast, Camille. Give Lora a chance to explain. We have the advantage that she spoke to Anna before Brassard. Let's use it."

Advantage? He never said anything about it being an advantage before. "I thought you were angry I went to Anna's," I said to him, still a bit miffed about his earlier silent treatment.

Laurent turned the full force of his gaze on me. "Angry? You went into the house of a possible murderer, Lora. Alone. Angry is too small a word for what I was feeling. And if you get any ideas about meeting with her on the sly again, I'll pull your cute little ass off this case. But I was hoping you'd learned something at least. Something Anna wouldn't tell the police. You still have a lot to learn as a PI, but that big heart of yours has a way of gaining people's trust."

Probably Laurent meant that last bit as a compliment, but I didn't like hearing his assessment of me as a PI. It was obvious now that it wasn't just anger making him quiet before, though. It was the anticipation of a hunt. He was like Camille that way. They both grew hushed and still when stalking their prey. I looked at their expectant faces and wished I had more to tell. Maybe Laurent's call about my investigation capabilities was fair. I'd had the opportunity to pump Anna for info, but I hardly got anything. Instead I'd talked cupcakes and hair.

I pulled off the stretchy band holding my pony tail, the tightness of it starting to bother me, and my hair fanned out down my back. "I've already told you everything there is to tell."

Camille drummed her fingers on the table. "You said that before. But you left out Anna's need for speed that time."

"It's not speed," I said. "It's Prozac. The shakes and stuff are just side effects. It's anxiety medication. And it's common. Something like seventeen million Americans take it. Anyway, now I've told you *everything* everything."

Laurent pulled his chair closer to mine. "Then start again from the beginning."

I suppressed a sigh. This was one of his old cop techniques. Make interviewee spill his or her guts, flush out details, start again. Spill, flush, repeat—cop mantra for getting the dirt out. No shampoo required.

But I did as I was asked and went over my conversation with Anna again. When I was done, Laurent momentarily rubbed at his temples and Camille got up to refresh her coffee.

"Was Anna's hair really bad?" Camille said from over by the counter. "She should see my cousin Albert at *Ciseaux*. He can work miracles."

With such a large family, the Carons had people working in just about every major sector and Albert owned a hair salon. I'd seen his work before and wasn't impressed. Like a good cousin, Camille talked him up—family being the glue that held life together for all the Carons. But I'd noticed Camille had her own hair done at a nearby place on Rue Rachel rather than trek it over to Albert's place in Westmount.

"I thought Anna's hair looked great," I said. "I think she just has a problem seeing it for what it is herself."

Camille came back to the table with her coffee and the box of remaining truffles from her buy the other day. "Body image problems?" she asked, referring to Anna.

I peered into the box. Two truffles left. "Mother issues, I think."

Camille nodded understanding, reached into the truffle box, and popped one into her mouth. I frowned. That left only one and I really needed a truffle. I eyed Laurent, hoping he'd leave the room, and I could grab the last chocolate without guilt. He caught me looking and met my eyes.

"We could split it?" I suggested.

He leaned forward to get a look at the truffle. The Caron sibs frequented the same *chocolatier* a lot and could identify flavors of even the most similar truffles just by studying the tiny details in markings, similar to how type enthusiasts could recognize specific fonts. "Looks like a champagne," he said to me. "One of your favorites, no?"

I nodded, my mouth starting to water in Pavlovian response to the champagne and chocolate combo trigger.

"Me too," he said.

Of course he had to say that. I already felt guilty for not doing a great job handling Anna and disappointing him. I couldn't deprive him of his favorite truffle, too. I issued a down command to my saliva glands. "You take it."

Laurent reached into the box, pulled out the chocolate, and handed it to me. "*Non.* We split it like you said before."

I placed it on a leftover empty plate on the table and went to grab a knife from the cutlery stand, but Laurent stopped me as I stood up.

"No need to dirty a knife," he said. "Just bite half."

I looked at the truffle, wondering if I could bite just half of it. The truffles were generously sized but equally generously scrumptious. I shrugged, picked it up and did my best to bite it evenly then passed the remainder to Laurent who managed to stretch his portion into two bites. Show off.

He swallowed the last bit and said, "You see. Teamwork, Lora. That's the key. Just like with Anna. You chat with her, pass the information to me, and together we pull out the clues."

Hmm. "Clues about what exactly?" I asked him, glancing at Camille to see if she had any inkling what he was getting at. She sat quietly sipping her coffee and shrugged.

"You tell me," Laurent said. "Start again at the beginning."

I MADE IT through the grilling and out of the office with barely enough time to get home to my early dinner date with Adam. Since I had evening work again at the *Danser* studio, Adam and I had planned to squeeze in some quality time together beforehand.

One of the plusses of having some flexibility in our schedules was being able to time shift. Not in the big, sci-fi kind of way, but in practical ways that didn't bind us to living our lives confined to regularly scheduled programming. Like Netflix, we'd learned the benefits of on-demand living and made the most of it.

Adam's car wasn't in our driveway or parked nearby on the street when I got home. I sighed with relief and pulled into our lane, no longer in fear of being the rotten egg who made it home last. I made my way over to the front door and inside where Pong greeted me with her usual dachshund-sized body check, pausing occasionally to fling herself into me as I shed my winter gear. Then she escorted me through the house to the back door lest I forget her need to romp around the yard and take a potty break.

I was done filling Pong's bowl with kibble and just letting her back inside when Ping came dashing down the stairs and pushed her cat whiskers into the dog bowl. The sound of pellets hitting the metal bowl worked better than an alarm clock to rouse Ping from her late afternoon nap. Never mind that these particular pellets were designed for dog tummies. To Ping, food was food. Pong sat back on her haunches and fixed anxious eyes on her bowl, experience having taught her that a long canine snout was an easy target for quick claw Mcgraw. Not that Ping usually used her claws when the two tangled. But she'd done it enough to leave a lasting impression when she first moved in and the two were establishing their boundaries.

"Hey," I said to Ping. "That's not your food."

Ping extracted one piece of kibble and ran into the hallway, getting only a few feet before dropping the nugget onto the wood floor. Pong wasted no time staking claim on her bowl as I went to retrieve the piece of kibble. Ping walked away, circling back to the kitchen through the living room/dining room route and meeting me there just in time to watch me pour cat food into her own bowl.

Both pets were done eating and were vying for the water bowl by the time I had dinner started. Nothing fancy, just a couple of tofu burgers heating in the oven alongside a pan of sweet potato French fries. With some sliced tomato, a few leaves of lettuce, and some grated mozzarella topping the burgers, I figured we'd be good to go.

Half an hour later, I sat at the candlelit dining room table facing an empty plate, phone in hand, trying for the third time to reach Adam who was a no-show. I left yet another message and decided to start eating without him. Laurent would be picking me up in less than an hour, and I still needed time to change. I carried my plate into the kitchen, filled it with food, and went back to the dining room. But I couldn't get much of my meal down. It wasn't like Adam to be so late for our scheduled dates, at least not without calling, and worry started to creep in. Chances were he was stuck in traffic or got waylaid by his boss, but neither of those should have kept him from calling. I gave up on my food about halfway through and put the rest in the fridge along with Adam's portion, which is exactly when I finally heard Adam's key in the lock.

"I'm sorry, hon," he said, rushing in, barely taking time to remove his boots.

As he made his way over to me, I caught a whiff of perfume. Expensive perfume. "Where were you?" I asked him, my worry quickly morphing into something far less kind.

He planted a quick kiss on my lips, and I held my breath to keep from inhaling the perfume fumes oozing off of him. He didn't have to tell me where he'd been. I already knew. Only one person we knew was more intent on spreading her scent than a dog marking his territory. Adam's old college friend Tina—damsel in distress *par excellence* and the wart on mine and Adam's relationship that just wouldn't stay away.

Adam slipped out of his coat and draped it over a kitchen chair. "I was with Tina."

I folded my arms across my chest. "And you couldn't call?"

"I didn't have a chance," he said, moving over to the water cooler and draining it of a glassful which he drank down like a man who'd just eaten a chile pepper. "So what's for dinner?"

"Dinner's over," I said and started for the stairs. "I have to go to work."

Adam followed me up to our bedroom and stood in the doorway. "Look, I'm sorry. It couldn't be helped."

Right. It never could when it came to Tina. I went into the walk-in closet, rifled through the Bunny clothes, and selected the most flirty outfit—a hip hugging black skirt that fanned into frills towards the bottom and a fuchsia blouse with a plunging neckline Camille had insisted I buy. And I teamed them with a set of intricately patterned black stockings and a black lace bra with a matching garter belt and panties.

"It's big news this time," Adam said.

I stayed in the closet and started changing my clothes. "It always is," I called out to him.

"No, really," he said. "Tina asked me to be a godfather."

I toddled out of the closet in my underwear, only one stocking on, holding the other one. "What?"

Adam crossed the room and sat on the bed. "She's pregnant, Lor. And she wants me to be the godfather for the baby."

Tina pregnant? That was a surprise. She and her third husband, Jeffrey, had been having some problems a couple of months ago that had dovetailed into a case I was working. She had moved in with us for a bit, and once she'd left we hadn't heard from her since. At least not that I knew about. But that was classic Tina. She only popped up when she wanted something. Which was still too often as far as I was concerned—she asked for more favors than a lobbyist on Capitol Hill.

Adam grinned. "It's exciting, isn't it? Me. A godfather."

"Sure," I said, still a bit stunned. "Who's going to be the godmother?" I knew for sure that Tina would never ask me. Adam had been her gallant hero way before I entered the picture. I was just a bit character she hoped would be written out of their story in the next chapter.

"Jeffrey's sister," Adam said. "But Tina doesn't really want her involved."

Of course not. The only female allowed to star in Tina's life was Tina. Not even a sidekick best girl friend for her. This baby better be a boy or it won't stand a chance.

Adam reached for my hand and drew me to him. "This isn't just another Tina stunt, Lor. This is me becoming a godfather. This is important."

And important enough to render him oblivious to my Bunny lingerie. I could see another kind of excitement glistening in his eyes, though, and I couldn't dampen that. Even if it did involve Tina.

"Sure," I said. "I get it." And I did. He was getting the chance to be one of the village people in this kid's life. And not the singing kind in the goofy costumes, but the ones on the front lines. He probably imagined himself dishing out sage advice and taking the kid to cool concerts. And I'd probably get used to the idea. Eventually. In the meantime, I had months to practice my "I'm good with it" face until I'd have to trot it out in public when the baby was born and Adam's godfather duties kicked in. If he even had real duties. Nowadays, it seemed like being a godparent was more of an honorary title.

"I'm so glad," Adam said. "And the best part is that Tina's already almost six months in, so it won't be long until I meet the little one."

Six months in? That meant I only had three months to practice my "I'm good with it" face. I leaned sideways so I could see myself in the mirror on the closet door and tried on an enthusiastic smile. It came out less "I'm good with it" and more "I just lost the Oscar to the beauty queen with no talent." I definitely needed more practice.

The doorbell rang and I rushed to finish dressing. "That'll be Laurent," I said to Adam. "Could you tell him I'll just be a couple minutes."

"Sure," Adam said, getting up and heading downstairs.

I went back into the closet to get some Bunny shoes. The dance instructor had said to bring the right shoes to the lesson. Just what he meant by that I wasn't sure. But since it was winter, I hadn't been thinking much about shoes when Camille and I were shopping for Bunny's wardrobe, and I'd only picked up one pair. Black pumps with more heel than I was used to wearing. I would have a hard enough time walking in those, let alone dancing, but it was either those or a pair of my own shoes. And I didn't think ballet-style flats, running shoes, or Birkenstocks would cut it. I had no choice but to take the new shoes and hope I didn't make too much of a fool of myself.

I dashed into the bathroom for a pit stop and to put on my Bunny makeup then ran out to the top of the stairs where I froze, looking down into Adam's reddening face and Laurent's apologetic one.

"What's this about you being pregnant?" Adam asked me, control in his voice.

I touched my belly, suddenly remembering that Bunny was supposed to be pregnant too. Pretend pregnant, but pregnant. Laurent must have told Adam. I waved the Bunny shoes clasped in my other hand and started down the stairs trying to appear casual. "That's just made up as part of my cover. Nowhere near as exciting as Tina's real pregnancy," I added in hoping to rekindle Adam's earlier mood and avoid an argument.

The muscles on the side of Adam's neck flinched as his eyes finally registered my Bunny ensemble. Whatever had been said between the two men in my absence seemed to have popped Adam out of his cone of godfatherly excitement and back into reality. Now I wished I hadn't channeled my own earlier anger into wearing Bunny's hottest clothes all in one shot. Not because they annoyed Adam, but because it made it harder for me to downplay my role as Bunny.

"This for that hooker case? You could have told me," Adam said.

Laurent tried to hide a smile, and I stopped midway down the stairs and shifted my weight from one stockinged foot to the other.

"It's *not* a hooker case. And I was going to. I just didn't get the chance yet."

"Right," he said, his tone dismissive enough to let me know how he felt without having to add more words and get into a full-fledged fight in front of Laurent.

One of my shoes dropped and tumbled down the rest of the stairs, and as I clutched the remaining shoe to my chest, I felt a bit of my own earlier anger returning. Why did I have to keep appeasing Adam about playing Bunny? It was part of my job for goodness sake.

I didn't need to apologize for that. And if I was supposed to trust him with Tina and her future offspring and makeshift family that so did not include me, then Adam would just have to trust me with Laurent and his pretend baby too.

Both men bent to retrieve my shoe, nearly bumping heads as Adam lunged for the advantage before Laurent moved aside to let him have it.

I zipped down the rest of the stairs and wedged my hand between the two men to grab the vestibule door handle. "Let's go," I said to Laurent, wrenching open the door.

Laurent looked from Adam to me, then followed me into the entryway to put on his boots while I layered on my winter wear.

Adam shoved my shoe at me. "I'll wait up," he said and moved in to plant a kiss on my mouth that landed on my jaw as I turned for the front door.

The tone in Adam's voice made his words seem more like a threat than a nicety, and I opened my mouth to tell him not to bother as I went out, but the cold outdoor air stole my breath and I never got the chance.

TWELVE

"**WHAT DID YOU** have to go and tell him for?" I said to Laurent when we were safely ensconced in the Léon car and out of the blistery wind that wafted snowflakes to and fro, making everything look as though icing sugar was being sifted over the city.

Laurent adjusted the windshield wipers and pulled out. "He was going on and on about a baby. I thought he knew."

"Adam was talking about Tina's baby not Bunny and Léon's. Couldn't you tell the difference?"

Laurent smiled. "Sorry, eh. I only have one baby on my head right now."

"On your mind," I corrected him. "Not on your head." Considering my French was nowhere near as fluent as Laurent's English, I had no business correcting him but somehow fixing his mistake made me feel better.

"Your Anglophone does not like your job anymore, Lora?" he said, amusement in his voice.

I took off my hat, pulled down the visor, and checked my hair in the tiny mirror. I had been in such a hurry to get downstairs, I'd forgotten to put my hair back and it was a mess of static cling and dry winter frizz. "He's just not keen on this Bunny business," I said, stopping short of mentioning Adam's reservations about my faux engagement to Laurent. Ordinarily, I wouldn't have said anything at all about Adam's feelings, but I was in no mood to weigh my every word. Still, I felt guilty right after I said it. Like I was being disloyal somehow. "Adam's actually very supportive of my work," I added in to temper my comment. "He was thrilled I was able to get a job and stay in Montreal." I replaced the visor and squinted when the headlights of the cars coming towards us in the adjoining lane hit my eyes.

"That's good," Laurent said. "Not every mate understands this kind of work."

I glanced over at him, wondering if he was speaking from experience, but he said nothing more and kept his eyes focused on the road as he guided the Léon car through the snow.

Then I got to wondering if Laurent's comment was as much about me as it was about Adam. I hoped not. I didn't want Laurent to think I'd let a row with my boyfriend distract me from work.

So as we neared the dance studio, I took some deep breaths to change gears and focus. Priorities, Lora, I told myself. Deal with work now and Adam later. That should be easy enough. After all, I had a plan for the night and had every intention of sticking to it. Especially since my plan only had one goal: finding out who else at the dance studio might have wanted Peter dead, identity thief or otherwise. If Peter really was murdered, I may be the only one who believed Anna didn't do it, and I wasn't about to let her take the blame.

"YOU'VE ALMOST GOT it," Cindy said to Laurent as they finished up some fancy footwork, their hands clenched together and held high, their bodies facing each other two feet apart.

I sat on a metal chair off to the side, arms folded across my chest and tapping my foot to the tune of some song I'd never heard before that was quickly becoming familiar the more times it got played. The foot tapping was partially an automatic response to the tempo and partially a means to keep my feet from going numb. Every time the song started up again, I uncrossed my legs and switched sides to keep the circulation even.

As far as I could tell, nothing had changed in the last three start-overs. Laurent had the moves down as well as Cindy. The song—which I took to be the Roch Voisine one since I didn't recognize the singer—was slow for the most part with some fast bits that made for some challenging transitions. In between, a lot of the choreography blurred together, repeating steps. At first, I'd watched carefully, hoping to learn by osmosis. But as time dragged on, I lost interest. And patience. I couldn't see how we were supposed to get our real work done if this was how things were going to go all night.

Aside from a brief chat given by Sylvain when we first arrived, we'd spent the rest of the time separated from the group, which now included two new members who took up the slots vacated by Anna and Peter. The new duo—Ben and Violette, a fortysomething real estate power couple with flawless caramel-colored skin dressed in equally flawless sweaters and expensive jeans—had sat next to us when we'd all assembled. Right after Sylvain introduced them, they took turns checking their cell phones while the rest of the group stayed quiet and solemn as Sylvain went on to offer condolences about Peter. Adding in that anyone who needed to talk about the accident could speak with a counselor the dance studio had on call who could be seen free of charge.

Probably that last bit was being offered on the advice of a legal bigwig. But it also made it clear that our lessons would go on and talk about Peter during class time was not expected to be part of them. Which meant even when all of us came together at the end of each lesson, it would be tricky to ferret out clues about who else here might have wanted Peter dead. Between that and the no-direct questions undercover thing, I was starting to feel like I was playing that kid's card game where the only way to guess the murderer is to catch him or her in a wink.

When the Roch Voisine song began again and I realized I was still not being called into action, I got up and headed out to find the ladies' room, tossing Laurent an open-handed wave on my wait out, letting him know I'd be back in five minutes. I thought I'd stretch my legs and touch up my Bunny makeup, but when I got into the hall and found a sign indicating that washrooms were to the left, I found myself instead taking a right to the marble staircase that connected the three levels of the building. I peered down, trying to remember which step I'd been on when Peter started to fall. To get a better sense, I walked down a few stairs but couldn't bring myself to go any farther. It had been hard enough to come up the staircase on our way in and pass the spot where Peter's body had landed. Seeing things from this direction made it all come back to me, and like an instant replay, the sights and sounds of the night of the fall filled my head.

"Still awful, isn't it?" I heard from behind me, and I turned to see Juliette leaning against the banister that ran along the side of the open stairwell and led to the next flight up.

I nodded at her.

She leaned over the railing to keep her voice low, her long, dark hair slipping from behind her back to fall forward. "Sébastien and I weren't sure we wanted to come back, but there weren't a lot of other options. Most dance studios only offer lessons, not unique choreography like Sylvain. And it would be hard to get in anywhere else. There's only so much time before our wedding, and Sébastien has to work around his business trips."

I tried to remember what line of work Camille had listed in the case file about Sébastien but drew a blank. "What's he do again?" I asked her, making my way back upstairs.

"Finance," she said. "With the bank."

"That's it. And you're a teacher, right? What grade?"

"*École primaire*," she said. "Grade five. At ten or eleven years old, the kids are old enough to be interesting but not old enough to be delinquents."

I laughed. I had liked Juliette on our first meeting. She reminded me a bit of a calm, less bold version of Camille.

"I came out to look for Cindy," Juliette said. "Have you seen her?"

"She's in there." I pointed at the door to my and Laurent's rehearsal room.

"Thanks. We've been waiting half an hour for her. She's supposed to be showing us our choreography so we can practice, only we haven't seen her since the demonstration."

When we'd first all been shuttled to our individual rehearsal spaces, Sylvain and Cindy had given us each a demonstration of the dance we were to start learning this lesson. Then each of them was to work with us one-on-one to walk through the steps. With only two of them and four couples to work with, they were each supposed to work with two couples—getting one started then moving on to the next and popping back and forth to oversee the practice time of both. Seemed once Cindy got her hands on Laurent, she had lost track of time and borrowed some from Juliette and Sébastien's instruction period.

Juliette went over to the door I'd pointed to and looked through the small glass window insert near the top. "Cindy's in with Laurent." She turned towards me. "So what are you doing out here?"

I moved closer and raised myself on my toes to glance through the window. Even with Bunny's heels, it was still a stretch for me to reach my head high enough to see through the glass. Inside the room, it seemed Cindy and Laurent had finished up another cycle, and I watched as Laurent went to get his water bottle. I ducked out of sight and backed away from the window before one of them spotted me.

"I was just taking a break," I told Juliette in answer to her question. No sense telling her I was taking a break from doing nothing. Especially when it had given me the opportunity to talk to her. An opportunity I wasn't going to miss. Undercover rule number three was not only becoming my favorite, it was proving the most useful. Last lesson, Juliette seemed happy to share gossip about Peter, and I was hoping she'd know more. "But then I got to thinking about Peter's fall and how awful it was," I said to prod her.

Juliette reached over and patted my shoulder like she was comforting a student who forgot his lunch. "You were in front of me, I think. You probably saw more than I did. All I remember is hearing a commotion and then seeing Peter at the bottom of the stairs. That was awful enough. For his fiancée it must be a nightmare. On the outside, she looks okay, but inside, it must be *insupportable*."

I was surprised to hear her mention Anna. "You know his fiancée?"

Juliette shook her head and her hair shook with it. "No. I saw her here earlier. She came to pick up a refund check for the lessons. She was very appreciative of everyone's help at the accident and mentioned you'd even made a condolence visit to her. She was trying to put on a good face, but her upset was still clear. Poor girl."

I was glad to hear I wasn't alone in my sympathy for Anna. "I know, she must be devastated. You'd think Peter of all people would have been the last person to slip on the stairs," I said, sticking with the accidental fall take on things since the suspicious death side was still on the qt. "With all his times at the dance studio, he probably could have managed the stairs in the dark."

She shrugged. "Anybody can have an accident, I suppose. But it's eerie that it happened so soon after the last one."

I felt the hairs rise on the back of my neck. "What last one?"

"You didn't know?" Juliette said. "Some woman was found unconscious in a bathroom stall and died later in the hospital. Couldn't have been two or three weeks ago. She was part of the last group. That's why Sébastien and I thought about not coming back. One death is bad luck. Two is creepy."

Creepy maybe. Coincidental certainly. I wondered why this was the first I was hearing of it. "You're right. I'm surprised anyone came back. I didn't know about the woman. Was she attacked?"

She shrugged again. "No idea. I only know what I overheard Sylvain and Cindy talking about last time. Sébastian and I were the first couple to arrive and the room has a bit of an echo. With no one else around, it was hard not to hear snippets of their conversation."

Juliette seemed good at that. Overhearing other people's conversations. Which was lucky for me, but also something to remember so I'd be careful when chatting about the case with Laurent within Juliette's earshot.

The door opened beside us and Cindy stepped out. Flushed, she nearly rushed right by without noticing us. "There you are," she said to me. "You better get practicing. I've got to get started with my next couple." She zipped off, not bothering to wait for me to answer or for Juliette to accompany her.

"I'd better go," Juliette said. "Or she'll be snapping at me too."

If Cindy treated all her female students the same way she treated me, Juliette needn't have worried about being late. She'd be warming the bench for most of what was left of the lesson.

118

TO CAP OFF the evening, everyone gathered in the large room where we'd had the initial meet and greet. I'd already told Laurent Juliette's tidbit about the dead woman in the washroom. Neither of us knew what to make of it yet, and when we took our chairs, I sat near Emmaline and George, the only other couple who had been part of our original group, hoping I'd get a chance to talk to them and see if they knew more. But instead Cindy motioned to Laurent and me almost immediately, and a spark of heat rushed to my neck, making its way higher.

Cindy was over at a table in the corner and turned her back to us as she fiddled with an iPod and docked it in a speaker. She turned our way again and motioned to us, this time a look of impatience on her face.

My cheeks grew hot and my heart quickened. I never should have agreed when Laurent suggested we volunteer to do our dance first. It had sounded right when he said if we got our performance out of the way we could concentrate on the case the rest of the night. But I was no dancer. I couldn't dance in front of the whole class. I could dance in a crowded club no problem. But not like this with everyone looking at me. I'd die of fear and embarrassment first and never get the chance to do any more work on the case.

Laurent stood up beside me and reached his hand out for mine.

I took a deep breath and got up, adjusting my blouse to minimize my girls. Then I took his hand and followed him over to take our positions. A flashback of summer camp and kids laughing at my hokey-pokey played in my head and I pushed the memory away. I wasn't a shy little girl any more. I was an adult. I was a PI. I was *not* going to let a little fear of dancing in front of an audience blow my cover. I could do this.

Our song started, a soft guitar playing with a strong voice coming in almost immediately, and I instantly froze. All the dance steps I'd learned in the little time we'd had to practice going AWOL. The sound of my pounding heart competing with the beat of the music. I took another deep breath and tuned back into our song, which wasn't the least bit hokey-pokeyish, and tried a step. But my legs clearly hadn't left the shy little girl me behind because they nearly gave out.

Laurent squeezed my hand, and I looked up to face him.

His eyes met mine. "*Je m'excuse*," he said, raising his voice to be heard above the song. "Can we start the music again? I missed my timing."

I held his gaze and mouthed a "thank you." Sweet of him to cover for me like that, but I wasn't sure starting over would help me any.

Laurent tightened his arm around my back, pulled me close, and whispered in my ear. "Don't think about what you're doing. Look only at me and follow what I do."

We took our positions again, and I tried to focus on him and only him this time. When he moved, I moved, feeling a bit like I was trying to match my own mirror image. Little by little, my stomach unclenched and my feet picked up the pace. I was no Ginger Rogers but gave myself brownie points for not losing a heel or throwing up. By the time Roch belted out the second refrain from *I'll Always be There*, I felt like I could even risk looking away from Laurent and check up on the group.

Our fellow students were sitting attentive and quiet despite Sylvain and Cindy having another argument off in the corner. With the music playing, I couldn't make out a word they were saying, so I tried to maneuver Laurent closer to them when we got to our big move in the last half of the dance. I only managed to shift us over a few feet before I felt Laurent pull me to him roughly, not a step I remembered being part of rehearsal. I felt his hand skim over my chest and looked down to see that one of my girls was on the verge of popping out. Laurent readjusted the fashion mishap by the time I'd registered it, and he resumed our routine so seamlessly anyone who didn't know our choreography well would never notice the glitch. Still, by the time our song came to an end, I knew my cheeks had reddened again from more than sheer exertion.

Sylvain rushed over to me when I took my seat. "*Ça va?*" he said. "Oh. *En anglais*, eh. You okay?" He paused, then threw a nasty look Cindy's way. *"C'est trop là! Elle est enceinte. Tu ne devrais pas la faire tourner."*

Cindy's face made an unsuccessful attempt at looking puzzled and from the end of the row Juliette said to me, "Oh, congratulations, Bunny."

I guessed Juliette had heard whatever Sylvain had said to Cindy and that whatever that something was it had to do with me. Thankfully, it couldn't be about my slip-ups on the dance floor. Nobody offered congratulations for those kinds of things. I felt myself relax some, relieved I survived our dance number, fashion mishap and all.

But when I looked at Laurent for clarification of Juliette's comment, he dropped his eyes to my belly and back up, and I felt nerves flair up again. Oh no. Madame Shakiba must have told Sylvain about Bunny's pregnancy. We never even saw the woman, but her hands-off approach to our pseudo wedding planning didn't seem to extend to our pseudo family planning. I forced a smile and thanked Juliette.

Emmaline stood to take her turn at dancing and paused to straighten her clothes. "When are you due?" she asked over the empty chair between us.

Due? Darned if I knew. I picked a date way off in the future, figuring I couldn't pass for too far along. "End of July," I told her.

She looked at my belly, the smile fixed on her face nearly as tight as the bun pinning up her black hair. "A summer baby," she said. "How nice." Her eyes skimmed over to Laurent and back. "What a lovely instant family you'll all make," she added before running off to join George on the dance floor.

Sébastien leaned forward in his chair beside Juliette, grinned at Laurent, winked at me, and called out, "He shoots, he scores, eh?"

Ugh. Just what I needed. A hockey metaphor for my fake conception.

Laurent wrapped his arm around my shoulders and smiled. "I cannot take all the credit. It's the nature of Bunnies, no?" He gave my shoulders a squeeze. "N'est-ce pas, *mon petit lapin*?"

I shot him a look. Wasn't I embarrassed enough for one night?

The music started up for George and Emmaline's dance and everyone grew quiet as Shania Twain's *From This Moment* filled the room. The couple began to sway and gradually glide around the room in ballroom style, their bodies stepping in technical perfection, their faces in deep concentration. It was hard to believe they'd just learned their dance number during the last hour or so. They danced impeccably, in sync almost until the end when George miscalculated a move and his foot landed on Emmaline's pristine red pump. She screeched and scowled at him before resuming her posture to finish out the dance, slinking back to her seat when they were done.

"I'm sorry," George whispered to her when he returned to his chair between mine and Emmaline's. "It was just one little mistake. Lighten up."

"I'm fine," she said back to him through gritted teeth and reached down to brush off the smudge his shoe had left on her pump.

"I thought you guys were really good," I said to get them talking during the lull while the music was loaded for the next dancers. "What a perfect song, too. Wish I'd thought of it."

Emmaline straightened. "Thank you."

"It's too bad we won't get to see Peter and Anna's dances," I added, getting down to business and trying to gear the conversation around to Peter. "They had some good song choices too." I didn't actually remember their songs, but I did remember they were Céline Dion ballads. You can't go wrong with Céline Dion at a wedding.

George turned my way. "Yeah. Peter was a great dancer too. You wouldn't know it to look at him, but he had a lot of grace."

Grace? Really? I never would have attached that word to Peter. Since we hadn't started our dancing before, I wondered how George knew about Peter's supposed dance moves. "Did you know Peter?" I asked.

"Oh yeah," he said. "He's the one who told us about *Danser* and Sylvain."

Emmaline placed her hand over George's forearm, her fingers sinking into the fabric of his shirt and causing some serious wrinkling. George paused and glanced in her direction.

"Shush," she said, pointing forward with her other hand. "They're starting."

I looked over at Laurent, and he winked at me. I had no idea what that meant. Did all Montreal men do this wink thing? This was so going to mess with my ability to identify the murderer if everyone kept winking. I decided to take Laurent's wink as a sign of encouragement. I waited until Juliette and Sébastien's song, a Frank Sinatra tune, was in full swing then leaned in toward George. "My curiosity is killing me," I whispered. "How did you know Peter?"

George tilted his head in my direction as though working a kink out of his neck and rubbed the back of his head. "Emmaline's sister," he murmured, talking out of the side of his mouth.

A jolt of excitement surged through me. Just what I was hoping to find. Someone with another link to Peter. "Were they a couple?"

He rotated his head from side to side, still working the kink thing. When his head cocked my way again he said, "Yeah. They broke up when she found out he was cozying up with Anna. Her sister took it hard. Emmaline doesn't like to talk about it." Then he veered off again, this time straightening his head and focusing on the couple dancing.

I was dying to know what happened after the breakup that had Emmaline in a snit, but the look on George's face said he was done talking about it too. I pretended to adjust my Bunny bangle, leaning forward some, and turned my head slightly to get a good look at Emmaline and size her up as a possible murderer. Had something really bad happened to her sister? Did she blame Peter? Enough to drug him? It would have been easy enough to do the way Peter was scoffing back cookies and coffee at the meet and greet. Anyone could have slipped something into his food and he'd probably never even have tasted it.

I sat back and let out a breath, watching as Juliette and Sébastien finished up their dance, thankful it was the last number of the night. I had what I came for and then some, and I was ready to go. I squirmed in my seat, suddenly painfully aware I'd never made it to the ladies' room earlier. That's when I remembered about the woman found dead in the washroom down the hall and that I hadn't just found another possible suspect tonight. I may have found another victim.

THIRTEEN

ADAM HADN'T KEPT his promise. He wasn't waiting up when I got home. He wasn't even home. And neither was his car. A note on the fridge told me he'd be back late but didn't say where he had gone. I didn't know whether to feel relieved that we wouldn't get into things again or annoyed that he'd walked out. So I chose option number three—to pretend I didn't feel anything at all. At least for the time being. My feeling well was tapped out for the day anyway.

I topped up the pets' water bowl, gave the dog her last-call walk, and went upstairs to take a shower. When I got out of the tub and into my robe, there was still no sign of Adam and pretending that I didn't care was wearing thin. I told myself it didn't matter where he was or what he was doing. But even I didn't buy that fib. I went back downstairs, grabbed a spoon, got some ice cream from the freezer, and ate straight out of the container as I leaned against the counter overlooking the backyard and watched the snowflakes fall. One murder suspect to defend and one to find was enough. Never mind an identity thief who may or not be connected. And figuring out if another possible victim was involved. I didn't need to be tousling with Adam, too.

I tossed my spoon in the sink, trashed the empty ice cream carton, and headed back upstairs, Ping and Pong following after me. If Adam wanted to play things this way, let him. I brushed my teeth, shed my robe, put on a nightshirt, and got into bed. The pets watched me then got into their respective beds too—Ping's a chair in the corner and Pong's a giant dog pillow on the floor. I shut off the lamp and within minutes light snoring drifted to my ears. None of it mine. I thrashed around for nearly half an hour then growled into my pillow. I couldn't stop thinking about Adam or the case.

Imagination mixed with reality in my head as images of Adam and Tina dripping holy water over a baby's head competed with images of Peter tumbling down the stairs at *Danser* and Anna being dragged off her porch in handcuffs.

I growled again and got up. Both pets breaking their snorefests long enough to peer at me as I left the room to go into my office and make use of my insomnia. I flicked on my computer, pulled up the case files, and opened Peter's. After learning about the woman dying at *Danser* and Emmaline's sister being Peter's ex, the possibility that Peter's death could relate to something more than identity theft gnawed at me. Not that I'd changed my mind about Anna. I knew in my gut she was innocent. But maybe there were other possibilities. Like his ex-fiancée.

Skimming Peter's file, I went straight to the updates Camille had added to the notes after Juliette's intel at the *Danser* meet and greet about Peter's serial relationships. I found his two ex-wives listed as his previous *Danser* partners along with one fiancée—Celeste Durocher.

Celeste didn't share the same last name with Emmaline which explained why she hadn't originally shown up as a connection between Emmaline and Peter. But the different last names didn't mean much. Different dads maybe. Camille had included some basic background on all the women and Celeste's notes had her currently residing in Paris with no recent trips back home. Okay, probably that left her off the list of suspects. But it didn't clear her devoted sister, Emmaline.

I skipped over to peruse Emmaline's info in the *Danser* file, looking for anything that suggested she was capable of murder. Nothing. But what did catch my attention was that Emmaline's family members only listed two older brothers, no sisters at all. I was sure I'd heard George right, so I made a note to ask Camille about it later and went back to read about Peter's two other exes. One still lived in Montreal, the other in Québec city. Both of them were remarried and neither had any kids with Peter or seemed to have contact with him. That didn't rule them out completely as suspects but pushed them down the likely list. Especially since

Camille had added supplementary notes that both women had already been questioned by the police and dismissed. Which unfortunately brought things back to Anna, so just to be thorough I moved on to check her info. Not much new to learn there. Her occupation was listed as accountant and her immediate family consisted of her mother, her sole surviving parent. No siblings. Anna had no criminal record and no big debts outside of the mortgage on her duplex. And she'd been with Peter about seven months, living together for two.

I sat back in think mode and turned to look out the window above the loveseat on the wall left of my desk. Then I swiveled back to my monitor to check Peter's file again, wondering about his store. From what I could tell, the place was a notch up from a convenience store, and it was located on a residential street not far from Anna's duplex. I took note of the address thinking I'd swing by in the morning. Maybe speak to his employees, real casual like, not formal interviews or anything. Nothing that could get me into trouble with Camille and Laurent. After all, a store is a public place, and a gal can shop anywhere she wants, right?

A car door slammed outside, and I looked back at the window. I went to peek out to see if it was Adam coming home but saw it was just Mrs. Feldman from across the street slogging a path in the snow from her driveway to her front door. I dropped the curtain and went back to my computer to check one more thing before I gave up for the night. I closed out all the files and tried googling for information about the woman who died at *Danser*. No news stories or other matches turned up. I sighed, my late-night probing not getting me very far.

Another car door slammed out front, and I checked outside again. Still no Adam. But I was done waiting up. I powered off the computer and headed back to bed. Alone.

The refrain from the Roch Voisine tune I'd heard for much of the evening popped into my head as I drifted off to sleep, and I wondered who exactly were these men who promised *"I'll always be there"* in songs women like me wanted to believe? Those weren't real men. Real men weren't always there. Real men went out and left notes that said squat about where they were. Notes scribbled on stickie paper and left on the fridge that held the dinner they didn't come home in time to eat. Notes, women like me crumpled up and threw in recycling, hoping our real men would have a good explanation when they finally got home.

I WOKE THE next morning with Adam's arm nestled around my stomach, his quiet, even breathing wafting in my ear. I checked the time. Nearly seven thirty. I closed my eyes again, remembering I had to meet Camille at the office around nine to head over to our second tea reading session with her aunt Claudette. I had to get up if I was going to make it in time. Only I didn't want to move and wake Adam and start my day with another fight, so I slowly removed his arm from my waist as delicately as I could, slipped out of bed, and put on my robe.

"Hey," Adam said, following up his words with sounds of the bed linens rustling.

I turned to him, wishing I'd cleared the room before he had woken, unsure what mood to expect or what mood I wanted to project. "Hey."

"Really sorry about last night," he said. "I don't know why this Bunny thing bothers me so much. I'm trying to deal, really I am."

Hmm. An apology. That was a promising start. I offered a tentative "okay" and waited for him to go on.

He patted the bed. "Why don't you come back for a bit?"

So much for the promising start. Did he really expect his little apology to solve everything? He still hadn't accounted for his MIA status until the wee hours of the morning. Or two-thirty eight a.m. to be precise, when I'd woken to find him crawling into bed and I'd feigned sleep in response to his asking if I was up. I had no intention of doing the prying, nagging girlfriend bit and asking him where he'd been. But I certainly wasn't going to let him off the hook without some kind of explanation. Let alone join him in bed.

"Can't," I said, heading for the bathroom. "I'm meeting Camille."

A few minutes later, I heard Adam pass by the bathroom door on his way downstairs, the unmistakable sound of claws clacking on wood floors followed as Ping and Pong shadowed him. Another minute later, Adam was swearing, loud, and I headed downstairs to see what the fuss was about.

Adam stood in the sunroom with the door to the backyard ajar and drifts of snow at his bare feet. Pong bounded by Adam and ran outside, hopping happily in the snow until she got stuck, her short legs sinking into the snow and rooting her to one spot, her chin tilting up to keep her head from becoming immersed.

I snatched my old rain boots from the draining mat, shoved my feet into them, and waded out to rescue her. The sticky snow swallowed my boots and compacted beneath my weight. The perfect snow for building forts and snowmen and shaping into snowballs. But not so much for navigating in unlined rubber boots barely protecting bare feet. I retraced my steps as quickly as I could, Pong in my arms, and slipped by Adam still working to push the errant snow back outside with a broom.

Releasing the dog, I yanked off my boots and moved into the kitchen to warm my feet on the throw mat in front of the sink. "I don't think either of us is going anywhere today," I said.

Enough snow out of the way, Adam closed the door, and headed for the hall. "It's just snow, Lora. I'll grab some clothes and clear a section of the yard for Pong to use."

I looked out the window at the mounds of snow tall enough to dwarf the garbage can sitting by the shed. Just snow. Back in New York, if we got half this much snow schools closed, activities were called off, and there was a run on cocoa.

Adam came back into the kitchen fully dressed and zipping up his parka. "I'll take care of this. You go ahead. Get ready for your meeting."

"I'm going to tell Camille I can't make it," I said. Not that I felt too bad about that. Another tea reading with talk of impending danger was the last thing I needed.

"Really, Lora. You don't have to cancel. The roads are cleared already. I checked out front. It's not that bad. It looks worse here because the snow drifted. Out front, it's only deep where people piled snow they shoveled out of their driveways and sidewalks."

We hired the same guy to shovel our pathways in the winter as we did to take care of our lawn in the summer, and I knew our excess snow would probably already be piled into one of those snowbanks by now too. But those weren't the mounds of snow I worried about.

I snagged the portable phone from its stand on the counter and headed to the living room to look out front. Sure the roads were cleared enough to make out that they were roads. But they still had a coating of snow that showed tire tracks, not pavement. I dialed Camille's cell number and waited through three rings before she picked up.

"*Allô*," she said, her voice nearly a shout over background noise.

I explained about the snow and the roads.

"*J'arrive*," she said. "I'm picking you up. Didn't you get my message?"

I hadn't checked my messages in ages. "No. What message?"

"On the Bunny phone. It doesn't matter. I'll be there soon, okay." There was some more background noise and she disconnected.

I walked back to the kitchen, put the portable phone away, and made myself a bowl of cereal of puffed rice and soy milk. Glancing out the window, I wondered if I could talk Camille into making a pit stop by Peter's store for a little clue shopping before we went to her aunt Claudette's. The run by Peter's store was the one thing I hadn't been happy to lose to a snow day. Maybe now with Camille driving I wouldn't have to. She had way more experience at winter driving. Adam told me once that just clearing snow costs Montreal about $150 million a year. That's almost four times what New York City spends. I never drove much back in New York at all, let alone through $150 million worth of snow. But Camille did. Every year. So I was more than happy to let her play chauffeur for the day.

I carried my bowl upstairs to my office and retrieved the Bunny phone to check Camille's message and found three new voice mails. I started the first one. Sure enough, it was Camille telling me she'd be picking me up. I moved on to the second message and listened as Anna told me everything was set with the transfer of the cupcake order. All I had to do was get in touch with the bakery and make a deposit. Which meant I'd have plenty of sweet treats to last me until spring since it turned out the cupcake bakery was not one of our suspect suppliers. It also meant Laurent would need to handle any payments involved to protect our covers, so I jotted down the contact information Anna left, toggled over to email, and sent it off to Laurent.

If Anna knew she was suspect numero uno in Peter's death, she didn't sound it. There wasn't the slightest note of anxiety in her voice. I hoped that wasn't just the Prozac working. I hoped that meant I still had time to find some evidence to widen the police investigation. Convincing myself that phone calls didn't count as meetings, I tried calling Anna back to get a better read on her but got her voice mail, so I disconnected and went back to check my third message. Which turned out to be from Madame Shakiba telling me I had to choose my wedding invitations that afternoon at two o'clock at her office and drop off the album she'd lent me along with my preference list for my wedding dress.

This was good. Maybe Camille could go with me for that too. So far Madame Shakiba had been two for two in matching us with suspect suppliers, and I was eager for another chance to size her up and more confident about facing down her glare since I'd survived my dance performance the night before at *Danser* with nearly all my dignity.

Madame Shakiba's message went on to recommend I not bring my groom along to our meeting because we'd need to discuss my dress choices, which she needed direction on right away so she could arrange our shopping asap. Right, probably to leave time for all the adjustments the dress would need.

The giant binder of wedding dresses Madame Shakiba had given me still sat untouched on one of the shelves behind my desk. I hauled it onto the desk and flipped through the pages while I finished me cereal. My instructions were to pinpoint three to five styles that I liked and bookmark them. Each page of the book had a full-page image of a model wearing a wedding dress. Some with veils, some holding bouquets, some dreamily gazing off. And each bride appeared as beautiful as the next. Narrowing my options down to under half a dozen would be tough.

"What are you looking at?" Adam said, as he wandered into the room. He crunched a bite of a breakfast bar, his work outside and the morning pet care apparently complete.

I spooned out the last of my cereal. "Don't get yourself in an uproar, but I'm looking for a wedding dress for Bunny."

"Let me help," he said, seating himself on the loveseat under the window. "Shift the book over here, and we'll look together."

I eyed him skeptically.

"Really, Lora. This is me being supportive. See?" He smiled broadly. "No fangs or anything."

I smiled despite my lingering annoyance with him over his late-night absence. I didn't know exactly when Camille was showing up and hadn't planned on continuing my dress browsing once I'd done eating, but if he was making an effort to be more accepting of my role as Bunny it was only fair to meet him halfway. I passed him the book, and he pointed to a plain dress with three-quarter sleeves.

"This one's nice," he said.

Not a choice I would make for Bunny. Or for me, for that matter. I sat down beside him and shifted the book so it was centered between us. "It's okay," I said and turned the page. After about twenty more pages and no agreement in taste, I started thinking there was a reason brides didn't take their future grooms dress shopping. Aside from superstition, that is.

The doorbell rang, and I asked Adam to get it while I got dressed, thankful for the reprieve in both the perusing and the punishing weight of the book on my legs.

A few minutes later, I heard the shower start and Camille appeared at my bedroom door, two takeout coffees in hand, and offered one to me. "*T'es prête?*" she asked.

I accepted the coffee she held out. "No. I'm not ready." I pointed at my closet. "I don't know what to wear. I'm being me at Claudette's and Bunny the rest of the day. How am I supposed to make that work? I don't know if I'll have time to come home and change."

Camille put her coffee down on my bureau along with her purse, and she wandered into my closet.

I went in after her and watched as she slid hangers back and forth and fingered clothes stacked on white metal shelving. "Laurent tell you what we found out at *Danser*?" I asked her.

She pulled out a sweater from a pile, clicked her tongue at it, and rammed it back in the stack. "*Oui, oui.*"

I wasn't surprised at her answer given how early Laurent started his days. "Any news yet about the woman who died?"

"Helen Wong," Camille told me. "Twenty-nine. Died from a complication of diabetes. Went into some kind of coma or something from her medication not working right and didn't get help in time."

My chest felt heavy. That was so sad. "So it was an accident," I said.

Camille slipped a dress from the rack, eyed it, and put it back. "Apparently."

"What about Emmaline's sister? The one who was engaged to Peter? I couldn't find much about her in the files. And there was no mention of a sister at all in Emmaline's info."

"That's because they're not sisters exactly. They're ex-stepsisters. Emmaline's mother was married four times. Celeste is the daughter of the second husband. Short marriage, no current relationship. That's why the connection between Celeste and Emmaline didn't show up. *Mais*, Celeste's in the file as one of Peter's exes. She's in Paris, that one, and she hasn't been in the country for months. She has a good job and a new boyfriend. Young, hot, and rich. *Probablement* by now she is thanking God for her new life without Peter."

Wow. Camille must have dug a lot deeper to get the extra info. And fast. Not surprising, though. Missing the sister connection, step or not, that linked Emmaline to Peter probably ruffled more than Camille's feathers. However remote the link was. Camille would have flown to Paris herself and grilled Celeste in person if she thought her reputation for thorough frisking was at stake.

Camille pulled out a pair of my jeans and a pale blue scoop-neck sweatshirt so shrunken that I rarely wore it unless it was laundry day. She turned and held the sweatshirt up to me.

I crinkled my nose. "That's old," I said. "And it's got a giant cat face on it. You think that's stylish enough for Bunny?"

She walked back over to my bedroom bureau, opened her purse, whipped out a pair of tiny scissors, and started to cut off the collar rim of the shirt.

"Hey," I said, catching up with her and grabbing for the scissors. "What are you doing? You'll ruin it."

Camille held the shirt up, squinted at it, and proceeded to have at it with the scissors again. "You said it was old, no?"

"Well, yeah."

She held the newly styled shirt out to me. "Try it with the pink bra I gave you."

I sighed, took the shirt, and got dressed, barely able to squeeze the shirt over my head and shimmy it down into place. Standing in front of the full-length mirror on the closet door, I tried to adjust the new neckline. The pink lace from the top of the bra showed no matter which way I pulled. The shirt hugged my body so tight, there'd be no chance of accidental slippage so lace would be all that showed, but still.

Camille removed a small white silk scarf from her neck and tied it around mine. "Now, where's the Bunny bracelet?"

I got the bracelet from the top of the bureau where I'd put it the night before and slipped it around my wrist, realizing only then that the Bunny engagement ring was missing. My heart skipped a beat at the thought of losing it before I found it sitting just where I'd left it. On my finger.

"*Tourne*," Camille said, stepping back to get the overall effect.

I let out a breath and turned to face her.

She scanned me and nodded. "*C'est beau ça.*"

Adam came into the room redressed in the same jeans and sweater he'd thrown on to deal with the snow and smelling of soap and shampoo. He stood beside Camille and looked at me. A muscle in his cheek pinched, but he didn't remark on the outfit. "You girls going soon?" he asked.

"I guess so," I said, wishing I'd had time to talk Camille into questioning him about his whereabouts the night before. Unlike me, Camille had no problem putting men through their paces. And if she didn't get what she wanted that way, she had other ways of making them talk. Non-verbal ways she'd learned while she was picking up her first major fashion accessory—her black belt. Not that I wanted Adam roughed up. But a little inducement to talk wouldn't hurt.

The phone on the nightstand next to me rang, and I picked up. I listened a minute then held the phone out to Adam, my arm stiff but my voice neutral. "It's for you. Tina wants to know if you'll meet her at Ikea instead of her picking you up. She said she's too tired from your movie date last night to drive all the way into the city."

Adam took the phone, his face at least having the good sense to look a bit sheepish.

Now I knew where he'd been. And with whom. Too bad Tina hadn't waited another five minutes before calling. It would have been much more satisfying to sick Camille on him to get the information.

MY MIND WAS still on Adam and Tina when Camille turned onto Avenue Fielding not far from Loyola park. It had taken some convincing to get her to make a minor detour over to Peter's store before we headed to her aunt's house, so when she made a couple more turns, stopped the car, and swore, I figured Camille was just letting me know she still wasn't thrilled about the request. Then I saw what she was looking at.

"Uh oh," I said, releasing my seat belt and pulling on my door handle to get out of the Jetta.

Camille was two steps behind me when my boots hit the snowy sidewalk. We both stood and stared at the blackened windows of Peter's store framed by newly scorched brick. The area out front nearly an ice slick. The place had either recently been hit by fire smothered by mega doses of water or Peter's decorator had steered him very wrong.

"*Merde*," Camille said.

I nodded. "Yeah." My eyes shifted upwards to the two floors of apartments above the commercial section of the building that held Peter's store. The apartments looked untouched. Whatever fire had hit the main floor seemed to have been contained quick enough to avoid spreading too far. Even the pizzeria that neighbored Peter's mini market had only minimal damage.

Camille pulled out her cell and placed a call, cupping her hand around the phone and turning towards the car, probably to help break the sound of the wind.

I baby-stepped my way over the icy snow to get closer to the store, trying to see inside through the less blackened areas of the windows. Wasn't much to see. Metal shelving units, items strewn on the floor, lots of water damage, large hole in the wall towards the back.

A woman came towards me, cigarette dangling from her lips, puffy purple coat held closed with her arm, gray curls poking out from under her hat. She pulled the cigarette from her lips with exposed fingertips, the rest of her hand sheathed from knuckles to wrist with worn knit gloves. "Store's closed, honey," she said.

I met her hazy gaze. "Yeah. Looks like a fire."

"Sure was. I came home last night and couldn't even get into my apartment." She made an offhand gesture towards the upper part of the building with her cigarette hand, then stretched her arm out towards the road. "Fire trucks took up half the street. Damn bus dropped us off blocks away. Had to walk the rest of the way, then stand out in the cold."

Hmm. A fire in an empty store. Faulty wiring maybe? "They tell you what caused it?"

"Nope. Figured it didn't affect the rest of us." She puffed at her cigarette and coughed. "Bet it won't stop our insurance from going up, though."

I looked at the scorched sign above Peter's store and scanned the other storefronts again—three in all with a dry cleaner at the far end and the pizzeria in the middle next to Peter's market. "Anyone hurt?"

She shook her head. "Nah. Happened after everything was closed." She pointed to the pizza place. "Even Franko closes by eleven. And this store hasn't been open for days. Heard the owner died. Damn shame. Place wasn't much, but it was handy and always had my cigs in stock."

"Did you know the owner?"

She stepped back a bit and took a drag of her cigarette, her eyes narrowing to slits and assessing. "You a friend of his?" she asked me.

I wondered what answer would get me more information and gambled on a no.

She took another drag before answering. "The guy was a bit of a schleb to tell you the truth. Always trying to sell me something I didn't need. Always trying out new things and pushing it on customers. Latest was some vitamin crap." She shook her head. "Do I look like I need vitamins?"

Good thing that was a rhetorical question because I'd have to side with Peter on that one. I smiled, the cold hitting my teeth, and looked back to see if Camille was done her call yet. She was back in the car, but her mouth was moving and I thought I saw the phone's umbilical cord winding down from her ear. Probably escaping the sound and bite of the weather. She looked up and waved at me to get back to the car.

"I gotta go," I said to the woman. "But it's been nice talking to you."

She raised both eyebrows at me like I must not get out much. "Yeah, I gotta get back in and feed my cat anyway." She glanced over her shoulder when Camille beeped at me to hurry up, and as I turned to go, the lady tapped my arm and passed me a cigarette. "Looks like your friend could use one of these to tide her over 'til you find another store. There's a *dépanneur* down thataway," she said, pointing south with her finger, the tip purple from the cold.

I took the cigarette and thanked her, feeling bad for depleting her stock but knowing she'd be offended if I refused her generosity.

She dropped her cigarette butt towards the snowy curb, grinding the butt with the toe of her boot, and watched me get into the Jetta before turning and rounding the building to go in the side door.

Camille eyed the cigarette when I got into the car. "I had no idea Bunny was a smoker," she said.

"It's not for me." I held it out to her. "It's for you. The woman I was talking to said you looked like you could use it."

She took it like she was giving it serious consideration. "Maybe we both could. I just got off the phone with Luc. This was no accidental fire. Someone torched the place."

Geez, Peter couldn't even catch a break when he was dead. Even his store wasn't safe from whatever bad mojo was going around.

"Any idea who?"

She turned her key in the ignition and pulled out. "Not yet. Started in the back where Peter had a small office off the stockroom. Looks like someone lit a pile of boxes on fire, and the flames spread from there."

Someone covering up a robbery maybe? "Was there a vault in the office?"

"Luc didn't say. Only that the fire happened overnight and was contained fairly quickly thanks to a passerby calling it in. Money in the register was untouched and no sign of forced entry."

That last bit caught my attention. "I don't suppose Peter had an employee with a key who juggled fire as a hobby and liked to practice in the back room?"

Camille smiled. "*Non*. One part-time employee with no key, and the guy's been away on a ski trip all week." She glanced at me as she drove. "Only one other person had a copy of the key."

Uh oh. She didn't have to tell me who. Had to be Anna. "That doesn't mean she used it last night," I said.

"Doesn't mean she didn't," Camille said, stopping in front of her aunt Claudette's house.

FOURTEEN

I CHECKED TO make sure my coat was done up all the way, rubbed my gloved hands together, and looked out the car window to check Camille's progress. We'd arrived at her aunt Claudette's to find both the walkway and the driveway filled with snow, and Camille insisted on shoveling them both. I'd offered to help, but Claudette wouldn't hear of it. I didn't want to insult her, but one more minute of sitting in this car and I'd go batty. Or freeze to death. The waste of my time gnawed at me too. Every minute I spent sitting on my rump was another minute I could have been working the case. There wasn't much I could do sitting in a car. I'd tried calling Laurent to see if he knew more about the fire or Anna and couldn't get him. So I tried Anna again and still didn't have any luck reaching her, but this time I left a message to call me. The longer I sat the more antsy I got. I needed to do something. I spied two more shovels leaning against the garage and watched for Claudette to back away from the front window so I could make a beeline for one.

When I saw my chance, I got out of the car and trotted over to the shovel, figuring I could start working at the end of the driveway near the garage door where I'd be partially hidden from Claudette's view should she return to her post at the window. Camille finished up the sidewalk and began heaving snow from the other end of the driveway. It took a while before we met near the middle with the job done. And a few minutes more for Camille to pull her car off the road and into the driveway.

Claudette was waiting for us at the door with her poodle *Mignon* circling her ankles, and she ushered us in when we stepped onto her stoop. Her hair was pinned up again, and she wore a red cardigan, black slacks, and puffy blue slippers.

She pulled Camille down to her and wrapped her in a hug. *"Merci mon petit ange."*

Camille hugged her back, not too close to avoid dripping snow on her aunt or the floor, did the cheek kiss thing, and backed away enough to take off her jacket. She too had a sweater on only hers was a cream color that nearly matched her hair and contrasted well with her dark jeans.

"Et toi aussi," Claudette said, shaking a finger at me before kissing my cheeks hello.

Apparently, she'd spied me shoveling after all. I smiled at her as I took off my coat and boots. The finger shaking was good. Most of Camille's family elders had kind of taken me in as one of their own. With my parents gone, Camille's mom in particular had stepped up to fill the parental void whenever she saw me. Claudette too wouldn't hesitate to extend her generosity to me, but her pride made it hard for her to accept any help in return, so I was still treated as a guest on that score. But she'd never shake her finger at a guest in her home. The finger shaking was a sign of greater acceptance. I was progressing from someone who got treated as family to someone who she would let treat her as family.

Mignon rushed over to smell my boots, tracked the smell over to my leg, looked up at me, and tilted his little white head. Probably not sure what to make of the mix of Ping and Pong scents he was picking up on. I bent to give *Mignon's* back a quick pat, and he bit at the Bunny bracelet as though it were a toy.

"Arrête là," Claudette said, scooping the dog up and heading for the kitchen.

Camille and I followed and took our places in the same seats as the last time we'd been over. While Claudette settled *Mignon* and put the water to boil for tea, she and Camille chatted in French. I tried to follow their conversation, but they spoke too fast for me to catch much more than the odd word. Partway through, I gave up trying. Since they weren't speaking English like they usually did when I was around, I figured it was none of my business anyway.

140

When everything was ready and Claudette joined us at the table, she nodded in my direction and shook her finger at me again. Only this time, she pointed it at my chest and wagged it back and forth in the general direction of my breasts. "What is this? With the *dentelle, là*? Ordinarily, you do not wear clothes like that."

Claudette's heavy accent made all her TH blends sound like Ds—a common pronunciation that I was used to by now having lived in Montreal for nearly two years. But combined with the finger wagging and her tone, I felt a distinct emphasis on her last word I wasn't quite sure how to interpret. It didn't feel exactly judgmental or derisive, but there was something in it that immediately twigged my embarrassment meter. I looked down to my chest and got an eyeful of pink lace and realized I'd forgotten to adjust Camille's borrowed scarf to hide my cleavage until I had to play Bunny later in the day.

Claudette bumped her elbow against Camille's and let out a little laugh. "*C'est le nouveau gars, c'est ça?*"

I smiled, more out of confusion than anything else. I didn't have a clue what she'd said. No questionable tone this time, though, whatever it was sounded friendly. My eyes darted to Camille for an explanation.

Camille waved her hand in the air. "It's nothing, Lora. *Ma tante* thinks you're dressing for the dream man she predicted would come into your life." She turned to her aunt. "It's not for a man, *ma tante*. She's dressed for work."

Claudette placed a hand near her collarbone and waved her other hand in the air. "You don't believe, but you will see. The leaves know."

I could hear foot tapping and knew Camille was holding back from contradicting her aunt or giving the speech about women not dressing for men. Her cell phone rang, and she answered, her voice loud and with an edge of irritation. Camille's emotions were like air. They never stayed trapped for long without seeking another outlet. She got up and headed out of the room. "*Excusez-moi*," she said to us. "I have to take this."

That would be the prearranged call from Laurent. This was my cue that she was going off to snoop, and I was to keep Claudette occupied. My cup still had quite a bit of tea in it, so I took a large swig and followed it with another then extended my cup to Claudette to show her the small amount I'd left in the bottom. "Is that good?"

She nodded and guided me through the same swilling and turning steps as the last time before having me glide the cup over to sit in front of her. When she peered into it, her lips pinched.

"What is it?" I asked, dipping my head and leaning forward to see the tiny leaves of tea scattered at the bottom of the cup. Looked innocent enough to me.

"The danger," Claudette said. "*C'est très présent*. It's getting closer now."

I was hoping she wouldn't mention the danger thing again. It had creeped me out the last time. My job was to keep her busy with questions about what she saw, but I didn't want to ask for more details about that. Couldn't she see me redecorating or winning the lottery or something? "Hmm," I said. "Do you see anything else?"

"I see the danger is not just for you but another person also. Someone you know."

"Right. But anything *besides* the danger?" I asked.

"There is the same man."

Naturally. What's a woman's fortune without a man on the horizon? And not just any man, but a soul mate.

She nodded to herself. "And a trip."

Okay. That sounded like a much better topic. I could use a break from the cold and the snow. "Can you tell if it's somewhere warm and sunny?"

Claudette raised her eyes to me, her head still bent over my cup. "It does not work like that. I only see what I see. *La destination* is not clear. But you will not be alone."

Let me guess. It would be with the new man.

"I see too *des choix* coming up," she continued, stumbling for more words. "You will need to make choices."

Didn't everyone? That point was so vague I thought I could stretch a few more questions out of it. "Choices about what?"

"Big things," she said, staring intently into the cup. "Things that change your life."

Hadn't I already changed my life enough by coming to a new country, moving in with my boyfriend, and starting a new career? What other big things could there be?

Claudette let out a big puff of air, sat back, and crossed herself. "*Une cassure* is coming."

I furrowed my brows, not understanding. What with the crossing herself, it didn't sound like anything good.

She knocked her hands together and quickly pulled them apart, the sharp skin on skin action of her palms slapping together causing me to flinch.

"A break," she said. "You understand?"

I didn't really, but I saw Claudette was about to do the clap bang thing again, so I nodded, only to flinch for a second time when the ring of a bicycle bell sounded and *Mignon* immediately started a shrill round of yapping. A woman's face appeared in the slit between the curtains on the window of the back door, and the dog catapulted himself out from under the table and accompanied his yapping with a jumping move that went straight up and down as though he was on an invisible pogo stick.

Maybe in the tea reading business, a lot of callers came the back way, but it would freak me out too if faces suddenly appeared at my back door. Claudette shushed the dog, her expression unfazed, and went to tend her visitor. With the door open, I saw it wasn't a bicycle bell I'd heard but an old-fashioned crank ringer attached just below the window.

The lady leaned into the kitchen, nodding a greeting in my direction and said something to Claudette in French then passed Claudette a Tupperware container. The two women exchanged a few more words before the woman left and Claudette closed the door and slipped the container into a cupboard. She swung around to return to the table, stopping when *Mignon* scratched at the back door. Looking down at the dog, she huffed at him and let him out.

Only to rush out after him a moment later, shaking her head and pulling her sweater tighter around her.

I rubbed my arms, trying to warm myself from the drop in temperature the cold air wafting in had brought, and got up to see what had lured her outside. As I neared the door, I heard several thuds followed by a whoop, and looked out to see Claudette's two blue puffy slippers sailing through the air, her legs holding them aloft as her back slid down a short flight of snowy stairs and landed soundlessly in a mound of snow at the bottom. I yelled for Camille and ran for my boots, stuffing my feet in them as I ran back to the kitchen and out to Claudette.

"Are you all right?" I asked her. "Can you get up?"

Claudette tightened her lips like a child determined not to cry and shook her head. "My leg is hurt."

"*Ne bouge pas,*" Camille called to her aunt from the doorway then disappeared from view only to reappear in her coat and boots with her phone to her ear and shouting Claudette's address to whoever listened at the other end of the line. Probably a 911 operator. She disconnected, dropped the phone into her pocket, and made her way over to Claudette and me, pulling out a jacket that had been tucked under her arm and swaddling Claudette in it the best she could.

"*Mignon,*" Claudette whispered, pointing.

I followed her finger and saw *Mignon's* tiny head shivering above snow a few yards away, his body stuck just like Pong's had been, the tall, sticky snow apparently doubling as doggy quicksand. I dashed over to pull him out, having to dig around him some before I could free him. I cradled him to me and slipped by Claudette and Camille to take him inside and warm him up.

By the time the paramedics had come and were settling Claudette for transport to the hospital, *Mignon* had stopped shivering and was back to prancing around the house, excited with all the activity of Camille dashing around looking for Claudette's handbag and closing up.

I had suited up for outside and was waiting by the front door when Camille hooked a plastic bag onto my gloved wrist. "What's that for?" I asked her.

She secured the bag, turned, and bent down. "*Mignon*," she said, getting back up and thrusting the dog into my arms. "Just a few things to tide you over."

"Tide me over?"

"Well, someone has to take him. I have no idea how long it will take at *l'hôpital*. The ambulance people say *tante* Claudette has a bad break, maybe even a fracture in her hip. The dog can't stay alone."

Mignon fussed in my arms, intent on prying open the plastic bag with his snout. We stepped outside, and I saw a taxi slow as it approached the ambulance and pulled in behind, leaving at least a three car buffer in between.

"That's for you," Camille said to me, pulling out the giant Caron key ring she kept in her purse for emergencies. "I called it to take you home. I'm following *ma tante*."

I watched her lock Claudette's front door while I tried to keep *Mignon* from chewing through the plastic bag.

"Okay," I said and carefully started down the stoop steps, holding tight to the dog. When I reached the sidewalk, I turned back to Camille. "What about this afternoon?" I asked her. "I'm supposed to drop something at *Prêt-à-Marier* without Laurent. I thought you'd come with me. Should I go alone?"

Camille threw the key ring back into her purse and hurried over to her car. She waved her arm in my general direction. "*Oui oui.* You go. Just don't talk to anybody." She got into her car, slammed the door shut, and revved on her engine.

I squinted in the brightness of nearly midday light reflecting off snow and watched the ambulance pull out with Camille on its tail, then I turned my attention to the cab driver waiting for me. He took one look at the dog in my arms, his bushy eyebrows banded together, and he sped away.

"**DON'T LOOK AT** me like that," I said to the three furry faces gazing at me from their respective resting spots in my kitchen. I took a bite of my avocado and tomato sandwich and followed it with a corn chip. Not the best winter lunch, but it was fast. And given that it had taken me forever to get another cab after Eyebrowman deserted me, I had barely more than half an hour before I was expected at *Prêt-à-Marier*.

Mignon and Pong sat at my feet, panting and staring up at me. Ping sat on the chair beside me, her eyes mere slits. The dogs, exhausted from introducing themselves and a harried game of tag in the backyard, probably hoped I'd take pity on them and drop a scrap of food on the floor. The cat, spent from introducing *Mignon* to her claws and making sure he knew his rank in the pecking order, probably hoped I'd take pity on her and drop the new dog off someplace else. Preferably someplace far, far away.

"It wasn't my idea," I told them all. "But it's not so bad, right?" It was certainly better than whatever Claudette must be going through. The eeriness of which hadn't escaped me. Not five minutes had passed from the time she predicted a break coming to her taking that fall. Granted, she'd predicted the break when she'd been reading *my* tea leaves, but maybe tea reading was one of those read-between-the-lines things, and the lines could get blurred and miss their target. I only hoped Claudette just broke her leg and didn't hurt her hip. Hip damage could be serious business, especially at her age.

I finished my sandwich, tidied up, and debated whether or not I could leave the new furry friends all together alone in the house. I decided to risk it since the likelihood of any major fights breaking out at this stage was slim.

"You'll be good, right?" I said to them as I got ready to face the great outdoors again for my errand over to *Prêt-à-Marier*.

The giant book of wedding dresses clenched in my arms, I gave them one last look before I closed the vestibule door and headed out. I plodded over to the driveway and stopped in front of a huge white blob. My car. Completely covered in snow, the antennae sticking out and pointing north as though fingering the culprit. A high pitched wail suddenly pierced the air, and I looked around trying to place it. Probably it was someone's heater letting off steam from being overworked, but it sounded like someone in dire pain and I sympathized. My muscles were already starting to complain about my earlier snow shoveling at Claudette's. No way would I be able to rescue my car in time to make it for my appointment.

I started back for the house to call a taxi and wait in warm comfort. The wailing sound got louder as I neared my porch. Even with my hat on, the noise shot right through my ears and into my heart. It sounded like someone in deep mourning. Either that, or minutes away from death by torture. I went inside and came face to snout with the mourner. *Mignon*, stopping mid wail at the sight of me and wagging his tail.

"That so was not you," I said to him. "You're maybe ten pounds. Your body can't possibly create that pitch."

He wagged his tail some more.

I stepped back outside and waited. Sure enough, *Mignon* started up again. Two ladies passing by stared at me, their faces shifting between annoyance and concern. I skirted back in the house, and the wailing stopped again.

Okay, now I had two problems, no car *and* no freedom. Undercover rule number two flashed in my head: be prepared for anything. Right. I could do that. I could be prepared. Or at least I could troubleshoot after the fact. I was a champion troubleshooter. And this problem had an easy fix. First, I called a taxi, then I ran upstairs to my closet. A few minutes of rummaging later, I came back downstairs with a beach bag and an old blue pashmina. I scooped *Mignon* up and slipped him into the bag, using a bit of the scarf to create a cushion for him and arranging the rest of the fabric to cover the dog's body. Partly for insulation and partly for camouflage. No way was I going to lose another taxi today. I grabbed a few Milk-Bones from the box we kept for Pong by the front door and shoved them into my pockets for reinforcement. I was not above bribery to keep *Mignon* quiet. Whatever works. That was *my* undercover rule.

"LET'S JUST ZIP back to my office real quick, Bunny," Chantal said. "It's okay if I call you Bunny, right? Madame Shakiba wants us to call everyone by their last name, but that always feels so formal to me."

Before I could respond, Chantal started walking away. I followed her out of the *Prêt-à-Marier* reception and into a makeshift corridor between banks of cubicles. Her outfit of slim-legged slacks and a cashmere sweater topped with a small knotted scarf could have come from a 1950s Sears catalogue, and her short ponytail bounced as she moved.

"Umm. Bunny's fine," I said to her back. "But I just came by to drop off this book for Madame Shakiba."

Chantal broke into more of a speed walk. "Sure. She's out right now, but you can leave that with me. She left me strict orders to help you select your invites today, too."

Right. I'd forgotten that bit of Madame Shakiba's phone message. It would be tough to follow Camille's "don't talk to anyone" tactic if I had to schmooze paper stock and fonts. I was a sucker for both. I'd been known to haunt the aisles of Office Depot comparing paper weights and textures, and I had a secret belief that fonts had distinct personalities.

Chantal turned into a gap as wide as a doorway between a couple of room dividers meeting at a right angle. I was breathing heavy under the burden of carrying the wedding dress tomb and my poodlepack by the time I joined her.

"Omigod," she said, looking at my bag. "Is that a dog?"

I looked over to see *Mignon*'s nose tipped up, barely skimming the top of my beach bag. "Uh, yeah."

"You are so lucky Madame Shakiba isn't here. She'd have a fit."

My eyes flitted up towards the second storey loft in the back where the enclosed, private offices were bunched together in a tight row. Four slim rooms overlooking the main floor of cubicles, the last office belonging to Madame Shakiba. Her door was closed, the slender glass pane beside it dark. "Oh, I'm so sorry. Is she allergic?"

"God, no," Chantal said, sitting at her desk. "She just hates 'em. Between you and me, I think she's scared of dogs. Cats too."

I set the dress book down on the edge of Chantal's desk and sat in the wood chair wedged in between a file cabinet and a divider wall covered in fabric with a collage of wedding photos attached by pushpins. *Mignon* fussed as I pivoted his bag onto my lap, and I reached in to give him a calming pat.

Chantal sat forward, peering into the bag. "How cute."

"Thanks," I said. "He's not mine. I'm just dog-sitting. And I wouldn't have brought him, but I really thought I'd just be in and out."

"No worries. This won't take long." Chantal pointed towards the tomb I'd placed on her desk. "I see Madame Shakiba gave you her dress bible."

I nodded.

She dragged the book over to her and flipped through my marked pages. "Nice. Good choices." She stopped at a picture of a spaghetti strap number and tapped her finger on it. "There's a store on rue St. Hubert that sells something like this. I'd go for that if I was you. It's off the rack, but doesn't look it. Nobody would have a clue it was a quickie find." She sat back and pivoted her computer monitor to face her better. "Do we have your email addy on file? I'll just send you the store link and you can check it out."

I had no idea if Bunny's email address had been given to *Prêt-à-Marier*. "I'm not sure."

"Yup. Here is it," Chantal said, her eyes fixed on her screen and her fingers typing away on her keyboard. "Done."

A beep came from inside my purse when Bunny's phone got the email, and *Mignon* started barking and jumped out of the poodlepack. He danced at my feet briefly before going into his pogo stick act, adding a circle flourish and accompanying every second leap with a bark. Minus the bark, the dog could try out for the Bolshoi Ballet with a pirouette like that.

"Shush, *Mignon*, shush," I told him, slipping the poodlepack on the floor and bending to reach for him.

He scrambled away and dashed out of Chantal's cubicle.

I rushed out after the dog, chasing behind him as me made his way through the maze of cubicle corridors. He was surprisingly fast given his short legs. On the third bend, I almost caught up with him but lost him when he disappeared into an open vent. Just my luck. I crouched on the carpet and looked in, calling out to him in soothing tones. Two red eyes came into view, and I hoped they didn't belong to a rat.

"Here, doggy doggy," I said. Nothing. I smiled and carefully reached out my hand, ready to pull it back in a millisecond if a rat nose poked out. Every New Yorker I knew had fast reflexes where vermin were concerned. "Here, *Mignon*," I tried again. Still nothing. So I tried in my pitiful French. "*Viens ici, petit Mignon.*" This time the eyes tilted as though the animal cocked its head. I repeated my phrase and watched as the eyes came closer and *Mignon* came into view.

I backed away to give the dog room to come out, and he sped up and rammed me, his body shimmying back and forth in time with his tail. I picked him up and stood, looking him over. Dirt splotches smeared his white fur in spots, but otherwise he seemed fine. I gave his head a light pat. "Don't do that again," I told him. I added in a chin scratch and was surprised when I got scratched back. I shifted *Mignon* to get a better look at his head and noticed a strip of metal encircling the lower part of his mouth, a mini gold coin dangling from the metal by a chain stained with blood.

"Omigod."

I turned to see Chantal had come up behind me.

"Omigod," she said again. "That's Madame Shakiba's bracelet."

FIFTEEN

LAURENT CLOSED THE door of Michel's office and turned to me. "Tell me again how you found the bracelet."

I put the poodlepack down on the ground and let *Mignon* out to stretch his legs, hoping the leg stretching didn't turn to lifting on one of Michel's potted plants. "I didn't find it. *Mignon* did." Remembering I'd brought some Milk-Bones, I gave one to the dog.

Laurent leaned against the desk, folded his arms across his chest, and looked down at the poodle licking up bone crumbs off the carpet. "I've never seen that dog do more than yap. A couple hours with you and he's Scooby Doo."

I smiled. "Poodles are very smart."

"And very small," Laurent said. "Let's hope the team doesn't find anything else in that vent that was too big for Scooby here to drag out."

I pushed an image of Madame Shakiba's lifeless body out of my head. She couldn't possibly be in the vent. We'd smell a dead body. "You don't think they will, do you?"

"*Non.* But nobody has seen or heard from Madame Shakiba since yesterday, and she's not answering her cell phone. If the only trace of her is a bloody bracelet, that can't be good."

Not much about this day had been good. First the snowstorm, then Tina's call, then Claudette getting hurt, and now this. I was right, I should never have left the house this morning. I shouldn't have even gotten out of bed. I forced myself to look for a bright side and came up with two. "Probably people have only been calling her this morning. Madame Shakiba could just be running a personal errand or at a doctor's appointment. And her cell phone could be set to go to voice mail. Or her battery too low. That happens a lot."

Laurent smiled on that one. Maybe it didn't happen a lot to other people, but we both knew it happened a lot to me.

"And maybe she just snagged the bracelet on something again like she did when we first met her," I went on. "I bet that thing gets caught on everything."

"And the blood?"

"From a cut maybe. That thing's pretty sharp. She could have snagged it and cut herself trying to get free. Maybe it even broke. Has anyone checked? Maybe it broke, and she got frustrated and tossed it into the vent."

Laurent kept his gaze on me, his eyes weighing my words.

I started for the door. "Let's go see. I didn't get a real careful look before."

He stepped in front of me, the sweater hugging his broad chest filling my eyeline. "Aren't you forgetting somebody?"

I looked over to where *Mignon* was gnawing the leg of a side table. An antique table. "No, *Mignon*, no."

"You should go home and take Scooby with you," Laurent said.

I pulled *Mignon* away from the table leg and picked him up. "But I want to see the bracelet. And the cops are still here. I want to see if they fish out anything else from the vent."

Laurent took *Mignon* from me, placed him in my poodlepack, and looped the bag onto my shoulder. "I'll check and let you know. We've both already been questioned. It's natural that I would have come to meet you, but it will look odd if we stay much longer."

"But you still haven't told me anything about the fire at Peter's store. And we should probably talk some more about Helen Wong, the woman who died at *Danser,* and Emmaline and her sister."

He steered me out the door and down the stairs. "Nothing new to talk about yet. *Puis,* I get the feeling Scooby there's wants are more pressing, and the next thing he needs to find is a fire hydrant."

"GEEZ, LORA, YOU could have talked to me before you got another pet. I thought we agreed after you brought Ping home, no more strays," Adam said, sitting down beside me on our living room sofa, his eyes on *Mignon* curled up on the floor. "The house is only so big."

He had some nerve sounding annoyed with me. He still hadn't explained word one about his secret outings with Tina. Plus, the house was way bigger than any cage a stray would get at a shelter. But that wasn't the point at the moment. "He's not a new pet. He belongs to Camille's aunt, and I'm just taking care of him for a bit. His name's *Mignon*. Isn't he adorable?"

Adam looked at *Mignon* with the same squint Ping did. "He's a poodle. I've never seen a multi-colored poodle before."

I bent down to brush at the dog's fur. "He's not. That's just dirt. He was helping on the case and got dirty."

"The hooker case?"

"Would you stop calling it that. The case has nothing to do with hookers." I went to the kitchen to wet and soap some paper towel to get the last of the smudges off *Mignon's* coat. "One of Michel's employees might be missing." Or dead, but I preferred not to believe that possibility yet. "The dog's the one who alerted us."

The doorbell rang, and *Mignon* went into his jumping and barking act. Not to be outdone, Pong started her intermittent barking routine. And somewhere upstairs, Ping was likely rolling her little cat eyes, wishing for ear plugs, and debating the merits of housecat life versus prowling alleys.

Adam answered the door to Camille who came in dressed all in black from her tuque to her Doc Martens. Not a good sign. Black clothes meant Camille was planning some alley prowling of her own. And when she played Catwoman, she rarely played alone.

"*Allez*," she said to me. "Go get ready. We've got work to do."

"What about dinner?" I said. "I haven't eaten yet."

Camille waved her arms at me. "*Dépêche-toi là*. We'll get something on the way."

I shot Adam a look putting an end to our conversation and dashed upstairs to change. After half a dozen times of scrambling to find black clothes to wear alongside Camille's Catwoman suit, I'd finally given in and bought a prowling outfit of my own—slim black leggings paired with a black turtleneck and a small pocket purse strapped across my torso. Batgirl to Camille's Catwoman, only in this case we were on the same side. I made a pretty good Batgirl, too. After all, we had a lot in common—we were both scrappy Gotham city gals who worked with men who made women swoon and sent bad guys to jail.

As I made my way back downstairs, it occurred to me that Camille made a good Catwoman too. They were both smart women who could hold their own with any man and knew how to handle trouble. Or make it. Whichever suited them. I wondered which one Camille had in mind for tonight and hoped it wasn't the second. Batgirl had a tough day and was in no mood for any more surprises.

"BREAKING AND ENTERING is illegal," I said to Camille. "I thought you said undercover rule number four was not to break the law." When Camille had expanded on Laurent's rules, she'd also added in number five—if you break any proceeding rules, don't get caught—and I had the eerie feeling that it would come into play now. I was also guessing Laurent probably didn't know about rule number five.

"We're not undercover," Camille said. "And we're not breaking, just entering. I've got the key to *tante* Claudette's house." She pulled the giant Caron emergency key ring from the black backpack she wore papoose-style. She held up the keys to make her point, and they glinted when a passing headlight went by.

I heard the automatic click of Camille unlocking the doors on her Jetta. "But we don't have a lot of time," she said. "Nia Papadopoulos will be back from bingo in less than an hour."

"Who's Nia Papadopoulos?"

"*Ma tante* Claudette's neighbor. She's a real snoop. I don't know how *ma tante* puts up with her."

I looked in the visor mirror to make sure all my hair was tucked into my hat. Working this far north, Batgirl also had a black cap and sleek black coat. We'd parked on a side street near Claudette's house and had to walk the rest of the way. The hair tucking was as much for warmth as concealment. "And why do we care about Nia Papadopoulos?"

"Because if she sees us, she'll tell *tante* Claudette we were here."

"So?"

Camille drummed her gloved fingers on the steering wheel. "So, we're not supposed to be. The doctors are keeping Claudette in *l'hôpital* for some time to see to her injuries. Her hip isn't too bad, but the break to her leg was not simple and her age and osteoporosis don't help. But Arielle already came by to get her some things for her stay. Me, I'm snooping, not helping."

We got out of the car, and as we trudged over to the house, our boots squeaking when they hit ice patches, I thought we should have dressed in white, not black, if we wanted to go unseen. Early sundowns and short days meant nothing. Even at night, the abundance of snow brightened the streets. Especially on Claudette's street, which seemed to have more than its share of street lamps. And less than its share of cleared sidewalks. Instead, a slender path in the center of the sidewalk had been forged by pedestrians before us. Barely wide enough to walk single file. And tough to keep an eye on while I scoped the area for witnesses who might report us to Claudette. That woman had me spooked enough with her tea leaves and predictions. I didn't need to find out what she was capable of if she caught wind of our little impromptu visit to her house sans invitation.

As we neared the house, Camille sped up and was on the porch so fast she was already inside by the time I caught up.

"Okay," she said, closing the door and taking off her boots in the dark entryway. "*Tante* Claudette keeps two lights on timers—one in the living room and one in the bedroom. We'll have to work with those." She pulled out her cell phone and powered it on so soft light glowed from it. "And these. They're not as bright as flashlights and don't give off the same obvious light stream."

Uh oh. She hadn't said anything about bringing a phone, and in my rush I hadn't thought to grab mine or Bunny's.

She looked at my empty hands and shook her head. "*Mais voyons*, Lora." She pulled out the old, extra phone she sometimes

155

carried for backup. The "sometimes" being when she knew she'd be working with me. My track record for not always making sure my phone was charged, or even always with me, still stuck even though I was better about both now. So long as I wasn't rushed out of the house, that is.

I took the phone she offered, flipped it open, powered it on, and the tiny screen lit up. Not as much light as a newer phone would have given off, but good enough to keep me from crashing into walls or furniture. "So what are we doing here?"

"Looking for money."

"Money?"

Camille shrugged. "Even at *l'hôpital, tante* Claudette won't let my mother visit. Her own sister. *C'est ridicule.* I have to get to the bottom of this feud, and I think it's about money. When I searched earlier, I found some bank records that showed *ma tante's* savings and investments were close to zero. They totaled thousands only six months ago. When I asked her about it, she kicked me out of her room at *l'hôpital.* I need to know where that money went." She started down the hall towards the bedrooms. "Look for anything worth anything, more financial papers, any big bills, anything that might tell us what happened to that money. And look fast."

I had never been into the private section of Claudette's house before and didn't know my way around, so when Camille disappeared into a doorway at the end of the hall, I turned into the room closest to me, letting the phone light lead me. In the faint glow, I made out a twin bed with purple flowered bedspread, a small white desk and matching tall bureau, a white rattan armchair in the corner, and bookshelves attached to walls here and there. Most of it stripped of daily necessities. Probably Claudette's daughter Arielle's room before she moved out. I poked around and didn't see any personal papers or anything of real value. Wasn't even a clock radio. Nothing interesting under the bed or in the closet either.

I moved on to the room across the hall, a sewing room by the looks of it. And unless Claudette had spent her loot on bolts of outdated fabric, this room netted me zero again. I went back out to the hall and bumped into Camille.

"Anything?" I asked her.

She shook her head. "*Toi?*"

"Nothing."

She blew out a stream of air and headed back towards the living room. "*Allez.* Madame Papadopoulos will be home soon, and we've still got the basement to check."

We went to the basement door and found it locked.

"*Merde,*" Camille said, tugging on the doorknob.

Guess there was no key on the Caron key chain for this door. Okay by me. Modern finished basements I didn't mind so much, but old ones had me thinking spiders and mold and things that go bump in the night.

Camille looked at me and must have noticed the smile that had found its way to my lips. "We're still going down," she said. "*Deux secondes.*" She reached into her sac and took out her toolkit—a small case that looked like a manicure set and held gadgets undercover rule number four probably shouldn't know about. She fiddled with a tool in the lock, and the door clicked open.

We went down the carpeted stairs and hit a large, wood-paneled room at the bottom. Two tweed sofas lined one wall, a recliner was stuffed in the corner, and a long faux maple wall unit faced them. The scent of beer and cigarettes emanated from the ratty shag carpet. The TV dated back to the early '90s, the knickknacks to the mid '60s, and the walls held yellowed newspaper clippings of hockey players I didn't recognize. The only thing that seemed new was a candle that smelled recently used and sat beside a picture of Camille's deceased uncle Yves that was on the mantel of the fake fireplace beside the recliner.

We gave the room a quick going over and found nothing. Only the wall unit had any storage space, and it was filled with books and old LP records with a turntable and speakers wedged in beside them. Camille did a quick walkthrough of the rest of the basement while I sat in the recliner and waited. She hadn't asked me to join her, and I was guessing this room was as finished as Claudette's basement got, so I wasn't eager to see whatever other old things were ripening behind closed doors.

"*Rien*," Camille said when she got back. "There's nothing here. Let's go."

I moved to get up and something hard knocked my spine. I reached back, threading my hand in behind the afghan draped over the chair, and pulled out the culprit. A laptop computer, sans cord.

Camille grabbed it and shoved it in her backpack.

"Hey. Can you do that?" I liked to bend the rules now and then as much as the next gal, but invading someone's privacy, not to mention taking personal property without permission, was pushing it even for me.

"Do what?" Camille said, checking under the afghan for more hidden treasures and moving on to frisk the sofa.

"Take the computer," I said.

"I'll put it back. If I had time, I'd check it here. But we have to go. Madame Papadopoulos will be home any minute."

I nodded and followed her back upstairs to the front door. We put on our boots, checked to see if the coast was clear, locked up, and hightailed it back to Camille's Jetta. Just in time to see Nia Papadopoulos pull into her driveway and get out of her car. As we drove past, I noticed Madame Papadopoulos crane her neck in the direction of Claudette's front porch before closing her own door. Camille was right. The woman really was a snoop. I just hoped she wasn't a good one because Claudette's porch light was on, and it hadn't been when we arrived.

SIXTEEN

"I DIDN'T TOUCH it."

"Well, I didn't do it."

I looked at Camille. "If you didn't and I didn't, who put that light on?"

She pulled into a parking slot in front of Starbucks, got out her phone, and pulled up her favorites list. "I'll get Laurent to go check on things."

"While you've got him, ask about Madame Shakiba and if there's any more news about the fire."

After a short conversation in French, she tapped her phone off and grabbed her bag from the back seat. "Let's get a coffee and take a peek at Claudette's laptop."

A coffee would be good. A brownie would be even better. We'd stopped for some sandwiches on the way to Claudette's but sandwiches weren't comfort food. I needed comfort food. "What did Laurent say?" I asked as we made our way over to the Starbucks entrance and went in. Or Café Starbucks as this one called itself.

"He's going over now."

We neared the counter and got in line. "No. About the fire and Madame Shakiba," I said.

"*Rien.* Just something about the wedding planner's bracelet not being broken."

So much for my theory about her throwing it into the vent. Not that I thought she would have left it there. She seemed too attached to it. But that's what had made it a good theory. She'd get the satisfaction of tossing it without the worry of someone collecting the

159

trash if she'd actually thrown it away. That way, she could retrieve it later when she'd calmed down. But if she was still missing and the bracelet was intact, Laurent was right. Things didn't look good.

"Bonjour, mesdemoiselles."

I turned my head to find the man behind the counter smiling at me. Rishi. I returned his smile and hello. Rishi was part-time Starbucks barista, part-time Masters student at McGill University, and freelance, self-proclaimed French tutor of yours truly. He originally hailed from India, and thanks to his ear for languages, he now spoke flawless French and somehow convinced himself that I could too. The fact that I was tone deaf when it came to languages didn't deter him in the least. Mostly because I hid my condition behind a smile and a nod.

Rishi looked from me to Camille. "The usual?"

We both nodded—the usual being a soy latté and brownie for me and an Espresso with a shot of whipped cream and a *chocolatine* for Camille—and Rishi placed our order.

"Vous semblez très absorbées ce soir, mesdemoiselles," he said. *"Grosse enquête?"*

Every time I came in, Rishi asked me about my work. And every time, he thought I was working on a big case. I'd become a regular at this Starbucks as soon as my last box was unloaded from the moving van, and Rishi welcomed my American self with an open heart and a curious mind. Over the time I'd been coming in, he'd learned I worked for a PI agency and now peppered me with questions when the mood struck. Problem was, Rishi's view of PIs came mostly from TV and movies. The Catwoman and Batgirl outfits Camille and I wore at the moment probably weren't helping dispel the myth.

"Just a girls' night," I said to him.

His smile thinned some, but he nodded as he passed us our food. "That is good. That will give you more time to practice your French, *n'es-ce pas*? How is it coming along?"

"Bien," I said. And it *was* good if you counted my recent exchanges with *Mignon*.

Camille waved to Rishi and stepped away to nab a free table.

I offered him a wave of my own as I started off to join her, adding in one last thing. "And thanks again for the book you gave me on irregular verbs, Rishi. It's been really helpful." Which was true. It was helping balance out a short leg on my nightstand.

His full smile reappeared and he waved his goodbyes. "You are very welcome. Next time, we move on to masculine and feminine agreement."

"Wow. I'm impressed," I said to Camille as I sat in the chair across from her. "I had no idea you Francophones had figured out masculine and feminine agreement. I had no idea there even was such a thing."

Her eyes rose from the laptop she was already busy perusing. "Only in grammar," she said. "Not in life. In life, men are nothing but trouble." She pivoted the computer so I could see the screen, and a photo of an older man came into view.

"I can't tell if that guy looks more like Harrison Ford or Sam Shepherd," I said.

"Probably both. I think it's a composite." She pointed to where the body and head came together. "And not a very good one. See the lines?"

"Who's it supposed to be?"

"Roland Marchand."

I bit off a chunk of my brownie. "And who's that?"

"*Ma tante* Claudette's new boyfriend."

I swallowed too soon, choked on brownie crumbs, and sipped my latté to ease the crumbs down my throat. "Her boyfriend? I didn't know she had a boyfriend."

"Neither did the rest of us."

Okay, so Claudette had been keeping her new guy under wraps. No crime against that. "What makes you think he's trouble?"

"Because he's the reason *ma tante* is nearly penniless."

MY HOUSE WAS dark, and the mail slot in my front door was crammed open with paper when I got home. I peeled off my outdoor layer of protection, pulled out the paper, and cracked open the vestibule door to find *Mignon* furiously wagging his tail. His eyes glazed, his mouth hanging open in a dry pant.

"You poor thing," I said to him and scooped him up. Adam must have gone out and left the dog. I'd forgotten to mention *Mignon's* little solitude phobia to Adam before I'd left but was surprised Adam had made it out of the house without noticing for himself. I walked *Mignon* into the kitchen and set him down in front of the pets' communal water bowl. He immediately set to lapping up half the contents and probably would have taken more if Pong hadn't circled in wait.

I got my own drink from the water cooler in the corner and took a look at the wads of paper I'd found in my mail slot. Notes from various neighbors expressing annoyance or concern about the wails emanating from our house. The last letter from Mrs. Millar, the one-woman neighborhood watch commando aka busybody across the street, threatening to call the police if the noise went on past ten o'clock.

I sighed and looked down at *Mignon*. "Looks like it's you and me, pup," I told him. "From now on, *mi* beach bag *es su* beach bag."

He wagged his tail and sat on my foot. Poor guy was probably homesick, too. I didn't want to tell him his overnight visit might be stretching into an extended stay until Claudette's doctors cleared her to go home. Instead, I tried to make sense of the emails Camille and I had read on Claudette's computer. Seemed that Claudette met her new beau, Roland Marchand, through an online dating site about four months ago. According to his letters, he lived in France, and from what we could tell they had yet to meet in person. Which explained how he got away with his celebrity-look-alike photo. People fudged their looks online all the time, but Roland had stretched the truth more than some and would probably have some serious "splaining" to do when the two finally laid eyes on each other in the flesh.

After two planned trips to Canada had failed, Roland had proposed to Claudette on Christmas Day, both of them promising not to tell their respective families of their upcoming nuptials until they could do it together. Meanwhile, Roland, an import/export guy, had enlisted Claudette to help him establish his business on her side of the Atlantic so everything would be up and running when he shipped himself over to reside with her on Canadian soil. And setting up the North American arm of his business apparently cost money. Lots of it. And Claudette was footing the bill.

If the computer held any more details, they'd stay hidden for the time being. The juice had run out, and Camille had dropped me at home and gone off in search of a compatible power cord for Claudette's aged laptop. Which left me with nothing to do but wonder about the unanswered questions about Claudette and her new beau. And about what happened to Madame Shakiba that had separated her from her beloved bracelet. And who had set fire to Peter's store and why. And if Helen Wong's death at *Danser* really was an accident. And if Emmaline had a thing for vendettas on behalf of her step sister. And where Adam was off to this time. And just how much caffeine was in a Starbucks soy latté and how long it would keep me up, my mind abuzz with questions.

I decided to get ready for bed and wait out the caffeine buzz tucked under my quilt with a good book. I went upstairs and into the bathroom. I scrubbed off Bunny's makeup, started the shower to warm, closed the bathroom door to lock in the heat and steam, and undressed. Wails punctuated by tiny barks started up in the hall. I yanked open the door to a panting *Mignon* and a pacing Pong, still barking.

"Oh no you don't," I said to *Mignon*. "This is too much." I waved my finger at him and backed it up with a stern "*non*."

Mignon turned in circles, wagging his tail, and Pong's barking grew louder. I scolded both of them, putting on a serious face. Just great. Just what I needed. Now Pong was getting anxiety lessons from a neurotic poodle.

"This is new."

I peered in the direction of the human voice slipped in between two barks to find Adam staring at me from the top step of the stairs beside the bathroom door.

"I had no idea this is what they taught you at doggy obedience class," he said. "If I'd have known the commands were given in the buff, I would have gone along."

I looked down at my naked body, rolled my eyes, closed the bathroom door, and went into the shower, happy to let Adam deal with the canine choir for a while.

Less than a minute later, the door opened, and Adam walked in. His head popped between the slit between the two shower curtains we used to enclose our claw-foot tub. "Want company?" he asked.

I was about to answer when the canine choir started up again.

Adam backed away from the shower. "What the hell is that?"

"Our houseguest and his back-up singer," I told him. "You must have closed the bathroom door."

Adam opened the door and the choir stopped. He closed the door and the choir started up again. He tried it two more times. "That's incredible."

He left the door partway open, stripped, and stepped into the shower with me. A draft filtered in as the open door let some of the steam escape the room, and he moved closer. "I didn't get a chance to tell you," he said. "I noticed you were low in ice cream, so I picked some up on my way home from the office."

"Is that where you were?"

He took the washcloth from me and soaped my back. "Yeah. We ran into a glitch with the game going out this month, and I needed to walk through things with the guy doing the music score. It's all good now."

"No Tina?"

"No. no Tina. And the only reason I didn't tell you about the movie and Ikea was because I didn't want to upset you. You seemed pretty pissed when I missed our dinner date because of the godfather thing, and I didn't want to get into things again."

Hmm. Not a great explanation but there was some male logic in it. "And you brought ice cream?"

"Yup."

"What kind?"

"Mint chocolate chip."

My favorite. He didn't bring the ice cream home to cross it off the shopping list. He brought it home to apologize. And it was a good apology too. Not as good as his next apology, but it ran a close second.

SOMEWHERE A PHONE was ringing. I ran out of my closet and listened in the bedroom doorway. The ringing was coming from downstairs. The Bunny phone. I ran down to get it, but it stopped by the time I found my bag. I reached in, pulled out the phone, and checked the missed calls. Laurent. Not good. He was probably wondering where I was and why I was late for work. I poured out the various pet kibbles and reached for an apple. Adam had already left, and I should have been at the office complaining about morning rush hour traffic a half hour ago. Instead, I was standing in my kitchen in gray stockings and a pink blouse eyeing the wet puddle on the floor I hoped was spilled water from the pet bowl.

I grabbed the phone again to see if it registered a message from Laurent yet. Nothing. And nothing from Anna. Disappointing but not necessarily worrisome. If the police were keeping an eye on her, chances were she was safe from harm. Whoever did kill Peter had to be smarter than to go after Anna with police floating around.

I toddled over to check Bunny's email inbox. There was a new message from Chantal at *Prêt-à-Marier* reminding me that with all the fuss that followed the finding of Madame Shakiba's bloody bracelet, I'd never chosen my invitations, and she asked me to drop by in the afternoon so we could get that done. A few messages down was the one she'd sent me with the link for the dress shop. I'd checked with Laurent and Camille and no dress suppliers were on our list of suspects, so I ignored the temptation to click through. Instead, I quit email, closed the phone, and tossed it back in my bag, hearing a ring just as I started walking away to finish dressing. Pong barked, and I realized this ring belonged to the doorbell, not the phone.

I wandered into the living room, peeled back an edge of curtain, and checked my porch. Laurent. The doorbell rang again sending *Mignon* into his pogo jumping routine accompanied by Pong's barking. I pulled the small throw blanket from my rocking chair and wrapped it around my waist sarong-style before heading for the door. Not perfect, but at least this time I was wearing underwear.

"Interesting look," Laurent said when he came in.

I smiled. "Wouldn't want to answer the door in inappropriate clothes."

He shed his boots and stepped into the hall, unbuttoning the long coat he'd left on over his jeans and revealing a blue dress shirt accessorized with a gun holster slung across his shoulder. Something must be up. Laurent was the only one of us with a gun and the only one allowed to carry one. Canadian gun laws were strict and handguns were a big no-no for most folks including PIs. And Laurent rarely carried his. It spent most of its time in a lockbox.

"No such thing as inappropriate with me, Lora," he said, a smile playing at the edges of his mouth. "It's the rest of the world you have to worry about."

No problem there. I worried about the world all the time, but not in the way he meant. Famines, earthquakes, global warming, and wars topped my world worry list. "What's up?" I asked him. Running late didn't usually garner me a home visit.

"Madame Shakiba is still missing, and it looks like you were the last person to hear from her. I need to play the message she left you. Where's your phone?"

I turned and headed for the kitchen with Laurent behind me. "Shouldn't we be out looking for her then?"

"We, Léon and Bunny, *non*. Léon and Bunny are more use in their roles, collecting information behind the scenes. With the circumstances of Madame Shakiba's disappearance, the police are looking for her. But us, we're keeping our efforts to find her low key."

I lifted my purse onto the kitchen table. "What about her family? Her husband must be worried sick."

Laurent sat and watched as I dug my hand in my purse and rooted around. "No husband," he said. "She was widowed three years ago. She has two kids—her son's in Iran on business and her daughter lives in Toronto and has four kids, the youngest not well.

They haven't been in touch with their mother in a week and are cooperating with the police, but there's nothing more for them to do."

I pulled a phone from my bag, but it was mine not Bunny's so I dumped everything out onto the table. My lip balm and a tiny bottle rolled when they landed, and Laurent whipped out his hand to catch them before they fell off the table. I spied the Bunny phone in the middle of my purse spillage, and we exchanged our finds. While Laurent checked my messages, I set the bottle and lip balm down and went to sop up the water on the floor before someone stepped in it.

"I can't get in," Laurent said. "What's the password?"

I got up and reached for the phone. "Let me do it."

He held onto the phone. "You don't trust me with your password?"

It wasn't that. I just didn't want to tell him the password. I had no imagination for passwords, and worse yet, no memory. Since this was the Bunny phone and I thought Bunny was too obvious a choice, I'd opted for Léon. Only if I told Laurent that, he'd take it as encouragement for his teasing, and I'd never hear the end of it. "Just give it to me."

Laurent shook his head and held tight to the cell. "Work phone. Someone needs access for backup."

Hmm. That sounded logical enough to be true. But the look in his eye told me it was a dubious argument at best. I picked up the portable phone from its stand on the counter and used the keypad to translate Léon into numerals. "Fifty-three, sixty-six."

He tapped it in and smiled. It took him all of a millisecond to translate it back. The guy was a detective, what did I expect?

"It means nothing," I said.

He winked at me and held up his hand in the "shush" position while he listened to Bunny's messages. He clicked off and passed me the phone.

"Any clues?" I asked him.

"Nothing jumps out. But something about it bothers me. Not sure what." He sat down at the table and surveyed my purse contents still spread out hilly nilly. He pointed to the bottle. "I thought you vegetarians were supposed to be healthier than the rest of us. What's that for?"

I picked up the vial. It was white with a torn label, a green checkered logo in the corner all that was left. And it wasn't mine. "No idea. Maybe it belongs to your aunt. Camille must have slipped it into my bag when we were at Claudette's last night."

I uncapped the bottle and peered inside. Capsules half filled the container. I closed it and set it down, something working its way to the front of my brain. "No," I said. "Camille couldn't have put it in my purse. I didn't have my purse last night. I was wearing my Batgirl clothes."

Laurent's eyebrows edged up. "Batgirl clothes?"

Omigod. Did I say that out loud? Where was the delete button when you really needed it? "I meant black clothes. I was wearing black like Camille. And I was carrying a pack not a purse."

"Then how did these pills get into your bag?"

I looked at the vial and wondered how long I'd been carting it around, my eyes gliding over to Laurent when he pulled a mini Ziplock from his pocket and extended it to me. I dropped the bottle into the plastic bag and watched him zip it closed. "I have no idea."

SEVENTEEN

"**REALLY, LORA. YOU** should have left Scooby at home," Laurent said, turning to go into his office.

I reached into my beach bag and stroked *Mignon's* back. "I couldn't. He cries. It's sad, and it bothers the neighbors." I put the poodlepack down on the floor, and *Mignon* squirmed out and set to sniffing the floor in reception. "Besides, I think he makes a cute mascot."

Laurent shook his head at the dog and closed his door.

I gave *Mignon* a reassuring smile, slipped my coat onto the back of Arielle's chair, adjusted the gray skirt I'd swapped for my makeshift sarong, sat down, and fired up Arielle's computer. My original plan for the morning was to dig into Emmaline's past some more and see if I could find anything on Madame Shakiba that might explain her disappearance, but the pill bottle that mysteriously appeared in my purse pre-empted my plan. It had me retracing my steps, trying to figure out when and how the pills got in the Bunny bag. And who put them there.

On the way into the office, I'd called Camille on the off-chance she knew anything about the pills. She didn't. And just to cover all my bases, I checked with Adam too who also knew nothing. But since I'd started clean with the purse when I started playing Bunny, I knew the bottle was a recent acquisition. And the bag had been unattended at two places: with Chantal at *Prêt-à-Marier* when I'd chased after *Mignon* and at *Danser* during the dance lesson and again during the group demo. Something told me the bottle had been planted deliberately, but I couldn't figure out why. Of course, there was always a slim chance the bottle got tossed into my bag by accident. But it was very slim. None of the women had bags like the Bunny purse, so no mix-up on that score at least.

Naturally, Laurent had suggested the pill planter was Anna. Considering the slew of pill vials I'd seen at her house, it was a reasonable suggestion. But not possible. My purse never left my lap or my attention while I was with her.

I settled into Arielle's chair and pulled up the case files. I sifted through each person's data again, looking for clues. After a half hour of perusing notes, I switched over to the Internet and ran Madame Shakiba and Chantal through my social sites and Google paces. I didn't find anything Camille hadn't already put in their files, so I gave up and strolled into Laurent's office. He was on the phone, his hand rising to the "hold on" position when he saw me, then falling when he clicked off from his call.

He leaned back in his chair, a distracted look in his eyes. "What's up?"

"I came for the pills," I told him.

He stood, went over to the blue sofa bed where he'd left his coat, reached into a pocket, and extracted the Ziplock with the pill bottle inside. "This isn't where you confess some addiction is it, Lora? I would help you, of course, but it would be a shock."

I smiled. "No." I held up the Bunny phone I'd brought with me. "I just want to take a picture of the bottle before you take it to the lab. That's the plan, right? To take it in for testing?"

He nodded and placed the Ziplock on his desk. "A picture is fine, but keep the bottle in the bag."

"Sure," I said, bending down to take my shot, then straightening to email it to my C&C account.

Laurent's phone rang when I was done, and I left him to his call, closing his door behind me as I went out.

Back at Arielle's desk, I grabbed the picture from my email and used it to run a Google comparison search on the logo. A few possibilities came back, and I combed through them looking for anything that looked like it could be connected to any kind of pill manufacturing. I hit a bingo at the bottom of the second page of results. I found a matching green checkered logo belonging to a company called Healthsups that sold a line of supplements. Clicking through to the link, the company website listed a post-box address in Detroit and an email address, no phone number.

I pulled up the photograph I'd taken of the bottle and enlarged it, trying to make out any other markings and was thrilled to see a faint "H" in a typeface that matched the Healthsups logo. I went back and browsed the company's website. It had an online catalogue of products ranging from basic vitamins to trendy supplements. No medications. As far as I could tell, the site looked the same as any other vitamin company's. Other than the lack of phone details, nothing raised any suspicions.

I grabbed the link and pasted it in an email to Laurent and Camille. I had just pressed the Send button when Camille stormed through the front door and blew into her office, yanking off her coat and tossing it into the window seat. *"Merde, merde, merde."*

I had a full view of her through her open doorway and watched her a beat to see if she was done. "Tough morning?"

She turned and looked at me. "She won't see me."

"Claudette?"

"Bien sûr, ma tante Claudette." Camille walked out my way. "Every day she gets mad when the doctors tell her to stay in *l'hôpital,* but she can't even go to the bathroom by herself. What does she expect? Crazy old fool. And now she refuses to see me, and she won't tell me a thing about her supposed fiancé Roland Marchand."

Camille's accent got stronger along with her emotions, and her syllables were coming out punched in odd places making me wish her words had subtitles. "I'm guessing you didn't learn anything more from her laptop either?"

Camille waved a hand in the air. *"Non, non.* It's useless. Laurent checked and *ma tante's* porch light came on by timer. A new one. So I went back after I dropped you at home and waited for Madame Papadopoulos to go to bed. I found the power cord for the computer, but there was nothing more on it." She turned to Laurent's closed door and crooked a finger at me. "He in a meeting?"

"Not in person," I said, glancing down at Arielle's phone system to see if his line still lit red. "But he's been on calls since we came in."

She tapped her foot, her eyes traveling south to where *Mignon* was curled up sleeping on top of the poodlepack on the floor near me. "*Pauvre petit.* You didn't need to bring him in. I can pick him up when *ma tante* finally goes home."

I started to explain about *Mignon's* aversion to solitude, but Camille's aversion to patience kicked in first. She stepped over to check Arielle's phone, took in the red button, blew out a breath, wrenched Laurent's door open, and went in. A few seconds later, Laurent's phone light went out and *Mignon* appeared beside me, perching up on his hind legs and stretching his front paws towards my lap. Poor thing was nearly shaking with distress. Couldn't blame him. Camille's voice was loud enough to be heard over a Zamboni clearing the ice between periods at a hockey game. I didn't have the sensitivity of dog ears, but I had human ones and I empathized. Camille spoke in clipped French, so probably *Mignon* and I both understood about the same amount of words, too.

Laurent came out of his office and headed for the kitchen with Camille close behind. Their conversation kept pace with their feet, and I understood enough to know the subject focused on Claudette, her mysterious new beau, and her daughter Arielle.

"*Tiens*," Camille said, coming back out to reception and snagging my coat from the hook near the kitchen door.

I sat back and looked at her. "What's up?"

She shoved my coat at me. "You're coming with me. Laurent says he can spare you for a bit, and I need you to help me with Arielle. She was due at *l'hôpital* over an hour ago, and she hasn't shown up. She's too busy with Jason to help her own mother. We're going to talk some sense into her and squeeze some information out of her."

Jason was a guy from Trinidad Arielle had been seeing for almost a year and recently shacked up with. He had a good education and a good job. And he was tall, dark, and dimpled and had muscles that belonged in a beer commercial. If Arielle was with him, chances were she wasn't so much busy as getting busy. Not that that would stop Camille from tracking her down. Or from dragging me along on her mission. So I stood to put on my coat, then I bent down to put *Mignon* into the poodlepack.

Camille wrinkled her nose at my beach bag, and I gave her the full skinny on *Mignon's* need for human companionship. Which turned her attention from me to Laurent.

He stood still in the kitchen doorway as she raised her eyebrows at him.

"Don't look at me," he said. "I've got a meeting with Luc at the PDQ and I'm not taking Scooby. When you catch up with Arielle, she'll probably want to keep him with her anyway."

I scratched *Mignon* behind his ears, feeling a sadness at the thought of passing him back to his family. He was clingy and needy and may have a slight bladder control problem, but I'd grown attached to him in less than a day. I knew he wasn't rightfully mine, but he was sure starting to feel like it.

ARIELLE LIVED IN a triplex not far from the C&C office. The area was predominantly a rental community made up of upper lower-class families. In summers, kids rode bikes on sidewalks and neighbors chatted on stoops. In winters, kids played hockey in the streets and neighbors shoveled each other's walkways. Houses were mostly multi-family units in mismatched styles, many attached in rows, the triplexes with long metal staircases that led to small balconies on the second floor that served two doors: one with direct entry for the second floor tenant and one with another staircase inside leading up to the top floor for the third-floor tenant. Arielle lived in one of the top-level flats, and it would be just my luck that that's where we'd find her.

Camille slid her silver Jetta into a space two doors down from Arielle's unit, unfazed by the fact that the Jetta was nearing a fire hydrant. She took off her hat, finger-combed her short blonde hair into spikes, touched up her lipstick, and got out of the car.

I joined her on the sidewalk and hoisted the poodlepack onto my shoulder as we picked our way through the snow to Arielle's staircase and headed up. When we got to the top of the stairs, I strained to catch my breath while Camille rang the doorbell.

No answer. She rang again. Still no answer. She rang a third time, this time depressing the button longer before letting it spring back. Still nothing. She pulled the Caron family key ring from her purse, flipped through the keys until she found the right one and inserted it into the lock. Seemed to me, the Caron key ring was getting a lot of use lately. And not for its intended purpose of emergency access. Normally I might question Camille about it, but there were extenuating circumstances here. I was cold and the poodlepack strap was digging into my shoulder.

Camille pushed the door open and called out, "*Allô*. Arielle, *c'est moi.*"

We went up the stairs that led to the inner door. This one wasn't locked. Camille opened it and called out again. We heard a faint rustling coming from the back of the house followed by a voice.

"Camille, *c'est toi*?" It was Arielle.

We both headed in the direction of Arielle's voice. "*Oui, oui.* I'm here with Lora," Camille said back, signaling a switch to English for my benefit.

We followed Arielle's voice to the end of a short hall and turned the corner into another short hall. At the end was an open door. The bedroom. We stopped dead in the doorway. Arielle and her boyfriend Jason were on the bed buck naked, her reddened curly hair splayed across the pillow, his black tight short hair glistening with sweat. They were also, umm, attached. I whipped my hands up to my eyes and turned to leave the room. Peep shows were definitely not my thing.

"Wait," Arielle said. "Don't go. We need help."

Slowly, I turned back around, keeping my eyes shielded with my hand.

Camille stood beside me, hands on hips. "*Mais voyons,*" she said. She moved closer to the bed, pulling me along beside her.

"We're stuck," Arielle said.

Stuck? Oh no. I was going to have to look, wasn't I? I peered out from one eye, keeping the other eye covered. Sure enough, upon closer look, Arielle and Jason were stuck together. They each had body piercings. Hers was on her nipple. His was in his tongue. And both were now joined together in "holy metalmony."

Camille and I looked at each other, silently contemplating the situation.

"First, we need to talk," Camille surprised me by saying. "I'll get you two apart if you tell me what's going on with your mother. I want to know why she canceled the trip to Europe with my mother, and I want to know about that new boyfriend of hers."

"Boyfriend?" Arielle repeated, shifting her body some to look at us. Not an easy task considering her hands were bound to the bed. A small squeal came from Jason, and Arielle moved back to her original position. "What boyfriend? *Maman* has a boyfriend?"

Camille nodded. "A fiancé."

Arielle shifted again. "A fiancé!"

Jason wiggled his fingers frantically. Which was pretty much his only moveable part considering he was on his knees with his hands handcuffed together behind his back and his thighs forced forward slightly because of the metal-lock.

Arielle moved back again. "Look, I don't know, okay. *Maman* hasn't told me a thing about her fight with your mother or about their trip. She said it was none of my business. That she was the mother and didn't need to explain. That was that. *Point final*. And I know nothing about a fiancé."

That was it then. To the Carons "*point final*" meant the case was closed. Even Camille knew that. Arielle was a dead end.

Camille moved to the bed, reached into the point of connection, and removed the nipple ring. Jason immediately sat back on his haunches and swallowed. "Thanks," he said when he was able to move his tongue again, following up his thanks with two successive sneezes.

Then Camille untied Arielle's hands too, got the handcuff key from the floor, and unshackled Jason. I just stood there and trained my eyes on the floor. I had never seen two people in the throes of it before. Not in the flesh. It was especially traumatic given that it was two people I knew and would have to see on a regular basis. It was an image I desperately wanted to clear from my brain. It was also an image I knew was seared into my memory for eternity. There was nothing I could do about it. So I did what anybody would do. I took another look. After all, if I was going to carry the image for eternity, I had an obligation to make sure the memory was faithful right down to the minute, or in this case not so minute, detail.

EIGHTEEN

"MERDE," **CAMILLE SAID** as she pulled into a parking spot down the street from my house.

"What's the matter?" I asked her.

She shot a look at *Mignon*. "We forgot to leave the dog with Arielle."

I reached into the poodlepack and rubbed *Mignon's* ears. "That's okay. I don't mind keeping him a while longer." Like forever.

"You can't cart him around everywhere."

"It's not so bad," I said, arranging the poodlepack and my purse so I could access the car door handle and get out. And it really wasn't bad. I got to spend time with a sweet dog. And as a bonus, I was getting quite a workout carrying him around and feeling less guilty about my lack of an exercise routine.

Camille got out of the Jetta and came around to the sidewalk on my side.

I opened my door and held the poodlepack out to her. "Hold him a sec, will you?"

She took the beach bag as I eased out of the car and rummaged in the side pocket of the bag for *Mignon's* leash, a plain, thin, blue nylon number. When I found it, I clipped it onto the dog's matching collar, slipped him out of the bag, and placed him in shallow snow near an evergreen shrub.

Camille passed me back the poodlepack and shut my car door.

"You want to stay for lunch?" I asked her. "I'm reheating some fettuccini Alfredo I got from that Italian place you like. It's got gobs of butter and cream. Just the way you like it."

177

She headed around to the driver's side of the Jetta, hesitating before getting in. "*Pas maintenant*. No time. I'm checking on a lead. I'd bring you with me if you didn't have to deal with your *ménagerie*." She closed the door and started the car, rolling the window down as she pulled out. "But not to worry. I'll talk to Arielle about picking up *Mignon* after she's done visiting her mother at *l'hôpital*. Then you'll have one less beast to deal with."

I smiled. Whenever that would be. After the tongue lashing Camille had given Arielle about familial duty just before we'd left, I'd be surprised if Arielle left her mother's side at all until Claudette was fully mended.

I waved to Camille as she drove off then I looked down at *Mignon*. He was still sniffing the shrub, finally lifting his leg, nose to the ground. He lasted maybe twenty seconds until he shivered and brought his leg back down only to alternate lifting the rest of his legs all the way home.

When I had my front door unlocked, I bent down to brush snow off his fur before taking him inside. Poor thing really needed a coat. Probably Claudette had one for him and Camille had forgotten to include it in his overnight bag. Considering the circumstances she'd been operating under when she'd gotten his stuff together, who could blame her.

"If you stay with me much longer, I'll buy you a new coat at the pet store," I said to *Mignon* as I took off my outdoor gear and put it away. "Something cute. Maybe something blue. And maybe booties too."

"Booties?" Adam said, opening the vestibule door before my hand reached the handle.

I flinched in surprise, not expecting him to be home.

"I was thinking something bigger than booties," Adam continued. "I mean, I am going to be the kid's godfather."

I stifled another flinch. Ugh. Adam must have only heard the tail end my conversation with *Mignon* and thought I was talking about buying something for Tina's baby. Which of course I would have to do. Eventually. But it wouldn't be easy. Nothing less than baby Dior would meet Tina's approval. No way could I get booties. Unless Manolo Blahnik made booties for babies.

"I was talking to the dog," I told Adam, squeezing by him and heading upstairs to make a bathroom pit stop.

Adam followed me up, a few feet behind Pong and *Mignon*, and stood outside the bathroom door with the rest of my entourage. "I was thinking about one of those cribs that grows into a bed," he said.

I came out of the bathroom and gave Pong a hello pat. "What?"

"For the baby. I was thinking of getting a crib for our shower gift."

"Un huh. That sounds nice," I said. And expensive. Neither Adam nor I made big bucks. We barely covered our expenses each month, let alone could afford posh gifts. The house had come with a second mortgage and some hefty repair bills.

He smiled. "You think? Because I'm torn between that and one of those Bugaboo strollers. I think Gwyneth Paltrow used those. Tina loves Gwyneth Paltrow."

I checked his face to see if he was joking. He wasn't. "Tough decision," I said, making my way downstairs to the kitchen. I didn't have much time to eat before I was due back at C&C and didn't have time to get into the pros and cons of choosing the right shower gift. And I definitely didn't want to get into another talk about Tina. I loved that Adam was the type of guy who was dedicated to his friend, but did his friend have to be Tina?

I heated up my fettuccini in the microwave and sat in my usual chair next to Ping, who sniffed the air when I settled in. Probably she was wondering if I was in the mood to share some of the cheesy goodness with a feline who'd had to put up with not one but two hyper canines lately.

Adam sat down across from me and looked down with a grimace when *Mignon* sat on his foot. "How long is the poodle staying anyway?" he asked me.

Since our last houseguest was Tina, I was thinking *Mignon* was an improvement. He didn't whine nearly as much, he didn't expect to be waited on hand and foot, and he smelled way better.

"I'm not sure," I told him, holding the rest of my opinions to myself. Maybe what Adam needed was more time with *Mignon* to get to know him better. Maybe I should leave the dog with him for the afternoon for a little one-on-one male bonding time. "You going to be home for the rest of the day?"

Adam cracked his knuckles, his eyes swaying between me and *Mignon*. "No. I have to run some errands before my dinner meeting."

"You mean you'll be out again tonight?"

"Yeah. Some producer wants to talk about a new game idea." He leaned across the table and reached for my hand. "I know. It sucks. Lately our schedules don't mesh at all."

I nodded, feeling the same way, only thinking it wasn't just because of work demands on his part. "Speaking of which," I said. "I've got to get back to the office. And I'm working tonight too," I said. I released his hand and got up to clear away my dishes, catching him watching me.

"You think this case will take much longer?" he asked.

I turned to face him. "Not sure. Why?"

His eyes scanned the low line of my pink blouse and the high line of my gray skirt. "No reason. Just wondering when things will get back to normal around here."

"GOOD, YOU'RE BACK," Laurent said. He pushed the front door closed behind him and strode over to Arielle's desk where I was working at her computer, doing more prying into suspects' Internet lives. So far, I'd learned very little, only that oversharing was still alive and well and out there for any Internet snoop like me to find. Unfortunately in this case, none of the oversharing was useful. Mostly it involved body habits, celebrity crushes, and youthful hangover confessions.

I smiled up at him. "Yup."

He started undoing his coat and didn't smile back. "We have to talk," he said, turning into his office.

I got up and followed him in, watching as he tossed his coat onto the sofa bed near his file cabinets. A yelp rang out, the coat started moving, and *Mignon's* head popped out from underneath.

I rushed over to pick up the dog and reset the coat. Laurent didn't seem like he was in any mood for doggy shenanigans.

"What did you want to talk about?" I asked.

Laurent stepped over to the sofa bed, lifted his coat, and scanned the couch. Probably he knew about *Mignon's* nervous bladder. Probably he was checking for damp spots. All must have been dry because he slid his coat to the end of the couch, sat down, and patted the cushion beside him. "Come. Sit."

I sat down, shifting my body to rest sideways on the couch to face Laurent, *Mignon* in my lap.

"Remember the woman who died at *Danser*?" Laurent said.

I rubbed *Mignon's* ears and the dog's eyes pinched closed like a purring cat. "Helen Wong," I said. "The woman with diabetes. She had some kind of problem with her medication."

Laurent nodded. "*Oui*. A drug interaction, actually. She mixed her medication with something called ginkgo without checking with her doctor first. It messed with her insulin and by the time someone found her unconscious in the bathroom and got her help it was too late."

I moved my hand down to stroke *Mignon's* back, curious where Laurent was going with this.

"According to the police files," he went on, "her death was ruled accidental. They found a bottle of the ginkgo at her apartment and think she was taking it for a while. Only her fiancé said he knew nothing about it when I spoke with him."

That must have been one of the calls keeping Laurent busy earlier. "Maybe she didn't tell him," I suggested. "Isn't ginkgo some herbal supplement? That's like taking vitamins to most people. Not something most of us talk about, we just take them with breakfast and get on with our day." I still remember biting the heads off my Flinstones vitamins when I was a kid, the purple and pink ones being my favorite. The orange I left to last hoping I wouldn't have to eat them, and I always believed that if I'd have had siblings I would have gotten away with it.

"It's possible," Laurent said. "But there's more. Peter's final autopsy results are in. They pinpoint exactly what substance killed him. It was ginkgo."

My hand stopped moving and *Mignon's* eyes eased open slightly. "You mean along with the Prozac? Some kind of drug interaction like Helen Wong?"

"*Non.* In Peter's case, it was just ginkgo. Ginkgo seeds, actually."

I smiled. "This is good news, right? Not for Helen or Peter, of course, but for Anna. This could clear her of involvement, right?"

Laurent sat forward, his knee bumping mine, rousing *Mignon* to jump off my lap. "*C'est possible.* Especially if the two deaths are related. It definitely complicates things," he said, his face showing none of the enthusiasm of mine. "This particular brand of ginkgo is not sold in stores. Only on the Internet."

"What kind is it?"

His eyes latched onto mine. "It's from a company called Healthsups."

"Right," I said, recognizing the name straight away from my own earlier detective work. "That place in Detroit."

Laurent's eyebrow twitched. "Good research. Only it's not really an American firm. The company works out of Asia, but they use an American address on their website."

He went quiet a beat, and realization hit me.

"So the pills we found in my Bunny purse, they're from the same company?"

He smiled. "*Oui.* Not just from the same company, but the same supplement. The bottle I took to the lab was filled with ginkgo." His eyes slipped to *Mignon* who'd come back and jumped into my lap again.

"Wow. Fast lab," I said, my mind trying to make sense of this new development.

"Things go faster when they check for specifics. And this ginkgo was very specific. It belonged to a batch that had been recalled."

Uh oh. "For what?"

"The batch was tainted with fresh ginkgo seeds."

I looked down at *Mignon* as he settled on me. "I don't get it. If the supplement was made from ginkgo and ginkgo has seeds, what's the problem?"

"The problem is the seeds can be deadly. Ginkgo supplements need to be made carefully. Most with leaves. Some putting seeds through a process to make them safe for use."

"And this ginkgo wasn't safe? It was recalled?" I thought back to my browse of the company's website. "I didn't see any recall notice on the Healthsups site."

"It's there," Laurent said. "It was a voluntary recall, and it's public knowledge. It's announced in their News section."

That could explain why I didn't see it. When I'd been checking the site, I'd been focused on products not publicity. "But who would want to put recalled ginkgo into Bunny's bag? And why?"

Laurent reached over and gently tugged a strand of my hair. "That's what we need to find out."

I contemplated that, not liking the ginkgo link to Peter and Helen's death. Or its sudden appearance in my Bunny bag. None of that was feeling like a coincidence. "How?" I asked.

I massaged *Mignon's* tiny head as I spoke, my fingers moving aimlessly along the dog's fur until I touched on wet cloth and bent to find a strip of fabric hanging out from the side of the his mouth. I eased his mouth open and pulled out a soggy sock. My eyes trailed to the duffel bag in the corner of Laurent's office. It was stuffed with hockey gear and unzipped partway. I was also guessing it was minus one sock.

Laurent stood and pulled me up, putting his hand to the small of my back as I cradled *Mignon*, and steered me and my poodle friend out of his office and closed the door. Then he lifted the dog out of my arms and put him on the floor. *Mignon* looked up, his head shifting back and forth in time with his tail as he looked from Laurent's face to mine, before he scampered over to the poodlepack nearby and curled up on top of it.

"For starters, you'll need to find a babysitter for Scooby tonight," Laurent said. "He's not coming to *Danser* with us."

I looked over at *Mignon*, already snoozing. Ordinarily, I would leave him with Adam but with his dinner meeting running until goodness knows when, not to mention Tina back in the picture luring Adam out on secret outings, that didn't seem wise. I didn't want to come home to a note-filled mailbox again. "He'll be fine with us," I said. "I'll keep a close eye on him."

"*Non*. Not tonight. Tonight you won't be the one keeping an eye on anyone. I'll be keeping an eye on you."

I raised an eyebrow at him as he moved in closer and picked a strand of chewed off sock from my shoulder.

"Two people are dead and ginkgo is the only link. We may not understand the connection. But someone out there does. Someone who planted that ginkgo on you. Which means either that someone is setting you up or sending you a warning."

"A warning? A warning about what?"

"My guess is a warning to butt out and stop asking nosy questions."

I'd been careful about my questioning for the most part and couldn't see anyone pegging me as nosy. "That's a pretty big warning if the stuff is killing people. And if the someone who planted it is just hoping I'll take the stuff and end up like the first two who did, that's a pretty sloppy murder attempt."

"Right. That's why if we're lucky, they're more interested in setting you up."

I thought about how I was closest to Peter when he fell. And how I'd been to Anna's house not two days after his death. And how I'd been the last one to hear from the missing Madame Shakiba. And how "my" dog had been the one to find her bloody bracelet. And how the ginkgo in my bag might not look so good to a cop. I didn't think any of it really made me look guilty of wrongdoing, but to someone looking for a patsy to throw suspicion on it might make me a good candidate. "How is someone wanting to set me up a lucky thing?"

Laurent's eyes flashed. "Because we're going to let them."

NINETEEN

OKAY, SO NOW I had to be fun, flirty, pregnant, *and* a decoy. Fabulous. I was still struggling with the first three. "Get a grip, Lora," I said to my reflection in the bathroom mirror. Only I had come home to ramp up my Bunny look, so the eyes looking back at me belonged to her not me. And for a second I could have sworn Bunny winked at me. That couldn't be good.

Probably it was just nerves I told myself as I went to get dressed. I pulled out a Bunny skirt and some dark stay-up stockings. I didn't want to go the garter route again. The garter belt itched me, and I figured stay-ups would work just as well. The skirt was royal blue, and I teamed it with a flowered white blouse I found in the back of my closet and finished off with Bunny's jewelry, swapping out the hoop earrings for heart-shaped fake diamond ones that dangled down nearly to my jawbone.

I gave myself a cursory once-over in the full-length mirror, avoiding eye contact with myself, and headed downstairs just as the doorbell rang. The dogs went into their barking routines, and I shushed them as I scooted around their dancing legs to answer the ring. Not that the shushing helped. If anything it seemed to prod them on to go louder. I opened the door to Camille who darted a look at the dogs followed by a sharp "*arrête*" command and was rewarded with silence.

"I'm double parked," she said to me. "Is *Mignon* ready?"

Camille was the only dog-sitter I could round up on short notice. She had no pets of her own and dog-sitting was the last thing she wanted to do, but *Mignon* was family, and she'd do just about anything for family. Especially Claudette, who was still stuck in the hospital in pain, Arielle now glued to her bedside. I bent to pick up the dog and put him in the poodlepack.

"*Non, non,*" Camille said. "No bag. Just the dog. *Il y a des limites là.*" She cocked her head, looking at my legs. "Are you wearing stay-ups?"

I stood, *Mignon* in my arms. "Yeah."

She shook her head. "You need the garter belt. Stay-ups won't last long with the tall boots. The boots will pull them down and loosen the grip band."

"I didn't plan on wearing the tall boots. I'm wearing the ankle boots outside and bringing shoes."

She shook her head. "Just do the boots. No shoes. You can dance in the boots."

Fat chance. I could barely dance in the shoes.

"And what's with that blouse?" she asked. "I don't remember buying that blouse. That looks like it came off of *Little House on the Prairie.*" She yanked off her coat, tossed it onto my iron coat stand in the vestibule, and started undoing her own shirt. A lavender crochet number cut low on the top and high on the bottom. She held out the shirt to me. "*Tiens.* We'll switch."

"Why?"

She glared at me, and I glared back.

"I don't have time for this," she said. "Give me your shirt and just trust me."

I put the dog down and swapped shirts with her. Partly because I felt bad that she'd get cold standing there in only a bra and because I didn't want her Jetta to get ticketed, but mostly because I did trust her. Camille's confidence could come off bossy to some, but I knew better. She was smart and she had an annoying habit of being right. Plus, she was way more savvy about this stuff than I was.

Someone beeped outside, and Camille poked her head out. "Gotta go. I'm blocking the road." She threw her coat back on and held her arms out to receive *Mignon* and the small bag of his food I'd prepared, her eyes on mine as my right eye twitched. "*Mais voyons*, Lora. Don't be nervous," she told me. "You'll do fine. Just follow whatever Laurent tells you."

I closed and locked the door behind her and went to switch into my garter belt, thinking that last bit of advice could get me into a whole lot of trouble.

LATE AFTERNOON DARKNESS had already set in, stretching the evening ahead of me into one long night. I'd left a note for Adam on the fridge telling him I wouldn't be home until late. Laurent and I were making a pit stop by *Prêt-à-Marier* before it closed to see Chantal and talk wedding invites. If someone had planted the ginkgo on Bunny, it was at *Prêt-à-Marier* or *Danser*. And it was a good bet the someone didn't do it to share. Laurent figured we could flush out the culprit and catch them in the act if they tried to throw a little more trouble Bunny's way. In principle, the logic seemed sound, and I definitely liked the idea of finding someone to deflect the blame for Peter's death off of Anna. I just didn't like the idea of that someone throwing a little blame my way in the process.

"You're fidgeting again. You can't be cold, the heat is set on sauna in here," Laurent whispered to me.

"I'm not cold," I whispered back. "It's this damn garter belt Camille made me wear. I think it's giving me a rash."

He leaned over closer to me, his hand brushing my thigh. "Want me to check?"

I pushed him back to his own chair. "No! Just sit over there and ignore me."

He smiled and sat back. We were waiting for Chantal while she finished up with another couple. She'd ushered us into a sectioned space down the way from her cubicle. The space was larger than hers and an oblong maple table sat dead center surrounded by six chairs, a matching breakfront flat against the far dividing wall, and a buffet on the other side. All of it looking like a dinette set from an estate sale.

"This whole thing is crazy anyway," I said. "How could anyone want to frame me for anything? Anna's already a suspect in Peter's death and Helen Wong's death wasn't even investigated."

"Nothing's public yet about Peter's murder or Anna's involvement. This isn't about what the public knows. This is about what the killer knows. And what he'll do to protect himself."

"He? You think the killer is a man?"

"Figure of speech," Laurent said, then quieted when Chantal finally appeared in the opening that served as the entrance to the cubicle.

Chantal paused a moment, her breath coming a bit fast. Her cheeks were red, her hair in shoulder-length brown pony tails over each ear. And her hoop skirt poked out below a tight sweater, the effect giving her the shape of a feather duster. She took a few deep breaths then made her way over to the table and took a seat across from us.

"So glad you guys could come in," Chantal said. "We really need to get moving on things for you." She opened a laptop computer she'd brought with her and eyed the screen. "In Madame Shakiba's, umm, absence, I've taken over your file. We really need to lock down your invites today, but there's so much more to do. And we don't have much time. I was hoping we could just run through a bunch of things while you're here. Sound good?"

I nodded. "Anyone have any idea what happened to Madame Shakiba?" I asked her. I knew we hadn't heard any updates yet, but someone had to know something and her assistant was as likely as anyone. Plus, I wanted to gauge her reaction to Madame Shakiba's disappearance.

Chantal lowered her voice. "No one knows a thing. It's spooky. It's like she just vanished. Part of me wishes they'd close the place down until she turns up. But another part of me is grateful to work and keep my mind off of it, you know?"

Hmm. Nothing odd about that answer. Or how she was coping. Anna was dealing with Peter's absence by plunging into work too. "I know what you mean."

She smiled, her lips forming more of a pinch than a grin. "So let's focus on you and making your big day all it can be, okay?"

I nodded again and listened as she listed everything we had yet to arrange—from dress buying and honeymoon booking to suit rentals and thank you notes. We went through the items one by one, and I did my best to make decisions, allowing her to guide my choices and crossing my fingers that I wasn't making any arrangements that Michel couldn't undo or cover. I also filled her in on decisions already made like the flowers and the cupcakes I'd taken over from Anna, and Chantal took it all down quickly and efficiently. None of her behavior seemed out of the ordinary to me, and she hadn't shown any extra interest in me or my Bunny purse. But I had no idea if Laurent had other observations to add. He sat quietly until the topic of the honeymoon came up, when he leaned forward and told Chantal that he had that covered.

Chantal turned a conspiratorial smile Laurent's way. "Ah, a surprise for your bride I bet."

He pulled me close and stroked the back of his hand on my cheek. "*Oui*, I have lots of surprises in mind for *mon lapin*."

I gave Laurent's leg a warning knock under-the-table. He tapped my leg back and added a squeeze to my thigh. The man could so not take a hint.

Through it all, Chantal went right on smiling, and I couldn't help comparing her smile to Madame Shakiba's judgmental glower. Chantal was exactly what a bride wanted in a wedding planner. She was upbeat, thorough, knowledgeable, and skilled at giving direction. We'd covered way more ground with her in fifteen minutes than we had in our initial one-hour session with Madame Shakiba.

"Great. All we have left then is the invitations," Chantal said, glancing down at her laptop then getting up and going over to the buffet behind her, sliding open a drawer, pulling out a few stacks of cards, and bringing them back to the table. "Have a look at these," she said. "It's way easier to tell color and texture from seeing them in person. You wanted pink, right?"

"Right," I said, reaching out to look through the cards she'd placed on the table, all in various tones of pink. I made a show of sifting through them then passed her a simple pale rose one with some etching at the side. "This is good."

"Wow," she said. "That was easy. I wish all my couples were as decisive as you. And what about the inscription?"

Laurent and I looked at each other a beat, each registering that the other hadn't prepared anything.

"Can I email that to you later?" I said.

Chantal nodded. "But latest tomorrow morning okay? I've got to get the order in."

She went on to ask for registry details to include in the invitations. Since I didn't know the local shops popular for bridal registration, I let Laurent answer that one, hoping he wouldn't embarrass me again. He gave her a name I didn't recognize, and she made a note, no comments or conspiratorial smiles this time to my relief.

Behind Chantal, a man appeared at the entranceway and knocked on the side of the buffet in lieu of a door. He was late thirties, Asian, and dressed in gray suit pants, a white dress shirt, and a tie. From the employee info I'd seen on the *Prêt-à-Marier* website, I recognized him as the other wedding planner, Kai Chin. The one Michel didn't want us to investigate. "Sorry to interrupt, Chantal," he said. "But a guy's waiting for you at reception."

Chantal turned to look at him. "Thanks, Kai. Could you ask him to wait in my office."

Kai agreed and headed off with a wave. If he knew or recognized Laurent, he didn't show it.

"That must be my boyfriend," Chantal said, darting a look at her computer. "I didn't realize it was so late, but we're good for today, right? Just don't forget to send me the invitation copy, okay?" She wound down her laptop, closed the lid, and stood.

Laurent and I stood too, me stumbling as my left foot buckled, tingling with numbness. My foot had gone to sleep while I was sitting. Probably the stiletto boots. They propped my legs higher than I was used to and played with my circulation. I righted myself and headed out behind Chantal, walking lopsided, favoring my good leg, with Laurent a few feet behind me. I stumbled again as we moved down the cubicle corridor and felt hands grab my arm to steady me. Moist, cushy hands far too cold to be Laurent's. I looked up to find Benoît from *Bon Souper* smiling at me and standing in the entryway to Chantal's cubicle, and I stumbled once more, this time from surprise.

"SO BENOÎT IS Chantal's boyfriend," I said to Laurent as we chugged along slushy streets in the Léon car en route to *Danser*. "Another coincidence? Like the picture of Peter at *Bon Souper*?"

"Maybe."

I knocked him on the arm with the back of my hand. "Oh, c'mon. We both know it's more than that. She's one of the people we're supposed to be watching *and* she's dating a guy from one of the suspect suppliers. That's got to be more than a coincidence."

Laurent slid his eyes over to his arm and back to the road. "It's nothing more unless we find a connection to the case."

I rolled my eyes. Mister stickler. One of the things I learned working as a social worker is that feeling are facts to the people who have them, and I had a habit of trusting my feelings and following my instincts. But in the PI biz, only facts were facts. Instincts were considered hunches until proven to be more. At least mine were. Laurent and Camille's hunches seemed to qualify as educated guesses. I hoped eventually mine would too.

"I'm surprised Camille didn't put this in the file," I said.

"She would have if she'd known."

True. But how could she not have learned Chantal and Benoît were a couple when she gathered preliminary background on the case? Or when she went over Chantal's computer at *Prêt-à-Marier*? There had to be emails or something between the two. Camille was good. Missing the remote stepsister connection between Peter's ex and Emmaline was one thing, but this coupling should have been obvious. The fact that it apparently wasn't upped Chantal higher on my list of suspects, much as I hated to admit it. I liked Chantal and up until this little tidbit came to light, I hadn't seen anything that got me thinking she was linked to the identity thefts or Peter's death. And I hadn't even considered her connecting to Helen's

Wong's. But the way Chantal whipped up my email addy the other day reminded me she had access to a lot of personal information on her clients. Information ripe for identity theft.

"Do we know if Helen Wong was working with *Prêt-à-Marier?*"

Laurent nodded. "She was. With Madame Shakiba."

"Well then, see. There is a connection to the case. Was she an identity theft victim too?"

"Not her, but her fiancé was."

I shot him a "duh" look, excitement starting to brew. "Well see. This must be it. Chantal must be involved. And maybe her beau Benoît too."

Laurent pulled into the parking lot at *Danser* and cut the engine. "*C'est possible.* But not a good idea to jump to conclusions too soon. You can miss other possibilities if you do. Who knows what the rest of the night will bring? Remember, both Peter and Helen died at *Danser.*" He reached into his inside pocket and took out a tiny gizmo the size of a watch battery only square, and he leaned over and started to unzip my boot.

"What are you doing?" I asked him.

He dropped the gizmo into my boot and re-zipped me. "It's a transmitter, so I can track you if you're out of my sight."

Was that why Camille insisted I wear the boots? "Why would you need to track me?"

"In case we get separated and something happens."

Hmm. "Something like what?"

He shrugged. "Not to worry. It's just a precaution. Probably nothing will happen."

His words would have been a lot more reassuring if they hadn't come out of his poker face. One thing I was learning about the Carons was that the only time they hid emotions was when they were protecting something. In this case, I was getting the eerie feeling like I was the something Laurent was protecting.

TWENTY

EVERYONE HAD LEARNED their dances for the night and was gathering in the big room for show time. Laurent sat next to Sébastien, seemingly deep in conversation, my Bunny bag abandoned on the chair on his other side. I was positioned over by the refreshment table with instructions to chat up Sylvain. Or as Laurent put it: use my do-gooder charm to crack him. So far, it wasn't going well. So far, all I'd managed to crack was a fingernail when I'd gripped my coffee mug too hard.

I squelched a squirm, my garter belt itch flaring up, and tried another tack. "Your studio is really impressive," I said to Sylvain. "How long have you had it?"

Sylvain patted the Baryshnikov wave in his hair. "Five years."

"Wow. You're so young to be so successful."

"Dancers are young. But most of us have been building our careers since we were small kids. Me, I've been working over twenty-five years."

If he was mid thirties like I thought, that would peg him at about ten when he put on his first ballet shoes. "Still," I said. "Not everyone makes it."

He nodded and smiled. "That's true."

"And not everyone can choreograph."

He smiled some more.

"And so well with such tricky music," I said. "I don't know how you and Cindy do it."

Sylvain lost his smile. "Cindy does not choreograph. Cindy is only an instructor."

Ah. Sore spot. Bingo. I feigned a confused look and went into a fib. "Oh. Really. While she was teaching us our dance, she gave me the impression she'd created it."

Sylvain's eyes panned the room for Cindy. And mine followed, finding her going through a move with the new guy who replaced Peter. Judging by the vein making itself prominent on Sylvain's forehead, I was guessing it was a no-no for her to work with anyone outside her assigned student couples. Cindy was supposed to teach Laurent and me, and Juliette and Sébastien. The new guy belonged to Sylvain.

"*Excuse-moi*," Sylvain said to me, already bustling away and making a beeline for Cindy.

Less than a minute later, new guy was benched, and Sylvain and Cindy were going at it by their table again. Their little *tête-a-têtes* were becoming a running bit during our classes. But this one included some looks my way. Looks that did not look happy. Which meant my mission was a success. I managed to agitate Sylvain *and* Cindy. In one shot.

I drained my coffee and strolled over to the chair beside Laurent, turning my attention to Emmaline and the other betrothed couples around me. Since I had spent time with our fellow students during the last lesson, Laurent wanted me to focus one-on-one time with staff this session. But I was still getting a bad vibe from Emmaline, and in the spirit of staying open to possibilities, I wanted to keep tabs on everybody else too. Especially now that I was offering myself up as bait. The plan being to dangle myself around to see if whoever had decided to play hot potato with the ginkgo and dropped it in Bunny's purse would be moved to up the ante. At the moment, everybody looked innocent and bored as they sat waiting. Everyone except Cindy and Sylvain.

Laurent threw his arm around the back of my chair when I sat and rubbed his fingers into the back of my hair, never breaking his conversation with Sébastien. I took the hair rubbing as acknowledgment of a job well done. Not that I'd exactly cracked Sylvain, but I definitely chipped something.

When the music finally started for the first demo of the night—Emmaline and George's dance—Cindy had kitty-cornered her chair at the table she shared with Sylvain and was scribbling furiously in a notebook. And by the time Laurent and I took our positions to dance to our first Bryan Adams' tune, the slow one not the stripper one, Cindy sat with her arms folded across her chest, notebook hugged to her heart. I tried not to stare as I waited for our music to begin, barely even registering my stage fright this time. I really wanted a look at that notebook.

And between trying to figure out how to get my hands on the book and watching the Bunny bag to see if anyone approached it, I completely fumbled my footing when we began our number. But at least I hadn't fumbled from fear this time. That had to count as progress. Laurent squeezed my hand and locked eyes with me, and I mouthed an apology and tried to focus but goofed again a few steps later.

He pulled me tighter, bringing his mouth to my ear. "What?"

Not tall enough to reach his ear, I motioned towards Cindy with my eyes.

He nodded and dipped his head to whisper in my ear again, his hot breath tickling, "Don't push it. Remember rule number one."

An idea forming, I scooped my hands behind his neck and drew him down to me in an improv move. "And you, rule number two," I countered.

Laurent straightened, shooting me two raised eyebrows as Bryan sang out something about loving someone and lonely nights.

I smiled and shimmied out of Laurent's arms, keeping hold of his hand while I did a slow turn, moving us closer to Cindy and Sylvain's table. I caught the look of confusion in Sylvain's face, probably wondering what the turn was doing in his choreography. And, as his face went darker, probably wondering if Cindy had messed with his work. I looped back to Laurent's arms, skimming my hip on the side of his leg to quell a garter belt itch, and then stretched back out for another turn, accidentally on purpose bumping into the table just as Sylvain reached out to shut off the music.

"*C'est quoi ça?*" he said, glaring at Cindy. "What did you do to my dance?"

She glared back at him. "I don't know what they're doing. I didn't teach them that."

"Well, who else?" Sylvain said.

Cindy threw her notebook down on the table and yelled something back at him in French.

And while the two of them went a few rounds, I inched closer to the table, pulling Laurent with me for cover, and snatched the notebook. My outfit had no pockets and no easy hiding place, so I wedged the book down the front of my skirt and started to step away when I heard Cindy's voice behind me.

"Hey. Wait. Where are you going?"

Damn. So close. I cringed, stopped, and turned an innocent face towards her. "Bathroom," I said, clamping my hand over my mouth and clutching my belly with the other hand, remembering I had a fake baby in there who would come in handy about now. I started walking again, faster this time, hoping to clear the room without more interference, the hand clutching my belly helping keep me from dropping the book.

When I got to the ladies' room, I rushed into a stall, locked it, and pulled out the notebook. Up close, I saw it was a yearly agenda, a full page dedicated to each day of the year with a tiny calendar alongside spaces for common notations like birthdays and appointments at the top, leaving the remaining two-thirds of the page lined but blank. Every page up until current day was filled with Cindy's scrawl. In French. I could only make out a few words here and there in the bottom sections, mostly food items I'd seen on French labels in the aisles at my local grocery store. But up top, Cindy had crossed out three of the categories next to the mini monthly calendar and entered her own headings. Those were easy to figure out. She had one for weight, one for calories, and one for mood. The weight and calorie slots filled in so far had one entry each, but the mood slots all had a slew of little circle faces beside them—some happy, some sad, some angry—in various order. Some days had only a few faces. Others had rows of faces that went well beyond the allotted space.

I flipped through the rest of the agenda. Nothing else was filled in. No phone numbers, no appointments, nothing. Probably Cindy used her cell phone to organize her life. Probably she could have stored this info in her phone too if she was tracking a food allergy or counting calories. There were excellent phone apps for that. This was something more than a food diary.

A high-pitched creaking suddenly echoed through the bathroom, ricocheting off the tiles. The sound of rusty hinges. Someone was easing open the door. I sucked in a breath and froze, nearly dropping Cindy's book into the toilet. Quiet footsteps drew close to my stall, black pumps coming into view. The thought of Helen Wong discovered unconscious in this very same bathroom, maybe even this very same stall, flashed in my head, and I hoped the last thing she ever saw wasn't black pumps.

"You okay, Bunny?"

I blew out a breath of relief when I recognized Juliette's voice.

"Fine," I called back, stuffing the agenda back down my skirt as quietly as I could, strapping it in place with the garter belt. Camille was right, lingerie really was a great PI tool. The garter belt did a great job of helping me hide the notebook. And as a bonus, the notebook created a buffer between the itchy fabric and my skin. I sent Camille a mental high-five on the lingerie call, gave the toilet a flush, and slid the stall lock open.

Juliette had made her way over to the mirror above one of the three sinks and was touching up her mascara when I walked out. She wore a green sweater that looked hand knit over stretch jeans that fit like a second skin, hugging her narrow hips as she leaned over the sink.

"Everything good?" she asked me, talking to me through her reflection in the mirror.

I washed my hands and yanked a paper towel from the dispenser between us. More habit than necessity since I'd only used the stall to sneak a peek at Cindy's book without any looky loos in eyeshot. "Sure. Everything okay back there?"

She switched her mascara for her lipstick and touched up her mouth, waiting to answer until she'd blotted her lips with a tissue. "Ben and Violette should be finished their dance by now. They were the last to go."

That meant we'd be wrapping up, and if Cindy hadn't already missed her book, she'd be looking for it soon. I wished I'd had my bag with the Bunny phone in it, so I could have taken pictures of some of the entries and given the book back. Now I would have to borrow Cindy's notebook until the next lesson. Well, not me. Bunny would have to do the borrowing. I would never do such a thing.

The door burst open and let out a screech, the old hinges begging for oil again, and Emmaline strode in. She slung her purse on the counter by the third sink and checked herself in the mirror, re-tucking her red blouse into her long, black skirt. *"J'ai mal à la tête. Quelqu'un a du Tylenol?"*

"Je pense que oui," Juliette said, scrounging through her handbag. "Headache," she said to me in case I hadn't understood Emmaline. I had. Camille talked about being *mal à la tête* now and again. Mostly when she was accusing someone of causing it.

Juliette pulled out some Midol from her purse. "Sorry, I only have this," she said, holding it out to Emmaline. "You want one?"

Emmaline rubbed her temples hard. *"Merci, merci,"* she said. *"Deux, s'il te plait."*

Juliette popped out two tablets and passed them to Emmaline who threw them in her mouth and bent to drink water from the tap.

"Those two are incredible," Emmaline said when she stood again. "All they do is fight. My sister was crazy to send me here."

"Your sister?" I said, innocently as though I had never heard of her stepsister, Celeste, or the ex-engagement to Peter.

Emmaline looked my way. Her bangs like dark, heavy clouds over stormy eyes. "My sister took lessons here with a man she was going to marry. The fiancé turned out to be a bastard. The lessons she raved about."

"At least she found out he was a bastard before she got married," Juliette said.

198

Emmaline nodded and turned to go into a stall. "Damn straight. And she got to see him pay for it, too."

Juliette's eyes trailed Emmaline to the stall then turned back to the mirror and winked at me. Just when I thought I'd get through a whole night at *Danser* sans winks. Now the women were doing it too.

THOSE WERE HER exact words," I told Laurent when he pulled the Léon car over several blocks from *Danser* and parked. I had my head bent over Bunny's purse, my hand sifting through the contents for unfamiliar additions. "I'm telling you, Emmaline is happy Peter's dead." With everything else going on, I hadn't had a chance to do any more digging into Emmaline and was starting to regret it. Nobody ever warns you about the sister of the woman scorned but maybe they should.

Laurent flipped on the overhead light. "I'm not worried about Emmaline. Camille found nothing on her. She's angry, yes, but that doesn't make her a killer. And she didn't even know Helen Wong." He reached his hand out towards me. "Let me see Cindy's book."

Finding nothing in the Bunny bag, I pulled my hand out and undid my seat belt. Then I opened my coat and reached into my skirt for the notebook. It was jammed in tight by the garter belt and bent from my sitting position that held half the book on my legs.

"Need help?" Laurent asked, leaning towards me, his eyes fixed on the top of my skirt.

I slid down in my seat, straightening my midsection to make it easier to pull the book out. "No. I got it." I sat up, flattened the bend in the book, and passed it to Laurent.

"It's hot," he said, opening the book and flipping the pages.

I shot him my second "duh" look of the night and scratched at my belly before re-closing my coat. With the freezing temperatures in the car, the book wouldn't stay warm for long. I glanced at the notebook and leaned in so I could see what page Laurent had stopped at. "So what's it say?" I asked him.

"Not much. Just complaints. Things people do that bother her."

"Bother her how?"

He read a few entries, flipping pages and translating for me. *"He's putting me down again, I feel horrible, really want Oreos. She criticized everything—my clothes, my makeup, my boyfriend, skipped dinner. Failed driving test again, ate half a cheesecake."*

"And today's page?"

Laurent skipped ahead to the last page that was filled in. "It's about Sylvain not respecting her talent and her wanting to quit and eat pudding." He closed the book, gave it back to me, started the car, and pulled out. "Nothing in there about poisoning people with ginkgo."

I stuffed the book into my bag and put my gloved hands out to warm on the burst of hot air that spewed from the side vent. The book wasn't just things that bothered Cindy. It connected food to feelings. Could be Cindy was keeping track for her own purposes, but my guess was that the book was for showing to someone. Probably a therapist. Cindy was as skinny as a stiletto heel but clearly had a habit of emotional eating. Got me thinking eating disorder. A serious one. The notebook may not be shedding much light on the case, but it was shedding light on Cindy, and I was starting to see her from a whole new perspective.

Laurent pulled onto my street and slowed the car. There were no free spots near my house, so he stopped in the driveway. He got out his phone and checked his messages then stretched over to me, unzipped my boot, stuck his hand in, and withdrew the tracking gizmo he'd dropped in earlier. "You haven't been wearing the locket from your mother," he said. "Where is it?"

I was startled by his mention of my mom's locket and touched he remembered it. "I took it off to play Bunny. Why?"

He slipped the gizmo into my glove. "Put this in the locket and go back to wearing it. Always."

I looked down at the glove, feeling the gizmo bump through the cotton with my other hand. It was small enough to fit in the locket for sure, but the idea of wearing it all the time bothered me. And seemed like overkill. No one had shown any interest in me all night. Nothing out of the ordinary anyway. Even with my poking at Sylvain and taking Cindy's book. Nobody had dumped anything new in my

Bunny bag either. Which is what I explained to Laurent when I tried to object.

And that's when he told me about the text he just got from Camille telling him Madame Shakiba was found late this afternoon. Dead. Her body wrapped in a carpet and left in a laneway dumpster. No personal effects, just a vial of ginkgo in her coat pocket.

TWENTY-ONE

THE NEWS WENT public the next morning. The media was all over it. I got my first eyeful on a local TV morning show. Thankfully, there were no pictures of Madame Shakiba's body. But there were plenty of the alleyway where she was found. Mere blocks from *Prêt-à-Marier* in a residential section. Lots of multi-family houses backed on to the laneway, so the police thought there was a good bet someone saw something and were encouraging the public to call in to the number flashing at the bottom of the screen.

Adam strolled into the living room from the kitchen, cereal bowl in hand, and looked at the TV. Probably hoping for some Saturday morning cartoon fun, but this day was not shaping up to be about fun. It was shaping up to be about work. I didn't usually work Saturdays unless a case called for it but this one definitely did.

"This about the hooker case?" he asked me.

I grimaced and looked down at my Bunny outfit for the day. Tight, hipster jeans and a clingy white sweater with pink sparkles lining the V in front. Not conservative but not hooker. "It's about Michel's case," I said. "There *is* no hooker case."

He sat down beside me on the couch. "What happened?"

"One of Michel's wedding planners died." An ache tugged at my chest as I spoke. It was the first time I'd said it out loud and somehow it made it real. And the more real it got, the more sick I felt. Madame Shakiba may not have been the most likeable person I'd ever met, but she didn't deserve to have her life end this way. Nobody did.

"In that alley?" Adam asked me.

"I don't know if she died there, but she was found there." I explained about the carpet and the bloody bracelet *Mignon* had found at *Prêt-à-Marier*, leaving out the ginkgo find. The police hadn't made that detail public yet, and I didn't know if I was allowed to either. But they were releasing probable cause of death. Head injury. Hard to imagine it was accidental given Madame Shakiba was found wrapped up in the carpet like a burrito.

"I knew this case was trouble," Adam said, putting his bowl down on the coffee table. "You need to back out. It's too dangerous. Let someone else find out who offed Peter and the wedding planner. You're a social worker, you're supposed to help live people not dead ones."

"Hey, dead people deserve help too. And I'm not a social worker anymore, I'm a PI."

"A PI's assistant," Adam corrected.

"A PI in training," I re-corrected.

The doorbell rang, and Ping lifted her head from my lap where she'd been napping to shoot Pong a look when she barked. I shifted Ping to the cushion beside me and went to get the door. When I opened it, *Mignon* bounced in with Camille holding his leash out to me.

"Take him or I'll ship him off to grand-mère in Trois-Rivières," she said. "He barks every time I get a text, refuses to eat, and put teeth marks on Bell's new TV remote." She closed the door behind her, kicked off her boots, and slipped her jacket off and draped it on the coat stand.

"Your grandmother is eighty-three years old," I said to her. "And she already has two dogs. I think three would be pushing it. And I thought you already gave mister big TV the boot."

Camille repositioned the belt on her black tunic and waved a hello to Adam from the hall as she headed to the kitchen. "I need a café. Please tell me you made coffee. Strong coffee."

I unclipped *Mignon*, and he trotted off to play with Pong. "I didn't. But I've got a pot of green tea."

Camille shook her head at the pitiful offer and let out a throaty noise of frustration.

"Wait," I said. "I've also got chocolate chip muffins." I pulled one out of the tin on the counter and held it up. "See? Lots of chips. Hardly even any cakey bits."

"Fine," she said, pulling a cup from the cupboard and taking a place at the table.

Adam came in, set his empty bowl in the sink, and kissed my cheek. "I've gotta go out. But don't think we're done talking about the hooker case."

Camille arched an eyebrow at us.

"Adam means Michel's case. He just calls it the hooker case because of the Bunny clothes," I explained.

Camille rolled her eyes. "Anglophones. You think showing a little skin is a sin. Relax already."

"I'm fine with Lora showing a little skin, it's a lot of skin I have a problem with," Adam said. "And only in public. In private, she can show all the skin she wants." He grinned at Camille. "We Anglophones aren't the prudes you Francophones think we are. You should know, you're dating one of us."

Camille stopped, mug midway to her mouth, eyes narrowing.

I pointed to the clock over the stove and started easing Adam out to the hall. I had no idea where he was off to but stopping to ask was probably not in either of our best interests. "You better go," I said to him. "Or you'll be late for sure." And probably limping too if he didn't leave and Camille had time to explain her philosophy on being in a relationship and how she felt about people who referred to her liaisons as dating.

He waved a goodbye to Camille on his way out, headed to the front door, and left.

I sat down across from Camille and poured the remaining tea from the teapot into my cup. "Okay, he's gone. So what *is* going on with Puddles?" Probably I should have been asking for news of Madame Shakiba first, but truthfully I was happy for the opportunity of a temporary diversion.

Her eyes lost some of their squint, and she took a bite of her muffin, waiting until she was done chewing to answer. "*Rien.* He wouldn't leave and he was willing to walk *Mignon*, so I let him stay."

I smiled. Camille didn't let people do anything. If she'd really wanted Puddles gone, he'd be gone.

"It means nothing," she said, echoing the phrase I'd said to Laurent about the Bunny phone password. But this was entirely different. When I'd said the same words, I'd meant them.

"You could have asked Arielle to take care of *Mignon*," I said.

"I did. She wouldn't take him. Jason is allergic."

Hmm. Poodles were one of the more hypoallergenic breeds but Camille wouldn't know that, and it was still possible Jason really was allergic to *Mignon*. Some people can't tolerate any breed. But now that I had the dog again, it would be interesting to see how long Puddles and his big TV stayed around.

Camille stood and cleared her dishes, skirting around *Mignon* and Pong on her way to the sink when they zipped through the room as they chased each other. "You shouldn't have to keep the dog long. According to Arielle, *ma tante* says she's going home today."

I wouldn't hold my breath on that one. Seemed to me Claudette thought she was going home every day. "You learn anything more about her computer fiancé?"

Camille shook her head. "*Ma tante* still won't talk about any of it. But it's crazy. Not only has she run through her savings to bankroll Monsieur Roland Marchand, but she took out a mortgage on the house. If she can't make the payments, she'll lose it. She's lived in that house since she married at twenty-one. She wouldn't know how to function anywhere else. I have to find Marchand and get her money back."

I understood completely. I just hoped Camille wouldn't be too busy trying to help her aunt to work on Michel's case. With two people dead—three if you counted Helen Wong—and the identity thief still out there, I worried the body count would go up. And I didn't have a clue where to focus my attention. There were so many balls in the air on this case, I couldn't get a firm grip on any of them. "So what's on the agenda today?" I asked.

"Laurent's at the PDQ to get more details on Madame Shakiba," Camille said, making her way back to sit across from me at the table. "And Michel's closed down *Prêt-à-Marier* for the day."

Closed it down? Hmm. Just when I'd gotten up early to snitch a wedding invitation template from the Internet and email it to Chantal for Bunny and Léon's inscription text, substituting our cover names and fudging parental ones. Now I wondered if I'd hear back from her, and I'd really hoped to connect with her too to ferret out more info about her relationship with Benoît.

"How's Michel handling the news about Madame Shakiba?" I asked.

Camille shrugged a dismissal. "Michel is Michel. Him too I should ship off to grand-mère." She pointed at me. "And you too if you don't wear your locket."

My hands checked my neck and found it bare. "Laurent told you about putting the tracking device in my locket? I meant to wear it. I mean, I will when I go out."

She shook her head. "*Non, non.* You wear it always. Even to bed. There is a murderer on the loose. A murderer who took the time to single you out and drop his calling card in your bag."

"No one singled me out. They singled out Bunny."

"Same difference," Camille said, waving her hand in the air, dismissing my distinction.

I resisted the urge to argue with her and got up to wash the teapot and load the dishwasher. When I was done, I did a quick tidy of the rest of the kitchen. "Anyway, the police will probably find the murderer soon now that Madame Shakiba's been killed. What about fingerprints? Didn't they find any on the ginkgo bottle from my bag?"

Camille tapped her foot under the table. "Yours and some smudged ones, but no idea who they belong to."

I went to sit across from her again. "I think we need to look more closely at Chantal and Benoît. Laurent tell you they were a couple?"

"*Oui, oui.* A surprise, no? That didn't come up in her background search. And there were no pictures or notes with him on her computer at *Prêt-à-Marier* and no link on her Facebook page or anywhere else. But maybe on her phone. She always had her phone on her that one so I never got to check it."

206

I thought it was odd too that nobody seemed to know about the relationship. Even Kai, the other wedding planner, someone Chantal worked with every day, had referred to Benoît as "some guy" when he talked about him waiting for her at *Prêt-à-Marier*. It's not like the twosome were celebrities trying to preserve their privacy from Paparazzi. It didn't make sense that they were keeping things quiet. Unless, of course, they were pulling a modern Bonnie and Clyde act and didn't want to be linked publicly.

"Benoît's not much of a talker but Chantal is," I said to Camille. "I'm sure I could learn more about them if I had a crack at her. Any ideas how I can see her now that *Prêt-à-Marier* is closed for the day?"

Camille stood and started for the front door. "*Peut-être.* I'll think on it. But first we have a stop to make." She opened the vestibule door and started putting on her coat.

"What kind of stop?" I asked her.

"The kind where you have to wear your locket."

I PEERED OUT through the windshield dotted with droplets of snow, Camille's borrowed black wig and blue-rimmed glasses making it hard to see. I brushed the bangs aside to better study my surroundings. "What is it you want me to do exactly?" I asked Camille.

"Just distract Luc."

That wouldn't be easy with Camille around. Luc's focus rarely strayed far from her when she was within his radius. I looked up the street from where Camille had parked her Jetta at the end of Madame Shakiba's block in Côte-Saint-Luc. It would be a bit of a trek up the street of townhouses over to Madame Shakiba's three-storey unit. I pegged the development to the '70s or '80s, the string of houses giving off a distinctly suburban vibe not common in the city core. Not that Côte-Saint-Luc was core exactly, it fringed more to the west.

I pressed the glasses back up my nose to keep them from falling off. On Camille they'd looked naughty librarian, on me they looked school marm. "You think a disguise will help?"

"The disguise isn't for Luc. It's so nobody sees Bunny at Madame Shakiba's house."

So that was the deal. I was going undercover from being undercover. And apparently moving up in the PI world by adding more tools to my toolbox. I fingered the wig bangs back into place and reached for the poodlepack.

Camille sighed. "You should never have brought *Mignon*. They won't let you in with a dog."

"Don't worry. I draped another layer of pashmina at the top of the bag, and he's sleeping. They won't even know he's here."

I got out of the car and waited for Camille to close up her Jetta and join me on the sidewalk. It had snowed nearly every day for over a week and even with some clearing, the layers had frozen together in spots making the sidewalk both bumpy and slippery. I had to plant my feet wide apart to straddle a snow clump just to keep my balance.

"Try to get Luc in the kitchen," Camille said to me as we started walking to the house.

"And what are you going to do while we're in the kitchen? The place will be crawling with cops."

She laughed. "You watch too much TV. It won't be crawling. They'll be a few. And none of them will care that I'm there. Being Laurent's sister has its advantages. To them I'm just a consultant. They won't pay the same attention to me as Luc would."

Nobody paid as much attention to her as Luc. Not even Puddles. All men noticed Camille, but only Luc counted her as his first love.

"Okay," I said. "So what won't the other cops not be paying attention to you doing?"

"Madame Shakiba is the only employee whose computer I didn't get to search. She had a laptop and had it out of the office each time I was there. I searched her office, but it was bare bones. Not even many personal touches, just one small framed picture on the corner of her desk of her kids when they were teenagers. Odd, no? She worked for *Prêt-à-Marier* for over fifteen years, before Michel even bought the business. You'd think some personal possessions would make their way into her office. I didn't even see an emergency umbrella."

I hadn't noticed anything either now that I thought about it. Didn't even catch the family photo. "Her office *was* small," I said. "Maybe she just didn't like clutter."

Camille shrugged as we made our way up the steps to Madame Shakiba's front door. Before we could knock, the door opened and Luc faced us, barely registering my new look. Camille moved in fast to kiss his cheeks hello—part mature ex-lover, part genuine greeting, part destabilizing gesture. And before I knew it, we were wearing protective covers over our boots and standing in Madame Shakiba's foyer taking in the smell of cops and saffron.

I waited while Luc and Camille had a short conversation in French, letting my eyes wander to the paintings on the living room walls off the foyer. Huge, colorful tableaux set off of white walls like they were hanging in a gallery, all of it extending into the open dining room at the far end. The furniture in the rooms formal, elegant, and lightly padded. The wood gleaming from years of regular polishing.

When my eyes wandered back to the foyer, they landed first on Camille's smiling face and then Luc's flushed one.

"It's good, Lora," Camille was saying. "Luc has a few minutes to talk to you now."

I tried to keep my face from showing my confusion. I understood she was setting up a way for me to keep Luc out of her hair while she looked for Madame Shakiba's computer, but I didn't follow about the talk. I racked my brain for a topic worthy of interrupting his work day. On a murder investigation.

Camille started shoving me in the direction of the kitchen doorway to our right. "Don't be shy, Lora. Luc understands. He won't say a word to Adam about his little problem. Luc's mother is a sex therapist. He knows lots of tricks that could help."

Sex therapist? Adam's problem? Omigod. What did Camille tell Luc I needed to talk about? I turned to ask her, but she was already closing the kitchen door behind me and Luc, who looked just as dazed as I felt.

I went to sit down at the glass table set in front of patio doors overlooking Madame Shakiba's small backyard, piled high with snow-drift waves covering everything but the barbeque top. Luc caught my arm before I sat and explained about contaminating evidence related to a crime. So instead, we both stood in the center of the immaculate room of white cabinets, marble countertops, and stainless steel appliances. Him, arms folded over his sculpted chest, slight blonde stubble barely shadowing his face, and me clutching the poodlepack to my chest, hot, pink cheeks shadowing my face.

"Umm. Yeah. About Adam," I began, searching for something to tell Luc that wouldn't mortify me. "We're having some problems."

Luc held up a hand. "*Arrête.* Look, I told Camille I'd talk to you, but I can't. Not about this. It's not my place. You understand?"

Relief wafted over me, and I nodded. "Sure. Yes. No problem."

Relief registered in his face, too, and he let his arms fall to his sides, his left arm resting on his shoulder holster. "Good. Okay. You understand, eh?" he said again. "I can't get in the middle. It's not right."

"Sure. Right," I said, nodding some more and wondering what middle he couldn't get into.

Mignon stirred in the poodlepack, and I shifted the bag back onto my shoulder to free my hand so I could slip it in the bag and keep the dog's head from popping up. I still needed to keep Luc busy until Camille showed up, and I didn't want to get myself thrown out. "So some case, eh?" I said to keep the conversation going. "Do you know what killed Madame Shakiba?"

Luc's cheek muscle tightened, and his biceps and pecs tightened along with it. Cop stance was setting back in. "Head injury," he said, keeping to public information.

"Do you know where it happened?" I was pushing my luck with my question but maybe that was soon to be public knowledge, too. "Since we found her bracelet at *Prêt-à-Marier*, I thought it might have happened there."

Something worked behind Luc's eyes and they traveled to my poodlepack. "Have you got *Mignon* in there?" he asked me.

Probably Camille would want me to lie. But I couldn't. Especially not to a cop. So I nodded. "But he's staying in the bag. He won't be pulling out any bloody bracelets here," I added with a reassuring smile.

Luc's brows furrowed, and he starting edging me out of the room. "*Tabarnak.* And what about Camille, eh?" he said. "What about her? Is she looking for bloody bracelets?"

Uh, oh. He was on to us. "Of course not," I said. Not lying exactly. How many bloody bracelets could Madame Shakiba have?

Luc hurried out of the room, darted his head around the main floor, then dashed up the stairs to the next level. I followed, huffing a bit from the weight of the poodlepack. We found Camille sifting one of her vinyl gloved hands through Madame Shakiba's nightstand drawer in the master bedroom. The massive canopy bed in dark mahogany beside her and its matching bedroom suite had me thinking of an old Vincent Price movie. I took a step back to the hallway when Camille and Luc got to whispered shouting in French. And when *Mignon* started scratching at the bottom of his beach bag, I got to thinking it might be a good idea to take a few more steps away and get him outside.

When I got downstairs, the front door was open and uniformed men and women streamed in and out, so I darted back into the kitchen and paused at the patio doors to remove my boot coverings and put on my gloves before sliding open the door, stepping out, and placing *Mignon* in the shallow end of a snow wave a few feet from the fence. *Mignon* immediately set to sniffing and lifted his leg to relieve himself, melting away some snow at the base of the barbeque. I waited a minute to see if he had anything else to do and was about to pick him up when he pushed his nose into the snow for some serious sniffing that took him around the bend into a small sheltered enclave for garbage cans and recycling bins. To the right of the trash storage was a door I was guessing led to the garage that separated Madame Shakiba's townhouse from the next one in the row.

Mignon stuck his nose deep into snow collecting to the side of the garbage can, his tiny paws tunneling alongside his nose. Seconds later, his snout emerged carrying a waded up scarf with bits of it trailing out the side of his mouth.

"No, *Mignon*, no," I called, rushing to collect him. I picked him up and wrestled the scarf from his mouth. It was woolen with traditional plaid in tones of red. I held it in one hand and tried to get *Mignon* back into the poodlepack with the other.

I had most of him in and was rounding the doors when Camille and Luc poked their heads out at me. I gave them an "everything's fine" smile, slipping the rest of *Mignon* in the bag, and waited for them to step back so I could put my foot coverings back on and go in. They didn't move. Instead, they stared at the scarf dangling from my hand and fanning out from the wind. I glanced at it, only noticing then the huge dark stain near the end. Blood.

I looked over at *Mignon's* panting little head, nose upturned towards the scarf, still on the scent.

Camille and Luc still stared at the scarf, too.

"Well," I said. "At least it's not a bracelet."

TWENTY-TWO

"SEX PROBLEMS? REALLY? Was that the only thing you could come up with?" I asked Camille. We'd stopped to get some Chinese takeout on our way back to the C&C office and were setting out the containers on the kitchen counter for self serve.

Camille pulled out an egg roll and dangled it towards *Mignon*.

"He can't have that," I told her, snatching it up.

"He should get something," she said. "He found the best clue of the morning."

Camille's own search had netted nothing. Madame Shakiba's computer was nowhere to be found. We'd learned the same was true for her cell phone, too. But Camille felt vindicated knowing a member of our team had trumped the police by finding the bloodied scarf. Hopes were high the scarf would yield important evidence once *Mignon's* saliva was discounted. Given its snow coverage, the police guestimate was that the scarf had been al fresco for thirty-six to forty eight hours, which conveniently matched the time when Madame Shakiba went off the grid.

Nothing else was found after the police searched the rest of the yard. Ditto when they did a second search of the garage. That turned up nothing but some gardening supplies and shelves of tools and labeled plastic storage bins, most of the latter now off the shelves and scattered around the cement floor with their contents spilling over. So *Mignon's* find was the pièce de résistance of the day.

I went out to Arielle's desk where I'd left the poodlepack, took out a Milk-Bone from the outer pocket, and brought it back to Camille. "If you want to give the dog something, give him this."

213

She took it and tossed it to *Mignon* who missed catching it then darted over to the spot on the floor where the bone landed and gobbled it up.

"And stop avoiding my question," I said to her. "Why did you have to tell Luc Adam had sex problems?"

"It worked, didn't it," she said, grinning. "What did you tell Luc anyway? Was Adam too small or too soft?" Camille's words didn't exactly answer my question. But her grin did. Clearly she was enjoying her jab at Adam's manhood. Probably getting back at him for his earlier comment about her dating Puddles.

I washed the dog bone off my hands, filled my plate with rice and vegetable chow mein, and went to sit at the table. "Neither. Luc didn't want to hear about my sex problems. He said it would put him in the middle. Any idea what he was talking about?"

Camille shrugged, grabbed an egg roll, dipped it in sauce, and took a bite, still standing by our improv buffet.

"Who's being put in the middle of your sex?" Laurent said as he slipped into the room.

I closed my eyes briefly and made a mental note to get Laurent a bell to wear around his neck for his next Christmas gift. "Camille made up a story for Luc that I was having sex problems, and he said he didn't want to help me with them because it would put him in the middle. Any idea what he meant?"

A fleeting look passed between Laurent and Camille before he made the same dismissive shrug she'd given me a minute before. Then he grabbed a plate from the cupboard, loaded it with food, and sat across from me. "So are you?"

"Am I what?"

"Having sex problems?"

I sighed. "Of course not. It was a diversion tactic so Camille could snoop through Madame Shakiba's house."

"I heard about that," he said between mouthfuls. "The whole station was talking about Scooby there. Thinking maybe he should join the force."

I looked over at *Mignon* stretched out on the mat by the sink, chewing an edge of the carpet while he watched the counter above as though food might drop at any second. He'd look pretty cute in a doggy police hat. At least until he chewed holes in it.

"You hear anything else at the station?" Camille said, still grazing at our buffet.

Laurent pivoted his chair a bit so he could see her. "They've been running checks on all the *Prêt-à-Marier* employees and suppliers, and so far nothing."

"What about the dance students?" I asked.

He shook his head. "They ran them too. Nothing."

Hmm. "Meaning what? Nobody has a police record?" I hoped my question didn't seem naïve, but I wanted to be clear. This didn't seem like news to me since Camille had already run checks on pretty much everyone.

Laurent looked in my direction. "Right."

Which still didn't tell us anything. Even murderers have to start somewhere.

"And the ginkgo they found with Madame Shakiba," Camille said. "Does it match the others?"

"*Oui.* But it doesn't look like she took any. Still, they're reopening Helen Wong's death and contacting her family to see if her bottle is around for testing."

"So that gets Anna off the hook finally, right?" I said, the words nearly spilling out of me. "I mean, with the other deaths, she doesn't even make sense as a suspect anymore. The police have to admit that, right?"

Laurent finished his last forkful of food and sat back. "*Probablement.* It doesn't explain how Peter got the Prozac, but Anna's been telling the police that Peter was under stress and dipping into her prescription. They're starting to believe her."

I smiled. I was happy my instincts about Anna had been right and somewhere deep down inside of me an "I told you so" wanted to let loose, which surprised me because I wasn't usually the "I told you so" type.

"And if the Prozac didn't kill him," I said, "what does it matter how he got it? It's wrong to share prescriptions and all, but I don't think it's a criminal act."

Really, if it wasn't for the ginkgo showing up in my Bunny bag and with Madame Shakiba's body, I'd have to wonder if the ginkgo deaths were criminal acts either or just unfortunate accidents; just innocent people unlucky enough to get hurt by another unsafe product that found its way to market before someone discovered the risks and ordered a recall.

But there was no mistaking Madame Shakiba's death as an accident. And the ginkgo in her pocket had suspicious written all over it. And as much as I hated to admit it, Chantal had risen to my number one suspect. After all, she was the only one who knew all the victims. I couldn't deny that logic.

"Anyway, I have another theory about who started all the trouble," I added, pausing when I saw a look pass between Camille and Laurent before I plowed ahead. "Maybe Chantal was skimming personal information from *Prêt-à-Marier* clients and passing it on to her boyfriend Benoît to sell. Maybe that's how the Greniers got the money to kick-start *Bon Souper* again."

Camille put down her fork and crossed the kitchen to sit in the chair beside mine. "That's good. I like that. And maybe Madame Shakiba caught Chantal so they killed her."

"Right."

Laurent leaned back in his chair, stretching his legs out under the table, his foot bumping mine. "And the ginkgo in Madame Shakiba's pocket?"

I came up blank on that one and looked over at Camille.

"*Mais, peut-être* they tried to get her to take it, and she refused so they had to hit her over the head instead," she said.

Laurent glared at her and she glared back, topping her glare off by saying, "*C'est possible.*"

"And Benoît?" Laurent said, turning his attention back to me. "You think he's in on it too. And that one or the other of them killed Peter and possibly Helen Wong?"

I mulled that over. It was possible. "Maybe Peter and Helen figured out the scam too. I mean, that gives Chantal and Benoît motive. And Chantal did have access to my Bunny bag. She could have dumped the bottle of ginkgo in it when I left the bag in her cubicle and chased after *Mignon* the day we found Madame Shakiba's bracelet."

Laurent caught my eye. "More hunches?" he said.

I scowled at him. "I think it's all more than hunches. I think it all makes good sense. It might even explain the fire at Peter's store. Maybe he had some evidence against them, something they wanted to destroy." The fire had been niggling at me, and I'd been trying to figure out how it fit into everything. The police still had no leads on who set the fire or why, so this seemed as good a theory as any.

"But how did they get in without a key?" Laurent said. "And if Peter had evidence, wouldn't he have passed it to the police when he reported his identity stolen?"

I was about to throw back an answer when I noticed something twinkling in Laurent's eye and realized he wasn't simply poking at my theory, he was spurring me on. Probably everything I was saying was something he had already thought of himself, he just wanted to see if I could find my way there on my own.

I hesitated and looked at Camille for support. "I don't know," I said. "Maybe they found a hide-a-key for the store. And maybe Peter was using the evidence to blackmail them."

Laurent shook his head, his eyes shifting to neutral. "Blackmail may be a leap. We have found nothing that suggests Peter was blackmailing anyone."

"*Mais alors. C'est possible, no?*" Camille said, getting up and moving to stand beside my chair, one hand clasping a wood spindle behind my back.

"*Oui,*" Laurent admitted. "It's possible. But we need more than possible to go on. All this talk is just a list of possibilities. We need proof."

His last remark was punctuated by the front door buzzer ringing and *Mignon* jumping up to bark.

Camille shot the dog a look and he went quiet, his feet dancing in place. She went to the door and came back with Michel. He was minus a suit this time, khakis visible under his coat instead, but wringing the same crinkled hat in his hands. He barely made it to a kitchen chair before his legs gave out from trembling. He tried twice to speak, getting out only a few French words before stopping and starting over. But once he finally got going, he raced through a monologue worthy of a Shakespeare play, accompanied by the fitting dramatics in the form of facial expressions and hat mauling.

"Some clients have been robbed," Camille explained to me when I shot her a quizzical look after Michel's rant petered out.

"Another identity theft?" I said.

She offered the egg roll box to Michel. He waved his arm and shook his head.

"*Non, non,*" she said, starting to put the leftover food away. "A couple has been robbed in their house. They were supposed to go on their honeymoon but the groom got too sick to fly. They got home to find their valuables gone along with packages of wedding gifts not even open yet. With the identity thefts, what happened to Peter, Madame Shakiba's death, and now this, Michel thinks someone is out to get him."

Him? All these horrible things were happening to other people. How could Michel possibly take any of it personally? It all definitely affected him, but if someone had it in for Michel I doubted that someone would use all these other people to send a message. If someone wanted to get Michel, chances were he'd be got by now.

I glanced over at Michel and the Charlie Brown curl that had formed again on his forehead. Maybe Camille and Laurent were right. Maybe he should be shipped off somewhere until this was all over.

TWENTY-THREE

THIS ISN'T HOW I expected to be spending my Saturday night.

"Ready?" Laurent called out to me.

I tugged up the top of the black dress Camille had lent me. Better, only now it was shortened to mid thigh.

There was a knock on the bathroom door. "*Eh, là*. We're going to be late for our reservation," Laurent said.

I gave myself one last look in the mirror, fingering my locket. Camille had gone heavier with the eye makeup this time but lighter on the lipstick, and I nearly felt like I was missing a layer of camouflage. I opened the bathroom door, and Laurent stepped back into the office reception, his eyes scanning what there was of the dress.

"Camille left this for you." He passed me a black evening bag with tiny beads covering the front.

I looked inside to find she'd filled it with essentials only. The lightweight of it felt odd after carrying around the poodlepack. "What about *Mignon*?" I said.

Laurent reached for my Bunny coat and held it out for me to slip into. "Scooby's got the night off. He went home with Camille."

Lucky dog. A night off sounded good. I let out a wistful sigh as I snuggled into my coat, part of me wishing I was snuggling into a blanket on my couch with a romcom and a cup of cocoa.

"Usually I don't get that reaction from my dates until after dinner," Laurent said, his fingers straightening my coat collar as he made his way around to face me.

That's when I noticed his suit and dress shirt, unbuttoned at the neck. And his hair, not tamed exactly but tidied. He pulled his coat off its hook and put it on. The coat too looked formal and tailored. "You're taking this evening seriously," I said.

He put his hand to my back and ushered me out. "I'm taking your theory seriously. If you're right and Benoît and Chantal are responsible for the identity thefts and Madame Shakiba's murder, we have to approach them with care. We don't want them to suspect we're anything but a couple out for a romantic dinner."

"So that's what you wear for romantic dinners?" I asked as we made our way down the street to the Léon car.

He turned his head towards me, an amused grin setting in. "*Ça dépend*. Romance is different for different people. I dress to suit my date."

As his date for the evening, I thought his clothes were a notch dressier than Bunny's. Or maybe he just looked better in his.

We got into the car and pulled out, on our way to *Bon Souper* where Camille's recon told her Benoît and Chantal were spending the evening. I still hadn't heard anything back from the email I'd sent Chantal with the Bunny and Léon invitation script. With Madame Shakiba's death announced, it didn't surprise me that invitations slipped down on Chantal's priority list, but connecting with her hadn't slipped down on mine. If anything, it had risen all day and now sat at the top.

This time the *Bon Souper* building parking wasn't as crowded, and we only had to go down one layer to find a parking spot. The elevator too was less busy, and we made it up to the restaurant just in time to make our reservation. Our table was near the fireplace with a partial view of the bar. But so far, no view of Benoît or Chantal that I could see. Then again, Camille's intel hadn't specified if they'd be dining or just on the premises.

I peered over my menu to the porthole doors near the bar, wondering what else may be beyond them besides the kitchen. I reached for my water glass, working on a way to gain access to the great beyond, when a warm hand wrapped around mine. I looked down and back up into Laurent's eyes.

"The order is good for you, *mon lapin*?" he said.

Beside Laurent, a formally dressed waiter stood, pen poised over a tiny pad.

Uh oh. I must have been too lost in thought to notice Laurent and the waiter discussing our meal choices. Or the waiter's approach, which seemed to be from along the fireplace wall where he now stood, an expectant look on his face. My lips formed into a slight smile as I glanced between the two men. "Um, which bit of the order exactly?"

"The pasta primavera and green salad," Laurent said.

I smiled wider and looked up at the waiter. "Sure. Sounds great." And it did actually. I hadn't eaten anything since lunch and Chinese food never filled me for long. "Your primavera doesn't have meat, does it?"

The waiter shook his head and gathered our menus, whisking both them and himself away. I watched him disappear behind the porthole doors and watched some more as other staff flitted in and out from the great beyond.

"Patience," Laurent said.

I turned to him, my face innocent. "I'm patient. I'm patiently trying to figure out how to get into the kitchen."

"The kitchen?"

"The kitchen, the office, the stockroom, whatever's behind those doors." I kept my voice low and restrained myself from pointing.

"You think that's where they are?"

"Well, they're not out here," I said.

He sat back, his glass of before-dinner wine in his hand, and winked at me. "Not yet."

The groupie friend Laurent had met on our first visit to *Bon Souper* came over and asked if we'd like more wine. She'd brought us our initial round when we'd first sat down, and I hadn't even touched mine and Laurent had only sipped at his. Refills were clearly not needed. But the flush of her face told me she wasn't necessarily an unobservant server, more a vigilant groupie.

When Laurent reached for my hand and declined her offer, her look of disappointment almost had me feeling sympathetic.

"I think I'll make a trip to the ladies' room before our food comes," I said when the groupie was gone, not that I needed to go so much as I was feeling fidgety. I slipped my hand away from Laurent's, edged my chair back, and stood, clutching the purse Camille had lent me for the evening.

Laurent stood too, came around to my side, and pulled my chair back some more as he bent down to whisper in my ear. "The restrooms are to the right of the bar, *not* through the kitchen doors."

I felt my forehead crinkle. Did he seriously think I was going to pull the whole lost bit and head for the porthole doors? I was better than that. Not that I wouldn't have tried it if there wasn't a steady stream of servers coming in and out who were sure to stop me with polite redirection. But there were, so I wouldn't.

I meandered my way towards the bar, panning for Chantal or Benoît, my eyes taking in the picture of Monsieur Grenier and Peter as I got closer. Maybe it was sentimentality because he had died, but I was starting to warm to Peter. He was starting to remind me of a St. Bernard dog minus the hair. Kind of scruffy and lumbering with a bit of a drool.

I passed through an archway into an alcove bearing a discrete sign with old-fashioned stick figures of a man and woman, an arrow below pointing left.

"Oh, Bunny," I heard as I followed the arrow around a corner into a short hall. I looked in the direction of the voice and saw Chantal standing at the end of the hall outside a door marked "*privé.*"

"Hey," I said, caution barely keeping me from breaking out into a full smile at having come across her.

She walked over to me. Her hair was pulled into a ponytail and she wore a charcoal gray dress, minimal makeup, and a hand over her heart. "Did you hear?" Tears welled in her eyes. "Madame Shakiba is dead."

I nodded, completely losing my urge to grin and not trusting myself to speak, seeing her moist eyes making me instantly emotional, too.

"I just can't believe it," she said. "I didn't know her that long and she could be difficult to work for, but she was my mentor, you know?"

I nodded again. I didn't know what to make of this outpouring. I was all set to size Chantal up as Madame Shakiba's co-murderer. This was throwing me off. The tears seemed genuine and so did the surprise.

The door behind her opened and out walked Benoît, wearing jeans and a sweatshirt, his own genuine surprise appearing on his face when he looked at me. One of his knees showed through a tear in his jeans and what looked like a mustard stain was encrusted near the shoulder of his shirt, so I was guessing he wasn't on bartender duty.

He came up to Chantal and put an arm around her shoulder. The stiffness of the move anything but casual. "You okay?" he asked her.

"I was just telling Bunny about Madame Shakiba," she said.

His eyes moved to me then back to her. "I thought we agreed you were going to take a nap in my mother's office while I finished my paperwork." With his free hand, he dug in the front pocket of his jeans and pulled out a ring of keys. "Was the door locked?" he said as he shifted them both towards another door marked *privé*, this one across from the washrooms, and tried the doorknob. It turned and he let the door swing open and edged Chantal inside before facing me again.

"I don't mean to break up the girl talk," he said. "But Chantal really needs some rest. She's had a busy day with the police and everything."

"Sure, of course," I said, slowly stepping towards the ladies' room. I felt disappointment sinking in at the thought of losing my crack at Chantal. I didn't think I could handle facing both of them, but Chantal on her own seemed doable so I tried to think of something to keep him from shuttling her away. But I wasn't fast enough, and the *privé* door closed shut behind them and I lost my opportunity.

I went into the washroom and used the facilities while I thought about my next move. Problem was, I had no idea if Chantal was just a good actress or if she really was upset. I needed more time with her to figure that out. Which meant I had to get into that room and talk to her. Alone. Without Benoît acting as bodyguard.

Hoping Benoît had left Chantal alone to nap, I left the ladies' room and went to listen at Madame Grenier's office door, shifting to lean against the doorframe and pretend to adjust my boot when a diner came through the hallway en route to the restroom. When the hall cleared, I got into my listening position again, this time staying long enough to make out muffled voices coming from inside the room. Probably Benoît still with Chantal. I pressed my ear against the door, trying to make out what they were saying, until footsteps echoed behind me and I pulled away to lean against the wall again, feigning a need for support. This time, it was Laurent entering the hallway at about the same time that the guy in the washroom came out and left.

Laurent shot me a quizzical look, and I held up a finger in the quiet position then pointed at Madame Grenier's office door and mouthed, "they're in there." He leaned in and listened a beat then pulled me back around the corner, clearing us both from the hall just before the door opened.

How did he do that? I'd been listening and had no idea anyone was headed for the door. Laurent must have ears like *Mignon*.

But now I could hear footsteps on the tile floor of the hall, footsteps that were coming towards us and not the dainty steps of a woman. I grabbed at Laurent to head back to our table, afraid Benoît would be suspicious to find me loitering around. In one swift move, Laurent used the hand I'd extended to his to spin me around and pin me to the alcove wall in a kiss. Not a polite peck kiss, but a kiss kiss. The kind that stops time and raises a gal's body temperature.

Dimly, I heard the footsteps slow then start up again and move past us.

"Um. What was that?" I whispered when Laurent released me. I smoothed my dress and put a hand to my face, hoping it hadn't flushed. The kiss had caught me off guard. Except for Adam, no other man had kissed me in over three years. And never like that.

"An extension to rule number one," Laurent whispered back. "Sometimes, we have to do whatever it takes."

Hmm. It was hard to argue that logic. Especially when it was my own undercover rule. But I doubted Adam would buy the "in the line of duty" line if I told him Laurent and I kissed. I wasn't even sure I bought it. A peck kiss, maybe, but a kiss kiss? "Wasn't that a tad extreme?" I said, my voice still low, my insides still filled with lingering heat.

Laurent rubbed my shoulder, his mouth forming into a small smile. "Realism, *mon petit lapin*. Couples don't steal a moment alone in a public place to overcome the passion for a handshake."

And with that, he laced his fingers through mine and led me back to our table where we found our waiter grimacing, two steaming plates in his hands.

The waiter shot a pointed look in the direction of our salads sitting untouched on the table.

I sat and moved my salad plate off to the side and gestured in front of me. "Sorry. You can just put the pasta here." I smiled. "We'll eat both," I assured him.

He placed one primavera on the table in front of me and another in front of Laurent who had taken his seat and followed my lead by sliding his salad aside. Then after asking if we wanted anything else, the waiter whisked himself away again when we said we were fine.

I picked up my fork, plucked a cucumber from my salad, and ate it. The cool taste mingling with the taste of Laurent's wine still on my tongue from his kiss.

Laurent leaned his head midway across the table. "So? Did you learn anything?"

It took me a moment to get what he was referring too, my mind still clouded with the events of the last few minutes. Then between a few mouthfuls of dinner, I explained to him about my interactions with Chantal and Benoît and my plan to go back and talk with Chantal alone. I could see Benoît now, talking to the bartender on duty behind the bar, and I wondered if he'd be kept busy long enough for me to scoot back and slip in to see Chantal.

Benoît's head turned and our eyes met. I had the urge to turn away but smiled instead. After all, our first meeting had been friendly and our second at *Prêt-à-Marier* hadn't changed that. Benoît didn't smile back and his attention transferred to the bartender when the man gestured towards something near the sink.

"Why don't you go over to the bar and get us some drinks?" I suggested to Laurent. "I'm sure our waiter won't mind."

Laurent kept his gaze on me. "What's going on in that pretty little head of yours, *mon petit lapin*? You want me to keep your friend busy?"

I lifted the napkin from my lap, dabbed it at my mouth, and nodded. "Five minutes," I said. "Just long enough for me to get to Chantal." I watched his eyes as he weighed my request.

"Too late," he said. "Your target is leaving."

I followed his glance towards the bar just in time to see Benoît head into the alcove beside it, a drink in each hand. An idea came to me and I grabbed my glass of water, spilled it on my dress, and tried not to shudder at the sudden cold dampness seeping onto my skin. "Back in a minute," I said to Laurent as I rose and rushed for the washroom, hearing Laurent sigh as I left our table.

Benoît was nowhere to be seen when I zipped through the alcove, but three seventysomething women were crowded in the hall outside the washrooms talking to the ladies' room door in hushed French. I could hear crying on the other side of the door, and one of the women waved me away as I tried to make my way around them. My hand was holding my wet dress away from my body some, and her wave caught me off balance. I knocked into another woman who jostled, sending me back towards the deep end of the hall where I bumped into the "*privé*" door and stumbled into the room as the door fell open. The women were so intent on their own drama that not one of them seemed to notice mine.

I felt pudgy, cold fingers grab my arm.

"*Maudit câlice*," Benoît said, shaking his head at me. "*C'est privé ici.*"

"I'm sorry," I said. "I know I'm not supposed to be in here. It was an accident." I gestured at the wet blotch of fabric covering the right side of my chest. "I came to get a drink out of my dress and got pushed in. I'm really sorry."

Benoît took a deep breath in and out and massaged the side of his head with one hand. "*Non, non. Je m'excuse.* I'm tired, eh. I didn't mean to yell."

I looked at the circles under his eyes, each one purple like a fresh bruise and sagging like a tiny saddlebag. He looked pale, too, which was offset by the burgundy walls of the small, windowless room. A plain desk sat behind him, file cabinets lined one side wall, boxes the other, and there was a door in one corner and a rolling chair in the other. Probably the latter pushed away from the desk when Benoît had quickly gotten up to greet his uninvited visitor.

He poked his head out into the hall and said something in French to the group of women still clustered and wrangling. When they didn't respond, he stepped out, pushed his way between them, and repeated himself. A few fevered words later, the ladies' room door opened and a lean woman came out. She was older than the others, her back straight, and her walk deliberate as she headed towards the exit. The rest of her womenfolk resumed their chattering and followed her out towards the restaurant.

I knew soon I'd be thrown out along with them, so I took a moment to scan the room around me, my eyes skimming over the desk to the two glasses I'd seen Benoît carrying and an open laptop beside them. Then my focus landed on a small bottle with a checkered logo sitting by the phone. A green checkered logo that was becoming all too familiar.

Benoît moved back into the room and tracked my gaze. Then he locked eyes with me and clicked the door shut behind him.

TWENTY-FOUR

"SERIOUSLY," I SAID, my heart picking up a loud thump as I tried to edge around Benoît towards the door. "I didn't mean to disturb your work." I pulled at the wet spot on my dress. "But thanks so much for freeing up the washroom. This spill really needs to be cleaned or it'll never come out." Since the spill was water, this was a fib. But he didn't need to know that.

Benoît stood rigid, blocking the door, watching me.

I smiled my best "c'mon-we're-all-friends-here" smile and thought I saw something soft flit through his eyes.

"Benoît, you in there?" a quiet voice said through the door.

For a second, we were both silent, and I thought he might not respond.

Someone tapped at the door and tried the handle. "Benoît?"

That time the voice was louder, and I recognized it as Chantal's.

"Is Bunny in there with you?" she said. "I've got her fiancé here and he's looking for her."

Relief went through me at hearing her mention Laurent. I wasn't sure why Benoît had locked us in his little office, but I really didn't want to stick around to find out.

Benoît turned, flicked the lock in the doorknob, and opened the door. He stood aside, and I took barely two steps out before Laurent pulled me to him and tucked me under his arm.

Chantal gave us a tired smile. "You weren't kidding about that *coup de foudre* thing. You two can't even bear to be apart, can you? Good thing we're getting you married soon." She focused on me. "Oh, I meant to tell you, Bunny, I did get your email this morning and sent it off to the printer. No worries on your invitations. I put a rush on them, so you'll have them within a few days." She stopped as her voice caught in her throat. "I made sure to do it as soon as I was done talking to the police. Madame Shakiba wouldn't have had it any other way."

"ARE YOU SURE it was the same logo on the bottle?" Laurent asked me on the car ride home.

"Absolutely."

"And it was ginkgo?"

That I didn't know. The bottle had been too far away to make out any writing on the label. "I don't know," I told him. "But it could have been."

Laurent went quiet and drove several blocks before he finally spoke, his voice almost too low to hear. "What were you thinking going into that room alone with him?"

"Excuse me?" I said.

He kept his eyes on the road. "You shouldn't have gone off like that."

His accent was getting stronger the way Camille's did when she got emotional. Not typical for Laurent. His English was better than Camille's and his voice calmer, usually leaning towards playful.

I looked over at him, not sure what to say. When I'd seen Benoît go off with two drinks, I'd thought he was taking one to Chantal and it could be my chance to get in to see her. Maybe offer to sit with her to help her de-stress while he finished his work. My plan had been to stage another run-in using my wet dress as an excuse for being back in the vicinity so soon. My plan had *not* been to get pushed around by a bunch of old ladies and find myself trapped in a room with Benoît and what was likely a not-so-healthy supply of poisoned ginkgo at the ready.

"I'm sorry," I said, trying to catch Laurent's eye. "I was trying to follow rule number three, but I screwed up. I didn't mean to."

He still didn't meet my eye, but I thought I saw the muscle in his jaw unclench so I went on. "But I got a good clue, right? I mean if

Benoît has the same ginkgo that could be some of the proof you wanted, right?"

Laurent jerked the car over to the side of the road in front of a clothing store on the main strip near my house. Most of the building fronts were dark, everything but restaurants and convenience stores closed. The street lit by snow and the occasional street lamp, not many people out and about.

He cut the engine, released his seat belt, and turned to me. "*Oui*, it might be a useful find. But not worth putting yourself in danger."

"I wasn't in danger really," I said, un-clicking my seat belt too so I could pivot his way. "You were right there. Plus I'm wearing my locket." I undid my coat near the top and pulled the locket out, feeling a sudden need to show I hadn't acted thoughtlessly.

Laurent slipped off his gloves, reached out one hand, and fingered my locket, the back of his knuckles brushing my skin. I looked down as he brought up his other hand and opened the locket. He removed the tiny tracker inside, leaned closer, and turned the locket upside down. "She's very beautiful your mother. You look a lot like her."

The locket had a tiny black and white photograph of each of my parents on either side. My dad had given the locket to my mom on their first wedding anniversary, and she'd worn it every day until she died. The pictures were upside down to the rest of the world, but upside right when she opened the locket to look inside while it was on her neck. Which she did frequently, telling me once that every time she opened and closed it, she liked to think the two got to share a kiss.

"Thanks," I said to Laurent, watching him replace the tracker, close the locket, and sit back.

His eyes searched out mine and held them. "Your mother, what would she think of your new job?"

Surprised by the question, I took a minute to think about it and felt a smile come to my lips. "She'd love it," I said. "She had a thing for adventure. Always told me it was better to live a life with passion than with complacency or indifference. That I get to help people and have adventures doing it would thrill her."

Laurent blinked, watching me a beat, then turned to face forward in his seat. Without another word, he belted up, started the car, and got us back into the slow flow of traffic.

"What else did you see in Benoît's office?" he asked me.

I did up my coat and cinched my seat belt, happy to move on if he was. "Nothing much. Some file cabinets, a laptop. There was a door in the back, a closet I think."

I rubbed a hole in the condensation that had formed on the window beside me and looked out, remembering the moment of panic I'd had when Benoît had shut us into the room together. Not wanting to linger on that too long, I replayed the rest of my time with him as the Léon car went another block and pulled onto my street. Just as Laurent slowed the car to a stop between two minivans parked in front of my house, I bolted up, snapping my seat belt hard against me.

"Wait," I said. "I did see something. The laptop on Benoît's desk. It had a big scratch across the front. Over the logo. Just like Madame Shakiba's computer."

TWENTY-FIVE

I ROLLED OVER and checked the clock on the nightstand again. Five to six. Ten minutes since the last time I'd checked. I'd woken at five to go the washroom and hadn't been able to get back to sleep since. Beside me, Adam breathed evenly, his eyes closed in sleepy bliss. Sometimes I stole moments to watch Adam sleep just like that. This morning, I had the urge to poke him so I could have company in my insomnia. Which I took as a cue to give up trying to snooze until the alarm went off at seven and hefted myself out of bed instead.

I tiptoed into the hall, the pets lifting their heads and fixing me with droopy eyes as I left the room. I made my way to the bathroom, splashed water on my face, and blinked at myself in the mirror.

"What's wrong with you?" I asked my reflection. "You did good. You should be happily sleeping."

My reflection didn't respond. No surprise since the question was completely unnecessary. I knew exactly what was wrong with me. As soon as Laurent told me he was passing on my sightings of Madame Shakiba's computer and the checkered-logo bottle at Benoît's office to the police so they could take things from there, I'd felt cheated. Like I had run three-quarters of a race that suddenly got called off. I wanted to see things through with Chantal and Benoît myself. I wanted to be the one following up on things. Which was ridiculous. This wasn't about me and what I wanted. This was about murder. Definite police territory. We'd done our bit. If there were arrests to be made, that was their job.

"After all," I said out loud, "we're *working* with the police, not *competing* with them."

Something warm and soft settled onto my foot, and I looked down to find *Mignon,* his brown eyes staring up at me from his face of curly white fur. I bent down and scooped him up. "What's the matter, pup? You can't sleep either? You homesick?"

I carried him over to the bedroom, snagged my robe from the back of the door and some socks from the floor, and went downstairs.

"May as well go out," I said to *Mignon* as I set him down in the kitchen. He trotted after me into the sunroom and out the back door I held open for him, did his business, and trotted back in. One at a time, he shook snow off each of his feet then he headed for the food bowl and stared up at me again.

As quietly as I could, I filled the empty bowl with kibble, turning when I was done to find Pong and Ping had come up behind me. Both glared at me with wide eyes still a bit misty from sleep.

"Fine," I said. "As long we we're all up, why don't we all eat?"

After I gave Pong her turn in the yard and served pet kibble to all, I made some tea and grabbed a muffin from the tin.

"Hmm, this is interesting," I said to my entourage, who had done eating and taken their usual places when I brought my food over to the table and sat. I sipped my tea and scrolled through a series of at least six texts on my Bunny phone. All from Camille and streaming in around five-thirty, barely a half hour ago. And all in Frenglish, the mix of French and English Montrealers liked to use. Only Camille's version here was heavily weighted on the French side, and my written French skills were worse than my speaking ones. It was like reading someone else's secret code. One I couldn't crack. So I took a chance she had stayed up since texting me and tried her home line.

She picked up before the first ring finished. "*Con,*" she said.

"What?"

"Monsieur Roland Marchand," she said. "He's a *con.* You know, like a fool, an asshole."

Camille didn't swear a whole lot before breakfast, so I knew she must have found some pretty big dirt on her aunt's supposed fiancé.

"His real name is John Jones if you can believe it," she told me. "And he's from right here in North America. *Probablement*, he's never even been to France. Or anywhere outside his basement. He uses online dating and other social sites to find women, pretend to fall in love with them, and con them out of whatever they've got. There are at least twelve other complaints against him. And who knows how many other fiancées on his hook."

"That's good, right?" I said. "I mean not good that he does that, but good that there are other complaints. That makes it easier to get Claudette's money back, doesn't it?"

A throaty noise came at me through the phone before Camille spoke actual words. "Claudette will never see her money. It's gone. Along with John Jones. He's retired his Roland Marchand personality and moved on. That's why *ma tante* hasn't heard from him. He's a snake. He slithers away when the cops get too close to finding him. He sheds his skin and creates a new one. Even when the police do catch up with him, there's very little chance they'll recover what he took. And with so many victims to compensate, it would take forever to sort out who gets what of whatever they could find."

"But they must be able to track where she sent him money. Even if it was through online banking or something. There's got to be a record."

"*Oui, oui.* There's a record of closed accounts. And she has notes from when she mailed him things by post, but all the addresses belong to other people. The police have tracked all that for his earlier victims, too. *Le con* had his deliveries sent to the addresses of people he didn't even know. Then they were collected by someone else, one of his slimy snake friends *probablement*."

That didn't make sense to me. "Why would complete strangers accept mail for him?"

"They weren't complete strangers. They didn't think so anyway. Like *tante* Claudette, they thought they were involved with him.

When his mail was delivered that made the relationship more real. That much I got from *ma tante*."

"So she finally spoke to you about it?" I asked.

"Not exactly. But I got into her room at *l'hôpital* and told her what I found out about her Prince Charming. She couldn't hide all her reactions. And now she'll have to talk to the police. Once she calms down and realizes there are other victims, she will help. She may suffer her own pain alone, but she would never let others suffer alone."

Even though I hadn't known Claudette my whole life like Camille had, I knew that to be true. Claudette spearheaded most of the charity drives at her church and volunteered at various local non-profits when she had time. Like all the women in the Caron clan, she had a fiery spirit and when she channeled it for good it was mighty powerful.

"*Attends*," Camille said. "I have a beep."

The beep meant she had another call. I heard a click as she switched over to her other line to check it, and I took advantage of the break in our call to finish my muffin and swig some tea.

She clicked back a couple minutes later. "Lora, *tu es là*? You there?"

"Mmmhmm," I said, muffin muffling my voice.

"They're gone," she said.

I swallowed. "Who's gone?"

"Benoît and Chantal. Luc just told me. They cleared out before the police got to them."

APPARENTLY, BENOÎT AND Chantal weren't all that was gone. The laptop I'd seen in Benoit's office and the supplement bottle pulled a vanishing act too. Which put a serious crimp in things and left us still with no proof of anything.

But none of that deterred Camille. She was more determined than ever to get some solid answers as she surveyed Chantal's office at *Prêt-à-Marier* and began rummaging through drawers and file cabinets.

Michel stood in the doorway to Chantal's cubicle and watched. "*Il n'y a rien là*," he said.

Camille paused in her search and glanced from me to Michel, shooting him a purposeful look. "English, Michel. And I know we found nothing here before. But we have to look again. We have to be missing something."

I sat in Chantal's chair, *Mignon* in my lap as I systematically went through computer files, and I was not happy. As much as I'd wanted to see the case through to the end, I didn't want to be back to square one. Plus, Camille had already given Chantal's files a thorough combing when she played computer doc, so I suspected I was wasting my time. And I was right. I didn't find anything. Nothing out of the ordinary anyway. I printed out and pocketed the few documents with personal contents, but none of it seemed concerning. Just notes Chantal made to herself, more event planning tips and work shortcuts than anything else. I still didn't find any emails sharing confidential tidbits with Benoît. Or any emails at all with Benoît. Not even in the mail trash. But Chantal did have access to client files. And all client files included personal information, some of which could be useful to an identity thief. Which was a scary thought considering how much personal information we all had stored in company or government databases somewhere. All it takes is one corrupt employee and poof, out goes our data to the highest bidder.

Only, as I sifted through Chantal's bookmarks of various wedding-related sites and her browser history that showed pages of cute animal videos, before-and-after house makeovers, and romance books excerpts, I had a hard time pegging Chantal as a corrupt employee, let alone a murderer. But I reminded myself that sometimes it's the people that seem nice and trustworthy who make the best scammers.

Camille slammed shut a file drawer, and *Mignon's* head popped up nearly headbutting me in the chest.

"*Deux minutes*," Camille said, walking towards the hall. "I'm getting a *café*."

I yawned. I wasn't usually up before dawn, let alone on the job before seven. But Camille insisted we meet at *Prêt-à-Marier* immediately, and I'd dressed to go right after we got off the phone. A coffee might be just what I needed. "One for me too, please," I called as she left.

Since Michel still had the *Prêt-à-Marier* suite closed down, with employees doing any necessary work from home, I doubted Camille would find coffee on the premises. Probably she would have to go to a café nearby to find coffee to her liking, and her two-minute time out would stretch into more like twenty minutes. I yawned again and wondered if my measly cup of tea at breakfast would keep me alert until reinforcement arrived.

Mignon fidgeted and I stroked his ears, hoping he'd resettle. Instead, he hopped off my lap and went over to scratch at the poodlepack I'd left by the chair in the corner. He went a few rounds in circles then curled up and lay down, and I put my mind to thinking of the best use of my time while Camille was gone.

Seemed to me Michel was right and this search was getting us nowhere. There was nothing here. And we hadn't found any clues when we'd gone through Madame Shakiba's office either. Or the rest of the place. Even my foot was getting bored with the search and had fallen asleep.

I stood to get my circulation moving, doing some bends and stretches, stopping mid flex on a neck curl when I heard a pop followed by a loud snap. And not a good kind. My hand went to my neck only to realize the snap hadn't come from there. The realization took maybe a millisecond. Just long enough for something to crash into me. Hard. Hard enough to send Chantal's chair rolling away and knock me off my feet, thrusting me face-first onto the floor, taking whatever hit me along for the ride.

TWENTY-SIX

FROM MY HORIZONTAL position on the floor behind Chantal's desk, I couldn't see much. I pivoted my head as best I could when I heard feet coming towards me, and I blinked at two brown loafers coming into view.

"Omigod," Michel said in his heavy French accent.

Behind him, black Doc Martens raced into my eyeline. "*Ben voyons*, Michel, help me get that thing off her."

A few seconds later, the weight above me was replaced with air, and a chill went through me when coolness hit the sweat that coated my back. I focused on breathing and tried to ignore the sensation of my clothes growing soggy and clinging to my body like layers of wet papier mâché.

"Anything hurt?" Camille asked me. "Can you get up?"

I tried to speak but nothing came out, my lungs still shell shocked from my fall.

She bent down beside me, and I slowly moved my hands into push-up position, raising myself up partway as her hands steadied my arms and helped me onto my feet.

"What the hell happened?" she said.

We all looked down at the rectangular hunk of grated metal now leaning against Chantal's desk. Then almost just as simultaneously, we turned our attention upwards toward the huge hole it had left when it plummeted from its rightful place in the ceiling.

Camille stepped over to the hunk of metal and examined it more closely. "*Merde*. That thing's iron. It could have killed you, Lora. We should get you to *l'hôpital* to check for internal damage."

Probably that was an exaggeration. But it would have been nice if Michel's penchant for all things antique hadn't extended to his vent gratings. That thing was not cheap, flimsy metal. I rubbed my tailbone area and winced. My lungs were back to moving air, but I was plenty sore.

"No. I'm fine," I said. The last thing I wanted was some unnecessary trip to the ER that would take hours. I knew the soreness I felt would intensify later and bruising was probably already setting in, but I didn't feel any broken bones or more serious pain. Luckily, the brunt of the weight had landed on my derrière. If that hunk of junk had hit higher up on my body, things could have been a lot worse. A little pain and bruising I could live with.

I looked over at the poodlepack to check on *Mignon* and didn't see him. "But where's *Mignon*?" I said, scanning the room and hoping he hadn't darted off somewhere.

Michel and Camille scanned along with me, but I spotted the dog first, nosing something over by Chantal's chair now sitting in the far corner of the cubicle. "Never mind. I see him." I stepped towards *Mignon* and stopped when I saw what had caught his interest. I pointed his way, watching his tail wag furiously as he switched from nosing to pawing his new toy, a large mottled bag. "And it looks like the little guy made another find."

CAMILLE PULLED VINYL gloves from her pocket and picked up the bag. "This wasn't here before. Did you put it here, Lora?"

"Nope. It must have fallen when the grating came down. I saw a bag like that in Madame Shakiba's office. I think it's her purse. Someone must have stashed it up there."

Camille raised an eyebrow at me and looked at the bag with greater interest. "Call Laurent, Michel."

Michel didn't move, his eyes fixed on the hole in the ceiling.

She nudged him with her elbow. "*Vas-y* already."

He started, picked up the phone on Chantal's desk, and dialed with a jittery finger.

I moved closer to where Camille was placing the bag on the edge of Chantal's desk. "Laurent?" I said. "Not Luc?"

Camille shrugged and opened the bag. "Luc will get his turn later."

She passed me a set of gloves, and we both leaned forward to see inside the purse. Then one by one, Camille took out the contents, pausing to check out the identification in the wallet which did indeed belong to Madame Shakiba. As did the cell phone Camille pulled out next. Its tiny screen filled with a duplicate of Madame Shakiba's office photo of her kids when Camille powered it on. The screen also asked for a password, so Camille set it aside and continued sifting through the rest of the bag's contents.

"*Il arrive,*" Michel said, hanging up the phone and going over to sit in Chantal's chair. He placed shaky hands on the armrests, and took a deep breath, his Charlie Brown curl forming again and drooping onto his forehead. "Laurent is close. He will be here soon."

I offered Michel a smile of support and picked up Madame Shakiba's wallet Camille had discarded. It too was mottle-toned and rather hefty, probably owing to the vast amount of coinage in the change compartment. I unzipped it and peered in. There were enough coins to feed every parking meter within a block radius. I stuck my gloved hand in and rooted through the hard metal, touching on something softer in the bottom. I pulled it out and saw it was paper folded into a tiny rectangle just a shade shorter than the width of the change compartment. I opened it to the full size of a sheet of paper, a list of names and addresses were on it alongside phone numbers and dates.

"*Très intéressant,*" I heard as heat closed in behind me and I turned to see Laurent looking over my shoulder. Michel wasn't kidding when he'd said Laurent was nearby.

Camille leaned my way to see what I was holding that was getting Laurent's attention, and she smiled.

I panned my eyes from one to the other. "What?"

"The names three down from the top," Laurent said. "That's the couple Michel told us about. The one that was just robbed."

I SET DOWN the poodlepack beneath the window seat in Camille's office, moving slowly from the stiffness that was setting in as my muscles clamped to protect my injured backside. *Mignon* stepped out of the bag, shook himself, and toddled over to Laurent who bent to pat the dog's head before straightening again.

"So you think they were in cahoots?" I said. "Chantal, Benoît, and Madame Shakiba. All tapping *Prêt-à-Marier* clients for various crimes. And what? There was a fallout and Madame Shakiba was drummed out of the club permanently?"

Camille threw her coat in the window seat and went to sit at her desk. "*Peut-être.*"

Again with another "maybe." Putting aside what the fallout may have been about, if the rest was true, that probably meant their scam went beyond identity theft.

"Are you telling me everyone on that list was some kind of target?"

Laurent left the room, answering my question as he walked away. "Everyone on that list of names you found was a client of *Prêt-à-Marier*. And I checked with Michel. The dates listed match the honeymoon reservations they booked. If anyone wanted to break into their houses, knowing when they would be away would help."

So now we were talking property thieves too. Really? What were these people running? Some kind of crime ring? There had to be a better explanation. "Maybe the recent break-in was a coincidence. Any clients on the list with past honeymoon dates who have already been robbed?" I asked him.

He came back into Camille's office carrying a couple of ice packs and handed them to me. "I'm having Luc check that." He slid his eyes to Camille. "If he's not too angry, he'll let us know."

Camille avoided Laurent's look and grabbed the multi-colored slinky on her desk.

I put the ice packs down, took off my coat, and tossed it on top of Camille's. Laurent picked up the ice packs and pressed them into my hands. "For your back," he said. "You can apply them or I can strap them to you."

His eyes were fixed on mine, and I knew he wasn't kidding. He'd had plenty of hockey injuries over the years and could probably rig up his own traction with a pen and some Bungee cord. Strapping ice packs to my body would be easy.

I sighed and slipped the ice packs around to my backside as I sat, propping one against the window so I could lean against it and partially wedging the other one underneath me. I'd been trying to ignore the soreness the fallen grating had caused when it hit me and hoping it hadn't left my skin riddled with waffle marks, but I had to admit the cold packs felt good.

"Is Luc still mad about our snooping at Madame Shakiba's?" I asked Camille.

"*Non*," Laurent said. "Luc is angry we pilfered Chantal's office. The police were due there by eight to go over the place and seize her computer."

That explained why Camille had insisted we meet so early. Somehow she knew the police plan and wanted to beat them to *Prêt-à-Marier*. Probably Luc mentioned it when he told her about Benoît and Chantal absconding. Probably Luc was more angry at himself for letting it slip than at Camille. He knew how her mind worked.

Camille kept her focus on the slinky she tipped back and forth. "He'll be fine. They'll still get Chantal's computer."

She was right. They would. But only because she didn't see a need to take it. One day, I thought Camille was going to push Luc too far. Or Laurent. She had a way of stretching the rules that not many of us could get away with. But I hoped that day was really far in the future because secretly she was my idol.

"So what about the couple we do know was robbed? Maybe it's time we spoke to them," I said.

"Already did," Camille told me. "Last night. It's just like Michel said. They postponed their honeymoon because the husband got sick. A day later, they went out for a doctor visit and came home to find a window broken, their gifts gone, and some electronics and jewelry missing."

I got up and went to collect *Mignon* who had decided to busy himself by tugging at a snippet of fabric jutting out of the wardrobe in the corner. "Some electronics and jewelry?"

Camille rotated her chair towards me and frowned as I tried to free *Mignon's* teeth from the clamp hold they had on one of her scarves. "*Oui, oui,*" she said. "Not everything was taken. *Probablement* the thieves grabbed fast and took off."

I brought *Mignon* over to the poodlepack, circling wide around Camille so he wouldn't see the grimace she was shooting him.

The phone on Camille's desk rang, and we all stared at it without moving. Since Arielle stopped showing up for work, neither sib liked to man the phones. I'd seen them outwait each other too many times to count, usually giving in and answering it myself. But this time, after a moment of stillness, both sibs lunged for the phone, probably both thinking the caller was Luc. There was a scramble, the phone got knocked over, and they both pressed their ears as close to the receiver as possible. They listened a beat before backing off, and Laurent passed the phone to me.

"Hey, hon," I heard Adam say when I put the phone to my ear. "We've got a situation here." His voice dipped out and I could make out crying in the background. Female crying. "It's Tina. Her doctor wants her to go for an ultrasound and Jeffrey's out of town, so I thought I'd go with her." More crying in the background, louder this time.

"Umm. Okay," I said. "Is everything okay with the baby?"

His voice grew quiet and muffled. "The doctor thinks he picked up two heartbeats. He thinks Tina might be having twins."

"Twins? Wouldn't they already know that by now? And isn't that good news?"

"I'll explain later," Adam said. "I just wanted you to know where I'd be, you know, because of before, and I couldn't reach you on your cell."

"What do you mean?"

"I called you a bunch of times from the clinic, but you didn't pick up."

Adam only had the number for my cell phone, not the Bunny phone. But since I carried both, I should have got his call. "I never heard it," I told him.

The crying grew louder, some hollers thrown in. "Gotta go," Adam said. "Tina's really melting down." And he clicked out.

Camille and Laurent watched me hang up the phone, their expressions curious.

"It's Tina," I said. "She might be having twins." I stepped over to the Bunny purse I'd left on the floor and rooted through the contents looking for my cell phone. When I pulled it out, it was dead. Not a sign I was slipping into my old ways, I assured myself. Just a simple matter of forgetting to charge it. I'd been using the Bunny phone so much lately, it was a natural mistake.

I threw everything back in my bag and refocused. "Can I see that sheet again? The client list?"

Laurent had the paper in a Ziploc, folded in half to make it fit. I wanted to see the whole page, so I asked for some gloves and took the paper out of the plastic bag.

There was something familiar about the page. Not the names or other information, but something. I slipped the paper back into the Ziploc, reached into my pocket, and pulled out the notes I'd printed out at Chantal's office. I put each page of notes on Camille's desk, side by side, and saw what I was looking for immediately. Just to be sure, I removed the page from the Ziploc and held it up. All the pages, including the one from Madame Shakiba's change purse, had the same wavy streak running top to bottom through the words a third of the way into the page, creating a nearly separated effect. The text was faint here and there too. Most likely from being printed by a printer running out of ink. The same printer. Chantal's.

I showed my find to Camille and Laurent. "I don't think this list belonged to Madame Shakiba," I said. I thought about the excessive amount of coins in her change purse. "I think she was hiding it. I think our original theory was right. I think she caught Chantal and Benoît stealing client information and was gathering evidence."

Camille sat in her chair and picked up her slinky again. "Before they cracked her on the head and stuffed her purse in the vent, you mean."

"Right." I went back to rest against the window seat. "Although I'm not sure why the police didn't find the purse when they checked the vents after *Mignon* found Madame Shakiba's bracelet."

Laurent looked up from where he'd taken my place by the papers, his eyes meeting mine. "Different vent system maybe. Or maybe the bag wasn't there at the time."

The phone chimed again, and this time Camille snatched it before it finished its first ring. And this time it was Luc.

NOT ONE OTHER couple on the list had been robbed. Or as Luc had stressed, at least there were no police reports of any break and enters or stolen goods. Even though seven out of the twenty-three couples had long since been back from their newlywed getaways. Apparently, none of their homes had been targeted. And none were victims of identity theft either. Probably that blew the crime ring theory. Which was good because I never believed it anyway.

Camille hung up the phone and tipped back in her chair. Silent, her slinky abandoned on the desk.

I got up to take a break from icing my backside and went back to look at the list of names again, feeling my shoulders sag. "Maybe the list in Madame Shakiba's purse doesn't mean anything."

Laurent moved beside me. "Does it feel meaningless?"

It would be easier if I said yes, but that wasn't how I felt. "Not really," I admitted.

His eyes locked onto mine, prompting me to elaborate.

"I mean, it can't just be some random client list. Madame Shakiba wouldn't put that in her change purse. She was organized. Her office and her house were neat and tidy. Everything in its place. A change purse is not the place for work papers."

Laurent moved away from me and took the Ziploc containing the list and left the room. He came back a minute later with two sheets of warm paper and passed them to me. Each one had half the list of names on it—one the top portion, the other the bottom—photocopied from the original. Probably while it was still encased in Ziploc but folded writing-side up. Camille may have had no problem snatching possible evidence, but Laurent would make sure the original made its way to the police. Along with Madame Shakiba's purse and the rest of its contents, sheathed in its own giant Ziploc and still sitting on the floor by Camille's desk where she'd dumped it when we'd arrived at the office.

Laurent dropped another set of copies of the list onto Camille's desk. I thanked him for mine and went to sit in the window seat. *Mignon* wasted no time jumping into my lap, crinkling the papers. I pulled them out from under him and set the dog back down on the floor, my mind zeroing in on something.

"These names aren't alphabetical," I said, scanning the sheets. "And wedding dates or locations aren't even included. The list is organized by honeymoon date."

Camille tilted forward in her chair and grabbed the other photocopies on her desk.

Laurent smiled at me. "*Bien*. And what does that tell you?"

I looked from him to Camille. "Um," I glanced back at the list. "Well, it sure makes it seem like the dates the honeymooners are away are important, like we thought. Maybe some of the people who've already been away were robbed and didn't know it. Or didn't report it. Or maybe there's another reason the dates are important." Although I didn't have a clue how to find out if that was the case. Two of the only people likely to know the significance were MIA and the other was dead. And I didn't think suggesting a séance to contact the latter would cut it with Camille or Laurent.

Camille stood, went to the window seat, and retrieved her coat. "*Allez*," she said. "Let's go."

"Go where?"

"*Mais voyons*. To find out what's going on. One couple on the list is set to leave today. And another couple left last week and isn't due back for two more weeks. Both places are empty. What better time to check them out."

I had the feeling she wanted to play Catwoman and Batgirl again. And my Batgirl outfit hadn't been washed yet. Plus, I couldn't take *Mignon* home; Adam wasn't there. *Mignon* would have to play Scooby, and I wasn't sure we could mix characters from different worlds like that. "Now? In broad daylight?"

"*Absolument,*" she said.

TWENTY-SEVEN

I HUGGED THE poodlepack to me and slipped my hand in to check *Mignon's* body temperature. Still warmer than my hand just like the last time I'd checked. Which was a miracle considering we'd spent over half an hour parked in the C&C stakeout sedan across the street from the house that belonged to *Prêt-à-Marier's* couple on week two of their honeymoon. Thankfully, the day was warm for January, probably only a few degrees below zero, and the sun beaming down on the car helped too.

Beside me, Camille sighed and rolled her eyes. "*Arrête*, already, Lora. The dog is fine. He's got fur and scarves to keep him warm. *Puis*, you've been snuggling him inside your coat forever. The poor thing is probably sweating."

"Dogs don't sweat. They pant," I said, glancing at *Mignon* to make sure he wasn't panting. "How much longer you want to sit here anyway? We're conspicuous. Someone's bound to wonder what we're doing here. And nothing's happening." Which was true. When we'd arrived, Camille had gone over to check the house for signs of trouble and found none. Ever since, we'd been stuck in the car, periodically revving the engine to generate some heat and watching for signs of suspicious activity. And there'd been zip. The only excitement so far had come when a group of kids walking by had argued over whether they should ice skate before lunch and toboggan in the afternoon or the other way around.

For the bazillionth time, Camille scanned the house with her mini binoculars. "We should have gone to the other house. *On arrête*. No more coin tosses with Laurent. *Probablement* he is having more luck with that place."

I couldn't help smiling. Probably Laurent was just as bored staking out the other house, but sometimes it was fun to witness their sibling rivalry still thriving and well in their thirties. As an only child, it gave me a bit of a vicarious rush.

Mignon poked his head out of the poodlepack, his feet dancing on my thighs doing the Twist and Snout. His version of the Twist and Shout aka I need to go out. Now.

I pulled his leash from the side pocket of the bag and clipped it onto his collar. "*Mignon* needs a walk. Be back in a sec." I opened my door to get out and held back a grimace. It did not feel good to move around on bruises, let alone with the extra weight of a dog adding pressure. And as time passed, the muscles in my lower back were going deeper into protection mode, feeling tight and stiff and anything but limber. Probably I was lucky I wasn't in full spasm.

Camille reached over and clutched my forearm. "*Attends*. I'll do it. You stay put. Fine. Pffft. You're not fine. I should have taken you home."

Either Camille was psychic or I hadn't held back my grimace as well as I'd thought. She got out, whizzed around to my side of the car, and snatched *Mignon* before I could protest.

I sat back and watched her walk up the street, her boots squishing the slushy snow. We were in Hampstead, a mostly English well-to-do family neighborhood with large, well-kept houses and large, well-kept cars in the driveways. She moved past the house we were watching—smaller than the ones on either side of it, more a starter home for the well-to-do in training, with painted white bricks matching its painted white fence, maroon shutters framing its windows, and a quaint front porch screaming charm with its swing at one end and antique milk crates stacked at the other. Camille made it a few more houses, but the fairer weather had brought out well-dressed kids to spend part of their Sunday in the fresh air, and one of the kids raced over to pet *Mignon*. Camille briefly stopped walking, tapping one Doc Marten in the mushy snow. She made it a little farther up the street before more kids surrounded her and the poodle. This time she picked up speed, the crowd of kids keeping up with her and growing. I smiled as I watched her disappear around the corner, so focused I nearly missed the flash of a hooded jogger dashing by me and up onto the porch of our stakeout house.

I whipped out my phone to call Camille but saw she had left her bag with her cell in it on her seat, so I flung open my door as the jogger made a beeline back my way, a package under his arm slowing his gait. I was working out what to do and angling my way out of the car by the time he reached me.

He stopped short to avoid ramming into my door and our faces met through the window. "*Toi*," he said. "Not you again. *Maudit câlice*."

I recognized the voice and the face at the same time. Benoît. I opened my mouth to call out, but he dashed around the door and pushed me back in the car, and my voice caught when I landed on my bruises. In a flash, he slammed my door and rounded the car. I scrambled to lock the doors, only my sleeve caught on the gear shift and I wasn't fast enough. Benoît jumped in the driver's seat, threw Camille's bag in the back along with the package, started the car, and floored it.

In my side-view mirror, I saw Camille coming around the bend behind us with *Mignon* in tow. The look of shock on her face was the last thing I saw as we sped up the road.

I WANTED TO wrestle Benoît for control of the car but the gun he pointed at me had me reconsidering my options. I didn't want to end up like Madame Shakiba or endanger anyone on the street by doing anything that could make Benoît trigger happy. He'd used the driver's master panel to activate the window locks on the car, and the one time I'd tried to mouth for help to a pedestrian, he'd gunned the car for the lady barely missing at the last minute. I'd learned my lesson, but I knew we couldn't get far without stopping and I could try something else. Benoît had been ignoring the speed limit and the stop signs so far, but once he wound his way out of Hampstead, all the main streets had plenty of stop lights that were notoriously out of sync. We wouldn't get green ones for long.

Only we never made it out of Hampstead. We'd gone mere blocks before Benoît turned into a driveway and docked the car in a garage he remoted closed. I scoped the car for a weapon, breathing deep to try to keep calm—lesson one in my crisis management course back in college and every yoga class I'd ever taken.

He held the gun steady and pointed it at my chest while he used his other hand to pull a roll of duct tape from his pocket. He set the tape between his knees to brace it, broke off a piece with his free hand, and covered my mouth.

I channeled my breathing to my nose and shook my head side to side to make it hard for him to tighten the tape.

"Stop moving," he ordered, poking the gun into my ribs.

I stilled, knowing he'd have to put down the gun and use both hands if he wanted to tape more of me and that's when I'd get my chance to make a move.

The door connecting the garage to the house flew open and we both turned towards it. Uh, oh. I'd forgotten about Chantal. With Chantal helping him, I saw my chance to get away fading fast. But it wasn't Chantal who walked out towards the car. It was Madame Grenier, holding a gun of her own. And hers looked longer and fancier than Benoît's. I'd seen enough movies to know why. It had a silencer attached at the end. Leave it to a woman to accessorize.

The look in Benoît's eyes told me he was nearly as dismayed to see his mother as I was.

They exchanged heated words in French as they got me out of the car and into the house. The garage entered into a mudroom with a laundry area at the far end, but we made a hard right and went into the kitchen and over to a door.

While his mother kept her gun trained on me, Benoît pulled out his duct tape again and bound my wrists behind my back and my ankles together. Then he opened the door and shoved me through the doorway.

Sweat broke out all over me, making my clothes soggy again beneath my coat as I hobbled forward into a narrow passage of darkness. It seemed insane that less than ten minutes earlier I'd been sitting in a car, bored, and now I was at the mercy of a gun-toting murderer, my body bound into a Tootsie roll.

The door slammed closed and locked behind me as I teetered and toppled over. I crashed down on my side, hitting wood floor, and then nothing. Nothing but darkness. Something tapped at my shoulder and I instinctively flinched and screamed, the duct tape covering my mouth stifling the sound and transforming it into a high-pitched cry in my ears. I heard a crash behind me and another wave of panic hit. My eyes pinched closed, and I forced myself to open them and blink, trying to adjust to the darkness. I needed to know what was going on around me even if a part of me didn't want to find out.

And the first thing I made out when I looked in the direction of the crash was another set of eyes blinking back at me.

TWENTY-EIGHT

THE EYES WERE big. Too big for rat eyes. Too big even for dog eyes.

As my vision accustomed to my dim surroundings, I made out a face around the eyes. A face dotted with dark smudges on the cheeks and puckered where duct tape covering the mouth pulled at skin. Around the body, more duct tape, and around the head, wisps of hair from a loosened ponytail that had been neat and tidy the evening before. Chantal.

She fixed me with a look of concern mixed with fatigue.

I nodded at her to show I was okay. Now that I could see better, I saw she was leaning against shelves that held rows of packaged paper towel. Above her head, I made out canned goods. On the floor nearby, a broken jar filling the air with the sweetened scent of strawberry. The whole room was walled in shelves with kitchen supplies. It was a walk-in pantry, and not large. It was a miracle I hadn't landed on top of Chantal when I'd been hurled in.

I searched the walls for a light switch and spotted one just past the jog near the door. Chantal must have followed my gaze because she nudged me again with her foot and gestured towards the ceiling with her head. I looked up and saw a naked socket sans light bulb, then I glanced back down into her tired, anxious eyes and wondered how long she'd been left like this without light or food or water or a bathroom. Worse yet, surrounded by food but unable to eat it with her mouth duct taped and her arms bound to her body. My hands had only been taped together, but Chantal's arms were flat to her sides held by tape wound around her body at the abdomen mummy style. Her legs too, bound the same way from above her knees to the bottom of her calves. Probably Benoît would have done the same to me if he hadn't been acting on the fly.

I pivoted myself into a sitting position and inched closer to her, feeling like a mermaid without the grace. And without the benefit of a big fin to cushion my aching derrière. I avoided the broken jam jar area completely in case glass shards had splintered off and scattered. Instead, I approached Chantal from the other side and gave her a more intense once-over as I got up close. Her skin was blotchy, her fingers swollen, the breath escaping her nose dank. She needed help. And soon.

With my fingers free, I figured I had enough maneuverability to remove the duct tape from her mouth. It wasn't much, but it was a start. I would have to stand up and back into her to do it, but it could work, so I swung my legs around and tried to stand, shifting onto my knees first then propelling myself up using my feet. I moved slowly, using my bound ankles to anchor my weight, ignoring the pain that shot out from my bruised muscles higher up and the slight dizziness starting to set in from overheating in my coat. Thankfully, the coat was still undone from warming *Mignon* with my body heat back in the car or I'd be in worse shape.

I got into position, crouching enough to reach her mouth, and held her skin down as best I could with one set of fingers while I peeled off the tape with the other. I was craning my neck to see behind me but mostly feeling my way, rushing near the end when I heard her whimper.

I heard her swallow hard as I turned around to face her, and she let out a small cough, her eyes glinting with tears and her nose starting to run.

"Omigod, Bunny," she said. "I can't believe you're here. We have to get out. I think Benoît's gone crazy. I think he killed Madame Shakiba."

I nodded at her. I didn't know about the crazy bit but the rest sounded right to me. Especially the part about getting away. But neither of us had a chance of getting far in our duct-tape ensembles.

I checked the tape around her midsection for an end piece I could begin to strip. I found it, but it wouldn't move. The layers beneath it were too thick and wound tight, covering at least six inches from top to bottom. It would need to be cut away. Only even if I could find something to cut it with, it would be hard to find a safe gap to slice it open. Unlike me, Chantal was coatless and the tape attached directly to her dress, which didn't leave much room between skin and tape. If my hands were in front of me and I could see properly, I might be able to manage it but not with my hands tied behind my back. Her legs, though, were a better bet. The natural gap between them left a nice space I could slip scissors into with no fear of cutting skin. If I had scissors.

"What are we going to do?" Chantal whispered. "He could be back any minute."

I needed time to think. I had no idea what to do. And I had no idea why Benoît had shut Chantal in the pantry. Was he paring down the team or was she an innocent pawn? Just whose side would she be on if I cut her loose?

I pivoted backwards again, reached for a set of juice boxes on the shelving, and broke one off from the set. Not easy with my attached wrists limiting my scope of movement, but my fingers did most of the work. After three failed tries, I pierced the straw through the box and held the box to Chantal's mouth. Later, I'd worry about whose side she was on. Now I'd get her hydrated.

I held the box in place until I felt her pull away.

"Thanks," she said.

If my own mouth weren't still taped shut, I would have told her to drink more. I moved the box closer to her again by way of suggestion but felt her head shake.

"I'm okay for now," she said. "I wish I could do something for you. I feel so helpless just sitting here. And I'm scared. I've never seen Benoît like this. It's like he's a different person."

But different from what was the question. I knew that by now someone may have reported his reckless driving, but even if they had and the police bothered to check out the complaint, it wouldn't be a big help since the license plate on the sedan was tied to C&C—

not to Benoît or the house we were in. And then there was his mother to think about. I had no idea how she fit in. What I needed was more information. What I needed was to get the damn tape off my mouth so I could talk to Chantal.

I looked down at her hands. Her mummy suit had her hands bound to her thighs but the tape stopped at her wrists, leaving her palms and fingers free. They didn't have much range of motion and the swelling suggested her circulation was low so probably they'd be stiff, but if I could get my mouth close enough, her fingers just might be able to rip off my tape. It was worth a try.

I maneuvered myself back down to the floor and placed my head near her right hand, hoping she'd get the idea. Almost straight away, she did and flexed her fingers some before grabbing hold of the tape and pulling as I turned my head to strip the tape off. I moved quickly and it burned like mad, but I told myself it was like getting a moustache wax. Only slightly more thorough. And even old ladies had moustache waxes. If they could tolerate the pain, so could I.

I tasted blood as I flexed my mouth when it was freed. Okay, so probably the old ladies didn't bleed when they had their moustaches waxed, but still. This blood seemed to be coming from a small split in my lip and would clot up soon.

"Bunny, omigod," Chantal said. "Are you all right?"

I nodded and shifted onto my knees and back to standing, feeling the blood drip from my lip. "I'm fine," I said, facing her. "But how about you? Are you hurt anywhere?"

"Not really, just sore."

I almost smiled. That was the same line I'd been handing out. Only in Chantal's case I hoped it was true. "What happened? How did you get in here?" I asked her.

"After you guys left the restaurant last night, Benoît brought me here. He did that a lot, so I didn't think anything of it. But then I think he must have put something in my drink at the restaurant because I fell asleep and woke up in this pantry."

"Do you know where we are?"

"Uh huh. The house belongs to friends of Benoît's family. They winter in Florida and his family watches the house for them while they're away."

That wasn't good. That meant the house wasn't likely on police radar. It also meant Benoît must be getting desperate if he'd bring Chantal to a place she knew and lock her up knowing she could identify the house later. Unless he was planning to make her into a carpet burrito like Madame Shakiba.

"Any idea why Benoît did this to you?" I said.

Chantal shook her head. "None." Her eyes pooled with restrained tears. "I thought we were like you and Léon. You know, that we had that *coup-de-foudre* kind of love. Benoît asked me out the second time we met and was really interested in me, you know, always asking about my work, how things were going. Most of the other guys I dated only talked about themselves. I thought what we had was special. He always wanted me all to himself. He liked to pretend we were secret lovers. Sometimes he'd come by my office at the end of the day with a picnic dinner. Everything was so romantic. I thought he loved me. And now this." Her hands flapped out from her hips in a feeble attempt to punctuate her words with a gesticulation.

The good news was that I believed Chantal and didn't think she was part of the identity thefts or whatever else was going on. Or that she was a threat to me. The bad news was that she was likely wrong. Men in love didn't drug and ditch their mates in pantries.

But I was starting to get an idea of what Benoît did love about Chantal. Her access to honeymooners conveniently leaving behind vacant houses. Or unused addresses to be more specific. It was the package Benoît had thrown in the C&C sedan that had tipped me off. I was sure he hadn't had it with him on his way over to the porch. Which meant he got it at the honeymooners' house. Somehow, Camille must have missed seeing it when she'd scoped out the place. But if Claudette's bogus fiancé could have packages delivered to his platoon of honeys, Benoît could be using his honey to get a platoon of addresses for his deliveries. Exactly why or what was in the packages I didn't know, but the idea definitely felt more like an educated guess than a hunch.

"What about you?" Chantal asked. "How did you get here?"

Briefly, I wondered if undercover rule number one should still apply and decided it did. I didn't see any benefit in telling Chantal the complete truth. Just like I didn't see the benefit in both of us screaming at the top of our lungs for help and angering the gun-toting Grenier family outside the door. Neither action would attract the right kind of attention.

I started to formulate an answer, pausing mid-thought at the sound of a loud buzz. My heart thumped as Chantal and I looked at each other, probably both thinking the same thing. Doorbell.

I hopped over to the jog in the wall leading to the door and got close enough to press my ear to the door. The doorbell went again, and I looked back at Chantal, rule number three going through my head as I reconsidered screaming for help. I didn't think about it for long, though. My attention went back to the door when it burst open and Benoît rushed into the tiny space and grabbed my shoulders.

"What the fuck did you do?" he spit at me. His hands moved lower on my body, rough and probing. Light streamed in behind him forcing my eyes to blink, and I cringed as his hands went through my pockets then tore aside my coat and patted down my body. "Where is it?"

"What?" I said, fighting to maintain my balance with my unileg status.

His face was red, his eyes shining with anger. "Your phone. Give it to me."

"I don't have one." I stopped at reminding him my purse had been left behind in the car along with Camille's. If he hadn't thought to go through our things, I wasn't going to give him any ideas.

He glared at me, so close I could smell the coffee on his breath and the perspiration on his clothes. I thought for sure he'd whip out new duct tape and seal my mouth. But either he hadn't noticed the old tape was gone or he was too angry about whatever had riled him to care. "Then what's your boyfriend doing coming to the door?"

Adam? No, he must mean Laurent. I glanced down at my chest. Laurent must have tracked me. With my coat covering it, I'd forgotten all about the locket with the tracker inside. "You mean my fiancé?"

Benoît's face pinched tighter, his arm swung, and he slapped my face. "Just give me the phone."

Tears welled in my eyes from the sting of the slap, blood dripped out from the reopened split in my lip, and I stumbled over and dropped to the floor.

Benoît stepped around me, his eyes darting over the pantry before he came back and loomed over my face.

I braced myself for another hit, rolling closer to the wall to steady my back and getting my legs ready to kick out at him. If Laurent was outside, he wouldn't stay out there for long. I just needed to hold Benoît off until help arrived.

"I did it, Benoît," Chantal said from over in the corner. Somehow during the scuttle she'd managed to wiggle her way to the far end of the space. "I called her fiancé."

He turned her way. "She doesn't have a fiancé," he said. "She's a PI. They both are."

Hmm. So probably he had gone through my stuff. Just how many phones did he think I carried?

"And *you* didn't call anyone," he went on talking to Chantal, moving over to her, sweat glistening on his forehead, a fist forming in his right hand.

"So what if she did?" I said to distract him away from her. "You said it yourself. We're PIs and we're on to you. We know all about your special delivery scheme." Maybe my hunch about that was wrong but what did it matter? I'd say anything at this point to keep him from hitting Chantal.

But the look on his face told me I was spot on. So I figured why not see what else I could get out of him. Plus, the more I kept him focused on me the less likely he'd turn on Chantal.

"And we know about Madame Shakiba," I said. Then I stretched it. "And about the ginkgo you gave your friend Peter."

Benoît's face went slack on that last remark, his eyes darkening. "You don't know anything. Peter was a fool. He did it to himself and screwed everything up. We had a nice thing going until he told his little girlfriend some thief ripped him off. Then he ups and dies. If it wasn't for his fuckups I wouldn't be in this mess."

"*Arrête, Benoît, viens,*" a woman's voice broke in from the doorway. Madame Grenier was standing just inside the kitchen, an unpleasant odor wafting in around her making me glad she was staying outside the pantry. She used the gun in her hand to gesture at Benoît. "*Il est parti mais il reviendra. Vite.*"

I understood enough to know she was telling him Laurent was gone but would be back. She wanted Benoît to go with her. To strategize or to hightail it out of the house before Laurent's return I didn't know.

Benoît met his mother's eyes but didn't move.

"Benoît," she said again, her voice oozing mother tone. She held a tissue to her nose and waited.

He skimmed the pantry again, hesitating, and looked at Chantal. "*Désolé,*" he said to her. "*Vraiment désolé.*"

I knew *désolé* meant sorry and could tell he meant what he said. Whether he was apologizing for using Chantal or for drugging her, taping her up, and stuffing her in the pantry, I couldn't make out. Not that I had much time to think about it because the shrill sound of breaking glass hit my ears, I saw Madame Grenier shudder, and then her gun fired into the pantry.

TWENTY-NINE

MY FIRST INSTINCT was to duck for cover, but I was already on the ground. I darted my eyes to Chantal to see if she was hit. She was unmoving, her eyes blinking at me. Benoît was on the move, though, dashing for the door, his own gun out now and pointed ahead of him.

I heard a grunt from the doorway and spun my head towards the noise just in time to see a Doc Marten zing through the air and Madame Grenier fall to the ground.

Benoît stumbled on my outstretched unileg, and my attention whirled to him, watching as he regained his footing and stepped back deeper into the pantry towards the shelves in the far end, his eyes assessing.

Then the room darkened, Laurent's body filling the doorway and blocking the light. His eyes found mine and he moved towards me, stopping when he got far enough in past the entryway jog to spot Benoît and his gun.

Benoît shouted something in French, too fast for me to catch the words, but it seemed Laurent had because he took a step away from me. Behind him, I caught sight of Camille quietly edging to the door, no sign of Madame Grenier with her. I darted a warning look her way and she slipped out of sight.

"*C'est fini, Benoît,*" Laurent said.

Benoît directed his gun at me. "*Non.*"

Laurent stood still, his eyes unreadable, his body taut.

I tried not to cringe under the point of the gun and shifted my gaze to Chantal. If I focused on her and her safety, I wouldn't have to

261

think about mine. I still couldn't tell if Madame Grenier's bullet had made contact with Chantal. There was no pool of blood on the floor and she was conscious, but her eyes remained fixed and she said nothing. Even her breathing was quiet. I needed to get closer to check on her.

Benoît moved slightly, dropping his gun from my head to my chest. I could tell his arm was tiring. Probably all of him was. I doubted he'd slept much if at all since the night before.

I slid my eyes to Laurent and waited. It didn't take long for him to feel my gaze on him and turn his dark eyes my way for an instant. Just long enough for me to wink at him before I lifted my unileg and rammed Benoît's shins as hard as I could. Benoît pitched forward and Laurent lunged to catch hold of his arm that held the gun. They struggled over me, the gun plummeted to the ground, and Camille appeared and snatched it up. Laurent had Benoît's head bent sideways and his arms behind his back and pushed him out into the kitchen where I heard the distinct sound of cuffs clinking into place.

Ambulance sirens wailed in the background and Laurent was back, leaning over me. He reached down, swooped me into his arms, and carried me into the kitchen just as Luc walked into the pantry and came out carrying Chantal.

I scanned her body for signs of a gunshot and didn't see any. My pulse started to slow and I let out several breaths watching her do the same as various cops swirled around. I closed my eyes to block out the activity for a moment and took in Laurent's heat, my ear resting on his chest and filling with the soothing beat of his heart. When I opened my eyes, Chantal was looking at me from the kitchen island where Luc had placed her.

"I guess it's true then," she said, finally speaking as Luc started to cut away the duct tape holding her legs.

I tilted my head at her. "What?"

"That you guys are really PIs and Léon isn't really your fiancé?"

Obviously undercover rule number one didn't apply anymore. The jig was up. "Umm. Yeah. We really are PIs. He's just my boss."

Her eyes wandered over to where Laurent's arms gripped me to him and she smiled for the first time since we'd been together. "Just your boss, eh? Could have fooled me."

I smiled back at her, part relief the pantry pistol party was over and part pride. Chantal's comment had to bode well for me. I'd not only managed to follow all the rules on my very first undercover case, but I'd clearly aced my Bunny role and been a convincing fiancée.

Hoping Laurent felt the same way, I turned my smile to him but he didn't smile back. He looked past me down at the floor as the unmistakable clickity-clack of claws crossing ceramic tile got louder and *Mignon* came into view, a ribbon streaming out from the side of his mouth. The ribbon was connected to a small rectangular box drooping below. *Mignon* wagged his tail and released the ribbon, and the box fell to the floor.

THIRTY

CAMILLE INSISTED I get my split lip checked at the ER. She balked when the paramedic said it didn't need further attention and took me to the hospital herself. Maybe it was because my injuries were crime related or maybe not, but I got speedy service and left with no stitches and assurances my lip and the rest of me would heal on its own over time. Chantal had been brought in too and released after they pulled some blood to check on the drug she'd been given and made sure she had no other damage.

By late afternoon, Camille and I were back at the office, and the first thing I noticed as we swung through the front door was that Arielle's chair was occupied. By Arielle. Her hair streaming free and cognac-colored under the desk lamp flooding it with light as she leaned over her keyboard, her fingers zipping away at the keys.

"You're back?" I said, more question than statement.

"*Oui*," Arielle said, not looking up. Either she was focused or she was embarrassed from the last time we'd seen each other while she and Jason were in "metalock." Whichever it was, I was glad. Seeing Arielle caught me off guard and flashbacks of sweaty body parts, piercings, and handcuffs hit me. I'd need a few minutes to get those under control before I could look her in the eye.

Camille waved her cell phone at Arielle by way of greeting, stopping mid wave when the phone buzzed in her hand. Probably another text from Luc. They'd been coming in off and on all afternoon updating her about what he could since the Greniers were brought into custody. Stickler that Luc was, he wasn't telling Camille nearly enough. We did know the Greniers were cooperating and already had legal counsel in place. And that the police were charging Benoît with Peter and Madame Shakiba's deaths as well as committing identity theft and various counts of fraud. But Camille wanted details, and Luc wouldn't give them.

What he did give her was grace for having smashed the glass in the kitchen door of the Hampstead house and broken in when she'd seen Madame Grenier pointing a gun into the pantry. Apparently, she and Laurent were supposed to wait for police before entering the dwelling. Camille argued she had the right to intervene and that the police should have shown up sooner if they wanted her to leave it to them. Of course, she always had some rationale for her rule breaking, but in this case I agreed with her.

Camille shifted her phone from hand to hand as she tugged off her coat and threw it on the edge of Arielle's desk. A second later, *Mignon* scurried out from behind the desk and over to me. I shed my own coat, hooked it onto a peg, and picked up the dog. His body vibrated slightly in my arms, so I went over to the poodlepack lying on the floor near Arielle's chair and pulled out a Milk-Bone. *Mignon* stopped shaking long enough to take a whiff of the bone, then he wiggled to be put down. I obliged, and he ran back to the poodlepack to chomp down his treat.

"So that's your secret," Arielle said, fixing *Mignon* with a look. "All afternoon that dog's been jumpy. I didn't know what to do with him. He's a handful that one. Thank goodness my mother is talking to my aunt again and letting her stay with her when she comes home from the hospital tonight. Someone will have to look after that crazy poodle when I drop him off."

I was glad to hear Claudette was well enough to leave the hospital and that the sisters' feud was finally over, but my heart sank at the thought of *Mignon* returning home. I wasn't ready to lose my poodlepack companion so soon.

Camille looked up from texting on her phone and caught my eye. "Not to worry, you can visit the dog whenever you want," she assured me.

That was the thing about best friends, they could always read you. And Camille was right, it's not like I was losing *Mignon* permanently, I was just giving up roomie status. Still, it felt a little like a breakup with a perfect guy. One you knew you had to let go, but thought about the rest of your life and always wondered if he was your soul mate. And just as I had that thought, Claudette's prophesy predicting a new man in my life came back to me and I smiled. She may not have got the man part right, but she did nail the gender. She'd been spot on about the danger too now that I gave her predictions more thought. And maybe even the *cassure*-break thing. Maybe that had nothing to do with her leg, maybe that was the grating falling on me. That just left the trip bit that hadn't come true. But three out of four wasn't bad. Spooky even.

I watched Camille, wondering if she'd believe any of it. Or if she did, if she'd admit it. Probably not. Camille was probably more like her aunt than she knew and could be just as prideful. Luckily, the pride thing also came with a high propensity for meddling, and Camille's meddling had ended the feud between her mother and her aunt. Which may not have brought back Claudette's money, but it brought Arielle back to work and restored family harmony. Not that Caron family harmony was ever pitch perfect—probably too many of the members were tone deaf from all the high-volume emotional outpourings they liked to share—but harmony didn't have to be in perfect sync to hum along in reasonable peace.

The front door opened a few feet behind Camille, and Laurent walked in, a large bag in one hand.

Camille clicked off her phone and faced him. "*Finalement*," she said. "Luc is telling me nothing. What happened?"

Laurent had gone to the PDQ when we headed to the hospital and had been incommunicado ever since. I thought Camille could give the man time to get all the way through the door before she pressed him for details, even though I too was curious. Especially about what was in the box *Mignon* had dropped at Laurent's feet.

Angling past Camille, Laurent stepped into his office and came back out sans coat and bag. His scruff was longer than usual, making it also appear darker and accentuating the tired look in his eyes. He went into the kitchen and got some coffee, Camille and I following him.

266

He poured out coffee for each of us and passed us mugs in turn. "Quite the case, this one," he said, crossing the room to sit at the table. "Turns out, Peter was not the innocent victim everybody thought. He and Benoît were business partners in a scam."

I tried not to smile too wide, sparing more pain to my split lip, but it was satisfying to know my first lead had meant something and there *was* a connection between Peter and *Bon Souper*.

"According to Benoît," Laurent went on. "Peter started the scam first. His store wasn't doing well, and he decided to cut expenses by stealing credit card numbers and using them to buy stock for his store. That way, his sales were all profit. To keep his buys from being traceable to him, he had them delivered to the addresses of strangers."

Hmm, interesting. I'd never heard of that before. Talk about creative business plans. "And let me guess," I said, joining Laurent at the table. "Peter used temporarily vacated houses for his deliveries and picked up the goods before the homeowners got back."

Laurent nodded. "*Oui.* But he had a hard time coming up with the drop points. That's where Benoît came in. He supplied the addresses."

"That he got from Chantal, eh?" Camille said, leaning in the doorway, both hands cupping her coffee mug. "And Peter? Where did he take the credit card numbers?"

"He stole them from Anna's clients so it wouldn't connect to him like stealing from his store customers might," Laurent explained. "Both men used girlfriends with access to personal information through their jobs. When they'd gotten all they thought they could from one girlfriend, they moved on to another. At first, they used the scam to fund stock to keep their businesses going. Sometimes buying supplies directly, sometimes buying small, expensive things like electronics or jewelry they could sell and turn into cash to use to buy supplies. Then they expanded to selling information to a network of identity thieves."

"Wait," I said. "That doesn't make sense. I thought Peter was a victim of identity theft."

"That's what he said. In reality, *non*. He set that up himself as a cover when some of Anna's clients told her their information had been stolen. Peter thought that if he said he was a victim too, she'd never suspect him. But when he reported his losses, Anna insisted he show her all his records so she could figure out how the theft happened. That's when Benoît got nervous that she'd spot the missing expenses and see that Peter's income couldn't support his store on its own. Benoît got Peter to stall while he came up with something to get Anna off the trail. Only the brilliant plan Benoît came up with was to replace some of Anna's Prozac capsules with ginkgo ones Peter had ordered for his store. He thought that by missing some of her medication doses, Anna's depression would take over and she'd be too sick to bother with Peter's problem."

"You mean Benoît didn't know the ginkgo was recalled?" I said.

"He claims no. He said Peter had been giving samples to everyone when the shipment came in, saying ginkgo helped with everything from obesity to Alzheimer's. Benoît said he doubted Peter even knew about the recall because he still had the ginkgo stocked in his store."

A flash hit me of the lady in the purple coat I'd met outside Peter's store. She had said Peter was always pushing something new. Maybe the ginkgo was one of the so-called vitamins he'd offered her. If so, refusing it was probably the best decision she ever made. Could be the first time preferring cigarettes to supplements saved someone's life.

"Only Anna was telling the truth," Laurent went on to say, "Peter *was* taking from her Prozac."

"And when he did, he took the ginkgo Benoît had added to the bottle and it killed him," Camille said, putting everything together.

Laurent nodded. "*Oui. Mais* Benoît didn't realize that. He thought Peter's death was accidental. But he worried about their association coming out after Peter died. They'd been careful not to be seen together in public, but Benoît had no idea how careful Peter had been about other things that linked them. So he started getting rid of anything that might tie him to Peter and bring the police around asking questions."

"So the fire at Peter's store. That was Benoît eliminating ties?" I said.

"*Oui c'est ça. Puis*, when Benoît went to the store to go through Peter's things, he saw the notification about the ginkgo recall. He panicked. He still didn't know that his Prozac swap had killed Peter, but he was afraid it would kill Anna. He set the fire to destroy Peter's business records and the leftover ginkgo. Then he broke into Anna's house to get the Prozac but it was already gone."

"The police?" Camille said.

"Right. It was taken during the investigation of Peter's death."

"If Benoît was so freaked out about possibly killing Anna, why'd he go and kill Madame Shakiba?" I asked.

"He says her death was an accident. She caught him at Chantal's computer and confronted him, said she had evidence of what he had been doing and was going to call the police. They fought, and she hit her head. He panicked again and hid her bag and dumped her body, thinking with no identification it would take time for the police to figure out who she was if and when they found her. He had her computer and her house keys and figured it would buy him time to find whatever evidence she had against him and get rid of it."

I peered out towards reception where *Mignon* rested on the poodlepack he'd relocated to the hallway. "So the scarf *Mignon* found at Madame Shakiba's was Benoît's? He dropped it while he was searching her house?"

"*Oui*. Scooby did good. That's a key piece of evidence."

Maybe *Mignon* really should join the police force. He was definitely good at finding things. Which reminded me of the box he dropped at Laurent's feet after the pantry incident. "And what about the box the dog brought you? The one with the ribbon? What was in that?"

Laurent grinned. "Ah, *oui*, the box. Diamonds."

Camille arched an eyebrow as we exchanged a look.

"A diamond bracelet to be exact," Laurent said. "It was in the package Benoît was picking up at the honeymooners' house. He had the delivery guy leave it in a crate on the porch so it wasn't out in the open, but he didn't want to leave it there long. He was planning to buy a lot of supplies with the money he'd get selling the bracelet. It had been delivered the day before, but he'd been too busy to get to it, what with dealing with Chantal and the person he calls the little thorn in his side." He looked at me. "That's you, *mon petit lapin*."

"Me? What'd I do?"

"He blames you for having to hide Chantal. He was searching Madame Shakiba's computer for evidence of his *Prêt-à-Marier* doings when you burst into his office. He wasn't sure what you'd seen and wanted Chantal to disappear until he knew if you were a threat. Then you go and show up as he's picking up his diamonds. He said his mother pegged you as trouble the minute she saw you and she was right."

Hmm. I wasn't that keen on his mother either. Especially after she threw the pantry party for Chantal and me and shot off her accessorized gun. I crossed my arms over my chest. "She doesn't seem completely innocent herself."

"*Non*, it was her idea to stash Chantal at the house of her friends, the Snowbirds. She was running damage control. Like she did when Benoît missed picking up a package that was sent to the couple who stayed home from their honeymoon."

"She broke into their house and stole all that stuff?" I said.

"Not her personally. She made Benoît do it and to take other things so it would look like a break-in. They had to get the package so no one traced it to the stolen credit card number or her son's scam could come out. Her husband had run the restaurant for years dabbling on the wrong side of the law with little trouble. She intended to do the same. Even if it meant doing away with a couple busybodies stowed in the pantry. Just two more business deductions to her."

I cringed and grabbed for my coffee to wash down the bile rising to my mouth. I'd wondered what the Greniers had planned for Chantal and me, but now that I knew I'd rather have been kept wondering.

Laurent reached over and swept a finger over the skin below my mouth. "It hurts a lot?" he said, probably mistaking my cringing as a sign of pain.

"A bit," I told him, fibbing a little and grading on a scale, the lip not hurting nearly as much as the rest of me. My lip had swollen near the split, my cheek was tender, my hair was a mess, and I didn't smell daisy fresh. Luckily, nothing else showed on the outside that would give my fib away. At least not anywhere he could see.

He removed his finger and sat back. "And if you go home to clean up and change, do you think you're okay to go out?" he asked me.

Camille went to get more coffee, shooting me a look, her protective instincts making a mother bear's seem slow. But I ignored the look and nodded at Laurent.

"Good," he said, standing and reaching out to help me up. "Bunny and Léon have one last appearance to make."

I STOOD AT the bottom of the marble staircase and looked up, gathering the ends of my dress in my hand. The dress Laurent had given me to wear was blue, sleek, ankle length, and showed merely a hint of cleavage. Bunny does ballroom, I was guessing. In deference to my aching backside, Laurent had also passed me matching shoes with only a two-inch heel. They were surprisingly comfortable but still had me wishing for an elevator.

"This is silly," I whispered to Laurent who stood beside me, arm steadying my elbow. "We already know who's responsible for Peter's death and who swiped personal info from Michel's *Prêt-à-Marier* clients. What are we doing here?"

Laurent leaned in close to my ear. "Benoît swears he didn't put the ginkgo in your purse. And he claims he doesn't even know who Helen Wong was. I don't like loose ends."

Of course Laurent didn't like loose ends. That's one of the things that made him a good PI. And I didn't like hearing about loose ends either. If my own ends hadn't been in such pain, I'd have cared even more about the loose ends. As it was, the end grabbing my attention at the moment was mine and it was none too keen about having to hike it up a flight of stairs.

"*Bonsoir,*" Sylvain said when we made it to the second floor and walked into the meet and greet room. The room was full of people.

271

Probably enough for at least six or seven dance lessons worth of students, the calculation sending my stomach into knots. No way would I be able to dance in front of all these people, bruises or no bruises. Not if it was a one-couple-at-a-time thing. And definitely not if I had to dance to our stripper song, and that was the only song we had left to learn.

"*Viens,*" Juliette said, coming towards us, a drink in her hand. "We've been waiting for you to get started."

Get started? Get started with what? I grabbed for Laurent's hand and clenched it.

"I forgot to tell you," he murmured to me as he gave my hand a quick squeeze before releasing it. "Tonight's lesson was canceled in lieu of a wake for Peter." He took my coat and slipped it onto the rack, following it with his own.

Juliette smiled wide. "It's more like a party to celebrate Peter," she said, her bionic ears obviously still working. "It's all Anna's doing." She slipped sideways and gestured towards the table in the back where Sylvain and Cindy usually sat. The table was covered in a white cloth and sets of white candles surrounding several framed photos of Peter. Anna stood to the side of the table speaking with someone I didn't recognize.

I'd been so preoccupied since I got my pantry jailbreak that I didn't know how much about Peter and his death was public knowledge yet. I had figured not much since Laurent said we'd still be playing Bunny and Léon. But Anna had to know the truth by now, didn't she? She had to have been told that Peter had put her accounting business at risk by stealing personal information from her clients. She had to know he was using her. She had to know about the recalled ginkgo that could have killed her. Yet, she looked every inch the grieving almost-widow.

I navigated my way through clusters of people and metal chairs set out in rows as I went over to see her. Her hair was pulled back, her bangs wispy over her puffy, red eyes. She wore a long-sleeved black dress that hung from her body long and straight like a flapper frock. Her only jewelry her engagement ring and gold stud earrings. And for the first time since I'd met her, her body was still.

She turned from the woman she had been speaking to and greeted me. I leaned in and gave her a small hug and she hugged back, her frail arm pressure making the hug feel like a limp handshake.

"I'm glad you could come," she said when we drew apart. Her eyes moved to my left. "Both of you."

I felt Laurent's warm hand touch my back and his body close in on mine as he gave his condolences to Anna.

The music quieted and Sylvain moved to stand in front of the table and asked for everyone to take their seats, repeating himself in French then English, and stopping when people began to quiet and sit.

Laurent led me to the last row of chairs. We sat on the aisle, giving us a good view of Sylvain and our fellow mourners, including our fellow students scattered in couples throughout the middle rows. Sylvain introduced a cousin of Peter's who stood and explained that Anna wanted to have a gathering to celebrate Peter in the last place they'd spent time together, and he thanked Sylvain for agreeing to host the event. The cousin was an Anglophone like Peter and spoke only in English when he went on to give a eulogy with a mix of memories and humor. The kind that made you wish you had known the person. Nothing in it about Peter being a patsy playboy or a shady shopkeeper.

When the cousin was done, a few other people spoke. Nobody I knew. Anna sat in the front row and from my vantage point, I could see half her face, her head nodding at times, a tissue coming up now and then to dab tears.

After the last tribute, a song filled the room, some folk rock sixties tune growing louder thanks to Cindy's doing over by the iPod set up on a small table near the back wall. Between the emotion of the song and the occasion, I couldn't help sniffling back a few tears, Laurent's hand quick to wipe away the few that crept down my cheek before I turned away in embarrassment. I didn't want him to think I was some big softie. Probably PIs weren't supposed to cry at criminal's funerals.

When the song was done, Sylvain stepped to the front again and invited everyone to stay and join the family for a reception of food and dance, and people began emptying out the rows haphazardly, small groupings intermingling.

Some men started disassembling the rows of chairs and Laurent went to help, leaving me free to scan the crowd. I'd been thinking about the loose ends and had a good idea who could tie them up and was busy looking for my target when Emmaline stepped in front of me, blocking my view.

"Quite the show this evening," she said, her voice condescending, her eyes mocking.

I felt a quip coming to my lips in response to her sarcasm. Maybe Emmaline had a right to harbor resentment about her stepsister and Peter's breakup, but this so wasn't the time. Whatever kind of person Peter was or wasn't in life, he still had friends and family who deserved to mourn him in peace. And he was still Anna's recently departed fiancé in his death and this service was as much for her as it was for him.

Laurent was suddenly at my side, and he rested his hand on the back of my neck. More Caron sign language, and I caught my quip before it flew out of my mouth, happy my tongue holding skills hadn't left me. "Yes," I said to Emmaline, pretending I hadn't picked up on her putdown. "It was a lovely service."

Emmaline turned her heavy banged look my way, her eyes sizing up my outfit for the evening before finding their way to my face. "*Oui*," she said. "Lovely," the word not sounding the same on her tongue as it had on mine.

"It's a bit unusual," George added in from beside her. "But I like it. And Peter would have too. Especially the dance idea. He really did love dancing. Anna's got a lot of class to do this."

Emmaline's nails did a major wrinkle job along the forearm of George's suit. He frowned and stripped her fingers from him.

I tried not to smile. Maybe the guy was developing some backbone.

274

Color flooded Emmaline's face and she muttered something to George in French and stalked off. George made a sorry gesture with his arms and went after her. So much for backbone.

I waited until they were both out of earshot then leaned over to Laurent. "I need you to do something for me," I said.

He moved his arm down my back. "Garter belt itch again?"

"No!" I said, subtly stopping the descent of his hand. "Come with me to the food table." I crossed the room to where I'd finally spotted my quarry. "I need you to listen to Sylvain and Cindy and tell me what they're saying."

Sylvain and Cindy were hovering at the end of the table in one of their little tête-a-têtes.

I pretended to peruse the selection of sandwiches and vegetable platters while Laurent edged in near enough to overhear them.

After a minute, Laurent's lips grazed my ear with his words. "It's the same as in Cindy's book," he told me. "More talk about food."

"Are you sure?" I whispered. "What exactly?"

"Sylvain thinks Cindy has had nothing. He says if she doesn't eat, he'll fire her." He paused. "Now Cindy is telling him to mind his own business. Only not in those words."

I nodded. Exactly what I thought. Now I just had to confirm it. I nudged Laurent back to signal I wanted some space, turned towards Cindy, excused myself for interrupting, and asked if I could speak with her privately.

Sylvain's Baryshnikov hair wave dipped into his eyes when he rolled his baby blues at Cindy as he left with a sigh, and Cindy turned to me, her arms criss-crossing over her chest, her hands rubbing the sleeves of her dark dress.

"Well?" she said.

I decided to go for the direct approach, undercover rules or not. I figured at this point, I'd earned a little slack. "I wanted to talk to you about the ginkgo you left in my purse," I said.

Her face paled some and her body stiffened. But I went on, trying to put her at ease and make the whole thing sound like no big deal. "I was going to give it back to you, but I found out it was bad so

I threw it out. I'm sorry, but I can get you another bottle if you'd like."

Her stance shifted and she bent closer to me, lowering her voice. "Forget it. I don't want it," she said. "Peter was always coming around offering stuff to everyone. I only took the ginkgo to be nice." And she turned on her heels and walked away. Which was fine by me, I heard all I needed. I slipped back over to the food table where Laurent was putting together a plate of vegetables and dip.

"*Alors?*" he said.

"Cindy's the one who played hot potato with the ginkgo. I'm guessing she was hiding it from Sylvain."

He slipped a hand into mine, his other carrying his food, and led me towards two empty chairs lining the wall. We sat and he passed me the plate of vegetables. "Tell me," he said.

"Remember Cindy's food diary?" I asked him. "It wasn't just complaints. I think she's got an eating disorder. And judging by Sylvain's threat to fire her, I'd say it's an issue with her job. It's pretty common with dancers. You said Peter told everyone ginkgo was good for everything from obesity to Alzheimer's. My bet is Cindy planned to use her freebie to help control her weight, and she didn't want to get caught with it under Sylvain's watchful eye."

Laurent smiled at me and plucked a carrot from my plate. "That your PI take or your social worker one, *mon petit lapin?*"

"Both." I told him. "But it's purely my professional PI opinion that Helen Wong probably got her ginkgo from Peter too. Cindy said he offered some to everyone. The fact that Helen died was probably an unfortunate accident. It's possible even that Madame Shakiba got her ginkgo from Peter too but just never took any. We have no idea how long it was in her coat pocket."

Laurent slid his hand onto my leg. "*Pas mal,*" he said. "Your hunches are getting better."

I returned his hand to him and smiled. "Not hunches," I said. "Educated guesses."

"*C'est super fun, eh?*" a man said, plunking into the chair beside mine. "For a wake," the man added quickly. It was Sébastien, sweaty and smiling, with Juliette taking a seat on his other side. Vaguely,

I'd noticed one of his and Juliette's rehearsal songs playing while I'd been talking to Laurent, and from the looks of it they'd been dancing to it.

Sylvain leaned over me and launched into another one of his French conversations with Laurent, his eyes periodically darting between my cleavage and my fat lip until I got fed up and walked away. I didn't want to hang out at the food table again, so I skimmed the room, spotted Anna sitting alone in the corner, and headed her way.

"This was a great idea," I said as I joined her. And it was too. Probably the best wake I'd ever been to. I wouldn't call it super fun like Sébastien did, but Anna had managed to create a really festive vibe despite the circumstances.

She nodded. "It was the right thing to do." She focused her gaze on mine. Her eyes sad but clear. "I know, you know. About him, about you. About everything."

I thought as much. It was my turn to nod.

She scanned the room. "And none of it matters to me. I know what he did was wrong, but he was still the best thing that ever happened to me. He was the first person to really see me. And he supported me. I had horrible anxiety attacks when he met me, and he helped me get over them. I was even able to stop my medication a couple weeks ago. The withdrawal was no picnic but now my whole life will be different because of Peter." She paused. "I owed him this. You know, before everyone else finds out what he did. He deserves to be remembered for more than his mistakes."

I smiled. Anna was good people. She had to be hurting from everything and she was still able to find the positive. Now I knew why I'd instinctively liked her. We were a lot alike. I reached out and squeezed her hand and she smiled back at me, then directed her smile upwards, and I turned to see Laurent had come up behind me.

"One last dance before we go, *mon petit lapin*?" he said.

At his words, I noticed one of our dance tunes—the slow Bryan Adams one—had started playing. I got up and walked out to the dance floor with him, hoping I'd remember the steps I'd learned and pleased when I did. I felt myself relax in Laurent's arms, listening to

Bryan sing about all the things you do when you love someone and all the sacrifices you make, and I thought it was a fitting song for the evening.

Concentrating on the lyrics, I let my eyes close then opened them again when I felt a tap on my shoulder. I lifted my head and Adam's face came into view.

"Hey," he said, his eyes searching my face then lowering to scan my body before moving back up. "I spoke to Camille and she told me what happened to you. I needed to see you. She said I could come pick you up if I didn't give you away. Pretend to be your brother or something. She said you were done for the day anyway." He shot a questioning look from my face to Laurent's.

"*Oui*. She's free to go," Laurent said, his mouth forming a small smile. He released me and shifted my arms to Adam who slipped in to finish the dance.

The winter cold still clung to Adam as he gave me a quick kiss on the cheek and started to slow dance, breaking from the choreography I'd learned at *Danser*. As we swayed, he asked how I was then filled me in on Tina and how he was indeed going to be a godfather to twins.

I told Adam how happy I was for him while I watched Laurent walk to the coat rack and put on his coat. He stood and looked back at me for a beat then shot me a wink on his way out. I winked back, without thinking. Then I smiled. Seems I'd caught the wink bug, and I didn't mind a bit.

Acknowledgments

This book was super fun to write. I'm a lucky gal to get to do what I love and luckier still to have a fab posse of people around me in life and in work. Many thanks to one and all.

To my beta readers Dana B. & Terry C. for their time, their encouragement, and their sharp feedback.

To Private Investigator John F. for taking the time to answer my many questions. Any creative liberties that appear in the story are entirely mine;)

To Richard S. for his unflinching belief in this series & for managing a completely unmanageable client.

To Fran J. for her endless support and great advice.

To Tyler P. and Sam D. for helping create a fab cover.

To Maud L. for fixing all the French bits. Your patience and guidance were invaluable.

To Amy and Rob at 52 Novels for making the book look spiffy.

To my mom and family for supporting my love of books.

To my in-laws for their support, and to my mother-in-law for all the unbridled enthusiasm and for never being afraid to rock the boat.

To my son for sharing my love of storytelling in all its forms.

To my husband for keeping the story of my life interesting and oh so worthwhile.

And to Montreal, its people, and the readers of this series: Merci muchly.

About the Author

Katy Leen is a native Montrealer who grew up on baguette and chocolate milk in a house full of pets and books. She writes the Lora Weaver mysteries and is currently working on the next book in the series.

Visit katyleen.com to learn more about Katy or to drop her a note.

Books in the Lora Weaver Mystery Series
The First Faux Pas

The Pas de Deux

Short Stories in the Lora Weaver Mystery Series
The Nearly Nixed Noël

Made in the USA
Charleston, SC
17 January 2015